Portia Da Costa is one of the most _____
authors of erotica.

    She is the author of *Continuum*, *Entertaining Mr Stone*,
Gemini Heat, *Gothic Blue*, *Gothic Heat*, *Hotbed*, *In Too Deep*,
Kiss it Better, *Shadowplay*, *Suite Seventeen*, *The Devil Inside*, *The
Stranger* and *The Tutor*, as well as being a contributing author
to a number of Black Lace short-story collections.

Also by Portia Da Costa

The
Accidental
Call Girl

PORTIA DA COSTA

BLACK
LACE

1 3 5 7 9 10 8 6 4 2

First published in 2013 by Black Lace, an imprint of Ebury Publishing
A Random House Group Company

Copyright © Portia Da Costa 2013

Portia Da Costa has asserted her right to be identified as the author of this
Work in accordance with the Copyright, Designs and Patents Act 1988

This novel is a work of fiction. Names and characters are the product of the
author's imagination and any resemblance to actual persons,
living or dead, is entirely coincidental

All rights reserved. No part of this publication may be reproduced,
stored in a retrieval system, or transmitted in any form or by any means,
electronic, mechanical, photocopying, recording or otherwise,
without the prior permission of the copyright owner

The Random House Group Limited Reg. No. 954009

Addresses for companies within the Random House Group can
be found at: www.randomhouse.co.uk

A CIP catalogue record for this book is available from the British Library

The Random House Group Limited supports The Forest Stewardship Council
(FSC®), the leading international forest certification organisation. Our books
carrying the FSC label are printed on FSC® certified paper. FSC is the only forest
certification scheme endorsed by the leading environmental organisations,
including Greenpeace. Our paper procurement policy can be found at:
www.randomhouse.co.uk/environment

Printed and bound by CPI Group (UK) Ltd, Croydon, CR0 4YY

ISBN 9780352346933

To buy books by your favourite authors and register for offers visit
www.randomhouse.co.uk
www.blacklace.co.uk

Dedicated to the real Mulder, a dear
feline friend now sadly missed.

1

Meeting Mr Smith

He looked like a god, the man sitting at the end of the bar did. Really. The glow from the down-lighter just above him made his blond hair look like a halo, and it was the most breath-taking effect. Lizzie just couldn't stop staring.

Oops, oh no, he suddenly looked her way. Unable to face his sharp eyes, she focused on her glass. It contained tonic, a bit dull really, but safe. She'd done some mad things in her time, both under the influence and sober, and she was alone now, and squarely in the 'mad things' zone. She'd felt like a fish out of water at the birthday party she was supposed to be at in the Waverley Grange Hotel's function room with her house-mates Brent and Shelley and a few other friends. It was for a vaguely posh girl who she didn't really know that well; someone in her year at uni, who she couldn't actually remember being all that pally with at the time. Surrounded by women who seemed to be looking at her and wondering why she was there, and men giving her the eye with a view to chatting her up, Lizzie had snuck out of the party and wandered into the bar, drawn by its strangely unsettling yet latent with 'something' atmosphere.

To look again or not to look again, that was the question. She wanted to. The man was so very hot, although not her usual type. Whatever *that* was. Slowly, slowly, she turned her head a few centimetres, straining her eyes in order to see the god, or angel guy, out of their corners.

Fuck! Damn! He wasn't looking now. He was chatting to the barman, favouring him with a killer smile, almost as if he fancied *him*, not any of the women at the bar. Was he gay? It didn't really matter, though, did it? She was only supposed to be enjoying the view, after all, and he really was a sight for sore eyes.

With his attention momentarily distracted, she grabbed a feast of him.

Not young, definitely. Possibly forty, maybe a bit more? Dark gold-blond, curling hair, thick and a bit longer than one would have expected for his age, but not straggling. Gorgeous face, even though his features, in analysis, could almost have been called average. Put together, however, there was something extra, something indefinable about him that induced a 'wow'. Perhaps it was his eyes? They were very bright, and very piercing. Yes, it *was* the eyes, probably. Even from a distance, Lizzie could tell they were a clear, beautiful, almost jewel-like blue.

Or maybe it was his mouth too? His lips were mobile, and they had a plush, almost sumptuous look to them that could have looked ambiguous on a man, but somehow not on him. The smile he gave the lucky barman was almost sunny, and when he suddenly snagged his lower lip between his teeth, something went 'Oof!' in Lizzie's mid-section. And lower down too.

What's his body like?

Hard to tell, with the curve of the bar, and other people

sitting between them, but if his general demeanour and the elegant shape of his hand as he lifted his glass to his lips were anything to go by, he was lean and fit. But, that could be wishful thinking, she admitted. He might actually be some podgy middle-aged guy who just happened to have a fallen angel's face and a very well-cut suit.

Just enjoy the bits you can see, you fool. That's all you'll ever get to look at. You're not here on the pull.

With that, as if he'd heard her thoughts, Fallen Angel snapped his head around and looked directly at her. No pretence, no hesitation, he stared her down, his eyes frank and intent, his velvet lips curved in a tricky, subtle quirk of a smile. As if showcasing himself, he shifted slightly on his stool, and she was able to see a little more of him.

She'd been exactly right. He *was* lean and fit, and the sleek way his clothes hung on him clearly suggested how he might look when those clothes were flung haphazardly on the floor.

The temptation to look away was like a living force, as if she were staring at the sun and its brilliance was a fatal peril. But Lizzie resisted the craven urge, and held his gaze. She didn't yield a smile. She just tried to eyeball him as challengingly as he was doing her, and her reward was more of that sun on the lips and in the eyes, and a little nod of acknowledgement.

'For you, miss.'

The voice from just inches away nearly made her fall off her stool. She actually teetered a bit, cursing inside as she dragged her attention from the blue-eyed devil-angel at the end of the bar to the rather toothsome young barman standing right in front of her.

'Er . . . yes, thanks. But I didn't order anything.'

There was no need to ask who'd sent the drink that had

been placed before her, in a plain low glass, set on a white napkin. It was about an inch and a half of clear fluid, no ice, no lemon, no nothing. Just what she realised *he* was drinking.

She stared at it as the barman retreated, smiling to himself. He must go through this dance about a million times every evening in a busy, softly lit bar like this. With its faintly recherché ambience it was the ideal venue for advances and retreats, games of 'Do you dare?' over glasses of fluids various.

What the hell was that stuff? Lighter fluid? Drain cleaner? A poisoned chalice?

She put it to her lips and took a hit, catching her breath. It was neat gin, not the vodka she'd half expected. It seemed a weird drink for a man, but perhaps he was a weird man? Taking a very cautious sip this time, she placed the glass back carefully and turned towards him.

Of course, he was watching, and he did a thing with his sandy eyebrows that seemed to ask if she liked his gift. Lizzie wasn't sure that she did, but she nodded at him, took up the glass again and toasted him.

The dazzling grin gained yet more wattage, and he matched the toast. Then, with another elegant piece of body language, a tilt of the head, and a lift of the shoulders, he indicated she should join him. More blatantly, he patted an empty stool beside him.

Here, Rover! Just like an alpha dog, he was summoning a bitch to his side.

Up yours!

Before she could stop herself, or even really think what she was doing, Lizzie mirrored his little pantomime.

Here, Fido! Come!

There was an infinitesimal pause. The man's exceptional eyes widened, and she saw surprise and admiration. Then he slid gracefully off his stool, caught up his drink and headed her way.

Oh God, now what have I done?

She'd come in here, away from the party, primarily to avoid getting hit on, and now what had she done? Invited a man she'd never set eyes on before to hit on her. What should her strategy be? Yes or no? Run or stay? Encourage or play it cool? The choices whirled in her head for what seemed like far longer than it took for a man with a long, smooth, confident stride to reach her.

In the end, she smiled. What woman wouldn't? Up close, he was what she could only inadequately describe as a stunner. All the things that had got her hot from a distance were turned up by a degree of about a thousand in proximity.

'Hello . . . I'll join you then, shall I?' He hitched himself easily onto the stool at her side, his long legs making the action easy, effortless and elegant.

'Hi,' she answered, trying to breathe deeply without appearing to.

Don't let him see that he's already made you into a crazy woman. Just play it cool, Lizzie, for God's sake.

She waited for some gambit or other, but he just smiled at her, his eyes steady, yet also full of amusement, in fact downright merriment. He was having a whale of a time already, and she realised she was too, dangerous as he seemed. This wasn't the kind of man she could handle in the way she usually handled men.

'Thank you for the drink,' she blurted out, unable to take the pressure of his smile and his gently mocking eyes. 'It wasn't what I expected, to be honest.' She glanced at his identical glass. 'It doesn't seem like a man's drink . . . neat gin. Not really.'

Still not speaking, he reached for his glass, and nodded that she take up hers. They clinked them together, and he took a long swallow from his. Lizzie watched the slow undulation of his throat. He was wearing a three-piece suit, a very good one in an expensive shade of washed-out grey-blue. His shirt was light blue and open at the neck.

The little triangle of exposed flesh at his throat seemed to invite the tongue. What would his skin taste like? Not as sharp as gin, no doubt, but just as much of a challenge and ten times as heady.

'Well, I am a man, as you can see.' He set down his glass again, and turned more to face her, doing that showcasing, 'look at the goods' thing again. 'But I'm happy to give you more proof, if you like?'

Lizzie took a quick sip of her own drink, to steady herself. The silvery, balsamic taste braced her up.

'That won't be necessary.' She paused, feeling the gin sizzle in her blood. 'Not right here at least.'

He shook his head and laughed softly, the light from above dancing on his curls, turning soft ash-blond into molten gold. 'That's what I like. Straight to the point. Now we're talking.' Reaching into his jacket pocket, he drew out a black leather wallet and peeled out a banknote, a fifty by the look of it, and dropped it beside his glass as he slipped off the stool again. Reaching for her arm, he said, 'Let's go up to my room. I hate wasting time.'

Oh bloody hell! Oh, bloody, bloody hell! He's either as direct as a very direct thing and he's dead set on a quickie . . . or . . .

Good grief, does he think I'm an escort?

The thought plummeted into the space between them like a great Acme anvil. It was possible. Definitely possible. And it would explain the 'eyes across a bar, nodding and buying drinks' dance. Lizzie had already twigged that the Lawns bar was a place likely to be rife with that sort of thing, and it wasn't as if she didn't *know* anything about escorting. One of her dearest friends had been one, if only part time and not lately, and Brent would most certainly be alarmed that she'd fallen so naively into this pickle of all pickles. She imagined telling him about this afterwards, perhaps making a big comical thing out of her near escape, and hopefully raising some of the old, wickedly droll humour that fate and loss had knocked out of her beloved house-mate.

Trying to think as fast as she could, Lizzie balked, staying put on the stool. Escort or casual pick-up, she still needed a moment to catch her breath and stall long enough to decide whether or not to do something completely mental. 'I think I'd rather like to finish my drink. Seems a shame to waste good gin.'

If her companion was vexed, or impatient, he didn't show it. In a beautiful roll of the shoulders, he shrugged and slipped back onto his stool. 'Quite right. It *is* good gin. Cheers!' He toasted her again.

What am I going to do? What the hell am I going to do? This is dangerous.

It was. It was very dangerous. But in a flash of dazzling honesty, she knew that the gin wasn't the only thing that was too good to waste. The only question was, if he *did* think she was a call girl, did she tell him the truth now, or play along for a bit? She'd never done anything like this before, but, suddenly, she wanted to. She really wanted to. Perhaps because the only man she knew from the wretched party she'd left, other than Brent and some other friends from the pub, was a guy she'd dated once and who'd called her uptight and frigid when she'd rebuffed a grope that'd come too soon.

No use looking like a pin-up and behaving like a dried-up nun, he'd said nastily when she'd told him to clear off.

But this man, well, there wasn't an atom in her body that wanted to rebuff *him*!

What would it be like to dance on the edge? Play a game? Have an adventure that was about as far from her daily humdrum routine of office temping as it was possible to get?

What would it be like to have this jaw-droppingly stunning man, who was so unlike her usual type? She usually went for guys her own age, and Fallen Angel here certainly wasn't that. She was twenty-four and, up close, she could see her estimate of mid-forties was probably accurate. A perfectly seasoned, well-kept, prime specimen of mid-forties man, but still with at least twenty more years of life under his belt than she had.

And if she explained his mistake, he might well just smile that glorious smile at her, shake her hand, and walk away. Goodnight, Vienna.

'Cheers!' she answered.

He didn't speak but his eyes gleamed a response.

I bet you know what to do with a woman, you devil, paid for or otherwise.

Yes, she'd put any amount of money, earned on one's back or by any other means, that when Fallen Angel was with an escort, it was no hardship to be that working girl.

And she couldn't keep calling him Fallen Angel!

On the spur of the moment, she made a decision. This was a game, and she needed a handle. A name, an avatar that she could hide behind and discard when she needed to.

Looking her companion directly in the eye, and trying

not to melt, she set down her glass, held out her hand and said, 'I'm Bettie. Bettie with an "ie". What's your name, Gin-Drinking Man?'

Apparently ignoring the offered handshake, he just laughed, a free, happy, hugely amused, proper laugh. 'Yes, obviously, you *are* Bettie.' Looking her up and down, his laser-blue eyes seemed to catalogue her every asset; her black hair with its full fringe, her pale skin, her lips tinted with vivid bombshell red, her pretty decent but unfashionable figure in a fitted dress with an angora cardigan over it. When she went out, especially to a party, she liked to riff on her superficial resemblance to Bettie Page, the notorious glamour model of the 1950s. And being an Elizabeth, Bettie was a natural alternate name too.

Having subjected her to his inspection, he did reach for her hand then, grip it, and give it a firm shake with both of his clasped around it. 'Delighted to meet you, Bettie. I'm John Smith.'

It was Lizzie's turn to laugh out loud, and 'John' grinned at her. 'Of course you are, John. How could you possibly be anyone else?' The classic punter's name. Even she knew that.

He rocked on the stool, giving his blond head another little shake, still holding on to her. 'But it's my name, Bettie. Cross my heart . . . Honestly.'

The way he held her hand was firm and no nonsense, yet there was a tricky quality to the way his fingertip lay across her wrist, touching the pulse point. She could almost imagine he was monitoring her somehow, but the moment she thought that, he released her.

'OK, I believe you, Mr John Smith. Now may I finish my drink?'

'Of course.' He gave her the glittering smile again, laced

with a sultry edge. 'Forgive me, I'm being a graceless boor. No woman should be rushed . . .' There was a pause, which might have included the rider, *even a prostitute*. 'But once I know I'm going to get a treat, I'm like a kid, Bettie. When I want something, I tend to want it now.'

So do I.

Lizzie tossed back the remainder of her gin, amazed that her throat didn't rebel at its silvery ferociousness. But she didn't cough, and she set the glass down with a purposeful 'clop' on the counter, and slid off her stool.

'There, all finished. Shall we go?'

John simply beamed, settled lightly on his feet and took her elbow, steering her from the crowded bar and into the foyer quite quickly, but not fast enough to make anyone think they were hurrying.

The lift cab was small, and felt smaller, filled by her new friend's presence. Standing, he was medium tall, but not towering or hulking, and his body was every bit as good as her preliminary inspection in the bar had promised. As was his suit. It looked breathtakingly high end, making her wonder why, if he was looking for an escort, he didn't just put in a call to an exclusive agency for a breath-takingly high-end woman to go with it? Rather than pick up an unknown quantity, on spec, in a hotel bar. Leaning against the lift's wall, though, he eyed her up too as the doors slid closed, looking satisfied enough with his random choice. Was he trying to estimate her price?

'So, do we do the "elevator" scene?' he suggested, making no move towards her, except with his bright blue eyes.

Oh yeah, in all those scenes in films and sexy stories, it always happened. The hot couple slammed together in the lift like ravenous dogs and kissed the hell out of each other.

'I don't know. You're in charge.'

'I most certainly am,' he said roundly, 'but let's pretend and savour the anticipation, shall we? The uncertainty. Even though I do know that you're the surest of sure things.'

Bingo! He does *think I'm an escort.*

Confirming her suspicions like that, his words should have sounded crass and crude, but instead they were provocative, exciting her. Especially the bit about him being 'in charge'. Brent had always said it was the whore who was really in charge during a booking, because he or she could just dump the money, say 'No way!' and walk out. But somehow Lizzie didn't think it'd be that way with Mr John Smith, regardless of whether or not he believed she was a call girl.

This is so dangerous.

But she could no sooner have turned back now than ceased to breathe.

'And anyway, here we are.' As he doors sprang open again, he ushered her out, his fingertips just touching her back. It was a light contact, but seemed powerful out of all proportion, and Lizzie found herself almost trotting as they hurried along the short corridor to John's room.

As he let her in, she smiled. She'd not really taken much note of their surroundings as they'd walked, but the room itself was notable. Spacious, but strangely old-fashioned in some ways, almost kitsch. The linens were in chintz, with warm red notes, and the carpet was the colour of vin rouge. It was a bizarre look, compared to the spare lines and neutrals of most modern hotels, but, then, the Waverley Grange Hotel *was* a strange place, both exclusive and with a frisky, whispered reputation. Lizzie had been to functions here before, but had never seen the accommodation, although she'd heard about the legendary chintz-clad love-nests of the Waverley from Brent's taller tales.

'Quite something, isn't it?' John grinned, indicating the deliciously blowsy décor with an open hand.

'Well, *I* like it.' Perhaps it was best to let him think she'd been in rooms like this before; seen clients and fucked them under or on top of the fluffy chintz duvets.

'So do I . . . it's refreshingly retro. I like old-fashioned things.' His blue eyes flicked to her 'Bettie' hair, her pencil skirt and her angora.

Lizzie realised she was hanging back, barely through the doorway. Now *that* wasn't confidence; she'd better shape up. She sashayed forward to the bed, and sat down on it, trying to project sangfroid. 'That's good to know.' Her own voice sounded odd to her, and she could hardly hear it over the pounding of her heart and the rush of blood in her veins.

John paused by the wardrobe, slipping off his jacket and putting it on a hanger. So normal, so everyday. 'Aren't you going to phone your agency? That's what girls usually do about now. They always slip off to the bathroom and I hear them muttering.'

Oops, she was giving herself away. He'd suss her out any moment, if he hadn't already. 'I'm . . . I'm an independent.' She flashed through her brain, trying to remember things Brent had told her, and stuff from *Secret Diary of a Call Girl* on the telly. 'But I think I will call someone, if you don't mind.' Springing up again, she headed for the other door in the room. It had to lead to the bathroom.

'Of course . . . but aren't you forgetting something?'

Oh God, yes, the money!

'Three hundred.' It was a wild guess; it sounded right.

Sandy eyebrows quirked. 'Very reasonable. I was happy to pay five, at least.'

'That's my basic,' she said, still thinking, thinking. 'If you find you want something fancier, we can renegotiate.'

Why the hell had she said that? Why? Why? Why? What if he wanted something kinky? Something nasty? He didn't look that way, but who knew?

'Fancy, eh? I'll give it some thought. But in the meantime, let's start with the basic.' Reaching into his jacket pocket, he slipped out the black wallet again, and peeled off fifties. 'There,' he said, placing the notes on the top of the sideboard.

Lizzie scooped them up as she passed, heading for the bathroom, but John stayed her with a hand on her arm, light but implacable.

'Do you kiss? I know some girls don't.'

She looked at his mouth, especially his beautiful lower lip, so velvety yet determined.

'Yes, I kiss.'

'Well, then, I'll kiss you when you come back. Now make your call.'

2

Something Fancy

Well, well, then, 'Bettie Page', what on earth did I do to receive a gift like you? A beautiful, feisty, retro girl who's suddenly appeared to me like an angel from 1950s heaven?

John Smith considered having another drink from the mini bar, but, after a moment, he decided he didn't need one. He was intoxicated enough already, after the barely more than a mouthful of gin he'd drunk downstairs. Far more excited than he'd been by a woman in a long time, and certainly more turned on than he'd ever been with an escort before. Not that he'd been with a professional woman in a while. Not that he'd been with a lot of them anyway.

It was interesting, though, to pretend to Bettie that he had.

Sinking into one of the big chintz armchairs, he took a breath and centred himself, marshalling his feelings. Yes, this was a crazy situation, but he was having fun, so why deny it? And she was too, this unusual young woman with her vintage style and her emotions all over her face. That challenging smile was unmistakeable.

'Bettie, eh?'

Not her real name, he was sure, but perhaps near to it.

She looked the part for Bettie Page, though. She had the same combination of innocence, yet overflowing sensuality. Naughtiness. Yes, that was perfect for her. But *how* naughty? As an escort she probably took most things, everything, in her stride. Surely she wouldn't balk at his favoured activities? And yet, despite her profession, there was that strangely untouched quality to her, just like the legendary Bettie. A sweet freshness. A wholesomeness, idiotic as that sounded.

How long had she been in the game, he wondered. What if she was new to this? She was certainly far younger than his usual preference. His choice was normally for sleek, groomed, experienced women in their thirties, courtesans rather than call girls, ladies of the world. There might be a good deal of pleasure, though, in giving something to *her* in return for her services, something more than simply the money. Satisfaction, something new . . . a little adventure, more than just the job.

Now there was the real trick, the deeper game. And with any luck, a working girl who styled herself as 'Bettie' and who was prepared to take a client on the fly, after barely five minutes' chat, was bold enough to play it.

Suddenly he wasn't as bored with life and business as he'd been half an hour ago. Suddenly, his gathering unease about the paths he'd chosen, the insidious phantoms of loss and guilt, and the horrid, circling feeling that his life was ultimately empty, all slipped away from him. Suddenly he felt as if he were a young man again, full of dreams. A player; excited, hopeful, potent.

When he touched his cock it was as hard as stone, risen and eager.

'Come on, Bettie,' he whispered to himself, smiling as his

heart rose too, with anticipation. 'Hurry up, because if you don't, I'll come in there and get you.'

When Lizzie emerged from the bathroom the first thing she saw was another small pile of banknotes on the dresser.

'Just in case I have a hankering for "fancy",' said John amiably. He was lounging on the bed, still fully dressed, although his shoes were lying on their sides on the carpet where he'd obviously kicked them off.

'Oh, right . . . OK.'

Fancy? What did fancy mean? A bit of bondage? Spanking? Nothing too weird, she hoped. But it might mean they needed 'accessories' and she had none. You don't take plastic spanking paddles and fluffy handcuffs to the posher kind of birthday party, which was what she was supposed to be at.

'I don't have any toys with me. Just these.' The words came out on a breath she hadn't realised she was holding, and louder than she'd meant to. She opened her palm to reveal the couple of condoms she'd had stashed in the bottom of her bag. 'I wasn't originally planning to work tonight, but the event I was at was a bit tedious, so I thought I'd take a chance in the bar . . . you know, waste not, want not.'

What the hell am I babbling about?

John grinned from his position of comfort and relaxation. A tricky grin, as sunny as before, but with an edge. He was in charge, and he knew it. Maybe that was the 'fancy'?

Something slow and snaky and honeyed rolled in her belly. A delicious sensation, scary but making her blood tingle. His blue eyes narrowed as if he were monitoring her physical responses remotely, and the surge of desire swelled again, and grew.

She'd played jokey little dominance and submission games with a couple of her boyfriends. Just a bit of fun, something to spice things up. But it had never quite lived up to her expectations. Never delivered. Mainly because they'd always wanted her to play the dominatrix for them, wear some cheap black vinyl tat and call them 'naughty boys'. It'd been a laugh, she supposed, but it hadn't done much for her, and when one had hinted at turning the tables, she'd said goodnight and goodbye to the relationship. He'd been a nice enough guy, but somehow, in a way she couldn't define, not 'good' enough to be her master and make her bow down.

But golden John Smith, a gin-drinking man of forty-something, with laughter lines and a look of beautiful world-weariness . . . well, he *was* 'good' enough. Her belly trembled and silky fluid pooled in her sex, shocking and quick.

Now was the moment to stop being a fake, if she could. Maybe explain, and then perhaps even go on with a new game? And yet she could barely speak. He wasn't speaking either, just looking at her with those eyes that seemed to see all. With a little tilt of his head, he told her not to explain or question or break the spell.

But just when she thought she might break down and scream from the tension, he did speak.

'Toys aren't always necessary, Bettie. You of all people should know that.'

Had she blown it? Maybe . . . maybe not. Schooling herself not to falter, she shrugged and moved towards him. When she reached the bed, she dropped her rather inadequate stash of condoms on the side table and said, 'Of course . . . you're so right. And I love to improvise, don't you?'

Slowly, he sat up, and swivelled around, letting his legs swing down and his feet settle on the floor. 'Good girl . . .

good girl . . .' He reached out and laid a hand on her hip, fingers curving, just touching the slope of her bottom cheek. The touch became a squeeze, the tips of his four fingers digging into her flesh, not cruelly but with assertion, owning her.

With his other hand, he drew her nearer, right in between his spread thighs. She was looking down at him but it was as if he were looking down at her, from a great and dominant height. Her heart tripped again, knowing he could give her what she wanted.

But what was *his* price? Could she afford to pay?

He squeezed her bottom harder, as if assessing the resilience of her flesh, his fingertips closer to her pussy now, pushing the cloth of her skirt into the edge of her cleft. With a will of its own, her body started moving, rocking, pushing against his hold. Her sex was heavy, agitated, in need of some attention, and yet they'd barely done anything thus far. She lifted her hands to put them on his shoulders and draw the two of them closer.

'Uh oh.' The slightest tilt of the head, and a narrowing of his eyes was all the command she needed. She let her hands drop . . . while his free hand rose to her breast, fingers grazing her nipple. Her bra was underwired, but not padded so there was little to dull his touch. With finger and thumb, he took hold of her nipple and pinched it lightly through her clothing, smiling when she let out a gasp, sensation shooting from the contact to her swollen folds, and her clit.

Squeeze. Pinch. Squeeze. Pinch. Nothing like the sex she was used to, but wonderful. Odd. Infinitely arousing. The wetness between her labia welled again, slippery and almost alarming, saturating the thin strip of cloth between her legs.

'I'm going to make you come,' said John in a strangely normal voice, 'and I mean a real one, no faking. I think you can do it for me. You seem like an honest girl, and I think you like the way I'm touching you . . . even if it *is* business.'

Lizzie swallowed. For a moment there she'd forgotten she was supposed to be a professional. She'd just been a lucky girl with a really hot man who probably wouldn't have to do all that much to get her off.

'Will you be honest for me?' His blue eyes were like the whole world, and unable to get away from. 'Will you give me what I want? What I've paid for?'

'Yes, I think I can do that. Shouldn't be too difficult.'

Finger and thumb closed hard on her nipple. It really hurt and she let out a moan from the pain and from other sensations. 'Honesty, remember?' His tongue, soft and pink slid along his lower lip and she had to hold in a moan at the sight of that too.

She nodded, unable to speak, the pressure on the tip of her breast consuming her. How could this be happening? It hurt but it was next to nothing really.

Then he released her. 'Take off your cardigan and your dress, nothing else.'

Shaking, but hoping he couldn't detect the fine tremors, Lizzie shucked off her cardigan and dropped it on the floor beside her, then she reached behind her, for her zip.

'Let me.' John turned her like a big doll, whizzed the zip down, and then turned her back again, leaving her to slip the dress off. He put out a hand, though, to steady her, as she stepped out of it.

She hadn't really been planning to seduce anyone tonight, so she hadn't put on her fanciest underwear, just a nice but fairly unfussy set, a plain white bra and panties with a little edge of rosy pink lace.

'Nice. Prim. I like it,' said John with a pleased smile. Lizzie almost fainted when he hitched himself a little sideways on the bed, reached down and casually adjusted himself in his trousers. As his hand slid away, she could see he was huge, madly erect.

Oh, yummy.

He laughed out loud. He'd seen her checking him out. 'Not too bad, eh?' He shrugged, still with that golden but vaguely unnerving grin. 'I guess you see all shapes and sizes.'

'True,' she replied, wanting to reach out and touch the not too bad item, but knowing instinctively it was forbidden to do so for the moment. 'And most of them are rather small . . . but you seem to be OK, though, from where I'm standing.'

'Cheeky minx. I should punish you for that.' He laid a hand on her thigh, just above the top of her hold-up stocking. He didn't slap her, though perversely she'd hoped he might, just so she could see what one felt like from him. 'Maybe I will in a bit.' He stroked her skin, just at the edge of her panties, then drew back.

'You're very beautiful, you know,' he went on, leaning back on his elbows for a moment. 'I expect you're very popular. Are you? Do you do well?'

'Not too badly.' It seemed a bland enough answer, not an exact lie. She had the occasional boyfriend, nothing special. She wasn't promiscuous, but she had sex now and again.

John nodded. She wasn't sure what he meant by it, but she didn't stop to worry. The way he was lying showed off that gorgeous erection. 'Do you actually, really like your job, then?' He glanced down to where she was looking, unashamed.

'Yes, I do. And I often come too. The things you see on the telly. Documentaries and stuff . . . They all try to tell people that we don't enjoy it. But some of us do.' It seemed safer to cover herself. If she didn't have a real orgasm soon, she might go mad. He'd barely touched her but her clit was aching, aching, aching.

'Show me, then. Pull down the top of your bra. Show me your tits. They look very nice but I'd like to see a bit more of them.'

Peeling down her straps, Lizzie pushed the cups of her bra down too, easing each breast out and letting it settle on the bunched fabric of the cup. It looked rude and naughty, as if she were presenting two juicy fruits to him on a tray, and it made her just nicely sized breasts look bigger, more opulent.

'Lovely. Now play with your nipples. Make them really come up for me.'

Tentatively, Lizzie cupped herself, first one breast, then the other. 'I thought you were going to make me come? I'm doing all the work here.' A shudder ran down her spine; her nipples were already acutely sensitive, dark and perky.

'Shush. You talk too much. Just do as you're told.' The words were soft, almost friendly, but she listened for an undertone, even if there wasn't one there.

Closing her eyes, she went about her task, wondering what he was thinking. Touching her breasts made her want to touch herself elsewhere too. It always did. It was putting electricity into a system and getting an overload in a different location. Her clit felt enormous, charged, desperate. As she ran her thumbs across her nipples, tantalising herself, she wanted to pant with excitement.

And all because this strange man was looking at her. She could feel the weight of his blue stare, even if she couldn't see him. Were his lips parted just as hers were? Was he hungering just as she did? Did he want a taste of her?

Swaying her hips, she slid a hand down from her breast to her belly, skirting the edge of her knickers, ready to dive inside.

'No, not there. I'll deal with that.'

Lizzie's eyes snapped open. John was watching her closely, as she'd expected, his gaze hooded. Gosh, his eyelashes were long. She suddenly noticed them, so surprisingly dark compared to his wheat-gold hair.

In a swift, shocking move, he sat up again and grasped the errant hand, then its mate, pushing them behind her, and then hooking both of them together behind her back. Her wrists were narrow and easily contained by his bigger hand. He was right up against her now, his breath hot on her breasts.

Bondage. Was this one of his fancy things? Her heart thrilled. Her pussy quivered. Yes. Yes. Yes. He held her firmly, his arm around her, securing her. She tried not to tremble but it was difficult to avoid it. Difficult to stop herself pressing her body as close to his as she could and trying to get off by rubbing her crotch against whatever part of him she could reach.

'Keep still. Keep very still. No movement unless I say so.' Inclining forward, he put out his tongue and licked her nipple, long, slowly and lasciviously, once, twice, three times.

'Oh God . . . oh God . . .'

His mouth was hot and his tongue nimble, flexible. He furled it to a point and dabbed at the very point of her, then lashed hard, flicking the bud. Lizzie imagined she was floating, buoyed up by the simple, focused pleasure, yet tethered by the weight of lust between her thighs.

'Hush . . . be quiet.' The words flowed over the skin of her breast. 'Try not to make any noises. Contain everything inside you.'

It was hard, so hard . . . and impossible when he took her nipple between his teeth and tugged on it hard. The pressure was oh so measured, but threatening, and his tongue still worked, right on the very tip.

Forbidden noises came out of her mouth. Her pelvis wafted in a dance proscribed. A tear formed at the corner of her eye. He dabbed and dabbed at her imprisoned nipple with his tongue, and when she looked down on him, she could see a demon looking back up at her, laughter dark and merry in his eyes.

He thinks he's getting the better of me. He thinks he's getting to a woman who's supposedly anaesthetised to pleasure, and making her excited.

Hard suction pulled at her nipple and her hips undulated in reply.

I don't know who the hell this woman is, but the bastard's making me crazy!

Lizzie had never believed that a woman could get off just from having her breasts played with. And maybe that still was so . . . But with her tit in John Smith's mouth she was only a hair's breadth from it. Maybe if she jerked her hips hard enough, it'd happen. Maybe she'd climax from sheer momentum.

'Stop that,' he ordered quietly, then with his free palm, he reached around and slapped her hard on the buttock, right next to her immobilised hands. It was like a thunderclap through the cotton of her panties.

'Ow!'

The pain was fierce and sudden, with strange powers. Her

skin burnt, but in her cleft, her clit pulsed and leapt. Had she come? She couldn't even tell, the signals were so mixed.

'What's the matter, little escort girl? Are you getting off?' He mouthed her nipple again, licking, sucking. Her clit jerked again, tightening.

'Could be,' she gasped, surprised she could still be so bold when her senses were whirling, 'I'm not sure.'

'Well, let's make certain then, eh?' Manhandling her, he turned her a little between his thighs. 'Arms around my shoulders. Hold on tight.'

'But . . .'

'This is what I've paid you for, Bettie' His blue eyes flashed. 'My pleasure is your compliance. That's the name of the game.'

She put her hands on him, obeying. The muscles of his neck and shoulders felt strong, unyielding, through the fine cotton of his shirt and the silk of his waistcoat lining, and this close, a wave of his cologne rose up, filling her head like an exotic potion, lime and spices, underscored by just a whiff of a foxier scent, fresh sweat. He was as excited as she, for all his apparent tranquillity, and that made her dizzier than ever. This was all mad, like no sex she'd ever really had before, although right here, right now, she was hard pressed to remember anything she'd done with other men.

'Oh Bettie, Bettie, you're really rather delightful,' he crooned, pushing a hand into her knickers from the front, making her pitch over, pressing her face against the side of his. His hair smelt good too, but fainter and with a greener note. He was a pot-pourri of delicious male odours.

'Oh, oh, God.' Burrowing in with determined fingers, he'd found her clit, and he took possession of it in a hard little rub. Her sex gathered itself, heat massing in her belly she was so ready from all the forays and tantalising gambits he'd put her through.

'If you have an orgasm before I give you permission, I'll slap your bottom, Bettie.' His voice was low, barely more than a breath. 'And if you come again . . . I'll slap you again.'

'But why punish me? If you want me to come?' She could barely speak, but something compelled her to. Maybe just the act of forming words gave her some control. Over herself at least.

'Because it's my will to do it, Bettie. Because I want you to come, and spanking your bottom makes me hard.' He twisted his neck, and pressed a kiss against her throat, a long, indecent licking kiss, messy and animal. 'Surely you understand how we men sometimes are?'

'Yes . . . yes, of course I do . . . Men are perverts,' she panted, bearing down on his relentless fingertip that was rocking now. 'At least the fun ones mostly are, in my experience.'

'Oh brava! Bravissima! That's my girl . . .' Latching his mouth on to her earlobe in a wicked nip, he circled his finger, working her clit like a bearing, rolling and pushing.

As his teeth closed tighter, just for an instant, he overcame her. She shouted, something incoherent, orgasming hard in sharp, intense waves, her flesh rippling.

The waves were still rolling when he slapped again, with his fully open hand, right across her bottom cheek.

'Ow! Oh God!'

John nuzzled her neck, still making magic with his finger, and torment with his hand, more and more slaps. Her body was a maelstrom, her nerves not sure what was happening, pain and pleasure whipping together in a froth. She gripped him hard, holding on, dimly aware that she might be hurting him too with her vice-like hold.

'Oh please . . . time out,' she begged after what could have been moments, or much longer.

The slaps stopped, and he curved his whole hand around her crotch, the gesture vaguely protective . . . or perhaps possessive?

'Not used to coming when you're "on duty"?' His voice was silky and provocative, but good-humoured. 'It's nice to know I managed to make you lose it. Seems that I've not lost my touch.' He pressed a kiss to her neck, snaking his arm around her back, supporting her.

Lizzie blinked, feeling odd, unsorted. She hadn't expected to feel quite this much with him. It had all started as a lark, a bit of fun, testing herself to see if she could get away with her pretence. She still didn't know if she'd achieved that, and she wasn't sure John Smith would give her a straight answer if she found a way to ask him.

Either way, he'd touched her more than just physically. He'd put heat in her bottom, and confusion in her soul.

For a few moments, she just let herself be held, trying not to think. She was half draped across the body of a man she barely knew, with several hundred pounds of his money in her bag and on the dresser. His hand was still tucked inside her panties, cradling her pussy, wet with her silk.

'You're very wet down there, sweetheart,' he said, as if he'd read her thoughts again. He sounded pleased with himself, which, she supposed he should be if he really believed she was an escort and he'd got her as dripping wet as this. 'And real, too . . . not out of a tube.' He dabbled in her pond.

'It's not unknown, John. I told you that . . . Some of us enjoy our profession very much. We make the most of our more attractive clients.'

'Flatterer,' he said, but she detected a pleased note in his voice. He was a man and only human. They all liked to be praised for their prowess. His hand closed a little tighter on her sex, finger flexing. 'Do you think you could oblige this attractive client with a fuck now? Nothing fancy this time. Just a bit of doggy style, if you don't mind.'

In spite of everything, Lizzie laughed out loud. He was a sexy, possibly very devious character, but she also sensed he was a bit of a caution too, a man with whom one could have good fun without sex ever being involved.

'I'd be glad to,' she replied, impetuously kissing him on the cheek, wondering if that was right for her role. Straightening up, she moved onto the bed, feeling his hand slide out of her underwear. 'Like this?' She went up on her knees on the mattress, close to the edge, reaching around to tug at her knickers and make way for him.

'Delightful . . . Hold that thought. I'll be right with you.'

Over her shoulder, Lizzie watched him boldly, eager to see if his cock was as good as it had felt through his clothes.

Swiftly, John unbuttoned his washed-slate-blue waistcoat, and then his trousers, but he didn't remove them. Instead, he fished amongst his shirt-tails and his linen, pushing them aside and freeing his cock without undressing.

He was a good size, hard and high, ruddy with defined, vigorous veining. He frisked himself two or three times, as if he doubted his erection, but Lizzie had no such doubts. He looked as solid as if he'd been carved from tropical wood.

'OK for you?' Jiggling himself again, he challenged her with a lift of his dark blond eyebrows.

'Very fair. Very fair indeed.' She wiggled her bottom enticingly. 'Much better than I usually get.'

'Glad to hear it.' He reached for a condom, and in a few quick, deft movements enrobed himself. A latex coating didn't diminish the temptation.

Taking hold of her hips, he moved her closer to the edge of the bed in a brisk, businesslike fashion, then peeled off her panties, tugging them off over her shoes and tossing them away.

'Very fair. Very fair indeed,' he teased, running his hands greedily over her buttocks and making the slight tingle from where he'd spanked her flare and surge. 'I'd like to spank you again, but not tonight.' Reaching between her legs, he played with her labia and her clit, reawakening sensations there too. 'I just want to be in you for the moment, but another time, well, I'd like to get fancier then, if you're amenable.'

'I . . . I think that could be arranged,' she answered, panting. He was touching her just the way she loved. How could he do that? If he kept on, she'd be agreeing to madness. Wanting to say more, she could only let out a moan and rock her body to entice him.

'Good, very good.' With some kind of magician-like twist of the wrist, he thrust a finger inside her, as if testing her condition. 'I'll pay extra, of course. I don't like to mark women, but you never know. I'll recompense you for any income lost, don't worry.'

What was he talking about? She could barely think. He was pumping her now. Not touching her clit, just thrusting his finger in and out of her in a smooth, relentless rhythm. And when her sensitive flesh seemed about to flutter into glorious orgasm, he pushed in a second finger too, beside the first. As she wriggled and rode them, she felt his cock brushing her thigh.

'Are you ready for me?' The redundant question was like a breeze sighing in her ear, so soft as he leant over her, clothing and rubber-clad erection pressed against her.

'What do you think?' she said on a hard gasp, almost coming, her entire body sizzling with sensation.

'Ready, willing and able, it seems.' He buried his face in her hair, and nuzzled her almost fondly. 'You're a remarkable woman, Bettie.'

And then she was empty, trembling, waiting . . . but not for long. Blunt and hot, his penis found her entrance, nudging, pushing, entering as he clasped her hip hard for purchase and seemed to fling himself at her in a ruthless shove.

'Oof!' His momentum knocked the breath out of her, sending her pitching forward, the side of her face hitting the mattress, her heart thrilling to the sheer primitive power of him. She felt him brace himself with a hand set beside her, while the fingers of his other hand tightened on her body like a vice, securing his grip. His thrusts were so powerful she had to hold on herself, grabbing hunks of the bedding to stop herself sliding.

'Hell. Yes!' His voice was fierce, ferocious, not like him. Where were his playful amused tones now? He sounded like a wild beast, voracious and alpha. He fucked like one too, pounding away at her. 'God, you're so tight . . . so *tight*!' There was surprise in the wildness too.

Squirming against the mattress, riding it as John rode her, Lizzie realised something. Of course, he had no idea he was taking a road with her that not too many men had travelled. She'd had sex, yes, and boyfriends. And enjoyed them immensely. But not all that many of them, throughout her years as a woman. Fewer than many of her friends, and hundreds fewer than an experienced escort.

But such thoughts dissolved. Who could think, being possessed like this? How could a man of nice but normal dimensions feel like a gigantic force of nature inside her, knocking against nerve-endings she couldn't remember ever being knocked before, stroking against exquisitely sensitive spots and making her gasp and howl, yes, howl!

Pleasure bloomed, red, white heat inside her, bathing her sex, her belly, making her clit sing. Her mouth was open against the duvet; good God, she was drooling too. Her hips jerked, as if trying to hammer back against John Smith as hard as he was hammering into her.

'Yes . . . that's good . . . oh . . .' His voice degraded again, foul, mindless blasphemy pouring from those beautiful lips as he ploughed her. Blue, filthy words that soared like a holy litany. 'Yes, oh God . . . now touch yourself, you gorgeous slut . . . rub your clit while I fuck you. I want you to be coming when I do. I want to feel it around me, your cunt, grabbing my dick.'

She barely needed the stimulus; the words alone set up the reality. The ripple of her flesh against his became hard, deep, grabbing clenches, the waves of pleasure so high and keen she could see white splodges in front of her eyes, as if she were swooning under him, even as she rubbed her clit with her fingers.

As she went limp, almost losing consciousness, a weird cry almost split the room. It was high, odd, broken, almost a sob as John's hips jerked like some ancient pneumatic device of both flesh and iron, pumping his seed into the thin rubber membrane lodged inside her.

He collapsed on her. She was collapsed already. It seemed as if the high wind that had swept the room had suddenly died. Her lover, both John and *a* John lay upon her, substantial, but

not a heavy man really. His weight, though, seemed real, in a
state of dreams.

After a minute, or perhaps two or three, he levered
himself off her, standing. She felt the brush of his fingers
sliding down her flank in a soft caress, then came his voice.

'Sorry about calling you a "slut" . . . and the other stuff. I
expect you've heard a lot worse in this line of work, but still
. . . You know us men, we talk a lot of bloody filthy nonsense
when we're getting our ends away. You don't mind, do you?'

'No . . . not at all. I rather like it, actually.' Rolling onto
her side, then her back, she discovered him knotting the
condom, then tossing it into the nearby waste bin. His cock
was deflating, naturally, but still had a certain majesty about
it, even as he tucked it away and sorted out his shirt-tails and
his zip.

'God, you look gorgeous like that.' His blue eyes blazed,
as if his spirit might be willing again even if his flesh was
currently shagged out. 'I'd love to have you again, but I think
I've been a bit of pig and I'll be *hors de combat* for a little while
now.'

You do say some quaint things, John Smith . . . But I like it.
I like you.

'Perhaps we could go again? When you've had a rest?'
She glanced across at the second pile of notes on the dresser.
It looked quite a lot. 'I'm not sure you've had full value for
your money.'

John's eyes narrowed, amused, and he gave her an odd,
boyish little grin.

'Oh, I think I've had plenty. You . . . you've been very good,
beautiful Bettie. Just what I needed.' He sat down beside her,
having swooped to pick up her panties, then pressed the little
cotton bundle into her hands. 'I haven't been sleeping too

well lately, love. But I think I'll sleep tonight now. Thank you.'

A lump came to Lizzie's throat. This wasn't sexual game playing, just honest words, honest thanks. He seemed younger suddenly, perhaps a little vulnerable. She wanted to stay, not for sex, but to just hug him, and hold him.

'Are you OK?'

'Yes, I'm fine,' he said, touching her cheek. 'But it's time for you to go. I've had what I've paid for, and more, sweet girl. I'd think I'd like to sleep now, and you should be home to your bed too. You don't have any more appointments tonight, do you?'

'No . . . nothing else.' Something very strange twisted in her mid-section. Yes, she should go now. Before she did or said something very silly. 'I'm done for the night.' She got up, wriggled into her knickers as gracefully as she could, then accepted her other things from John's hands. He'd picked them up for her. 'I'll just need a moment in your bathroom, then I'll leave you to your sleep.'

She skittered away, sensing him reaching for her. Not sure she could cope with his touch again, at least not in gentleness.

John stared at the door to the bathroom, smiling to himself, but perplexed.

You haven't been working very long, have you, beautiful Bettie?

How new was she to the game, he wondered. She didn't have that gloss, that slightly authoritative edge that he could always detect in an experienced escort. She was a sensual, lovely woman, and she seemed unafraid, but her responses were raw, unfiltered, as if she'd not yet learned to wear a mask and keep a bit of herself back. The working girls he'd been with had always been flatteringly responsive, accomplished, a massage to his ego. But there'd always been a tiny trickle of an edge that told him he was really just a job to them, even if they did genuinely seem to enjoy themselves.

But Bettie seemed completely unfettered by all that. She was full throttle. There was no way she could have fabricated her enjoyment of the sex; there was no way she could have faked the unprocessed excitement she'd exhibited, the response when he'd spanked her luscious bottom.

She loved it, and maybe that was the explanation. Most whores encountered clients who wanted to take the punishment, not dish it out. Maybe she wasn't all that experienced in being on the receiving end of BDSM? But she was a natural, and he needed a natural right now. Someone fresh, and vigorous, and enthusiastic. Unschooled, but with a deep, innate understanding of the mysteries.

He *had* to see her again. And see her soon.

3

Gorgeous

'Are you out of your mind, you idiot? Just because it's called "being on the game" that doesn't mean it *is* a game. You can't just play at it, Lizzie!'

Brent was furious. Lizzie got that. Her male house-mate had been an escort himself, on and off, and her wild escapade with John Smith must seem like a bit of an insult to him, and to men and women who lived the life and took it seriously.

She looked from one of her companions to the other, hoping for some support from Shelley, the third house-sharer. But Shelley was just gawping at her as if she was a space alien, as if a pod person had overtaken her normally moderately sensible friend.

'I meant to tell him, really I did. But things got a bit passionate, and there didn't seem to be the right moment.' Their black tailless cat, Mulder, leapt up onto her lap and automatically Lizzie began to stroke her. The rhythmic action, and the little feline's soft purr, settled and centred her. 'Also, it was patently obvious he *wanted* an escort. Not a one-night stand. No complications, know what I mean? If I'd told him he was mistaken, it might have been, "Oops, sorry, thank you and goodnight" . . . and he was far too gorgeous for that.'

Gorgeous was too small a word, though. Too simple. John Smith had a plain name but her instincts told her he was a complicated man. Very complicated.

'Ooh, I wish I'd nipped into the bar and seen him.' Shelley finally found her voice. 'The party was OK . . . but there wasn't much talent, and what there was seemed to be taken already. Same old story.'

Guilt tweaked at Lizzie. Not about John, but about abandoning her friends. If she'd stayed with them, they'd all have found a way to have a laugh, dud party or no dud party. Between them, she and Shelley might even have coaxed the old Brent out of hiding. The one who'd always had them in stitches with snarky remarks and razor-sharp observations.

But Brent was still frowning, his black brows low. They all three were sitting in the kitchen together, the morning after the night before, touching base. There had been no chance to talk in the taxi home from the Waverley because the driver had been the nosy, garrulous kind, asking questions in a slightly seedy way about their evening. Lizzie had feigned an exhaustion that hadn't been entirely faux, and once they'd got home, to the house they shared in a quiet suburban road, not too far out of town, Lizzie had scuttled to her room with yawned apologies to Shelley and Brent, not wanting to do anything but think about John Smith.

And she'd done nothing but think of him all night. Despite her tiredness, she'd lain awake, imagining herself still lying under him, being pounded. She could still feel him now, as if his flesh had imprinted itself upon her, as if his cock was there inside her still. As if his strong, deft fingertip was still on her clit as he spanked her.

Lizzie! Get a grip! Stop being a sex fiend!

But hell, yes, that spanking. She kept coming back to it, again and again.

And now, both Shelley and Brent were still staring at her. Shelley looked a bit lost in admiration, to be honest, but their handsome flatmate was cross. Lizzie knew why. He was worried about her welfare, and knowing what he knew about the life of an escort, she could easily see why he'd be concerned.

'I think you'd have liked him. You're a good judge of character. If you'd met him, you'd have known he was pukka.'

Brent's expression softened. 'I'm not that great a judge . . . not always.' He gave a shrug of his lean shoulders, and swept his dark hair out of his eyes. Eyes that could flash with wicked humour, but also show a terrible, terrible sadness. 'But still, this John Smith of yours . . . I mean, "John Smith", what the hell kind of name is that? At least he could have chosen something a bit more imaginative.'

Lizzie fished a card out of her robe pocket. A business card, plain white, with a name and a mobile number in a sharp, no-nonsense font and a tiny logo, an entwined J & S in the corner.

'It's his name. Really.' As Shelley craned for a look, she handed over the card to Brent, remembering her bark of astonished laughter.

'It really is my name,' he'd reiterated, smiling as she'd emerged from the bathroom, her clothing set to rights, even if her mind and her senses were still in turmoil. He'd changed into a long, dark blue silk robe, and the idea of his naked body beneath the thin, light cloth had almost made her beg him to let her stay.

But she hadn't. He didn't want that. He'd calmly and

composedly explained that all he wanted for the duration of his stay in the area – business stuff, looking over properties, acquisitions – was a beautiful and experienced woman to have sex with, someone who'd be comfortable with his 'preferences', and game for a bit of the 'fancy'. He was willing to pay, and pay well, particularly if she were to make herself available exclusively to him for the duration. He'd make sure that she was well compensated for any income lost by not seeing other clients.

Brent turned the card over in his fingers as Lizzie outlined all this to him, and Shelley listened, all ears.

'Ooh, just like *Pretty Woman* . . . You lucky bitch!' She grinned, and though Lizzie sensed a bit of genuine envy in her friend, she knew it was good-natured. 'Trust you to score a freaking millionaire or whatever, you jammy thing.'

'Well . . . on the face of it, it sounds like the ideal gig,' observed Brent. 'A high-roller with not too many strings attached, and hopefully not too weird. He doesn't want the girlfriend experience, then? No all-nighters?'

'Nope, just evenings. He's busy with what sounds like high-powered "tycoon" type stuff during the day, and at night he prefers to sleep alone.' Ignoring the word *weird* for the time being, she nevertheless experienced a pang. It was daft to want it, but the idea of actually curling up for sleep with John was suddenly infinitely appealing. Almost as much as fucking him, or feeling his hand strike her bottom. She could still smell the clean scent of him, and imagine cuddling against his warm skin, dozing off.

No, no, no . . . don't go there. This is what it is.

And that thing was a slightly crazy lark and a chance to broaden her sexual horizons with an interesting and very desirable man. A chance to be someone other than Lizzie

Aitchison, ordinary girl bored to death with office temping, and in a limbo of not quite having figured out what to do with her life, even at twenty-four.

'Probably for the best. You're playing with fire, my girl, and the less time you have the matches in your hand, the better.' Brent shrugged sagely.

Mulder the cat wriggled out of her arms, as if sensing her unease, and trotted off out of the room. While Shelley made 'Don't listen to him . . . tell me more!' faces behind his back, Lizzie eyed Brent, who'd got up to fetch the teapot and top up their mugs. It was easier to talk to his narrow shoulders about certain matters.

'Er . . . what do you know about BDSM? John seems to be into that sort of thing. He said he'd like to . . . well . . . experiment more next time.'

'BDSM? Yikes!' Shelley edged forward. She looked like a wide-eyed, slightly prurient pixie, with smudges of last night's mascara and her cap of ash blonde hair standing up in morning tufts.

Brent rolled his eyes as he set down the teapot on its mat in the middle of the table. 'Oh, please don't tell me he wants you to spank him? It's much harder than it looks in the films and on the telly. It's an art, and you can really hurt someone if you don't know what you're doing. Which, unless I know less about your previous adventures than you've told me, you don't.'

Eyes narrowed, he poured the tea, waiting; while Shelley seemed beside herself with excited anticipation.

'No, actually, it's the other way round. He wants to spank me . . . Um . . . to spank me again.'

'Oh my, we are already in deep, aren't we?' Brent studied her over the rim of his mug, his pale blue eyes worried. But he also looking vaguely admiring, as if she'd impressed him somehow. All three of the house-mates shared quite intimate confidences, but she and Brent were especially close, both emotionally and about their sex lives. Lizzie hoped it could stay that way. She couldn't bear to think they'd just hit a barrier with him when he needed both her and Shelley so much.

'Deepish . . . although I don't think he's a vicious sadist or anything. It's just a pain and pleasure thing with him.' She stared into her mug, imagining it was a glass of gin, crystal clear and with answers swimming in it.

'Do you even know what a sadist is? Or a dominant? They're a bit different, you know.' Brent's voice was sharp.

'Yes, I sort of get the gist . . . but it's all theoretical, from sexy stories and what have you. I've never had any practice, really, other than a bit of horsing around that didn't account to anything and ended up just getting rather embarrassing.'

'Er . . . what horsing around? You've never told me about this?' Shelley demanded.

Lizzie felt rather hot all of a sudden. It was OK talking to one or other of her friends about personal topics, one on one, but this was turning into something suspiciously like a being grilled by the panel situation. 'Er . . . don't you have a special gig this morning?' she asked Shelley, grasping a welcome straw that had just occurred to her. The two of them temped for the same secretarial agency, and she knew the other girl had something booked in for today, even though it was a Saturday. Double rate was always welcome.

'Oh shit! Fuck! Yes, I have and I'm going to be buggering well late!' Shelley flung herself off her stool, spilling tea in the process. Abandoning her mug, and grabbing a banana from the fruit bowl for a travelling breakfast, she made for the door. 'I want all the gruesome details later! I mean it! Promise?' she flung over her shoulder before disappearing out of the door and thundering up the stairs to her room.

'Promise,' said Lizzie, returning her attention to Brent now they were alone.

'You do need to be careful, love.' Worry was winning the battle in his eyes. 'You need to set firm limits beforehand. Establish a safe word. Especially if you're supposed to be an escort . . . Most don't tend to "sub" because they can't risk getting bruised and looking a mess for the next client. I've often been asked to dispense it, though. You know, women, and men too . . . when they read the latest hot book and they want to know what it feels like.'

Lizzie explained the general outline of John's proposition, and how he'd offered to compensate her on that score.

'Well, in that case, if you promise to stay safe, and keep your phone handy with my number at the ready . . . Maybe you should go for it, if only for one more date. Are you supposed to see this gorgeous, gin-drinking dominant of yours tonight, then? How are you communicating with him? You haven't given him your normal phone number, have you?' He glanced across at the twin electrical socket in the corner, with his personal iPhone, and his 'working' iPhone, both currently charging. He hadn't been on any appointments in a long, long time, but he still kept the phone charged out of habit. 'Escorts always have a separate phone, solely for "business".'

Lizzie reached for a biscuit, but took two, then another. She'd expended a lot of calories last night in all that writhing about and squirming in pleasure. 'Ah, I thought of that. I told him I'd just had my phone stolen, and that I wasn't officially working last night. I gave him my "Bettie" Gmail address so he could contact me . . . and I was going to nip to the phone shop today and get a cheap second phone.'

Brent looked admiring again. 'Well, at least part of your brain wasn't completely softened by lust. Shall we make a day of it? I'm not due in until the four-to-eight stint. We could have lunch, then hit the O2 shop? To spend some of your ill-gotten gains?' Brent sometimes worked on Saturdays too, in a garden centre, a job he'd dismissed as menial when he'd first grudgingly accepted it as a stop gap, but now seemed to have taken to.

'Absolutely. Unlike you two, I've got absolutely no work of any kind today, and I'd love to do lunch.' Lizzie's heart lightened, seeing something of the old Brent twinkle coming back. 'I need some new undies as well . . . something a bit more deluxe.' She paused again, and felt her blush intensify. 'And maybe a little detour into the Anne Summers shop . . . for a few, um, accessories. And a lot of condoms, of course.'

'Of course.' Brent looked solemn, but he was fighting not to laugh. 'One must be prepared for anything.' He reached across the table. 'If you're going to do this bonkers thing, you might as well do it right . . . and enjoy yourself. Especially if he's as gorgeous as you say.'

'Oh, he is . . . he is . . .'

'I'll make some breakfast, then we'll make plans.' Brent rose, lithe and handsome as he crossed the room. Lizzie still found him attractive, but in a detached sort of way. The two of them had enjoyed a fling very briefly, a year or two ago, but had soon realised they liked each other much better as friends, partly because Brent's true emotional preference was for men.

'Incidentally, how much did you charge?' he flung over his shoulder, rummaging in the fridge.

Lizzie named her price, and the bonus John had given her.

'Good grief, woman, you must have been good! That's as much as I'd have charged for an all-nighter. I can't believe you pulled down that amount of dosh for something you'd have done for nothing anyway. There's no justice in this world, you acquisitive little bitch,' he finished amiably.

'Well, I shan't keep it all. Just enough for the undies and stuff, and some for the rent and bills pot.' She remembered her guilt, not over the sex and the subterfuge, just about the money. 'I'm going to put the rest in an envelope and slip it through the letterbox at the Cats' Protection shop. Either that or keep it all and give it back to him when he goes.'

Brent shook his head. 'If you're going to do this thing, do it properly. He's obviously loaded and the money means nothing to him. So spend the money on yourself and on the lucky kitty cats, if you must.'

Maybe I will . . . Maybe I will . . .

But why did she somehow feel that she was the one who ought to be paying John Smith for her pleasure, rather than the other way around?

Don't look anywhere but where you're going, Belle had said in *The Secret Diary of a Call Girl*. Swan straight into a place as if you're meant to be there, head up, gaze forward, looking fabulous.

Well, yes, that probably worked beautifully in a huge cosmopolitan hotel in a big city, but the Waverley Grange was just a modest-sized country house hotel, and the staff on reception probably knew precisely who all their guests were, and who was or wasn't supposed to be in the building. Lizzie's heart thudded, and not from the delirious excitement of seeing John again. No, it was the fear of being called to account by someone that had her pulse hammering.

'I shouldn't worry, love,' Brent had said. 'The Waverley is a rum sort of place and they won't turn a hair over a guest sending out for an escort. They have regular fetish nights, and the bar is known as an upmarket pick-up spot. Hell, I've done appointments there myself, in the past.'

Still, Lizzie's nerves jumped when she forgot her resolutions and glanced at the reception desk. A tall, dark, slightly Latin looking man with long black hair was behind the desk. He wore a superb suit, something she might imagine John wearing, but just a tad flashier. The manager, she thought, and he doesn't half fancy himself. Dark eyes behind metal-framed spectacles appraised her, and he smiled slightly, but his barely perceptible nod seemed to be her pass to the hotel's interior.

In the lift, she tried to slow down her breathing, and checked her look in the mirror on the back wall. She'd gone for a businesslike vibe with a smart, navy blue suit she'd once got for a big interview, worn with a crisp white blouse. She hadn't got the job – there were a hundred people up for it – but she knew she'd looked fantastic on the day. Her hair was shining black, easily guided into its almost natural 'Bettie' style, her shoes were her highest heels, and she carried her most humungous bag that could still be termed a handbag rather than a tote. She didn't like to think what would have happened if the hotel manager had insisted on a security check, although if what Brent said about the Waverley was true, maybe almost everybody marched into the place with bags full of condoms, sex toys, spare lingerie, lubricants and goodness knew what else.

Reaching John's floor in moments, she drew in a big

breath and stepped out, remembering last night. She'd been with him, his hand at the small of her back, guiding her. Now she had to proceed under her own steam, with the choice to chicken out entirely at her disposal. She fingered the new phone in her bag, with John already listed as a 'favourite', along with Brent and Shelley. It would be so easy to call or text, politely declining. Brent would probably even know an alternative girl who'd be happy to take the gig.

No way!

At his door, she rapped firmly before second thoughts could grip her.

'Bettie! So glad you made it.'

Ah, she hadn't dreamed him. John Smith was just as handsome as she remembered, just as real. It seemed like a week since she'd seen him, a long week in which she'd spent most of her waking moments wanting him again, but really it was just twenty-four hours.

As he conducted her into the room, she wondered if he'd been aware of her doubts. Something quizzical in his expression seemed to suggest so, as if he were privy to her most intimate thoughts . . . and perhaps the depth of her deception? 'Nice to see you again, John,' she said, masking it all, and leaning in towards him, to kiss his cheek. Her lips brushed a faint hint of stubble, and he was dressed for business, apart from his abandoned jacket. Had he been hard at work doing whatever it was he did, even far into the evening?

'You look perfectly delicious, woman. That's a great outfit. Do you always dress for business when you're doing business?' He winked at her, his expression puckish and provocative.

'Doesn't do to look too obvious in my line of work. Keep

the goodies in a plain brown wrapper, so to speak.' She winked back at him.

'Speaking of business . . .' John crossed to the dresser and came back with a plump envelope. The cash sum, she presumed, that they'd agreed when she'd emailed her new phone number.

Knowing it was crass to count it in front of him, she said, 'Might I powder my nose before we . . . we get started?'

'Of course.' His blue eyes glittered. Had he heard the little hesitation? She still couldn't be sure he didn't suspect. He seemed to be almost humming with thoughts and secrets all the time, his smile open like the sun, yet hiding Lord alone knew what shadows and deceptions of his own.

In the bathroom, she counted the cash – all there – then texted Brent to say everything was OK and he mustn't worry. After a few deep centring breaths, she spent a penny, rinsed her hands, and refreshed her lip gloss.

Ready as I'll ever be. Now or never and all that . . .

She pushed open the door.

John was sipping a small drink. Gin, she supposed. She could detect a faint hint of its balsamic tang as he came close to her. 'Drink?' he enquired.

'I'll just have some water, please, if I may?'

'You are businesslike tonight, aren't you?' His grin was tricky as he opened a bottle and poured for her.

'Well, I'm in a service industry. I like to stay sharp and give value for money.'

'Admirable . . . admirable . . .' he murmured, watching her like a raptor as she took a few sips, then put aside the drink.

Another deep breath. 'So, John . . . what's it to be?'

His beautiful mouth quirked, then for just an instant, he snagged his plush lower lip between his teeth. Then even

though there was barely any visible sign of it, she sensed him
turn to steel in front of her. It was as if he grew an inch or
two, at least in aura, radiating power. She imagined him as a
demon, a bastard of the negotiating table, getting everything
he ever wanted with barely any effort.

'Well . . . first, indulge me, beautiful Bettie . . . Call me
"master".'

It was like being back in the lift again, but with the cable
cut. The word sent her plunging wildly, perhaps not down a
lift shaft but a hurtling roller-coaster plunge, a thrill of terror
ride. This was it. The game. She could play, or just give him
his money back and flee.

Never!

'Yes, master,' she said. Her voice was soft; he'd taken her
breath away.

He took her face between his two smooth hands and
looked into her eyes, the intensity of his scrutiny stripping
her. Still fully clothed she felt more than naked, all her hopes
and fears revealed. Then he kissed her, gently at first, then
more powerfully. Thrilling to her submissive role, she kept
her lips still, and pliant, receptive, passive. Her arms hung by
her sides as he ravished her with his lips and tongue, tasting
the soft interior of her mouth, subduing her, filling her to the
brim with the kiss.

'Good,' he said abstractedly, releasing her lips. 'Very good.'
Sliding his thumb across her face, he pushed that into her
mouth like a pacifier. 'Suck it.' As she obeyed, he let his other
hand glide down her body, over breast, flank and thigh, then,
tugging at her skirt, he hauled it up ruthlessly and cupped
her bottom cheek in a rough, rude grip. Her flesh was dough
to him, he kneaded it, fingertips digging in. After a second
or two, he pushed his fingers into her anal groove, rubbing

her there, teasing, pressing, his other thumb dragging at the corner of her mouth as she gasped, breathing hard.

'Such a delicious little strumpet,' he whispered, hard up against her, his breath wafting her hair as he massaged her anus through her knickers. 'Dirty little minx . . . You like this, don't you?' He probed her, pushing, pushing. 'I bet you'd like a cock in there, wouldn't you? Or a plug? A big fat black plug?'

Heat surged through every cell in her body. Goddammit, she was sweating, despite her industrial strength deodorant. Her head filled with visions of herself kneeling on the chintz covered bed, her bottom well up, heavily lubricated, while John pushed obscenely inside her rectum. Swaying, she was weak at the knees at the very thought of it.

'Answer me.' His thumb slid out of her mouth.

'Yes . . . yes . . . I'd like that.'

'Cock or plug?'

'Either . . . if it pleases you.'

He laughed happily, sounding almost boyish. 'Perfect answer, my darling.' He kissed her again, softer this time. 'We'll do that . . . play those games. Maybe not tonight, but soon.'

His lips plundered hers again, more rough kisses as he fingered her rear portal.

'Lovely girl,' he said at length, freeing her, setting her from him and looking her up and down again as her skirt slid back into place. 'And lovely suit too . . .' He touched her breast fleetingly through the crisp jacket. 'I think I'd like you to keep it on for a while.'

As she stood there waiting, he retrieved his drink and sipped a small mouthful before putting it aside. 'Will you bring that chair from over there into the centre of the room?'

He nodded to a very plain wooden upright chair that she'd never noticed before. Had it been there last night? She didn't think so. Had he requested it specially, for his devious purposes?

She set the chair in the centre of the room, a few feet from the bed, facing it.

'Now sit down, please.'

Trembling a bit, Lizzie took her place, arms resting on her thighs. John moved to stand directly in front of her, looking down. She tried to keep her eyes respectfully lowered, but she couldn't stop herself staring at his crotch. His erection was massive already.

'Naughty, naughty . . . you mustn't look at that. You can't have that for a while yet, much as I know you're wet for it.'

She was. She really was. Perspiration wasn't the half of it. Her expensive new knickers were already saturated with silky arousal. There wouldn't be any necessity for her to fake her enthusiasm with lube, no way.

'Sit very still. Eyes lowered. No peeking.'

He strode away, towards the dresser, and opened a drawer. Curiosity boiled. She wanted to see what he was taking out, but she managed to keep her eyes downcast, only stealing an oblique glance when he threw a few items on the bed. It looked like a handful of silk scarves, the substantial, men's kind, and perhaps some ties.

Bondage now? Well, she'd expected it.

Trailing a scarf, he came and stood behind her, and with no warning, drew first one of her arms then the other behind the chair-back. In quick, precise movements, he tied her wrists. The knot was firm, though not painfully restricting, but the positioning of her hands made her chest lift, and her breasts press against the fabric of her jacket and blouse. She was breathing hard as he went away, and then brought back another scarf.

This, he fastened around her eyes. It was a black scarf, in a tight weave. She could no longer see a single thing. As he adjusted it, he stroked her hair, tidying and smoothing.

What now? What now?

She could hear him moving about. She could almost hear him thinking, although not the actual thoughts. He was plotting, scheming.

He was close.

Strong hands settled on her thighs and she realised he was actually kneeling in front of her. Surely that was wrong? He shouldn't kneel to her; he was the master here. Then she had a flash of what he was up to, the second before he did it.

He pushed up her skirt, saying, 'Hup!' to make her lift her bottom from the seat so he could bunch the fabric around her waist, back and front. Next, he slid his thumbs in the elastic of her knickers and skinned them down in a brisk, ruthless action. The waft of his shirtsleeved arm seemed to suggest him tossing them away across the room.

'Sublime.'

Steps away again, then he was back at her, and with more scarves, he secured her ankles to the front legs of the chair, immobilising her with her crotch on show and her bare bottom and her pussy pressed to the wooden seat.

Oh God, oh God, oh God!

A sensation of light-headedness engulfed her, powerlessness and extreme excitement. It was like being very young again, right on the sexual threshold, and about to go all the way for the first time. Her heart thundered, and she almost wanted to cry, but in a good way. The very best way.

'Pretty as a picture,' said John roundly. She could sense

him still very close, crouching in front of her as if he were staring intently at her exposed bush. There was absolute silence for a moment, apart from his breathing and hers, which was far more rapid and fluttering, then she felt it.

A fingertip slid in amongst her pubic curls, parting her labia, to settle right on the tip of her clit in the very lightest ghost of a contact. Her hips jerked, pushing her forward, chasing pressure, but the touch was gone again as suddenly as it had occurred, and she sensed John rise to his feet in front of her.

'And now, I think I'll take a shower.' His footsteps receded away from her. 'Be a good girl while I'm away, won't you?'

Then the bathroom door opened, and closed, and she was alone.

4

Devil in the Dark

Lizzie tried her bonds, but she was firmly secured. How many woman had John tied up lately? Probably enough, because he seemed to know precisely what he was doing.

The room was very quiet. She could barely hear the sound of running water from the bathroom. Her head seemed to fill with scents: the room's pot-pourri, the ghost of John's cologne, the sudden, pungent musk of her pussy.

She could still feel his fingertip against her clit, and it ached for more, almost as if he'd brought her almost to the point of orgasm and just left her hanging. Her awareness of that tiny bud of flesh was out of all proportion. She couldn't stop thinking about it, nestled between her labia, the very nexus of her pleasure. Fondled and abandoned, almost screaming silently for contact, for him to return and rub it. She tossed her head, willing him to come back and masturbate her roughly to orgasm.

The emptiness of the room pressed down upon her. She tried to picture where everything was. The beautiful suit she'd seen hung on the wardrobe door. John's other things. There'd been a laptop, phone, a fine, hide-covered briefcase.

This was his space, temporarily, and she imagined him in it. Walking naked from the bathroom, drying his wheat-gold hair. Lying on the bed, touching himself, liking it, then wanking furiously. Had he done that since yesterday? Had he been thinking of her as he pumped his stiff cock?

Other visions came to her. Images of herself with him. Fucking, yes, but other things. How he might use her and play with her. There was a big, well-upholstered armchair in the room. He might thrash her over the back of that, and bugger her, as he'd intimated. Oh hell, what would that be like? So rude and dark and dangerous . . . Her back passage stuffed with his rampant erection. Her clit throbbed as she tried to imagine it, the tiny reaction entirely spontaneous.

He might bind her again, and gag her, then slather her bottom with lube and take her like a boy, making her grunt and sob with forbidden pleasure.

She wanted it. So much . . .

She wanted everything.

Silky arousal pooled beneath her where she sat. Helplessly, she oozed, a creature enslaved by her own senses. Wanton. Willing. Available.

Faintly, the shower teemed on, in the bathroom. What would happen if someone came to the door? Some hotel employee, perhaps with room service, and on getting no answer they might use their pass key to enter and find her here, bound, exposed, blind and available.

A waiter might come in and be unable to resist the delicious female dish presented to him. He might grab her crotch, just as she longed for John to return and do. Unknown fingers might push and poke at her, rubbing her clit to see if it were possible to rouse her against her will; perhaps wiggling into her vagina, mock-fucking her.

Groaning, she wriggled and rocked on the chair, imagining some stranger playing with her, crudely defiling her while John relaxed on the bed, watching the show. Perhaps he might issue instructions, *pinch her clitty*, *make her come*.

'Oh please,' she murmured to nobody in particular, longing to be used and fingered.

A door opened and every muscle in her body went taut. Was it the bathroom? Or was it the door to the corridor outside, as she'd feared . . . or yearned for?

Footsteps approached. They sounded as if they were heading from the bathroom, and muffled, as if made by bare feet.

John?

The hand she'd anticipated clasped her pussy, finger diving in, making her whimper and struggle. The pressure was firm, but not quite enough, devilishly measured to tease and taunt, but not grant climax.

In a cloud of familiar fragrance, a face nestled against hers, a cheek brushing her hair as the probing fingertip skirted her inner sex lips, her perineum, the margins of her entrance. She felt him scoop a little of her juice, rub it between finger and thumb, assaying her.

'Randy little trollop,' he whispered. 'You've made a mess on the seat with your wetness. You haven't got a bit of self-control, have you? You've just been sitting here getting hornier and hornier . . . What have you been thinking about? Cock, is it?'

Unable to speak, she nodded, wishing her hands were free so she could reach out and grab his crotch as he'd grabbed hers. As if he'd heard her, he stood up and edged to her side, abandoning her sex as he leant his pelvis against her arm. Through the cloth of her jacket, and whatever he was wearing, she felt him like an iron bar, jabbing at her, the mass of him intimidating.

'Have you been thinking about it?' He rocked, pressing harder, and holding her by the shoulder, keeping her steady. Damn him, was he getting himself off that way?

'Yes, I've been thinking about your cock, master. I couldn't help myself.'

She couldn't see his smile, but she could swear it was there. As best she could within the restriction of her bonds, she pressed herself against him, circling her shoulder to caress him.

'Be careful . . . be very careful.' He reached down and touched her lips, running his fingertip across the lower one. When she darted out her tongue to caress it, she tasted her own foxy flavour, and when he turned his hand over, she pressed a fierce kiss of fealty against his knuckle.

'What do you want, Bettie?' He spoke quietly, almost kindly.

She didn't have to think. 'To see you, master. If it pleases you.'

'It'll cost you, sweetheart. That and your naughty thoughts . . . it'll cost you in pain across your beautiful bottom.'

'I don't care . . . master.'

With a flick the dark scarf around her head flew away. It went fluttering to the floor, but she had no time to observe it. She could only look at John. He'd been a devil in the dark, but in the light he was an angel.

Not sure what she was expecting, she was caught by surprise at the sight of what he wore. Masters wore black, didn't they? Sombre, unrelieved, sometimes . . . Often, tight-fitting leather.

But John had on a very light, off-white shirt, made from

cheesecloth or some other floating fabric. It was open down the front, revealing a firm, well-shaped chest, a little tanned and with a scattering of sandy hair across his pectorals. A pair of old, very old jeans clung to his hips and thighs, their venerable state bordering on bleached white, and worn paper thin at the knees. His strong, narrow feet were quite bare. He'd been towelling his hair dry and it was all soft curls; his face looked fresh, his jaw newly shaved.

'Satisfied?' He struck an attitude.

'No.'

'No? What, then?'

He was a feast, and she wanted to gorge her senses on him. See every bit of him, touch every bit of him. Taste . . .

'I don't know . . . To touch you, I think. To convince myself you're real.'

His sandy eyebrows shot up. 'That's rather fanciful. Of course I'm real. But if you need convincing, yes, you can touch me, but I'll punish you all the harder for your whims, beautiful slave, believe me.' He moved closer, filling her head with the scent of his cologne. 'Do you think I'm worth it?'

'Yes!'

Leaning over her, his soft shirt brushing the side of her face, he reached behind her and unfastened her wrists. Freed, she reached for him, not sure what to touch or sample first. After a heartbeat's hesitation, she laid her hand against the muscle of his chest, fingers spread.

Oh, he was so warm, and his skin so smooth. She stroked, loving the crisp yet silky texture of his chest hair. Edging forward, she kissed him there too, unable to resist putting out her tongue and licking his nipple.

'Ooh, that's nice,' he crooned. 'Do that again.'

Circling with the tip of her tongue, she tantalised and

teased the little pink-brown bud, flicking at it, loving that it was erect, just like hers. When she started sucking, he held her head, compelling her to continue, commanding her to pleasure him in this small thing. Sliding her arm around him, she reached up to toy with his other nipple with her free hand, but he knocked it away, plucking at the little crest himself, squeezing and pinching. She could see the action out of the corner of her eye, and it inflamed her. He just didn't care. He did what he wanted, pleasuring himself right there in front of her, even though he was supposed to be playing the stern disciplinarian. When he murmured, 'Mm . . .' and shimmied against her, she almost came on the spot.

'I bet you give marvellous head,' he said, easing her away from him. 'I shall look forward to that. But first, I really want to punish you. Quite hard. Are you OK with that?'

Nodding furiously, she was too choked with lust to speak.

With a smile, he dipped down gracefully and unfastened her ankles from the chair. Again, it seemed bizarre that he should kneel before her, and yet when he straightened, he'd lost none of his dominant aura. He was the strangest master, not a bit like the way she'd anticipated a dominant man might be, but somehow his very unusual approach made him stronger rather than weaker.

He pulled her to her feet and drew her against him, holding her body tight to his as he took her in a rough, messy, annihilating kiss that decimated the finish of her clear lip gloss. His tongue owned her, and he held her head immobile, ravishing her mouth. When her arms lifted of their own accord to embrace him, he made a warning sound in his throat, then kissed her more savagely than before.

Against her belly, his cock was a knot of iron.

Then suddenly the kiss was over as abruptly as it had begun, and licking her gloss off his lips, John took her by the arm and propelled her to the bed. 'Lie face down, pussy near the edge. Stretch your arms out in front of you. You can grab the duvet if you need to.' As if she were an object, a doll, he adjusted her position as soon as she was prone, adjusting her thighs, parting them, making sure she was on show. The fact that she was fully clothed, apart from her bare bottom and her exposed pussy, only made her feel more deliciously subjugated. It was as if she was just an arse and a sex to him at the moment, the rest of her temporarily of little interest.

As he leant over her, she felt the brush of his floating shirt again. 'Don't feel you have to be stoic, Bettie,' he said, drawing a fingertip down her bottom cleft and making her squirm. 'In fact, I'll enjoy it more if you cry . . . or maybe even scream a bit.' His finger tickled her anus. 'I've been told the sound-proofing in this place is second to none, so you won't disturb anyone except me.'

Choked with lust, Lizzie rocked her pelvis against the bed. How could he stir her like this, with little touches, and soft, yet menacing talk? Her body was screaming already, aching for something to happen. She wanted to mash her sex against the mattress, work her clit against something, anything, and she could feel a wet patch forming on the duvet beneath her crotch.

She longed for him to push a finger into her vagina and fuck her with it, but though she had no doubt that in his eerie way he knew exactly what she craved, he didn't oblige her.

In silence, he walked away, and she could hear him sorting through objects in the drawer. Choosing something to use on her? She'd half expected a hand spanking was coming first, but now she suspected something more severe. Wanted it, really. She was afraid of pain – in fact she'd always been a baby about it – but perversely she was longing for it too. For the new experience, for the test. She wanted no half measures, and she knew that John Smith would not short-change her. After all, he'd paid her a princely sum in order to do exactly what he wanted with her. And offered a generous bonus, in case he marked her.

Oh, bring it on, you devil! Bring it on!

She heard a swish of something in the air, and out of the corner of her eye she saw what was producing the sound. A ruler. A simple blue plastic ruler, one of the very same bendy kind they had at home, and which she used for quick measurements on dress patterns.

'Do you need a safe word?'

What was he talking about? Then, it dawned on her. Goddammit, she was supposed to know all this stuff. It was supposed to be second nature. Straining to track him as he moved behind her, she could see the duvet out of the corner of her eye, and said, 'Chintz!'

'Good choice,' he said, sitting down beside her, half twisted sideways on the bed. Face pressed to the duvet, it was difficult to see him, but his presence overwhelmed her. His weight at her side; the scent of him.

'Your bottom is very beautiful, Bettie. But it'll be even prettier when it's red.'

With that he slapped down hard with the plastic ruler, right across the crown of both her buttocks, catching them both in one blow.

'Yowch!'

It hurt, God how it hurt! The ruler wasn't all that substantial but its flexibility gave an evil little flick to it.

Radiant heat bloomed in her flesh, sharp and keen, making her wriggle.

'Keep still,' he ordered, placing his free hand flat on the middle of her back, then lashing her again, this time landing two or three swift blows in quick succession.

Grabbing the duvet, Lizzie tried to hold still, but it was a trial. The heat was furious, much more so than she'd expected. It wasn't a bit like the pathetic, half-hearted spanking games she'd played with a boyfriend or two. This was real, unrelenting, and serious. John was working the plastic ruler methodically over her bottom, covering it in a pattern of strokes, not leaving any area unvisited.

'Oh . . . Oh . . .' she chanted, gripping fistfuls of the chintz duvet cover, straining every sinew to remain motionless but failing miserably. Her pelvis had a mind of its own, and she was circling and rocking, spreading her legs to try and rub herself against the mattress and get some ease for her throbbing clit.

John merely smacked her harder, catching her upper thighs above the tops of her hold-up stockings, angling the ruler to strike the inner slopes of her buttocks, close to her anus.

She wanted him to stop. She wanted him to go on and on. The blaze in her bottom was like white heat, warping her mind. Clutching madly at the bedding, she hauled herself forward a bit, got some purchase with her knees, then gyrated her hips, humping the mattress as the blows rained down. Her body in motion didn't seem to distract John from his purpose in the slightest. He just kept spanking, and spanking, layering the smacks now, making redder the zones that were already red.

'Come up on your knees now, Bettie, that's a good girl.'

Manhandling her, he lifted her up, and she sobbed when his thumbs dug into her punished flesh. 'I'll do your thighs now,' he said in an almost gentle voice, as if he were offering to apply sun cream or some other benison. In a couple of brisk jerks, he pulled down her stockings to the knees, then set about the tender skin of her thighs, lashing, lashing, lashing the ruler, patterning the newly revealed areas in just the way he'd already coloured her bottom.

'Oh God, oh God,' Lizzie chanted, burning with the flames of pain that licked her haunches. Yet still, she could feel her sex dripping, her arousal oozing down her legs, her labia puffed and pouting, her anus winking with each blow as she clenched herself. She was still moving when the ruler stilled, resting across her sizzling cheeks.

'Had enough?' Twisting, John inclined across her, then, with one last tap flung the instrument of her torment away. 'I think I have.' His lips settled against her hair, infinitely gentle. 'You're rather magnificent, you know. A natural. I'd never believe you were a working girl.'

She'd forgotten. She'd completely forgotten. Again. She'd been so into it, so swept away by the intensity. To her horror, a tear oozed out from the corner of her eye, running across her face.

John scooped up the moisture with his fingertip. 'I hit too hard. Didn't I? You're not really into this.' He leant and kissed the track of the tear, infinitely gentle.

For a moment, Lizzie felt as if she were floating up from the bed. She felt very odd. Even the burning heat in her bottom was distant. If she were to roll onto her back, reach up and draw John's lips to her own, she had a feeling she'd barely register her spanking.

'No . . . No, you didn't hit too hard. Not at all.' She

rolled, then hissed between her teeth. Hah, she *did* notice the spanking. In fact she far more than noticed it, but still, the clear blue of John's eyes, and the strangely solicitous expression in them over-rode the discomfort. 'I liked it . . . I actually liked it a lot. So sue me if I'm a kinky whore who gets off on her work.'

John smiled, interesting crinkles forming at the corner of his brilliant eyes. Why hadn't she honed in on slightly older men before? The fit ones were devastatingly attractive. Especially the sophisticated blond variety who were in their forties and gorgeous with it.

'I'm not complaining.' He brushed her hair back from her face where the black strands lay across her cheek. 'Why should I object to getting better value for money? A real response is worth a thousand feigned ones, and everything about you is a bonus, Bettie.'

'Well, at the risk of this turning into a mutual admiration fest, you're a pretty exceptional client, Mr Smith.' It wasn't a lie. He'd have been a gorgeous treat even if he wasn't her only client, faux or otherwise.

'Ah, but isn't it in the escorts' code that you *have* to tell all of us that?'

She guessed it was. Men always wanted to know that they were exceptional, even if they weren't, and if they were paying for a woman's company a little bit of ego stroking was all part of the service.

'Well, yes, sort of, but I try not to get myself into a situation where I have to say it . . . unless I mean it.' When he leant over her, looking into her eyes, she tried to shuffle away a bit, knowing she was in danger of revealing herself. The motion made her wince as the duvet cover scratched her tender bottom.

'Touché.' His hand settled on her bare belly, spread fingertips just brushing the edge of her bush. 'I suppose I'll never get a straight answer out of you, will I?'

Now was the time to tell him. But she couldn't quite get the words out. He seemed so relaxed and comfortable with the escort experience. Knowing she wasn't one would just make things complicated. Especially about the money. She resolved to put most of it aside from now on, to give it back to him eventually, apart from a bit for expenses. If such an obviously wealthy man like him had been courting her properly he would probably have spent far more on gifts and meals and whatnot anyway.

'What on earth are you thinking about, Bettie? You're frowning. If I didn't know better I'd think you were doing your expenses in your head.'

'No! No way! Sorry . . . I just got a bit distracted. I'm so sorry.' She tried to sit up, but his hand remained firm upon her, so she reached up and put her arms around his neck, drawing him down for a quick kiss. His lips were firm, yet evocative with that delicious velvet plushness too. With a dart of his tongue, he responded, kissing her back beautifully. Against her thigh, she felt his erection, still hard as iron.

'Would you like to fuck now, John?' She moved herself against him, ignoring the pangs in her bottom. They were fainter now, anyway, amazingly so. He seemed to be something of an artist where spanking was concerned. Maybe he knew how to lay it on without any lasting damage after all? 'Would you like me to take my clothes off?' His bare chest looked so nice, and she could only imagine how lovely it would feel to press her bare breasts against him as they embraced.

'No, not this time.' He brushed her hair again, then ran a fingertip down the dark lapel of her suit. 'I've a yen to have you while you're still wearing this. I love women in sexy suits. The more severe looking the better. The contrast between strict, crisp lines and wanton animal horniness really gets me going. The idea of a deliciously hot wet pussy beneath a flannel pencil skirt . . . mmm . . . irresistible.'

'Mine's not beneath . . . ah!' She gasped as he cupped her sex, gripping her roughly, a finger going determinedly for her clit.

'Near enough,' he said, a split second before kissing her again and massaging her pussy.

Lizzie writhed on the bed, rubbing her reddened bottom against the duvet, loving both the painful heat there and the heat John was creating between her thighs, playing with her. Whimpers tried to escape from her lips, but he absorbed them with his own, his finger working her tirelessly until she squealed into his mouth, coming intensely.

'Lie still,' he said as she lay panting, and she almost laughed. There wasn't much chance of anything else. She felt sideswiped, and all she could do was watch John as, to her surprise, he wrenched at his soft shirt and almost tore it off, then attacked his jeans.

Naked. He was naked. What a feast.

John Smith's body was lean and well-formed, beautifully proportioned. He didn't have the hard-cut muscle of a gym bunny in his twenties, but he was fit and toned, and she wondered what he did to stay that way. Probably a private trainer or two. She immediately felt jealous, hoping he didn't work out with a woman. Perhaps he swam; that was great for all-over condition.

'You're frowning again. I'm not in that bad nick, am I?' He grinned as he reached beneath the heap of chintz-covered pillows at the head of the bed, for a condom.

'No, you look great, actually. I was just wondering what you do to keep fit. I should really go to a gym or something myself.'

John paused, condom wrapper half torn open. 'Well, thank you, Miss Bettie. I suppose you have to say that, because that's in the whore's operating manual too. But at my age I'm still flattered.' He ripped open the package, and rolled on the contraceptive with admirable speed and dexterity, considering he was staring at her thighs, and her belly. 'And I'd say your own exercise regime is working perfectly. Your body's magnificent, sweetheart. Sheer perfection.'

Lunging forward, he lay between her thighs, kissing her again and stroking her hair. His weight pressed her to the mattress, stirring her fiery bottom, especially when he rocked his hips against hers, pressing his latex-covered cock between her sex-lips.

'What do you mean "my age"? You're not old, you stupid sod!'

Oh my God, why the hell did I say that? What a moment.

John laughed, but his mirth and her tactlessness didn't seem to hamper proceedings. With a smooth roll of his pelvis, he pushed into her, deep and easy.

'Well, that's not the usual sort of remark a man comes to expect just as he's slipping his cock into a woman, but as it's you, I'll let you off. Oh, and by the way, I'm forty-six . . . and a bit.' Grabbing her bottom mercilessly to adjust his angle, he made her gasp. 'And please don't say I don't look it,' he finished, bedding himself in to the hilt and burying his face in her hair.

'I wouldn't dream of it. And anyway, forty-six is nothing. You're still a young stud in your prime,' she panted, flexing against him, loving the feel of him inside her, even loving the pangs of pain in her bottom where he held on to her. Her sex clenched around him, ready, ready, ready to ignite into orgasm, she grabbed on to him as hard he held her.

'Good. I'm glad you think so,' he said happily, his voice gruff as he manipulated her sore thighs, almost doubling her up, pulling them up to rest on his hips. It seemed the most natural thing in the world to hook her ankles together at the base of his spine. She almost laughed. She was still wearing her high heels. They would dig into him but he didn't seem to care. Maybe he even liked it? Perhaps he liked feeling pleasure-pain as much as inflicting it?

Now there was a thing . . .

Their bodies raged at each other. John thundered into her; Lizzie bucked up against him, meeting each lunge, pounding her body against his, stimulating herself with the force of her own movements as much as with the furore of his.

He was in deep, so deep. He filled her completely and seemed to fill her more than physically. An emptiness greater than simply that of her sex was stuffed to the brim. Emptiness of her life, disappointments and failures, paths not followed, all were expunged in that moment of completion.

As her orgasm engulfed her, she laughed out loud. Full of a pure, unadulterated happiness that she wasn't sure she'd experienced since her childhood.

'Oh God, oh God, oh God,' she crooned, enchanted. And it was like an echo bouncing around the chintz-clad room; John chanting the same thing, the very same thing as he powered harder, his hips jerking like an infernal mechanism as he too reached his climax.

Afterwards, for a few seconds, she could barely breathe. Barely think. Only feel.

I've been laid waste to . . . and I love it, love it, love it. I . . .

As she lay holding on to his hot body, and savouring the weight of it, as before, a single tear trickled from the corner of her eye. Post-coital *tristesse*, she supposed, but it was no use wanting things to be different.

They were what they were.

5

No Princess Charming

'I'm sorry. I did it again, didn't I?' He heaved himself off her and flopped back onto the bed, at her side.

'Did what?'

'Behaved like a slavering beast. Hurled myself at you like an animal.' He sat up, grinning wryly as he dealt with the condom. 'You wouldn't think that I pride myself as a sophisticated lover, would you? I seem to turn into the King of the Jungle the moment I start to fuck you.'

'I'm not complaining. I like a bit of enthusiasm. And besides, I'm being paid.' Lizzie hauled herself up too, with some difficulty. She actually did feel a bit like she'd been mauled by a lion, although in the best possible way. Twitching her skirt down from its bundle around her mid-section, she wondered where on earth her knickers had got to. They were really nice ones, among the best she'd ever had. Catering to a high-class 'punter' had been an excuse to indulge herself.

Sitting with his arms around his knees, smiling at her, John said, 'Well, that's all right, then. But next time, I'll try to exercise a bit more finesse. And last longer, for one thing. I'm usually pretty good on the stamina front . . . but it's been

a while, and you really are so very beautiful. It's difficult not
to indulge my baser side.'

'Well, thank you . . . I think.' She smiled back at him,
loving the softer look she saw now in his perceptive blue
eyes. His honesty about his own sexual performance was
refreshing. And modest. In this quiet moment, it was bizarre
to think of the effortless way he'd dominated her, not all that
long ago. More and more, he unveiled his complexity.

Only moments ago, she'd resolved simply to enjoy the
game, and perhaps the prospect of a few more intense sessions
like this, with probably the most exciting and intriguing man
she'd ever met. But those subversive thoughts surfaced again,
yearnings for what she couldn't have.

What would it have been like if they'd met in the bar,
chatted, and then decided to spend the night together? Like
a normal couple?

Maybe they'd both be naked now, and curled in each
other's arms, preparing for sleep? His body was beautiful, but
she also sensed it could be comforting too. It was a long time
since she'd had an all-nighter with a man. God, it was a long
time since she'd been with a man at all. There'd been one or
two brief flings and flirtations since her short but basically
unsatisfactory love affair with Brent, but that was all. It was
no wonder she was all over John Smith like a cheap suit,
lapping him up.

She opened her mouth to suggest she knew not what, but
he pre-empted her, reaching out and brushing his thumb
along her lower lip. 'Still very pink . . . how do you manage
that? With other girls I've often ended up smeared with all
sorts of gunk.' He rubbed his own lip with his other thumb,
'But apart from a bit of stickiness, I've remained remarkably
unsmeared. What's your secret?'

'Lip-stain.' The desire to suck his thumb into her mouth again, and mimic oral sex, was hard to resist. Despite all her orgasms, she found herself wanting him again. 'It's like a pen. Sort of indelible until you use proper make-up remover. You draw it on, then put gloss on top . . . and I've got naturally rosy lips too. That helps.'

'Delectable,' said John softly. Lizzie glanced down. Was he hardening again? It looked as if he might be on the verge of it. 'I think next time we meet, I shall have to sample the esoteric delights of this mouth.' He slid his thumb to and fro, very, very gently. 'I should imagine it will be a very fine thing to slip my cock between such exquisite, indelibly pink lips.'

She stole another quick look at his groin. Yes, definite liveliness, definite thickening. 'I . . . er . . . I could stay a while, and you could have that sample, if you like?' He withdrew his thumb. His blue eyes narrowed a little. 'I mean . . . off the clock. A freebie. On the house.'

Oh God, I sound so desperate. No escort in her right mind would do that, even if she really, really liked the man. Especially if she liked him.

No, it wouldn't do to mix business with pleasure. She could see that in the expression on John's face. It was guarded now, distanced. Shit, she'd put him off.

But to her relief, he smiled. 'Well that's one of the sweetest offers I've had in a long time, Bettie, and I do appreciate it.' He leant forward and kissed where his thumb had been, very briefly, very lightly. 'But I don't do all-nighters. Sorry.'

Disappointment sluiced through her like a cold shower. That and anger at her own ridiculousness. He was a 'client' and she was a 'whore'. Or at least he believed she was. And he clearly wanted her out of the way now, as she was just a pleasant interlude for him. He wasn't the one who was deceiving anybody; it was simply what he'd signed up and paid for, nothing more.

'Never mind. I shouldn't have mentioned it. Not very professional of me, was it?'

'No, not really.' His voice was neutral, yet somehow almost challenging. Was this the moment to tell him?

The words rose to her lips but before she could utter them, he'd slid off the bed and lightly onto his feet, reaching for his blue robe.

'I guess you want me to leave now.' She could have kicked herself for the disappointed tone. Good Lord, she sounded almost petulant, like a spoiled kid who'd had her lolly pinched.

If he was annoyed, or tired, he didn't show it. 'No, you don't have to rush off, sweetheart. Unless of course you've got other plans?' Knotting his sash, he shrugged. 'I would love to avail myself of your services a little longer, but alas, I've got quite a bit of work I need to catch up on tonight, while it's fresh in my mind. You could have a drink before you leave, though, and give yourself time to decompress? If you like?'

He was just being nice now. How odd. Half an hour ago, he'd been so quietly imperious that she'd have crawled across the room on hands and knees to him, dripping with arousal. Half an hour ago, she'd been willing, more than willing, to accept the thrashing of a lifetime from him. Well, another one . . .

But now he wanted to see the back of her. Perfectly understandable. Time to make a graceful exit, as the best escorts always did.

'Now that's a very sweet offer too, but it's time I was on my way. I'll just slip into the bathroom, if I may?' She shuffled off the bed, surprised that her belaboured bottom was already feeling far less sore. Now, where were those knickers?

'Of course . . . and you'll be needing these.' John handed her the garment in question. How the devil had he retrieved them without her noticing it? Was he a magician of some kind, as well as a fabulous lay?

In the bathroom, she tried to analyse the expression she'd seen on his face. Had he been relieved she was ready to leave? Or disappointed that he had to send her away? He'd become inscrutable, even with his angelic smile.

Men! she thought, perched on the loo.

A few moments later, she was surprised when he offered her another envelope.

'Just a little something. For turfing you out like this.'

'But you've already paid me very handsomely, John.' She tried to push the money back into his hand, but he folded both of his around it, and her fingers.

'No, take it. I'd feel better.' His mouth quirked and he looked almost embarrassed. 'I do have to work . . . but . . .' His sigh wound like a breath around her heart. 'I have this quirk. About sleeping . . . I just can't go to sleep with a woman, escort or otherwise. I couldn't fall asleep with *anyone* in the room, not just women.'

Lizzie just stared at him. What on earth had happened to John Smith? For just a second his beautiful apologetic mask of amiableness had slipped and the starkest, darkest expression had crossed his face. It'd been a fleeting look of horror and now she *really* wanted to stay, to understand, and more than that, to comfort . . . but she could tell that was the last thing he wanted.

'I'm sure I could get a shrink to sort me out. Perhaps a hypnotist could talk me out of it, some charlatan or other.'

He shrugged, as if dismissing the odd blip in his mood, then gave her a smile that almost convinced her she'd imagined it. 'But I'm used to it now. It's a foible, a part of my psyche, and I suppose I'm just waiting for the day when Princess Charming kisses me better.'

Lizzie darted forward, intending to kiss his lips, but veering at the last moment to his cheek. She was nobody's Princess Charming, especially not in her current deceptive role.

But a few moments later, as she walked, alone, along the corridor of the Waverley, she dearly wished that, for John, she might have been.

Sunday morning. Lazy Sunday morning. Usually one of the best times of the week, with no work to do other than a bit of sewing for herself, and with Sunday lunch and often a trip to the pub to look forward to. Not a care in the world or, more accurately, a tacit agreement, in the house, not to think about cares. With plenty of sport and old films on the telly, Brent was always at his most cheerful on Sundays, and Lizzie and Shelley went out of their way to make sure he stayed like that, at least until bedtime when they could no longer help him stave off his demons.

But, sipping her tea, and looking at the pile of money she'd tossed onto the bed to count, not to mention last night's sexy underwear thrown over the back of the chair, Lizzie was thinking about cares. Specifically, a care in the form of a handsome and to all intents and purposes unattainable man by the name of John Smith.

'Sod!'

He'd not made another appointment. He'd not even promised to call about one. He'd just accepted her kiss on the cheek, caught her hand to dust one of his own across her fingertips, and then let her go.

I'm just an escort to him. We had a good time, but I'm interchangeable with any other escort. Maybe he did want me for the duration of his stay, but then changed his mind. The punter's prerogative. Brent had told her they were like that, whether they be male clients or female. They were just the same.

Lizzie took another sip of tea, absent-mindedly noticing there were now three cups on her bedside table. She frowned. Another lesser care to contend with. She'd have to do something about the Dumpster Room of Doom today as well. It was getting ridiculous. She was almost absurdly fastidious about her person, but hopeless at housework. An all-out onslaught on the clothes, the magazines, the books, all the sewing projects in various stages of completion, the piles of patterns she was adapting and, yes, the teacups, would take her mind off a certain gorgeous blond businessman.

Enormously fat chance of that.

Yes, she and John had shared a good time. Nobody could take that away from her. Not ever. She'd never forget her mad adventure of deception and kinky sex as long as she lived and she'd always be grateful for it. Some women, most women, would never even have that.

Sliding back down among the pillows with John's twenty pound notes all around her, she brought back a picture of him. Yes, he'd always be a memory to savour with his luscious blond hair, his quirkily handsome face and his exceptional body. Not to mention his deft, taper-tipped fingers and his solid, indefatigable cock.

And the things he did.

Squirming, she wriggled her hand down the back of her

pyjama shorts and fingered the skin of her bottom. Why didn't it hurt? It ought to. But somehow he had miracle skills, and seemed to know exactly how to smack in a way that was excruciating at the time, but soon faded. She knew there wasn't a mark on her, but she still felt the print of what he'd done to her, like an invisible tattoo, indelible, for ever.

She wanted to feel his slap now, again and again, so carefully aimed and delivered. Between her legs she felt herself moisten, as if she were back with him, enduring the rigours of that flexible blue ruler.

'John,' she sighed, closing her eyes, pinching the flesh of her buttock with one hand while sliding her other hand into her shorts at the front. Her bedroom door wasn't locked, but she'd heard Shelley go out for the Sunday newspapers, and Brent was dead to the world, fast asleep. He'd been out last night too, after his evening shift at the garden centre. But even if he'd been up and about already and likely to waltz in at any moment, she couldn't have kept from touching herself. It was as if John Smith was here in the room, standing over her, commanding her to masturbate in his name.

Behind her eyelids, she saw herself and him, not in the chintzy environment of his suite at the Waverley, but in some other place, darker, more forbidding.

A dungeon perhaps? She'd never been in one, not really. Maybe a club tarted up to look that way, but not the real McCoy.

In her fantasy, she was in an underground chamber somewhere. There was a brazier burning, and there were chains and fiendish implements hanging from the walls. Nameless, almost faceless people stood around; an audience.

John was there in a dark suit, with a dark shirt, looking both golden and ominous in his beauty. She herself was in a corset and high heels, much like the great Bettie Page herself might have worn in one of her bondage photo-spreads or even a private blue movie. Her stockings were fishnet, held up by suspenders. Her crotch was bare, no panties to protect or guard the modesty of her sex.

A heavy chain reached down from the centre of the low ceiling, with leather cuffs at the end of it. She was secured in them, and there was no slack; her arms were stretched up.

Oh wow, where was all this coming from? Slipping her middle finger between her labia she found herself sopping wet, just from the introduction to the fantasy. A little gasp escaped her lips as she flicked tentatively at her clit.

'Ah Bettie, you wicked girl,' her master seemed to say, his voice clear as if he really were in the room with her, prowling, watching. 'You get aroused so easily. Nobody's touched you yet and you're dripping. You need to be punished for being so easy and so horny.'

As she started to rub at herself, Dream John was the one with his hand between her legs, mastering her clit with rough, powerful strokes, then pinching it and squeezing it. Her legs flailed in the real world and the fantasy, and she jerked her hips. Turning onto her side, she arched her body and, reaching around from behind, slipped a finger into her vagina while still worrying her clitoris and pinching it as John did in her fantasy.

Another moan escaped her lips and the master of her fantasies said, 'Silence,' in his low, musical voice, 'or I'll stop your mouth.'

She moaned again, and some barely visualised person handed him a scarf, or maybe just a length of silk. After giving her one hard kiss, with a fierce jab of his tongue, he gagged her with the silk, tying it tightly at the back of her head.

'Now I'll be able to punish you has hard as you need punishing, without any interruptions and entreaties.' He was already punishing her, still pinching her clit while running his smooth, executive's hands over her bare buttocks where they were fully exposed by the short corset.

'I'm going to make these red and sore.' His threat was silk, like the scarf that stopped her mouth, and he kissed the side of her throat like the kiss of silk too. When his teeth closed delicately on her earlobe, she keened behind the gag, her sex fluttering.

'Dirty girl,' he whispered, 'you're not coming, are you?'

She wasn't yet, but she was barely a heartbeat away from it, both in the dream and in reality.

No, master. I promise. I'm not, she silently pledged, even though it would soon be a lie.

In the dream, he whirled away from her and an acolyte handed him a fearsome riding crop, which he swished once or twice in the air.

'And we begin.'

The pain was unimaginable. Literally. She had no idea what a crop would feel like. But she could remember the ruler and the fierce, sweet kiss of his hand on her bottom, and just the recollection roused her. Hot. Intimate. Relentless. His palm landing again and again became the crop landing again and again, blazing through her loins, making her run wet and her sex ache with yearning.

Rocking on her side, Lizzie fingered herself furiously, attacking her clit while Dream John's beautiful, implacable blue eyes stared into hers. Almost wrenching her wrist, she pushed her finger deeper inside her, and then, in frustration, withdrew it and added another, stretching herself.

'Dirty, dirty girl,' the phantom of John Smith said again,

'filthy, dripping wet, lascivious little trollop. You have no grace, no self-control. You're just a nasty, randy little harlot and you deserve to be thrashed until you scream.'

She was chanting the words herself, but he was with her, his expression blazing with the very lust of which she accused herself. In the fantasy, he'd created agony in her buttocks; in reality, the idea of him made her come.

'Oh, oh, God,' she gasped, burying her face in the pillow to muffle her moans and whimpers as her clit leapt and pulsed and her core clenched and clenched again around her fingers.

Oh, if only John were here now. If only he could climb into this bed with her, gorgeous, warm and naked. If only he could be lying behind her, dragging her fingers from her pussy, and then pushing in with his gorgeous cock. In, in, in . . . while his gracious hand cupped her from the front, stroking her clitty.

Oh John . . . John . . .

Wriggling, riding the waves, she tried to conjure him, but a jangling, jingling, ringing sound snatched him from her. She almost sobbed as he seemed to recede, as if hurtling away down a dark tunnel, leaving her behind.

6

Mucky Telephone Pervert

'Buggeration, fuck and fucking bugger!' she growled, snatching for breath, then hoped that Brent hadn't woken up and heard her.

Wriggling and scrabbling around she grabbed for the phone from her bedside cupboard, scowling and half prepared to hurl the damn thing across the room . . . until she realised it was her 'Bettie' mobile that was trilling, and apart from Brent, who was in the house, and Shelley, who would surely use her normal number, there was only one person in the world who could possibly call her on her second phone.

'H—hello?' She was still panting. Her chest was heaving. And between her legs, her sex was still rippling in exquisite little aftershocks.

'Hello, Bettie. Whatever are you doing that's making you so short of breath?' His voice was low and full of laughter, and he might as well have been in the room, standing by the bed, looking down on her. She had no cover across her, and he would clearly have been able to see what she'd been doing.

Good God, her free hand was still inside her shorts.

About to whip it out and make herself decent, she

hesitated, her mad, wicked ideas making her smile. 'Oh nothing,' she said, wriggling again and making adjustments. Her voice still sounded breathy.

'I don't believe you. You're up to something. I can tell from your voice. We had an exclusive deal – you're not with another client, are you?'

She could tell he didn't really think that. The teasing note in his low voice was unmistakeable.

Miles apart, they were already playing.

'On Sunday? How could you say that? I don't do clients on the Lord's day!'

He laughed now. No pretence of seriousness any more.

'Well, that's a shame, Bettie, because I was hoping to engage you again myself today.' He sounded very arch. 'I thought lunch, maybe, then some "afters"? All on the clock, of course.' He paused. Lizzie listened hard. Had he caught his breath too? What was *he* doing? 'But, of course, if you're at your devotions, I wouldn't dream of disturbing you.'

'I've finished now!' she blurted out. He was playing, but it was a delicate game and she didn't want it to end too soon.

'Yes, I think you have, and not long ago, either, judging by the way you were panting when you picked up the phone. God, I wish I was there with you!'

Oh, me too. Me too!

Picturing his cosy, fussy, chintz-clad room at the Waverley, she imagined him in his bed, just as she was in her bed. Did he wear pyjamas, or sleep naked? Was he holding his erect cock now; was he close to coming? His blond hair would be wild and tousled from sleep, and he'd have stubble too, all sexy and lovely.

'Oh, you wouldn't be very impressed with me this morning, John. I'm not done up. No make-up. My hair needs washing and I'm wearing ancient and very scruffy clothes.'

They weren't that bad, but she was painting a different kind of picture for him. 'Nobody would believe that I'm an escort, to look at me now.'

'Sounds delightful. Like the girl next door. Horny and unsophisticated. I'll bet that's a good look on you.'

'Oh, thank you very much.'

'You know what I mean, Bettie. And *you* don't know how to be anything but gorgeous. I'm holding my cock now, thinking of you in your scruffy pyjamas and with your hair all over the place, and none of that magical lip-tint.' He gasped. How close was *he* to coming? 'I can imagine your lips soft and pink, soft and rosy . . . Oh lordy, lordy, I'd love to feel them on me right now.'

'Mr Smith, are you wanking? I should charge you for this. Phone sex is still sex, you know.'

He laughed again, a free, happy sound. So young. Like a boy tossing himself off for his first sweetheart. 'Don't worry, I'll slip an extra hour's fee in the next envelope. It'll be worth it.'

'Well, in that case, carry on. Is there anything you'd like me to do or say, seeing as how we're on an appointment now?'

He exhaled. A breath? A sigh? A gasp of pleasure? 'Tell me where your hands are? Tell me what you're doing? What you've *been* doing?'

Truth? Or confabulation, for his benefit? Truth, she decided, well, partially. Swapping her phone hand, she adjusted her position again, for comfort. If she'd had half a brain cell, she'd have jumped up and locked her door – Shelley might come bounding in with the *Sunday Times* any moment, never thinking to knock – but somehow John's voice was too hypnotising and she just couldn't move.

'Well, at the moment I'm lying back against the pillows,

holding my phone on one hand and . . . touching myself with the other. I was masturbating when you called. I'd just come but I was wondering whether to go again . . . I . . .' She faltered. Could she tell him? He thought she was a prostitute, as brazen as brazen could be, but really she was just an ordinary woman, not a prude but not a sexual *raconteuse* either.

'Oh, Bettie, Bettie, don't hold back. I'll pay double your usual rate. Go on, make an old man very happy.' He chuckled, but his breath was light in the earpiece. She had no doubt that he was a hair away from coming.

'How many times do I have to tell you? You're not old, you idiot!' She laughed too. He was a brilliant, virile man, but even brilliant, virile men could be idiots and have their self-doubts. 'You're the perfect age, John, and the most fanciable man I've met in ages.'

Fanciable man *ever*, a subversive voice in the back of her mind piped up.

'Now, now . . . no flattery, beautiful Bettie. No falsehood. Tell me where your hands were when the phone rang. Tell me exactly.'

Somewhere in the banter, a new thread had emerged. Somehow, he'd suddenly morphed into that fierce, indomitable, masterful man again. The man who made her shudder in the most delicious way, and want to crawl on her knees before him.

'I . . . I was rubbing myself with one hand, and with the other I had a finger inside myself. Well, two actually . . . I like to do that. When I pleasure myself. I like something in me, you know?'

'Excellent. And how often do you pleasure yourself, Bettie? How often do you put fingers inside yourself and stroke yourself?'

That gave her pause for thought. In the normal run of things, she didn't masturbate all that often. It was only now, with John Smith in her life, that she seemed to feel like doing it all the time.

'Do you mean when I put on a show for clients, or when I do it for myself?'

There was a pause. She could almost feel him thinking, weighing her up, perhaps even judging her? The bastard, who was he to do that? A man who chose to pay for sex was no better than the woman who chose to sell it.

'For yourself, foolish girl, for yourself. As far as I'm concerned, you have no other clients.'

Yikes, does he suspect? He's no fool . . .

'I'm not a girl. I'm twenty-four. I'm a woman.'

A soft laugh issued from the phone. 'Indeed you are, and God, don't I know it.' There was a pause, and Lizzie thought she heard a rustling. What was he doing? Was he still handling himself? How close was he? 'You're also wilful and contrary and you're straying from the point. How often do you masturbate?'

'Often enough . . . several times a week. It depends how busy work is, you know?'

John sighed the impatient sigh of perhaps a schoolmaster with a wayward, recalcitrant pupil.

'What's the matter? Were you expecting me to be super horny, just because I'm an escort? Surely, you'd understand it might be exactly the opposite. Sex is work. Maybe I want to do other things in my spare time?'

There was a long pause. Damn, she'd killed the mood. He'd probably been grooving along nicely, stroking himself and climbing towards orgasm, and now she'd as good as thrown a bucket of cold water all over him.

'I appreciate your honesty, Bettie. Now tell me one thing. When you were with me, did you really feel pleasure? Did you come?' His voice was soft, honest . . . sympathetic. 'I won't be offended if you didn't. I thought you did. I hoped you did. But I guess in your business, you get to be a pretty good actress.'

'Honesty? Well, yes, John. When I was with you, I did feel pleasure and I enjoyed the games. I had orgasms. Lots of them.' She drew in a deep breath. 'And I can safely say I've never experienced that with another client. I'm sure you won't believe me, but with you, it has been different.'

It was all the truth. She'd never come with another client. The fact that she'd *never* had any clients and unless something very drastic occurred, she never would have any, was beside the point.

'I believe you, Bettie,' he replied, sounding happy. Sophisticated and worldly as he was, he was still a man, and men enjoyed having their prowess and their specialness praised.

'And I *was* playing with myself when you rang, thinking of you. God's honest truth.'

'Even better . . . Although I guess I've put you off now.'

'Not necessarily,' she said, realising that was true too. Just talking to him, listening to his velvety voice, was getting to her. She imagined him in the fantasy dungeon, then in his hotel room. So in charge. She wished he'd tell her to do something again now. Whatever it was, she'd do it.

'Is your finger still where it was?'

'Honestly, no. It was a bit uncomfortable, twisted around like that. I couldn't concentrate on talking to you like that, and I like to focus on your voice. You've got a very nice voice, Mr Smith. I bet all the girls tell you that, don't they?'

'It's true actually. I have been praised for my dulcet tones,' he admitted. She could hear him smiling again. 'Not by a girl, though, not by a long shot. But, there's one particular lady who did like to hear me talk dirty now and again.'

'Who was that?'

Damn, she was asking questions again, and that was bad form for an escort.

'An older woman of my acquaintance. I'll tell you about her sometime. Now, do you think we might resume our phone sex? I was enjoying it. Where are your fingers now?'

Lizzie sank more comfortably into the pillows, and slid her free hand back inside her sleep shorts. She was still hot, still wet. Still almost there, despite everything.

'One lot holding the phone, naturally . . . the others still in my knickers, in the usual place.'

'Wonderful! At the risk of sounding like the world's worst cliché of a mucky telephone pervert . . . what are you wearing? Do you wear knickers in bed? You said you were scruffy . . . How scruffy?'

Lizzie smiled to herself. He did sound like a telephone pervert, but in the most luscious and desirable way.

'I'm wearing a pair of soft jersey shorts and a plain white tee shirt. Nothing too glamorous, just sleep grunge.'

'Mm . . . I'm picturing the scene . . . white tee shirt. Thin cotton, with erect nipples evident beneath. Little, tight grungy shorts, with your hand inside them, fiddling about . . . And you're super wet, am I right?'

'Yes.' She was a swimming pond, almost ready to come.

'When you were masturbating before, what were you fantasising about? Tell me. What gets a woman like you going? What are your secret turn-ons?'

A woman like her? How little he knew. Or perhaps not?

He might have rumbled her and was playing her along. As an older man, and one infinitely more sophisticated than any she'd ever met before, he was difficult to read.

'A woman in my line of work? Well, I fantasise about sitting in front of the telly, in a puce velour tracksuit, eating crisps and watching *Countdown* . . . Now *that's* exotic to me!'

'Bettie . . .' His voice was low and warning, utterly thrilling. Just as it would have been in that dungeon she'd fancied him in.

'All right already . . . I was fantasising about being in a dungeon and you punishing me, if you must know. You and your kinky ways have warped my mind.' She was already back there, hanging on the chain, while John prowled around her, whip in hand, ready to lash.

'Am I more kinky than most of your clients, then? I would've thought you'd see all kinds, get asked for all sorts of things.'

'I do, but it's like we said . . . where punishment's concerned, it's usually the men who want *me* to thrash them. Being on the other end of the stick, so to speak, is a novelty.' And a gigantic turn-on. Her sex was dripping, making a damp patch on the back of her shorts. Impatient with them, she whipped them off and flung them away, spreading her thighs wide now unhindered. 'John, I just took my shorts off . . . do you mind?'

'But I didn't give you permission.' His voice sounded like navy blue velvet, rich and dark. She'd played right into his hands.

'Forgive me, master. Shall I put them back on?'

'No . . . leave them. Are your legs spread wide?' She could swear he could see her. How could he do that? Was he a remote viewer, or some kind of wizard?

'Yes, master.'

'Now, place your free hand on your thighs. Don't touch yourself. Just talk to me. If you disobey me . . . if you come . . . I'll know, and I'll punish you even harder next time we meet.'

Oh no! It wasn't the punishment that bothered her. She was suddenly yearning for that. It was the not touching. Her clit was throbbing, aching, yearning for contact. She could swear it was twice its normal size, swollen and sensitive.

'Do you understand me, Bettie?'

'Y—yes, master.' Her non-phone hand felt like a useless object pressed against her inner thigh, but she couldn't move it. She was immobilised by his will.

'So, let's talk about this fantasy dungeon of yours, and what you're wearing. I think you might have on a leather bikini with peepholes for your nipples and just a tiny little thong for the bottom half.'

Lizzie barked with laughter. Oh, he was a caution. Was he serious? Was that what he wanted to see her in? It sounded like a blue version of a *Carry On* movie outfit.

'Ah, so you think my wishes are funny, do you?'

'No! No! It was just a surprise. But you might be right . . . Now I come to think about it, I am wearing a leather bikini, yes. Yes, I am. And it's very skimpy, you can see everything. It makes me look more exposed than if I was naked.'

'That sounds like a very nice bikini indeed. And your nipples, perhaps they're rouged? A pretty red, to match your lip-tint and the stripes I'm going to put across your bottom?'

'Um, yes . . . yes they are.' She looked down at her nipples. They were very dark beneath the thin white cotton of her tee, poking against it, hard. Her hand tingled with another urge, to tweak and squeeze them, but she was forbidden to do that too, presumably.

'Excellent. And now, the leather knickers. I fancy that they're very abbreviated. Barely more than a few strips of butter-soft hide, you know? Just a little triangle at the front and a cord at the back, dividing your delicious buttocks and leaving them bare and available. Might that be the case, perhaps?'

She could see herself in this get-up. The corset she'd imagined before dissolved, only to be replaced by John's porno fantasy. She was hanging on the chain with her nipples painted red and her bum bare but for a single dark leather strip, snug and tight in her anal groove.

Oh God . . . She dug her nails into her thigh, pinching herself to keep from thrashing at her clit and making herself come. If only John were here and he would play with her. In her mind, the dungeon was forgotten and he was here, now, looming over her, kneeling on the bed and reaching down to fondle her pussy.

'Bettie? What are you doing?'

'Nothing, just admiring your choice in elegant undergarments for me.'

She heard a soft breath through the speaker. Not quite a laugh, not quite a grunt. Was he wanking? She thought he might be.

'Now, back to your leather panties. They're only tiny, and your beautiful dark bush is peeking out. Why is that so, Bettie? Most working ladies of my acquaintance are pretty scrupulous about their Brazilians. Some of them even wax it off completely. But you're relatively luxuriant down there.' He paused. He was challenging her again, testing her. 'Not that I'm complaining. I prefer it on you . . . but still.'

'I . . . Well, once, I had to take a client at very short notice, and I hadn't time to wax, and he loved it. He went wild.' She bit her lip, thinking fast. 'So I tried it again, with another punter, and he loved it too . . . so since then I've been a bit less . . . um . . . stringent down there. I've even got one or two guys now who'll pay extra if I let it get really shaggy.'

'Connoisseurs,' pronounced John roundly.

'If you say so.'

'I do, and my word is the law.' She could hear the laughter in his voice, but there was that edge too, the thread of dominance that made her feel light-headed. 'So, this dungeon of yours, let's hear a bit more about it? Are you chained up?'

'Yes, I am. There's a big chain hanging from the ceiling and I'm fastened to it, with my arms stretched up. I can only just reach.'

'Because you're wearing high heels?'

'How did you know?' She hadn't got as far as her feet, but if he was into her wearing a leather bikini, it wasn't much of a leap to imagine he'd want her in towering stilettos too.

'I have powers . . . Now come on, more detail.'

'It's very dark and gloomy and there are torches. More chains and whips, and instruments of torture hanging from the walls. And people too, watching the show. I can't see them properly. They're in the shadows, but they're all agog. Some of them might be masturbating.'

'Agog, eh? I'm not surprised. It sounds like my birthday in there.' He laughed softly, the sound of that just as sexy as his faux dictatorial voice. The way he switched from one persona to the other was breath-taking, and seamless. 'And me, what about me in all this? What am I wearing?'

'Er . . . it's dark . . . it's hard to see . . .'

'Do you know, I think I might be wearing leather too.

Skin-tight leather jeans and high boots, and a big belt. Nothing else, except maybe a studded collar?'

Lizzie exploded into laughter again, unable to help herself. John Smith was the most surprising man she'd ever met, both awe-inspiring and yet frequently hilarious.

'And again . . . she laughs. You're just asking for trouble, aren't you, Bettie? Don't you fancy the idea of me in leather trousers?' She could hear that grin again, that sunny, beautiful grin of his. 'Do you think I'd look like a dickhead?'

'Well, it's a bit of cliché, but you should be able to get away with leather, at a pinch. In fact . . . you look great!'

And he did. In her mind. The beautiful suit faded and she saw him clearly in the fetish gear, the black of it stunning against his golden beauty, the leather sleek over his thighs and arse, the collar round his throat a sigil of power. He didn't look like a fool or a cliché. He looked wonderful.

'Good answer . . . I think.' He paused, and she thought she detected a rustle. Him getting comfortable, ready to bring himself off? 'So, you're strung up from the ceiling and I'm strutting around in my leather strides . . . What next?'

'You whip me with a riding crop and it really, really hurts.'

'Oh, my sweet Bettie, you do tell the best stories. I can just imagine it . . . You twisting on the chain, struggling and writhing, your gorgeous body jiggling about as you try to avoid the blows. Tears on your face. Fire across your bottom. Crimson nipples peeking out of the leather. You're aroused and wet, and it starts to ooze down your thighs even while you're moaning for mercy. Your arse is on fire but suddenly you're begging and pleading for me to fuck you.'

He sounded breathy. He had to be pumping himself. He just had to be.

And his strictures forgotten, Lizzie was rubbing herself

too, pounding her clit as she clutched her phone so tightly she thought she might snap it in half. Her bottom lifted from the bed, blindly pushing her crotch at her hand as much as that hand was pressing back down. Heels gouging at the bed sheets, she jerked her hips.

'And I want to fuck you . . . but I want to hear you groan and cry a bit more first. So I crop you some more, criss-crossing the strokes, finding tender new spots. I whip your thighs, the outer curves of your bottom . . . the inner ones too. I catch you right across your delicious little arsehole and you scream.'

Biting down hard on her lip, so as not to actually scream, in the real world, Lizzie pressed down hard on her clitoris and the world went white with intense pleasure, an orgasm so ferocious it was almost brutal, laying waste to her as her sex pulsed like a heart.

She knew that John knew. She knew that he knew she knew. But he went on, pushing on, making the dream world all his own. 'And while you're still screaming, I let you down and then I fuck you on the floor, still in your chains, from behind. It's hard-packed earth beneath us, and you're on your knees. I have your pussy first, hard and fast. Your face is in the dirt as I thrust into you . . . but you're loving it, despite the pain in your bum. In fact when I dig my nails into the soreness, you come like a train, milking me and grunting like an animal.'

If only.

Rising to pleasure again, Lizzie wanted to fling the phone away and howl and curse, her vagina clenching on the empty air where John should be. Keeping silent was a more perverse agony than having her bottom beaten raw.

'While you're still climaxing, I pull out . . . then I thrust into your arse instead. In deep. Right in. God, that's gorgeous. So hot and tight. And when I rub your clit, you clench on me again, embracing me with your snug, luscious bottom . . . Oh, that feels so good . . . so good . . .'

Wriggling about, Lizzie finished herself, riding the last sweet ripples, fingertip wringing the last echoes of pleasure from her centre. Her chest was heaving, she was drenched in sweat. She felt like she'd been through a mangle, completely drained of sensation by the power of John's profane yet beautiful words.

But now he was silent. Dead silent. Was he coming? Was his spunk shooting out of him, anointing the Waverley's colourful chintz bedding?

Surely if he was climaxing, she'd at least hear heavy breathing?

'Are you still there?' she asked, aware that he'd certainly be able to hear her heavy breathing.

'Of course I am. Where would you think I'd be?' His voice was even, low, completely unruffled. And thoroughly annoying. He could control her with words, via a phone, but none of it seemed to have had an effect on him.

'Did you . . . did you . . . did anything happen?'

'Do you mean, did I come?'

'Yes, what the hell else would I mean?' He was so contrary, but somehow that made her hotter than ever rather than cooling her off him. She wished he was right there in bed, next to her, so she could pummel him, then jump astride him and ride his beautiful cock.

'No, Bettie. I didn't come. The object of the exercise was to make *you* come . . . Did you?'

She leapt up, searching for her shorts. She'd had enough of his controlling games for the moment. Dropping her phone she wriggled into her shorts and considered just hanging up on him. It was a stupid thing to do, and cutting off her nose to spite her face, but her emotions were suddenly in a whirl.

'Yes, I did. And you really are the most perverse pervert, I've ever encountered,' she growled into the speaker on retrieving the handset. 'You needn't think I'm paying *you* for all that, you know . . . Just because you like to play mind-games, it doesn't mean you're not taking up my valuable . . . and billable . . . time!'

'I wouldn't dream of short-changing you, Bettie, don't worry.' He paused, then named a sum for her recent services that made her gasp.

'That's ridiculous if you didn't come!'

'Indulge me, sweetheart. Sometimes the climax isn't everything, you know?'

'You're a very weird man, Mr Smith.' She couldn't help but smile. It was hard to stay cross with him long. That heavenly smile of his could melt the heart . . . even when you couldn't actually see it.

'You don't know the half of it, Bettie, but hopefully you'll soon find out. Will you have lunch with me, then? Here at the Waverley?'

She wanted to. It sounded so lovely, almost like a date. She imagined sitting across a table from him, sharing good wine and food and conversation. He was so handsome that every woman in the restaurant would envy her. It didn't matter that he was paying her for her company. They weren't to know that. They'd just think she'd pulled the most fabulous man in the county. Or even the country . . . or beyond.

But, there was a 'but'.

'I'd love to, but I usually spend Sundays just chilling out with my house-mates. It's sort of tradition, and . . . well . . . it's especially important now. Brent, he's one of them, he's very depressed at the moment.'

Jesus God, why had she blurted that out? What escort had a male house-mate? Or maybe escorts did have male house-mates? How was she to know? And Brent, a sometime male escort himself, had a couple of female house-mates.

'Well, why not bring them along?' replied John instantly, apparently not turning a hair. 'It doesn't have to be an appointment, just a pleasant lunch, though I'll still pay you for your time, naturally. Do they know what you do for a living?'

'Um . . . yes. Shelley's an office temp, but Brent's an escort himself. Well, a part-time one, sometimes. We're not involved or anything. Not now. We used to be an item, long ago. But now we're just friends. We're *all* just friends.'

Why, why, why was she telling him all this?

'Ask them, then. If you won't feel awkward, and you don't think they'll feel awkward. And I'll just save this massive erection until our next "date", instead.'

He was silently laughing again.

'Oh God, are you still hard. I thought . . . well . . . that you probably weren't, if you hadn't come.'

'Ah, Bettie, sometimes I like to prolong the anticipation. It makes the eventual pleasure all the sweeter and more intense.'

'But don't you mind? I mean . . . to be "wanting" like that?' She didn't have to imagine the sensation of frustration. She had it now, for him, and she'd only come moments ago.

'Not in the slightest. I'm a grown-up; I can wait for my treats. Now, shall I book a table for four, and your friends can join us if they feel like it, and if they don't it'll just be us, OK?'

Still dubious, Lizzie agreed. She seriously doubted Brent would want to do lunch under these strange circumstances, but she'd ask. Shelley would probably be aching to accept, but would still decline because she was a doll and would never put the mockers on another woman's action. John named a time, apparently not in the slightest doubt he could get a table, then said, 'Ciao, beautiful Bettie, see you soon.'

Staring down at the phone in her hand, Lizzie puffed out her lips, vaguely nonplussed.

John Smith might be gorgeous, but he was the oddest man. She didn't know what to make of him sometimes.

How on earth would a *real* escort handle him?

7

Déjeuner à Deux

Why did she feel so nervous? She'd been to lunch with a man before. It was silly to get all of a flutter like this, even if she did like him more than she'd liked anyone in ages.

The trouble was, this wasn't an 'appointment'. They couldn't have sex across the table, unless the Waverley's risqué reputation was even more extreme than she'd been led to believe. She'd have to spend time actually *talking* to John. And that would involve even more elaborate twists and turns to her fabrication.

That was, unless she decided to come clean over the soup or hors d'oeuvres.

She'd have to play it by ear, and if the right moment occurred, grasp it. Preferably when John had drunk a glass or two of wine to mellow him. Selfish as it seemed, Lizzie was relieved that both Brent and Shelley had declined John's invitation. Their presence would have created even more complications, and that was a fact. Brent, she was fairly sure, could be relied on to maintain her subterfuge, but Shelley, though meaning well, would probably have slipped up.

Even so, Lizzie still felt desperately worried about Brent.

Time just didn't seem to be doing its healing thing for her friend, and Brent had refused to even come out of his room when she'd tried to tempt him with John's offer. Worse, judging from the sound of his voice, she had a feeling he'd been crying.

'Look, I won't go. He won't mind,' she'd said. 'We can all go to the pub and have our usual lunch, and I'll see him some other time.'

'Don't patronise me, Lizzie. I can take care of myself. You and Shelley don't need to keep mothering me.' Brent's voice had been a growl. 'Just fuck off and have lunch with your rich stud, will you?'

'All right, I bloody well will!'

Lizzie sighed now, still worried despite knowing Shelley was at home and doing her best to whip up the jolly, laid-back Sunday mood. Brent did try to conquer his unhappiness, and mostly did a pretty good job of it, but she knew he still hurt badly, even though it was almost a year now since the loss of Steven, a man he'd been in love with. It had almost crushed him, and even though she and Shelley did the best they could, Lizzie knew their best efforts weren't achieving much. But still they both tried, and much as she'd love to linger as long as she could in the company of her delicious 'client' John, she'd decided not to stay *too* long at the Waverley today. No matter how fabulous the sex was.

And at least if Brent wouldn't come out of his room and talk to Shelley, Lizzie knew at least he still had Mulder for company. She'd heard him talking to their furry sweetheart, through the door, and she knew that the little feline's purr was a sovereign remedy for the deepest of the blues.

As her taxi drew up in front of the Waverley's handsome ivy-clad façade, Lizzie tried to orientate herself, and remember whether she'd seen a sign for the restaurant in the reception area when she'd last been here. It was barely twenty-four hours ago, yet still it seemed like a lifetime. Time seemed to be stretching and warping most strangely at the moment, and hours away from John Smith seemed like days, like weeks.

Where is it? Where is it?

Feeling ridiculously nervous, she cast her glance around the warmly welcoming lobby of the hotel. Her eyes skittered about and couldn't seem to locate signs for the restaurant. She felt certain she'd been rumbled as an escort – or at least a faux one – last time she'd been here, and it had been all right. But it still seemed a bit dodgy to draw attention to herself too much.

Ah, too late!

'Can I help you?' said the smiling young woman on reception, a twinkly-eyed blonde whose mischievous expression was both appealing and disquieting.

Damn, she knows.

'Yes, thanks. Could you point me in the direction of the restaurant. I'm having lunch with a friend.'

'Of course, it's over there.' The blonde pointed to a large, clearly visible sign saying 'Restaurant', and Lizzie suppressed her self-directed sigh. 'You're Mr Smith's guest, aren't you? I believe he's already in there, waiting for you at your table. *Bon appetit!*'

'Thanks.'

The naughty glint in the receptionist's eye seemed to suggest that she too found John Smith as toothsome as anything on the menu, but happily she didn't seem to be passing judgement on the handsome guest's appetite for working girls.

Taking a deep breath, Lizzie strode towards the dining room. She'd have to run the gamut of the Traditional Sunday Lunch diners. How many of them would have the imagination to divine her and John's secret? She'd just be a woman dining with her date, to them, even if half the staff of the Waverley seemed to believe she was an escort, even if she wasn't one.

At the threshold, she drew in a deep breath and scanned the room. Was he here, after all? Jumbo-sized butterflies skittered around in her chest, and she braced herself for disappointment, amazed how piercing that prospect was. But then she saw him, sitting at a table in a discreet bay window alcove. It was probably the nicest location in the room, and perfect for lovers, with a bit of privacy and a lovely view of the Waverley's beautifully manicured gardens.

The best table in the house. For me, supposedly a prostitute. Bless you, John; even if I were a working girl you'd make me feel like a princess.

And as he turned towards her, dazzling her with a smile that reached out across the entire length of the room, her heart lifted, and she smiled back, and began to weave her way between the tables, towards him.

She's a vision. Every time different. So beautiful . . .

John couldn't help but smile as Bettie crossed the room, heading towards him. She looked as fresh as springtime in her pretty vintage sundress, with its full, blue, polka-dot adorned skirt, and a little jacket modestly covering her creamy shoulders. There was a total innocence about her, a quality of being exquisitely untouched, despite the enthusiasm he knew she'd exhibit the moment he touched her. Her shiny black hair was pulled back in a 1950s pony-tail, and she wore barely any make-up, apart from her trademark lip-tint. He'd never seen an escort look quite like her. Which made sense, because he'd wager far more than he was paying her that she hadn't been long in the life. That she was still optimistically believing it was 'just temporary' and that she wouldn't allow herself to get trapped . . . or jaded.

He wondered how much she needed the money. He barely knew her yet, but he sensed she was a smart and savvy girl. Wasn't there something else she could do? Some career or other? A thought came out of left field. Perhaps he could sponsor her or something? Get her started in a small business, or perhaps fund a course? Support her in a way that was nothing to do with sex. She wouldn't be the only one, he thought, the old, familiar shudder of guilt rippling through him.

But if he did become her benefactor, would she . . . would she still see him as a lover too? He frowned. In a way he'd still be paying her for services . . . It still wouldn't be the same as her fucking him and succumbing to his hand just because she wanted to, without him giving her a penny? The cash meant nothing to him, but it would still be there, the elephant in the room.

Oh, get a grip, man. Don't get ahead of yourself. Just enjoy . . .

And there was much to enjoy as she seemed to glide towards him like an old-time movie star. His cock hardened at the thought of the games they'd played thus far. He'd not had this much fun with a woman in years, and his heart lifted, along with his flesh, in anticipation.

'Bettie! So glad you could come.'

The words were total honesty. Weird as their situation was, he *was* happy. Strangely light-hearted. Springing to his feet before the waiter could arrive and do the honours, he darted around the table to ease out her chair so she could sit. She nibbled her lovely rosy lower lip as she took her seat, looking a little nervous, but also excited. The little action made his cock lurch again and he resisted the urge to check himself. God, here he was in a public restaurant sporting a massive hard-on and she hadn't even spoken yet.

But something must have alerted her. Her black lashes fluttered, she glanced where he'd avoided, and her cheeks blushed rosy. 'Good grief, John, you are pleased to see me. Or is that a pistol in your pocket, as they say?'

'I blame you for that, Bettie, you shouldn't look so luscious. I've lost my appetite for lunch now . . . in lieu of something else.'

'Well, *I'm* hungry,' she replied pertly as he resumed his seat, but the way her eyes skittered to the general direction of his groin seemed to suggest she was having similar problems to the ones he was enjoying.

'I'm glad to hear it. I just hope they've got plenty of aphrodisiacs on the menu, to get you in the mood for what I'm hoping for as a dessert.'

She held his gaze, her eyes dark as she fussed with her napkin. 'Well, you can order all the aphrodisiacs you like, John, but I'm not sure I really need them. You know me. I love my job and I don't need any extra incentive, culinary or otherwise.'

Intent on her, he seemed to hear an odd little edge in her voice. That sense that she wasn't quite as sure of what she was doing as she was trying to project. That she was indeed a novice in her chosen profession.

He wondered how he could ask, without seeming to judge her. It would certainly spoil the mood, and while the philanthropist in him might have done it, the horny, selfish man with a raging erection just growled, *shut the fuck up*!

'Well, as long as you don't start refusing my money, Bettie. I always like to keep things on a professional footing. A fair day's pay for a fair day's work and all that.'

Her face was a picture. She parted her lips. Ran her tongue along the lower one in a way that made him want to wrench open his trousers and stroke himself furiously in her honour. He could see the battle in her eyes, and then, the triumph of the courtesan over the inexperienced girl. Her chin came up and her whole demeanour seemed to morph, become more sultry. More seductive.

Before his very eyes, she became 'Bettie' completely, the accomplished seductress – even though he'd bet all the money in the envelope stashed in his inner jacket pocket that it wasn't her real name.

So that was it. He only wanted the prostitute. He wanted 'Bettie' the working girl, not some ordinary woman who'd cost him nothing, but who came with complications. She couldn't blame him. Perhaps that was his life? Simple. Everything in boxes, including kinky sex. No hassle.

Well, that was what he would get. Maybe she'd send him the money back, when it was all over, when they'd never see each other again. It would be simple enough to discover a forwarding address from the hotel's reception, when the time came. Perhaps minus a little for 'expenses' and a charitable donation or two, just to show him.

'Oh, absolutely. No matter how much creative satisfaction one gets from a job, it's always nice to have one's talents validated by cold, hard cash.' She looked him up and down, taking in his expensive clothes and grooming and general air of wealth. 'You look like an obscenely successful man of business to me. You must understand that more than anybody.'

'Oh, I do . . . I do . . . Which is why I'm prepared to pay top dollar for you, my dear.' He patted his soft, slate-blue linen jacket, where no doubt 'the envelope' was tucked away in his inner pocket. 'You're my treat to myself while I'm staying here. My self-indulgence.' He favoured her with his most golden smile, and suddenly it was impossible to be vexed with him, or worried about being with him, or deceiving him. That delicious grin made all arguments invalid.

'A treat? Yes, I like that. It sums up my entire philosophy, John. I'm glad we see eye to eye.' Her voice sounded confident, worldly, assured, even to herself, but suddenly, inside, there were the strangest stirrings. Unsettling thoughts. Yearnings.

No, don't be daft. This is all there is. Enjoy the ride, you silly mare. There's nothing more.

'Excellent. Let's eat, then, shall we?' Still smiling and pleased with himself, John lifted his head a little and made the slightest gesture with his fingers and, just like in the movies, the waiter appeared at his side with menus, as if he'd been on tenterhooks, waiting for and watching the hotel's most favoured of all guests for the tiniest bit of body language indicating his requirements.

'Champagne, Bettie? Let's be a total cliché, shall we?' said John, quirking his eyebrows at her like another movie standard, the wicked Lothario.

'Lovely! But I mustn't drink too much if we're supposed to be going for a walk.'

He'd texted her earlier, suggesting more sensible shoes, rather than hooker heels, because the grounds at the Waverley were particularly green and tempting looking, and he fancied an after-lunch stroll.

'Very sage. We can't have you getting sloshed and falling over in the shrubbery, can we? I might accidentally fall on top of you, and then who knows what might happen?' He snagged his lower lip with his white teeth for a moment, and Lizzie's stomach quivered.

Ooh, a bit of al fresco . . . that *was* what he had in mind. She'd really been hoping so.

'I thought that was the whole idea, for you to fall on top of me. It's pretty much our *raison d'être* here, isn't it?' Feeling giddy before the champers had even arrived, she kicked off her shoe and ran her toes up and down his calf.

'Amongst other things.' His smile became darker, more saturnine and, under the table, he nimbly defeated her in a clever bit of footwork, so that the toe of his leather shoe was taunting her leg instead. Slowly, he slid it upwards, amongst the net petticoats that gave her skirt its bounce, pressing against the soft skin at the inside of her knee. He left it there a moment, almost threateningly, then withdrew again, punctuating the retreat with a shrug of his shoulders.

Lizzie opened her mouth to speak, but then the waiter scurried over, and there was the usual ritual dance over ordering food, and the Champagne. Despite her claim, her appetite was barely in existence. All she really hungered for was the man sitting opposite her, looking so cool and appetising in his smudged blue summer suit and toning shirt, with his worldly angel face and tousled blond hair.

If he'd asked her to have sex with him across the table, right now, she probably wouldn't have done it . . . but she'd be tempted. And the fantasy of it gripped her mind, irresistibly.

'What are you thinking about, Bettie?' he enquired once the wine was poured and they were alone again in their little cocoon of intimacy in a busy, crowded room.

'Just imagining myself on my back on this table with you hammering away between my thighs.'

John beamed. 'Well, I'll drink to that!' He clinked his glass to hers.

The Champagne was superlative, crisp yet somehow unctuous too. Lizzie was grateful for its cool, invigorating zing, and drank half a glass straight down.

'Remember the shrubbery,' John warned.

'It's OK. I can take it.'

Table. Shrubbery. Anywhere . . . with you.

To her surprise, he began to chat. Casual, light talk that, despite the fact she still wanted to eat him far more than the delicious meal they'd ordered, Lizzie found easy. Over the rosemary braised lamb cutlets, she was able to ask him about himself, and why he was staying at the Waverley, and she wasn't in the least bit surprised to discover he was indeed the very plutocratic tycoon, or whatever, that she'd suspected. He had a number of acquisitions ongoing in the area, a leisure complex, a shopping centre, a couple of light, artisan industry projects that had interested him. The way he talked about it all, in a natural, enthusiastic way, completely without any trace of ego, was enthralling. It was a different world to hers, like night and day, but he gave her a glimpse of it, and the way it both drove him and fascinated him.

In a natural pause, John seemed to study her, somehow in a completely non-sexual way, for a change.

'And your friends, didn't they fancy lunch with us, then? It would have been OK, you know . . . Well, just for lunch.' He winked.

'I asked them . . . but Shelley, well, she was tempted, but she's the soul of discretion and she doesn't, um, like to get in the way of things.' This was slightly perilous ground, but hopefully she was dancing over it OK. 'And Brent just wasn't in the mood. It would have probably done him good, though. He's not doing so well at the moment and he seems to be having a bad day. He . . . he lost someone last year, in a road accident, and we're coming up to the anniversary of it. He blames himself. You know how it is . . .'

Lizzie's tongue seemed to freeze, as she looked at John. His face was stricken again, in another of those weird, dark moments. She flailed around for something more to say, a slick way to change the subject, but before she could try, his expression altered, smoothing out somehow, and he said, 'What happened?' in a soft voice that sounded genuinely interested.

She found herself telling the story of Brent, and his lover Steven, and the smash that Brent believed *he* shouldn't have survived if Steven hadn't. From what she'd gleaned from other sources, Brent *wasn't* to blame, but no amount of telling him that would convince him. All he knew was that the love of his life was dead.

As she fizzled to a halt in her account, John reached over and lightly touched her hand. Good grief, she was supposed to be entertaining him, not telling him all this. But when she opened her mouth again to apologise, he cut her off.

'It sounds like you've been a good friend to him, Bettie, and done all a friend possibly could.' He looked serious. He wasn't just trying to sway the conversation back to her and himself. 'Perhaps he should seek professional help? I know a very good man. He's pricey, but he does see one or two National Health patients. Or I could put in a good word . . . He's London based, but it might be worth a trip, if Brent's willing.'

For a moment, intense curiosity gripped her. Had John had cause to see this good man? About his sleeping alone 'thing' . . . and possibly other stuff?

He smiled. Lizzie willed him to open up to her. *Go on, go on . . . tell me!*

'Do you want to call Brent now, and check he's OK?'

She shrugged, sensing the little crack of an open door being firmly closed. 'I should have called him anyway. He's my "safety" person.'

'I thought as much. Now phone him, or your friend Shelley, and put everybody's mind at ease. And then we can enjoy our lunch.' He quirked his eyebrows, in that characteristic way of his. 'And other things.'

He was right, and with a nod, she rose from her seat and made her way back to the foyer, not wanting to inflict a phone conversation on other diners.

'You all right?' Brent said fairly brightly, on answering. Lizzie was glad to hear what sounded like motorbikes in the background. Which meant he'd perked up considerably. In the background, she heard Shelley's voice too. *Is it her? Is it her?*

'I'm fine. I'm just worried about you.'

'Don't fret, love. I'm OK. I just felt a bit rough this morning but I'm fine now. I'm sorry if I was a git. We're all watching last weeks *MotoGP* on catch-up, even Mulder. The "thing" Shelley made for lunch was barely edible, so I'm afraid I ate that special Chinese dinner for one of yours out of the freezer.' There was a squawk of protest in the background, Shelley defending her culinary arts.

'I was saving that.'

'I'll get you another. Now, you, get back to your hot guy. All OK with him? Not too freaky? You *are* safe, aren't you?'

'Of course. We're having lunch. He's a bit frisky but I think he's a good guy, really. So don't worry.'

'You're playing a risky game, Lizzie. You should tell him.'

'I will . . . I will . . . soon. Now, put Shelley on.'

'What's happening? What's happening?' demanded Shelley. 'Any acts of desperate passion yet? And more to the point, has he rumbled you?'

'Nothing much. No. And, no. We're having a really delicious lunch, and we might go for a walk afterwards.'

Lizzie could almost hear Shelley's frustration. 'Well, that doesn't sound much like Belle de Jour. Sounds more like Sunday lunch with my Auntie Mae. I'm very disappointed in you. You're letting the side down. I thought you'd be banging him by now.'

'It's a busy dining room full of people, you dolt! John might be fond of call girls, but he behaves like a perfect gentleman and is a pillar of society in public.'

There was some tittering then about John's 'pillar', and after tasking Shelley with making sure Brent stayed cheerful, and assuring her friend that she was perfectly safe and would tell all later, Lizzie rang off. Brent's low mood still worried her, but at least Shelley seemed to have things under control and it sounded as they were having fun back at the house.

Which left her ready to *really* engage with John Smith.

'Everything OK?' He rose to his feet again as she arrived at the table.

'Yes, everyone's fine. They're watching *MotoGP* with our cat and scoffing my food. Situation normal.' She slid into her seat, watching John as she did so. Was he still concerned? 'And now I suggest you and I stop being so "normal"! Discussing the problems of someone you don't know from

Adam isn't really why you're here, is it? It's certainly not what you're paying for.'

John smiled and took a sip of his Champagne. 'Well, I'm not such a sex-crazed monster that I can't feel for other people's difficulties. But, yes, if all's well at home, I'd love to return to the business in hand.' He licked a drop of the wine from his lower lip. Good God, surely he knew how provocative that looked? 'And perhaps revisit our conversation this morning?'

'Oh that . . . What do you want to know? I told you everything at the time.' She picked at a little of her food, her appetite still languid. 'What I'm amazed at is you . . . not . . . well, *concluding*.' She glanced around. Everyone appeared to be concerned with their own dining companions and their own food and wine, but you never knew if some sly character might also be earwigging. 'That was weird, John, and I'm a bit insulted that you wouldn't do it for me.'

'Would you like me to do it now?' Blue eyes blazing, he beamed at her, laid down his fork and made as if to slide his hand beneath the table.

'No!' He was incorrigible. She half believed he might do it.

'What's the matter? Are you scared someone will know what I'm doing?' His hand was still hidden. 'Perhaps that's what I'm paying you for . . . to bear witness? To watch me? It doesn't always have to be you that's doing things, Bettie.'

Her eyes wide, she stared at him. At his face. At his arm and shoulder. After a moment, he half closed his eyes, the gorgeous fans of his lashes sweeping down, and he let out a little sigh.

Good God . . .

But then he withdrew his hand, took up his knife and fork

and casually started eating. 'I had you there, didn't I? You really thought I was going to do it, didn't you?'

Lizzie let out her breath. She'd been holding it, she realised. 'Well, yes, I did half wonder if you might. I hope you'll beg my pardon for saying it, but I think you're just a little bit crazy, John Smith.'

'I've been called worse,' he said amiably, pausing to take a sip of water. 'And if you really, really wanted me to do it, I would.'

Lizzie set her cutlery neatly on her plate. She couldn't eat any more, lovely as it was. This beautiful, slightly mad man had stolen her appetite. The only thing she felt hungry for was him. 'Perhaps in a more private setting it would be nice. I'd actually prefer to *see* you at it. You've got such a splendid appendage.'

He grinned, wicked lights in his eyes. 'Well, if you won't watch me, the least you can do is let me watch you. It's easier for girls . . . with their skirts.'

Heat sluiced through her veins. It was crazy . . . risky . . . mad. But she wanted to do it. Not just for the devilment, but because suddenly she was wickedly aroused. Desire knotted in her belly, plaguing her with that slow, heavy tug on her clitoris. Her heart was beating wildly, and her clit seemed to beat along with it in a silent siren song, calling to her fingers.

Mouth suddenly furiously dry, she took a sip of water. John's eyes bored into her soul.

'Oh, go on . . . Nobody will see.' He leant in closer. 'We've got the most secluded table, and the cloth is long enough to cover a multitude of sins.' He did his wicked thing with his tongue, gliding over his lip. 'I bet you wouldn't be the first one to do it here, not by a long shot. This place is the very den of iniquity. Dear God, you should see the in-house porn they have on the TV in the rooms.'

'Really?' Momentarily distracted, Lizzie wondered. Given what Brent had told her about the Waverley, anything was possible.

'Really. Now . . . are you going to oblige me, you gorgeous woman?'

Taking a deep breath, Lizzie let her hand drop to her lap, in what she hoped looked like an innocuous gesture. Then she reached down, as if looking for her bag or something she might have dropped on the floor, and as she did so, she adjusted the fall of the tablecloth so it spread in more concealing fullness over her thighs.

As John idly toyed with a floret of broccoli with his fork, his eyes flitted to hers, watching, monitoring, she began bunching her skirt and her petticoats up and up, working her way through the fullness of layers. It would have been easy with a simple, light summer frock and no slip, but the way she dressed was the way she dressed, and she would have to manage somehow.

Soon she found her stocking top, then her suspender, and naked skin. Wiggling her fingers, while at the same time trying to project a motionless calm, she inveigled her forefinger and middle finger beneath the elastic in the leg of her panties, and touched her bush.

'Everything all right, my dear?' John enquired archly, then turned towards the waiter who'd suddenly appeared from nowhere, to take their plates.

Sweat popped out on Lizzie's skin. She could feel it trickle between her breasts, and gather between her legs, blending with other fluids there. Her face must be rosy, and her cleavage too. Would the waiter notice?

'I think we're finished with this,' said John, leaning back and nodding to his plate and hers. 'Perhaps you'd give us five or ten minutes, and then bring the dessert menu, if you would?'

'Of course,' said the young man, efficiently clearing away. Were his eyes solely on his task? Or was he wondering why the female diner's face was so pink and why her hand was hidden beneath the cloth? Perhaps he was imagining what was actually happening? Perhaps that was his kink as well as John's, and he fantasised about beautiful women playing with themselves furiously beneath the voluminous damask tablecloths of the Waverley restaurant?

Lizzie gasped with relief when he sped away. It seemed like he'd been hovering over her half an hour, when really it was barely ten seconds.

'So, how far have we got?' drawled John, toying with the stem of his wine glass. 'Have we reached the heart of the matter?'

'Well, I don't know what you're doing,' replied Lizzie tartly, 'but I'm not quite there yet. I don't like to rush.'

'Admirable. But in this instance, I'd really rather like you to achieve your goal before our young friend comes back with offers of almond gateau and strawberries and cream.' He leant forward a bit, his voice sinking to a whisper. 'Touch yourself now, Bettie. Do it for me.'

She wiggled her finger, diving through her pubic hair. Things would have been so much easier if she'd been groomed to a skimpy Brazilian, but as John had stated his preference for a more natural look, she'd left it that way.

With a little gasp, she achieved her goal, her fingertip sliding and skirting her clit. Good lord, she was dripping, she was a swamp down there. It was a good job she was wearing a couple of layers of petticoat, to give buoyancy to her skirt, because if she'd been wearing just a thong beneath her dress, she'd have been sitting in a wet patch, her arousal was so lavish.

'Have you ever travelled in a tropical rain forest at all?'

The question was innocuous, but the demonic curve of John's lips told quite a different story. He was enquiring as to her condition. And he wanted an answer.

'No, but I can easily imagine the conditions. Hot. Wet. Everything lush and dripping.'

'Sounds wonderful. I'd love to be travelling there now. Perhaps you can describe a little more what it's like?'

She didn't want to talk about it. She just wanted to touch it. To fondle herself while looking deep into his provocative blue eyes. They were much darker now, with pupils dilated. He was as aroused as she was, and she could imagine that, under the tablecloth, he was as hard as a rock.

'You'll just have to use your imagination, John. It should be easy enough, if you've travelled in that area before. You know it's dark and warm and . . . um . . . humid. And there's a very sensitive little creature that hides in a grotto.'

He let out a laugh, shaking his head and, despite everything, Lizzie smirked too. It was all a bit silly, along with the sexiness, but somehow that was OK. There was a time for dark games, and rituals, but it was also good to act a bit daft sometimes too.

'Ah, yes, I've encountered that little beast, and a very tender and demanding little organism it is too. Capable of extraordinary responses.'

'Yeah, and especially to your investigations, Mr Attenborough. You seem to have exactly the right skills to get the best from it.'

John seemed to be struggling with a straight and studious face, as if it was hard not to laugh. 'Well, I'm not in a position for exploration right now, so maybe you could examine the little beast for me? Test its responses to stimuli?'

'I'll try.'

Blue eyes seemed to draw her in and invite her to drown in them. Almost dazzled, she adjusted the angle of her wrist, and settled her middle finger on her clit, feeling its heat, its swollen needy state. Now she was the one biting her lip as ripples of sensation – not orgasm yet, but not far from it – radiated out, washing through her body, from the point of contact.

Shuffling a little in her seat, while trying not to be noticeable in it, she bore down, opening herself to her own investigations. Her clitoris was so tense, poised like a trigger. She essayed a delicate stroke and her heart thundered.

'You need to master the little creature, Bettie. Take it in hand, but not let it get its own way just yet. Give it some delicate treatment, but try not to give in to its demands.'

Easy for you, you sod!

Both his hands were on the table, but she yearned for him to be in the same parlous condition, with his hand on his sex, almost at the tipping point. A few moments ago, she'd stopped him when she'd thought he might do it; now she wished she hadn't.

'Oh no, you had your chance. You told me to stop.'

Damn him and his bloody mind-reading act! How could he tell what she was thinking? Surely all her face revealed was excitement and arousal, with pink cheeks and bright eyes?

'You can watch me later, Bettie . . . when we go for our walk. I'll put on a show for you. At least I will . . . if it pleases me.'

The brilliant eyes were suddenly stormier, more forbidding. He'd been puckish until now, but in the blink of an eye, the master in him had appeared. His voice very low, for her ears only, he said, 'Stroke yourself . . . do it. That's what I want now.'

With infinite care, she flicked herself, keeping the pressure light and gliding on the copious slipperiness gathered in her sex. Mad energy flowed through her and she fought not to kick out her legs, work her bottom against the chair and tip her head back, moaning and gasping. She wanted to cup her breast through her dress and pinch her nipple in time to her strokes. She wanted to part her thighs wide, bear down hard, and massage her whole crotch against the surface of the chair beneath her.

But she couldn't. She could only look into John Smith's blue eyes and stroke her clit.

'Are you doing as I ask?'

'Y—yes . . .'

'Are you close?'

'Yes, very.'

Her breathing was shallow. Much as she wanted to press down, she also seemed to be floating upwards, lighter than air.

'Don't succumb just yet, but keep at your task.'

Finger working, working, she tried to look away from him, feeling the heat in her face bloom. But he tut-tutted and reached across the table to take her free hand, enclosing it in his, holding her wrist, his fingertip against her pulse point. He'd easily be able to feel the race and charge of her blood. He'd know her state from that alone, never mind her frantic eyes.

There were people all around them, yet they seemed to

be the solitary denizens of a special magic zone. Nobody was looking at them. Perhaps everybody had their own game? Perhaps they'd ceased to exist in the same continuum that she and John inhabited.

'Circle your fingertip,' he ordered, in barely more than a breath, 'circle it round and round, but remember, don't give in.'

The sensations were exquisite, yet also agony. Her whole body was one state of tension, holding back from pressing too hard, circling too hard, from battering her clit and surrendering into a huge orgasm. Still holding her wrist, John lifted his wine glass with his free hand and took a sip. She saw the moisture on his lips, and the undulation of his throat as he swallowed, and her desire surged higher.

'Stop. Remain still. Finger still touching.' As he drank a little more wine, he caressed her pulse point with his fingertip and it was exactly as if he'd taken over between her legs, the slow, tantalising stroke gliding against her clit, the action as stimulating as if she'd still been doing herself.

'Now . . . push your finger inside. Explore further. Sample the well. The way you did this morning.'

Crooking her wrist, she obeyed him, her body glowing with heat and her thighs trembling. She brushed her clit with her thumb, gasping.

'I wish I was there. I wish I was in you . . . deep in you . . .' His lashes fluttered. If a man could look sultry, he did, a perfect icon of fabulous male seduction. His voice dropped again, barely audible, a whisper, almost miming the words. 'I'd like to be in you right up to my balls, so snug in there, surrounded by you. Embraced by the feel of hot, wet silk.'

The words, the touch of her stroking finger on her pulse, it was all too much. She pressed a little harder with her thumb, and her body fluttered and melted in orgasm. Her spine trembled and threatened to give out on her, but John's hand tightened hard on hers, giving her strength and keeping her steady in her seat while the waves of exquisite sensation assailed her groin.

It wasn't possible to look at him. Of their own accord, her eyes were tight shut. But she felt closer to him than she'd ever felt to any man before. To any person . . .

'Yes, we'll see the sweet menu now, please.'

Lizzie's eyes snapped open and, to her astonishment, she saw the waiter standing just a few feet away. How long had he been there? What had he seen, or heard? How long had she been out of it, sitting in a blissed-out daze with one hand still in her knickers and the other in John's steadying grasp?

The handsome young man seemed unperturbed, unruffled. He'd either seen nothing at all, or he was used to such shenanigans at the racy Waverley. Watching his back as he retreated, Lizzie tugged her hand out of John's grip, and her other out from between her legs, and rubbed her sticky fingers furiously on her napkin, not sure why she was doing it, other than her fundamental desire to be dainty – and normal – for a moment.

'Why did you do that? I might have wanted you to taste yourself. I might have wanted to taste you myself.'

Her head snapped round, towards her companion, at the soft sound of his voice. He glanced momentarily at her hand, resting on the table now. She'd rubbed the spoor of her pleasure off her fingers, she was sure, but somehow she could swear it was still there, an invisible imprint of what she'd done at his behest.

'It wasn't hygienic. Not when I'm going to be eating.'

How prim that sounded, how old-fashioned. Almost hysterically, she imagined her old granny reprimanding her, saying nice young ladies don't touch themselves 'down there', and especially not when they're at table. Not that her grandmother would ever actually have acknowledged the existence of a 'down there' in the first place.

Lizzie knew she probably wasn't acting much like an authentic escort, who would have done anything for the client and probably indulged in activities infinitely more dubious than she just had. But the simple fact was that no matter how good her performance was proving to be, she wasn't really a call girl and she couldn't change some things that were ingrained in her.

'Still, you're very wilful for a submissive, aren't you?' persisted John, his smile golden and foxy. 'I'll have to punish you all the harder for that later. I believe we agreed on the phone you're in need of some discipline.'

The arousal that had barely faded suddenly surged back again. Her skin tingled as if it were aping the sting of punishment, glowing all over. She looked not at her own hands, but at his. They were at rest, relaxed now, but she knew they were hard, and implacable, when he needed them to be. Shuffling in her seat, she imagined their rigour on her bottom.

'Ah, but I'm only a submissive when I want to be one. When I'm on the clock. At other times, I'm my own boss, John. I do what *I* want.'

'But I'm paying you now, Bettie. The envelope's right here if you want it.' He patted his jacket, over the inner pocket area. 'You should do what *I* want, not what you want.'

The temptation to bob helplessly on the great sea of his will was almost irresistible. It was so much easier to surrender than to fight. She imagined touching herself again now, and then offering him the evidence, her head lowered respectfully as she held out her hand.

Oh, what a load of bollocks you do think sometimes, Lizzie Aitchison!

'Well, it's . . . it's a bit of grey area, I'd say. And probably better not to be seen exchanging money in a public restaurant, perhaps?' She looked him boldly in the eye, fighting the compulsion to be completely dazzled, as usual.

'So, you'll masturbate in a public restaurant but you won't take money for it. That's an unexpected rationale for a woman in your line of work.' He winked at her, then nodded towards the waiter now approaching with the sweet menus.

I'll have to tell him, it's no good.

The desserts listed seemed to total at least a billion calories each, but contemplating them was a welcome diversion. Sugar always helped her to think straight, and there was enough there to make even her into a genius.

'Ooh, I'll have some of that, please, it sounds divine!' She tapped the description of an insane concoction of chocolate, cake, fudge and whipped cream.

'Chocolate Paradise? Good choice, it's the chef's speciality,' said the waiter, beaming as if he'd created the wicked melange himself.

'I'll have that too,' John said, not even looking at the menu, 'I like the sound of a trip to Paradise.' His tone was normal, conversational, but Lizzie could still detect that sly, suggestive edge aimed directly at her.

A few moments later, they were both faced with a huge wedge of Chocolate Paradise and, for all intents and purposes, alone again in their private zone of intimacy.

'I'm glad you're not one of those women who turns down

pudding.' He took a bite of chocolate goo, with obvious, intense relish. 'It always seems so repressed to resist. It's just another sensual pleasure, after all.'

Lizzie narrowed her eyes. Gorgeous as he was, and adventurous, he'd let his inner chauvinist out from under wraps. 'Ah, so you're judging our entire sex because some of us want to eat healthily, and not get obese and be a burden on the health services?'

His fingers tightened on his spoon. Had she vexed him? Maybe he didn't expect this kind of thing from a woman he'd paid?

'I'm not saying that at all. It's just that some women of my acquaintance don't seem to be able to be in the same room as a calorie without getting nervous. I'm just happy you're enjoying your dessert . . . because it *is* yummy.'

'I'm not one of those women, John.' Especially if those women were working girls.

'No, you're not. You're not like any woman . . . or escort . . . I've ever met.' He leant forward, scrutinising her, chocolate pudding apparently forgotten.

I should tell him. I should tell him now.

Lizzie opened her mouth, the words, *I've something I must tell you* teetering on her lips.

'Come on, eat up,' he encouraged, all chocoholic again, spooning up his Paradise. 'I was looking forward to a stroll this afternoon, but I've a feeling it's looking a bit ominous out there, all of a sudden.'

She followed his gaze to the window, the gardens outside, and the rolling parkland beyond, in which the Waverley was set. It'd been bright and sunny before, but now clouds had rolled in. It wasn't exactly dark, though, not yet.

Around John Smith, though, the sun still seemed to shine.

8

Stormy Weather

Why haven't I told him?
   Is this a date?
   Are we going to do it outdoors?
   Will it rain?

The questions clamoured in Lizzie's brain as she hurried through the foyer from the ladies' cloakroom, heading for the front entrance of the hotel. John had said he'd meet her outside, and she'd tried to be quick, but then got involved in all kinds of maintenance of her personal grooming, and checking, checking, double checking. Mainly that she had condoms aplenty in her bag, wet wipes, clean knickers. Her whore's 'kit'.

She slowed as she left the foyer, looking for him. What if he wasn't there? He was entitled to change his mind; he was a punter, after all.

What if you just dreamed all this? It's crazy enough.

But she spotted him, standing at the edge of the stone terrace, hands in the pockets of his blue jacket, gazing out over the long lawns beyond. She'd expected him to be lounging on one of the benches, Mr Relaxation, but he had a vaguely troubled expression on his face, a stare that seemed to suggest he was seeing more than the grass, the trees and the slightly questionable sky.

About to call out, she almost reeled back when he turned towards her, bright as the sun again on this suddenly overcast day. His smile was all welcome, and showed genuine pleasure at seeing her, as if he too had been wondering about his 'date' doing a runner.

Looking up at the clouds, as she drew close, he said, 'I think we might be all right, don't you? And a spot of rain never hurt anybody anyway. Shall we walk?' He offered her his arm, in old-fashioned courtesy, and she took it gladly. Just touching him, even platonically, seemed to bestow a sense of equilibrium that she didn't have in her normal life.

They fell into step, walking companionably towards what looked like the beginnings of a rambling path through a thick copse of trees. As they approached it, Lizzie wondered whether other lovers passed this way from time to time, looking for a change of scene from the Waverley's cosy chintz and the classic claustrophobia of the hotel room.

When they reached the Rubicon between parkland and woods, John paused, unhooked her arm from his, and reached into his inner pocket. 'Lest I forget, in the excitement.' He drew out a chubby envelope and passed it to her.

Now, tell him now!

'John, there's something I really have to tell you.' She fingered the envelope nervously. Goodness, it really was fat. How the hell much was there in it?

'Uh oh, nothing serious right now, please.' He frowned, the pleat of his brow exaggerating the few faint lines there. 'I'm looking forward to a nice, healthy ramble and a bit of fun.' He winked again, broadly this time, favouring her with his 'Lothario from a sex farce' look. 'Know what I mean? Nudge, nudge . . .'

'Yes, I do . . . but really . . .'

She stopped, silenced by his forefinger against her lips. 'No . . . hush . . . Nothing heavy. I'm in charge here.' His voice was a low purr now, silky but implacable. That master was suddenly before her. No arguments.

'Yes. Yes, you are . . . I'm sorry.'

'No need to apologise. Well, not yet.' Before she could protest, he reached out and took her bag, opening it up and peering in.

Lizzie blushed. The knickers and the condoms were clearly visible, and John grinned, although he didn't remark on them, simply taking the envelope from her, popping it inside, and fastening the clasp again before returning the bag to her.

'There, that's all sorted.' He sounded pleased with himself as he took her by the hand and led her forward along the path.

They couldn't walk abreast now, because the way was uneven, but his grip on her was sure and firm and she felt strangely safe, even though a man she barely knew was leading her into deep undergrowth, far from prying eyes. At either side of them, trees stood close together, old and well grown, and within moments there was no sight of the lawns and the hotel behind them. It was like being on an expedition, a trek into the unknown. Birds sang, and the branches around them sighed. Rustling and scuffling was more problematical, and she gripped on to John's fingers more tightly, making him pause and turn towards her.

'Not scared, are you? I don't think there are any dangerous wild beasts around.'

'Except you, Mr Smith.'

He grinned again. 'Very true. Come on, just a bit further. I found a nice little trysting spot when I was out running this morning.'

Running, eh? She tried to imagine him pounding this path, wearing trainers and a vest and shorts. No wonder he was fit and powerful and lithe.

Pretty soon, they reached what must be the trysting spot, an open yet intimate clearing amongst the thick trees, where a single trunk had fallen, beside a small, weed-girt pond. It was mossy underfoot and, on a bright day, the sun would have shone down, illuminating the entire area, making it almost like a magical arena for activities sacred or carnal.

Immediately, John turned to her, took her bag from her shoulder and tossed it aside, onto the woodland floor. Grasping her in his arms, he brought his mouth down hard on hers, holding her body very tightly against his. As she wound her arms around him, opening her lips to let in his tongue, he gripped her bottom and pressed her pelvis to his.

God, he was hard. Really hard. As he savoured her mouth, tasting and jabbing with his tongue, he ground the iron-hard length of his cock against her belly.

'That's what I've been wanting to do since the moment you appeared in the dining room,' he murmured against her neck, breaking for a moment to kiss the skin there too. 'That and a whole lot more.' His teeth grazed the skin beneath her ear. 'All the time, I wanted to grab you, throw you on the table and play with you until climaxed . . . then stick my cock into you and fuck you until you screamed.'

Lizzie's hips jerked, pressing her sex against his, against that cock she knew beyond doubt *could* make her scream with pleasure.

But John Smith could make her scream and grant her pleasure in other ways too, darker ways. Did he want straight sex out here in the woods, or did he want to play?

As he took her mouth again, she surged against him, loving the way he made a rough sound of approval in his throat. They kissed for a few moments, and he ravished her with his tongue and lips until she was so dizzy with lust she could barely stand.

When he broke away, gasping, his eyes were wild and dark. 'Hell, this is no good. I can't think straight to do what I want to do. I've got to take the edge off.' His hand settled on her shoulder, pushing down. 'Get on your knees . . . now.'

Almost swooning, Lizzie sank down, barely noticing the dampness of the turf beneath her knees. All she could focus on was John, and his crotch, and his swift, nimble hands unfastening his trousers, then drawing out his erection before her eyes.

He was huge, and from this angle he looked bigger still. Without hesitation, or question, he gripped the back of her head and pressed the fat glans against her lips, pushing for entrance, stiff and imperious. 'Open up, escort girl,' he hissed, his voice low.

Thrusting, he pushed right in, filling her mouth with his hard flesh, ruthlessly jerking and shoving. It should have been demeaning, and uncomfortable, but had her mouth not been stuffed with him, Lizzie would have felt like shouting, singing in triumph. He was using her, yet it felt like rapture.

John gasped and growled, holding her still, fucking her mouth, ruthless and demanding. But loving it, she grasped his thighs, helped him to get deeper, miraculously not choking or gagging but relishing every inch and every thrust. She loved it too when he cried out, his snarling, swearing voice nothing like that of the urbane, civilised man she'd come to know. He cursed and grunted like a savage, and after just a few moments of furore, he jerked and jerked and jerked, and without pausing to ask, filled her mouth with his come, holding her tightly and compelling her to swallow.

His chest heaving, John swayed, but Lizzie supported him, holding him just as tight, his thick seed on her tongue, and his cock subsiding, still between her lips. After a moment, she let him slip out and, ever so delicately, and mindful of his sensitised state, she neatly licked him clean.

Between her legs, she ached for the flesh that she attended to, her sex dripping, but it would only be a matter of time before he was ready . . . ready again.

'Hell yes . . . that was good.' His voice was soft now, still a little breathless, and his hand was gentler against the side of her head, stroking and caressing. She felt him reach for the ribbon that contained her hair, and realised that when he'd been grabbing at her, in extremis, he'd half deconstructed her pony-tail. 'Exceptional . . .' He coiled the ribbon and slid it into his pocket, as if saving it for later, while her hair cascaded around her face in smooth, dark curtains.

She didn't move. He hadn't given permission, and he was in charge now. If nothing else, his show of dominance by fucking her mouth had defined their roles for the moment.

Still close, her ran his fingers through her hair, lifting the black strands and then letting them trail across his temporarily somnolent cock. It twitched a little, as if already beginning to revive.

'You, my dear, are the most superlative cocksucker, if you don't mind me being blunt.' He cradled her face, fingers still plunged into her hair, making her look up at him. 'The best I've ever had.'

'Well, I don't think I can really claim the honours, some-how. I wasn't really the active party in that little contretemps. More a convenient vessel than a star performer.'

He gave her an arch look. His eyes narrowed warningly. 'Sometimes it takes skill to be passive, and receptive, and you have that quality in abundance.' He stroked her head again, punctuating his assessment of her, then returned his attention to his clothing, tucking his cock tidily away. Lizzie felt a pang of disappointment, wishing he'd have given her a chance to show what she could do with lips and tongue.

'Take all your clothes off, Bettie. I want to see your luscious body naked.'

She'd half been expecting this, but still it made her heart thud. They weren't all that far from the hotel, and if they could find this walking path, any other guest or guests taking a stroll could too. And when she glanced upwards, the sky was very dark, the cloud thickening, low and heavy. They were in for a downpour soon.

'But it's dark. It's going to rain any minute.'

'Ah, but I wish it, Bettie. And I don't need the sun. *You're* the sun for me.'

For a moment there was an odd, almost confused look in his eyes, then he smiled.

I feel the same. You're my sun, John Smith. You're golden . . .

Even in the gathering gloom he looked like some wicked, gilded angel with his gleaming hair and his sudden, almost beatific smile. It scared her, but for him she'd do anything, everything. Stripping off her clothes in broad daylight, with a real risk of being discovered, was the least of it.

And he's paid you for it too. So jump to it.

The return to her thoughts of her deception, and her dilemma, brought apprehension for a moment, but the expectant look in John's eyes quickly banished that.

Trying to be smooth, accomplished and graceful, she began to strip. The air was still quite warm, but still she trembled as she stepped out of her shoes, then peeled off first her little jacket, then her sundress. She flung the clothes aside, not looking where they landed, no thought for the hours she'd spent at the sewing machine, creating them. Lifting her head, she looked John boldly in the eye, daring him to find fault with her light, lacy basque and matching knickers.

'Delightful, but all off, please. I want you bare as a wood nymph.'

She unhooked her stockings and rolled them down and off, then unfastened the basque too, tossing the whole lot after her dress. Then she stepped out of her panties and, when John held out his hand, she put them into it. 'I'll keep these. You won't need them for the rest of the day, because I'm going to spend most of the time spanking you or fucking you or playing with your pussy . . . That is, when you're not playing with it yourself for my entertainment.'

He sounded so ruthless, so wicked, but there was still that playful twinkle in his eyes. Her nipples hardened painfully with desire.

Sidling closer, he slid behind her and murmured in her ear. 'Fondle your tits for me, you gorgeous girl. I want to see your nipples standing out, really pert.'

He seemed to relish the broad, almost coarse talk. And so did she. He was an intelligent man of refinement, but even more thrilling when he was raw and direct. Licking her lips, she raised her right hand and took a nipple between finger and thumb, slowly rolling.

It felt as if the tiny organ was a switch that tuned her

desire to a higher pitch. Kinetic energy gathered in her pelvis and as she tweaked and plucked at herself, it became harder and harder to keep her lower body still. The urge to gyrate her hips, and thrust and rock in a lewd display, was almost agony.

'You want to move, don't you?' he whispered in her ear, 'You want wiggle your hips, and to be rude and crude, like some cheap stripper . . . You want to be like the real Bettie, exhibiting your body and wafting your crotch about to excite a drooling audience.'

She fought to keep still, tried to surreptitiously back off from the stimulation of her breast. 'Oh no, no, no . . . no cheating. Pinch your nipple. Pinch it hard. But if you move your hips even a millimetre, I'll beat you . . . You know that, don't you?'

Lizzie nodded her head. God, that was what she wanted. It was strange. It was bizarre. But she craved the lash. She wanted to offer her bare bottom to him and feel him create fire in it, thrashing her flesh without mercy. Against all reason, she wanted him to make her moan and sob in pain, as well as ecstasy. She wanted him to dispense both, and so intensely that she could barely differentiate between the two.

Squashing her nipple hard between finger and thumb, she gasped aloud and her hips jerked involuntarily.

'Wicked girl. You'll suffer for that.' His voice was joyous and he reached around her, pinching her other nipple, just as hard, making her moan and waft her pelvis to and fro, her lust over-tipping. Silky fluid trickled down her inner thigh, and her sex was awash, her clitoris distended and aching.

Gasping, she surrendered to the sensations, and felt John press himself close against her back and her naked bottom. His cock was like a knot of stone again, pressing against her crease as he reached around and cupped her crotch while his fingers still wrought distress on the tip of her breast.

'God, you're such a deliciously accomplished whore,' he said, lips in her hair. 'I love that you get so wet . . . so into it. You make it all so real for me.'

What was he talking about? Oh God, yes . . . again, she'd forgotten. But to her, it *was* real. Real sex. Real desire, so dark and twisted. For an instant, she wanted to blurt out the truth, but then squashed the urge. She just couldn't . . . she couldn't stop now, and get into something else entirely and lose the mood.

Not when he was stroking her clit, creating beauty with one set of fingers while hurting her with the other and making both sensations feed one voracious appetite.

When he pinched her in both places, nipple and clit, she came hard, knees almost buckling, leaning against him. Her voice assailed the sky, high and clear, soaring towards the clouds.

'Well, that was more than a millimetre,' he whispered as she tried to gather her wits, still half slumped against him, reaching back, gripping his muscular thigh to steady herself. 'That was a climax, you greedy woman, and I didn't give you permission to have one. I'm going to have to beat your bottom really hard for that.'

Lizzie whimpered, a little of it play-acting, but most of it real. Her pussy was still rippling but seemed to surge with new hunger. With a defiant swirl, she rubbed her bottom against his erection, feeling the bulge of him massage her anal groove.

'Oh, and you'll get that too, wicked Bettie.' His hips flirted, pushing his hardness at her. 'But not this afternoon, I think . . . Activities like that need a little forethought.'

He was right. But she was still disappointed.

'Don't worry . . . Soon . . .'

It was as if he'd read her thoughts. Read them again. And the idea of that made her sag against him, coming down from the high of her orgasm.

'Are you all right?' His voice was different now, real and not of their sexual world. He was concerned for her as a lover would have been, or a friend.

'Yes, thank you . . . I'm fine . . . If there's anything the matter, I'll always cry "chintz", don't you worry.'

He laughed softly, and caressed her, running his hands over her body. 'Such soft skin you have . . .' In a sudden movement, he held her by the shoulders and turned her, looking into her eyes. Then, unexpectedly, he shrugged out of his jacket, turned it lining side down and set it on the big tree trunk. 'Sit down.'

Taken aback, she obeyed him, wondering at his strange courtesy. They were playing dominance games, and that was a fact. She was his creature. And yet, like a knight of old, he'd laid down his modern equivalent of a cloak for her comfort.

'Are you sure you're OK?' There was still concern in his eyes as he stared into hers, cradling her face and taking her wrist in his free hand. 'You swayed there. I don't want you to pass out. What we do is intense.'

'I'm fine. Really I am.' She wanted to laugh, but she could see he was serious. 'What are you? A paramedic now?'

John smiled, but seemed reassured. He squeezed her hand and released her. 'I'll have you know I got badges for first aid when I was a boy scout. I know what I'm talking about.'

For an instant, she imagined him young. A golden adolescent with a mop of angelic curls. He must have been adorable. He was still pretty divine now, the seasoning of maturity only adding to his attractions.

'That's very reassuring,' she said, adding, 'Really!' when he raised his sandy eyebrows at her. 'And you've certainly still got the legs for the shorts.'

'Cheeky mare!'

Tentatively, she put her hand on his thigh, loving the firm toned feeling of his musculature, then slid it higher. Her knuckles brushed against his cock through the linen of his trousers, and that felt firm and toned too. More than firm. It twitched like a wild beast when she pressed harder.

'What are you doing, Bettie?' he asked softly, his eyes narrow and twinkling. He didn't touch her or stop her. His arms were relaxed by his sides now, hands loose on the surface of the tree trunk. He seemed to be challenging her, or perhaps tempting her into some unwary act.

'I...I thought we might resume our normal programming.' Unable to resist, she twisted her wrist and laid her full hand over his erection, glorying in its mass, the perceptible heat through the light cloth, and the jersey of his undergarment beneath. 'I wanted to check whether you'd recovered from the blow job . . . whether you were still in the mood.' She cupped him, searching for the details, the shape of his shaft.

'I'm always in the mood around you. Especially when you're as bold as this. Making free with me without permission. Any more, and I'll have to punish you, you know that, don't you?'

You were always going to punish me.

Not answering, she slid down his zip, and fished around inside, finding him. He was hot, hard and velvety, his tip a little moist with pre-come. Her mouth watered, and she wanted to suck him again, she found him so delightful.

Perhaps use a bit of her own skill this time, rather than just be a receptacle for his release. She imagined sucking on just the crown, taking just the glans between her lips to tease him. Playing around the little love-eye with the point of her tongue while she delicately cradled his balls.

But when she started to slide off the tree trunk, to kneel before him, he murmured, 'Uh oh . . . I want something different now. Maybe when we return to the hotel.'

She sat quiescent, waiting for his will, but with her hand still in his trousers, defiantly. As he studied her, with the devil-light in his eyes, a few fat drops of rain pattered down onto them from the darkening skies.

John felt the rain on his face as if it were a phenomenon happening to some other person. All he could think about was the soft embrace of Bettie's fingers around his cock. Her hold on him was light, yet at the same time, paradoxically, it had great weight. Weight of meaning, of feeling. He loved her touch. It felt right. Good. Clean.

He was tempted to let her suck him again, but the sight of her gorgeous nude body incited other urges. The curve of her haunch beside him, the exquisite tight round of her bottom where she perched on his jacket. They were so unbearably tempting to him. He imagined her face down over the tree trunk, her sublime rump offered to his hand, or perhaps to a switch. There were plenty of promising materials about, thin, whippy branchlets that would make the perfect instrument of punishment. In his mind her saw a red line across her creamy buttocks, and her hips churning as she fought the pain and pleasure both. She responded so divinely to discipline. She was a natural, despite the lack of experience she took such care to hide from him.

But he didn't care about that. Her zest for the game was obvious; she certainly wasn't hiding that. He hoped she'd tell him more of her story, and her background, in her own good time, and perhaps they could . . . well, he didn't know quite what, but maybe some other kind of arrangement.

Rain splattered down, faster now, and the drops were like jewels on Bettie's skin, diamonds on cream, and brilliant also where they clung to her dark hair, loose about her shoulders, and the equally dark curls of her exquisite bush.

'Perhaps we'd better go now?' she suggested, staring up at the glowering clouds visible through the break in the trees above them. For a moment, she closed her eyes as if savouring the rain, but still, below, she held him in that sweet, tantalising hold. It was like electricity. Not the lightning crash that might actually strike them any moment, if the weather deteriorated, but a softer, energising glow that made him feel strong and happy and young, like a boy, barely more than when he'd been that scout he'd told her about.

With Bettie, sitting here as the rain streamed down around them, the years, and the rocks and knocks along the path of his life, were all washed away. Everything seemed bright, and fresh, and new and full of possibilities.

'No, let's stay a while. You're not afraid of the rain, are you?' he teased, putting his hand on her wrist and, with some reluctance, prising her off him.

You're not afraid of me, I know that.

He took her hand, raised it to his lips, and kissed it, smelling his own aroused scent as he did so.

The look in her eyes as he set her hand down in her own lap confirmed the thought. She was eager, excited, enraptured. Everything magical.

No, I'm the one that's afraid. Afraid of what I might feel.

But that wasn't going to stop him playing the game, or sharing this exquisite, brief adventure. With an unexpected angel who'd fallen from heaven into his life . . .

'No, of course I'm not. And, after all, there's nothing on me to spoil, is there?' Lizzie looked down at her own bare body and laughed. Good God, she was sitting here naked in the middle of the woods, in an increasing rain storm, and it felt wonderful. The moisture on her skin seemed to combine with the heat in John's eyes to form a delicious, potent aphrodisiac. She wanted him more than ever now; either in her, or as the remorseless administrator of some as yet undetermined punishment.

'Nothing *could* spoil you,' he said, running his hand up her thigh, skin gliding on skin coated in water. 'And yes, I think we should resume. I'm suddenly consumed by an intense passion to whip your glorious bottom.' He squeezed. 'Now come on, let's have you over this incredibly convenient log while I select an implement.'

An implement? What implement? Her eyes skittered to the thin belt he wore. It looked rather cruel, as if it could bite fiercely. There wasn't much else, apart from his hand.

Taking her by the arm, first he urged her onto her feet, then edged her down again, until she was lying over the tree trunk, her belly and breasts pressed against the hard bark, protected only by his jacket. Her head hung down the other side, but fortunately there was a dip beyond, or else she'd have been distracted by the idea of beetles and spiders crawling in her dangling hair. She wondered about asking John to tie it back again, but it seemed he had another purpose for her ribbon. He fastened her hands behind her back with it, at the base of her spine.

'Beautiful,' he pronounced as the rain lashed down, pausing to cup her left buttock and give it a squeeze. 'Now lie quiet and be absolutely still. I won't be but a moment.'

Oh no, he's leaving me!

John strode away through the trees, in the direction they'd arrived from, and Lizzie was left, bared to the elements . . . alone.

9

The Lashing Rain

Where are you? Where are you?

The minutes stretched out. The rain poured down. Her skin and hair were wet through. The pit of her belly ached with desire. She could hardly keep still, even though he'd commanded her to.

Perhaps a little adjustment of her position would allow her to rub herself against the hard bark beneath her, through John's jacket, and stimulate her clit? Surreptitiously, she worked her hips, adjusting the angle, spreading her thighs, rocking. The result was worse. She was more roused, more needy than ever. If he hadn't tied her hands she'd be rubbing herself by now.

Testing her bonds, she found them firm, but not uncomfortably tight. He knew what he was doing. How many women had he tied up before? How many women had he punished?

Dozens, I'll bet. Who could resist him? Even if I hadn't had a curiosity about BDSM before I met him, I'd certainly be into it now.

She wriggled again, trying to get off, knowing she

couldn't. Unless, of course, she could will herself into it? But even John Smith and the fantasies he inspired in her weren't quite capable of that feat.

But still she rocked and jiggled, imagining him touching her, spanking her, fucking her. Even the sound of footsteps approaching couldn't stop her and she was still moving as she saw John appear in the periphery of her vision.

'Didn't I tell you to be still?'

She craned around and found him smiling indulgently. But for once, his beautiful grin wasn't what caught her attention. No, it was the thin, freshly cut switch he was slashing experimentally through the air. No great student of the natural world, Lizzie had no idea what kind of tree it might have come from, but it looked narrow and fierce and unsettlingly cruel.

Ignoring his query, she made one of her own. 'How did you manage to cut that? More boy scout skills?'

He approached fast, still swishing his new implement, and sweeping his wet hair back from his brow with his other hand. He was just as saturated as she was now, his expensive shirt and trousers drenched. But it didn't seem to bother him too much, and the way the sodden linen clung to his crotch only outlined the fact he was hard as rock again.

'I always carry a Swiss Army knife. You never know quite when you'll need one.' He slipped his hand into his trouser pocket, and drew out the famous knife in question. It was a small version, but obviously just as effective.

'Must be useful for all the stones in horses' hooves you have to deal with,' she shot back.

'I've used it for that in my time,' he replied equably, stowing away the knife and returning his attention to the switch, running his fingers along it then swishing it again.

Momentarily, Lizzie was distracted, though. John rode horses? What kind of life did he have, away from all this? She knew nothing of him, and suddenly wondered why the hell that was. The first thing she did, usually, when she met someone, was look them up on the internet, on Google and Facebook and Twitter, and yet this time, when finding a man's provenance would be critically important . . . she hadn't done it!

You're making me crazy, Mr Smith. You're making me lose it.

But as he laid the switch across the crown of her buttocks, she resolved to rectify her omission. She *would* find out who was this devil who'd bewitched her.

'So, how many strokes do you fancy?' He drew the thin wand over her skin, as if he were painting with the rainwater on the canvas of her body.

'Well, I rather thought that wasn't really up to me,' she replied, trembling wildly. Despite the rain, it wasn't really cold, but still she shuddered and gooseflesh popped up on her skin. This organic instrument of discipline was far more ominous than the hand, or the plastic ruler.

And yet John was a master. In every sense. She knew in her gut that he was supreme at this, and knew exactly what he was doing. He would only ever hurt her in the way she wanted and craved. In all other ways, he would take care of her.

'No, it isn't. I was just messing with you.' His smile was like a sunrise polished by the rain.

'Half a dozen. Just half a dozen. That thing looks vicious.'

'Ah . . . bold . . . For that, I might give you twice as many.'

You won't.

Somehow she knew that six was all she'd get.

'Are you ready?'

She nodded, choked with apprehension . . . and anticipation.

'You must be quiet and good and still and make me proud. Can you do that?'

She nodded, sincerely doubting she'd achieve any of it.

'Very well . . . then we begin.'

Before she had time to think, there was a high whistling swish and the first cut landed. Even though she'd no chance to brace herself, it didn't feel so bad . . . didn't feel like anything . . .

Then her heart started beating again and electric fire arced in a fierce agonising line across the crown of both her buttocks.

It was astonishing. It took her breath. Blanked her mind. A shrill cry breached her lips and echoed around the little dell, and to her astonishment she realised she was rolling to and fro on the tree trunk, her feet kicking madly.

Oh God, that was only one.

The second was better . . . or worse . . . she couldn't tell. It was just another line of fire that lay exactly parallel to the first.

'Oh God, oh God, oh God,' she chanted, twisting her hands in their bonds to try and grab herself.

'Don't do that,' instructed John softly, and she instantly desisted.

Another stroke fell, right on the under-hang of her bottom this time, and she shrieked and shot forward over the tree trunk, nearly plummeting head first over the other side of it.

As she flamed and burned, John paused and rested a cool hand on her heat. 'Steady, my lovely one,' he whispered, the touch like a blessing. Then he sought her fingers and coiled them with his for just a moment. A surge of strength coursed through Lizzie from the point of contact, and courage too. She quieted, fell still, braced by his benediction.

Then he was beating her again, the last three strokes. They were harder than before, taxing her to her limits, but she kept dead still and uttered not a word even though her bottom felt as if it were roasting in a furnace, and she couldn't tell where one stripe ended and another began.

The switch whistled through the air, but this time Lizzie saw it fly away across the dell, out of the corner of her eye.

Just six strokes. Exactly as she'd specified. She almost laughed, savouring a revelation in the pain.

Good God, I really am in charge, aren't I?

'Jesus, you're adorable.' John's voice came in her ear. He'd flung himself alongside her, heedless of grass and mud, and buried his face in her hair. Lizzie pressed herself against him, not caring that his body rubbed against the fire in her bottom, making her hiss through her teeth.

'I want you,' she whispered, her voice breathy, the wind still knocked out of her by the thrashing.

His lips pressed against her neck, hot with passion and, as he kissed her, she felt him working on the ribbon that held her wrists, to free her. Loosed, she rocked back on her knees, twisting to fling her arms around him and embrace him. Every move stirred the pain in her buttocks, but she didn't care. She even welcomed it. The fierce marks were another bond between them.

'Oh God, let's fuck,' growled John, starting to pluck at his shirt, then wrenching it open to send buttons flying amongst the grass and ferns and undergrowth. Leaping to his feet, he kicked off his shoes, tugged off his socks, then attacked his trousers, shucking them off and tossing them over the tree trunk.

When his boxer briefs went the same way, he stood before her, a god of fire and rain, his erection jutting from his groin.

Lizzie shuffled towards him, lured by that magnificent rod, but John put his hand on her shoulder. 'No . . . I want you to have pleasure too, my sweet Bettie.' He sank to his knees beside her, fishing into the pocket of his trousers across the tree as he did so. 'I want you to ride me into oblivion, you gorgeous goddess,' he said, producing a condom with a flourish. 'I want to see your beautiful body and your lovely face as I come.'

Rolling onto his back, apparently oblivious to mud and grass and twigs, and creepy crawlies various, he gestured to her, inviting her to join him. With a grin, he tossed her the condom.

All a jitter, and still constantly aware of her blazing bottom, Lizzie grappled with the wrapper, then prized out the fine contraceptive within. She half wondered if John wanted her to do the 'put the rubber on with the mouth' trick, but as she'd never done it, and suspected she'd make a not very authentic mess of it, she positioned the condom carefully over the fat tip of his cock and rolled it down as deftly and lightly as she could. He was close to the edge, she could tell, because he rocked back onto his elbows, his handsome face turned to the stormy heavens, his eyes closed. As she enrobed him, he opened his mouth as if to drink the rain that teemed onto his face.

Moving around with a thrashed bottom was uncomfortable, to say the least, but somehow the pain only seemed to add a lustre to the experience. Throwing her thigh across John's lean hips, Lizzie manoeuvred into position, raising high so she could grasp him by the head of his cock and present him to her entrance. He felt huge against her there, warm through the rubber, but she was swimmingly wet in a way that had nothing to do with the rain, so when she bore down, and he bucked up, he slid in easily.

'Oh God. Hell. Yes,' he proclaimed through gritted teeth, canting up and grasping her by the hips. His fingers caught a sore spot as he held her, and she grunted, but for once he didn't seem to notice, so lost was he in his own sensations.

Yes, yes, she answered him, but silently, wiggling in his grip and wanting him to reignite the fire in her stripes. They were badges of honour, and the soreness only stoked her desire all the more. The pain, and the pleasure of him, were indivisible, each increasing the other. She almost felt like inviting him to slap her bottom while his cock was lodged inside her.

John's blue eyes snapped open, their wild colour so glorious that her sex rippled around him. 'What is it, Bettie? What are you thinking? Tell me . . . tell me now.' He snagged his lower lip as she clenched on him, almost coming.

'I . . . I thought about you slapping my bum. Now . . .'

'Really?'

'Yes.'

Before she had time to change her mind, he fetched her a ringing slap on her sore left buttock and she shrieked, pain hurtling through her loins and turning to the sweetest bloom of ecstasy between her legs. Grabbing at John's shoulder, she loomed over him, reaching down and rubbing her clit as she came and came and came, mashing her body against his . . . and yes, riding him. Riding him hard.

Tossing her head, her hair flying around her, she rode the pleasure too. John made a harsh, almost ferocious sound, his hips thundering as hers did, lifting again and again as he came along with her. His hold on her was a death grip, tormenting her stripes, and the burn of it only drove her higher. As she soared, she was dimly aware of her own fingers, her fingernails, digging deep into the muscle of his shoulder.

But the madness couldn't last and, as she pitched forward, overcome, his arms slid right around her, holding her close, cradling her now, his embrace protective. For some minutes, she couldn't move, and neither, it seemed, could he. Wrapped together, they held on as the rain still teemed down and lashed their joined bodies.

Eventually, Lizzie blinked and reached up to sweep her hair out of her eyes. John's arms were still around her and his face buried in her neck, and when she looked down at his shoulder, so close to her face, she saw the clear print of her own fingernails, outlined in blood that trickled over his lightly tanned skin.

'I've hurt you, John,' she whispered, then lowered her mouth to his shoulder, kissing it better and tasting the copper of the blood.

Against her, she felt the shake of his body as he laughed softly and, as he shifted, his subsiding cock slid out of her. The feel of it thus was so tender and intimate that she blinked, aware that some of the moisture in her eyes was more than rain.

'Treasured battle scars, sweetheart,' he said, cradling her cheek and urging her to lift her head. His smile was beatific.

'Yeah, but it's a real injury, not pain for pleasure.' She hitched her hips a little, freeing him completely and feeling the glide of his fingers, too, on her punished bottom.

'Worry not, fair maiden.' He kissed her lips, softly brushing them with his. 'It's more than worth it. Far more than worth it. You could have scratched half my back off and I'd still be smiling.'

'But still,' she said, sitting up, then climbing off him to kneel at his side, grimacing at the twinges in her buttocks.

'Still yourself.' Straightening too, he pressed on her shoulder and made her turn so he could see her back view. 'Did I hit you too hard? Was it more than you wanted?' He reached around and touched the edge of one of her stripes, making her hiss.

'No, not more than I wanted . . . but more than I usually allow.' Which was the truth. She'd never allowed this before, because she'd never played this way.

'I'll compensate you for it.' He took her hand and kissed it. 'I'll make it up to you. Danger money, you might say.'

'Don't be ridiculous, John, you're already paying way over the odds.' She paused. Was now the moment, when he was feeling mellow and well shagged out? 'Look, I've got to tell you. I'm—'

He pressed the tips of his fingers across her lips, and looked skywards, allowing the rain to patter hard on his face. 'Not now, eh? I think we need to be moving. Let's get back to the hotel, and the hot shower and the hot towels, and maybe a nice hot toddy.' Lithely, he sprang to his feet and then, with no trace of self-consciousness, peeled off the used condom. 'Do you have a tissue in your bag, sweetheart? Ecology and all that.'

Clambering up somewhat less gracefully, she cast around for her bag, found it slightly sheltered under a tree and not too wet, and fished in it for tissues.

Their clothes had avoided the worst of the storm, under the arboreal canopy, but they wouldn't stay relatively dry long. The rain was increasing rather than slowing down.

Pulling a face, Lizzie wrapped the basque around herself, ready to hook it up.

'No . . . not yet.' John stayed her hand. 'Bundle your things up, as tightly as you can. We'll walk to the edge of the woods, put our clothes on, and then run as fast as we can across the park. That way, they won't get quite as wet.'

Lizzie opened her mouth to protest, then just laughed. Wild as it sounded, John's plan made sense. He nodded, pleased with himself.

'Lateral thinking, eh? Am I clever or what?'

You're a know it all, Mr Smith. But I don't mind a bit.

They gathered all their belongings and began to pick their way along the path, with John indicating the safest places to step with bare feet. It was one of the most bizarre episodes of her life, BDSM games with him notwithstanding, but she felt strangely safe, and nurtured, following his lead. And even though she was supposed to be watching her footing, a lot of the time she was observing the smooth flexion of his gorgeous male arse as he walked ahead of her.

'I know you're looking at my bum,' he called out, turning briefly and catching her in the act. 'If I wasn't trying to stop you treading on stones and twigs and God alone knows what else, I'd make you walk in front so I could watch your lovely bottom and admire my own handiwork.'

'You'll get the chance later,' she flung back, strangely excited. Despite everything, she wanted to exhibit herself to him. She was proud of the marks still. They were the sigils of his possession and her bravery.

At the edge of the park, they halted behind a thicket of bushes and dressed, at least partially. Lizzie thrust her basque into her bag as best she could. If she could keep that fairly dry, and her spare knickers, it was only her top clothes that she'd have to dry out when they reached the sanctuary of John's room.

'Come on, beautiful Bettie, let's run for it, shall we?' His expression was merry, like that of a wicked, playful imp and, clutching his shoes in one hand, he grabbed her hand with the other and urged her forward, out into the open.

Across the grass they hurtled, laughing crazily within seconds at the absurdity of it all, barefoot, squelching and sliding. It was so exhilarating that Lizzie barely felt where he'd beat her. Perhaps the endorphins or adrenaline or whatever it was had cancelled out the ache?

She wasn't sure which it was, but she was sure she'd have followed him anywhere. And at a run.

Please don't fall for him, Lizzie, she told herself, as he turned and grinned at her, making a sunny day out of a torrential rainstorm. *You can't* really *have him, and he only wants you for a while* . . .

But it was far too late for that. The deed was done. As they almost flew across the lawn, she'd already fallen.

10

Trust

The stripes were quite red, but nowhere near as livid as Lizzie had expected. Lifting up the back of the thick, fluffy white bathrobe, she checked them one last time before returning to the bedroom to join John. She'd just enjoyed one of the most delicious and welcome showers in her entire life. In the movies, they would probably have shared it, but she'd been grateful for a little time to herself.

Although John's room had been furnished and kitted out for a single, male occupant, a phone call to reception had produced a towering pile of extra towels, additional bathrobes, and a complementary basket of feminine toiletries and beauty products. She'd been able to pamper herself far more lavishly than she'd ever have been able to at home, in the process of washing away the last of the mud, twigs and leaves that had still been clinging to her skin despite the sluicing of the rain.

Tentatively, she touched one of the ruddy marks on her bottom. It was still sore, but not agonising. Goddamn, the man knew what he was doing! Even with a bit of branch he'd harvested randomly in the woods, he was a master of hand to eye coordination. Somehow, he'd managed to pull each stroke at the very last second, making it lighter yet still dramatic.

Letting the robe drop, she grasped the door handle.

John was sitting on the bed, bundled in another bathrobe, with his laptop across his knees. He seemed intent on something, and a cup stood on the bedside table at his side, along with a half-eaten scone on a plate. A trolley loaded with a lavish English afternoon tea had been delivered while she was showering.

'Feeling better? Ready for some tea?' John tapped a few keys and set aside his computer, then slid to his feet, coming towards her.

Wouldn't it be nice if this were real?

He slid his arm around her, gave her a kiss on the cheek and led her to the bed.

'Do you need a cushion? I didn't hurt you too much, did I?'

How cool would it be if I really had this gorgeous man as my boyfriend? He's handsome, intelligent, mature . . . and bloody hell, he's even rich too.

'No, I'm fine thanks. You're a very clever man, John Smith. I'm really nowhere near as sore as I thought I would be. You have a very skilled touch.'

'So I've been told.' He grinned, and when she made as if to sit where he'd been sitting, he halted her. 'Hang on a minute. I've got some balm that's sometimes useful in these circumstances. It's herbal, and I use it sometimes when my trick knee is bothering me . . . an old rugby injury . . . but it works just as well on spanked bottoms.'

'You played rugby?' She let him help her onto the bed, and to lie down on her front. This was a tantalising hint. She'd never have pegged him as a rugby player, but she supposed he might have the build for a winger, or whatever. The ones who ran and were fleet of foot.

'I did indeed. At public school for my sins.' As she got comfortable, he folded up her robe at the back to expose her. Curiously, the moment felt strangely asexual, just the action of someone who was familiar and comfortable. Someone there was no reason to be on edge or embarrassed with.

Even if he *was* an ex public schoolboy. The plot thickened.

'It'll feel a bit chilly. I've had it in the mini fridge. It works better that way,' he warned, then a moment later, he applied the first dose.

The ointment, and the way he applied it, was heavenly. His touch was light as a feather, delicately stirring the pain at first, then ameliorating it with the cool potion. The keenest, sorest spots seemed to back right down to a gentle, almost steadying glow. A sweet reminder of challenge and pleasure. He dressed each stripe carefully, methodically, and at the edge of her perception, Lizzie acknowledged the renewed stir of desire for him. But it wasn't strident. If he initiated sex again now, it would be nice. But if he didn't, it would also be nice.

'There, you're done.'

The terrycloth settled back on her bottom again. So, no sex, then? That was OK. She rolled onto her side and watched John wiping the ointment from his fingers with tissues. He walked to the waste bin and flung them in, then turned to the tea trolley.

Hmmm, he did have an erection. And when he saw her notice it, he winked.

'You don't seriously think I could touch your beautiful spanked bottom and not get hard, do you?'

'I don't know . . . You're an unusual man, John. I never know quite what to expect.'

'Of course I want you. I always want you.' With a quick smile over his shoulder, he inspected the teapot, and started preparing her a cup. 'Milk? Sugar?'

'Just a splosh of milk, please.' She watched him being mother with the tea things, then buttering her a scone. It was quite bizarre to see a dominant man with a hard-on being so domestic. 'It must be rather inconvenient in your business meetings and whatnot, always wanting me. Don't people notice?'

He came towards her, bearing his gifts of tea and confectionery. 'Ah well, I practise certain bio feedback techniques that keep the beast under control in such circumstances . . . although they don't work on my mind quite as well.'

'Crikey, I hope you haven't missed out on some barzillion pound deal because of me!'

He grinned. 'Don't worry, I've always managed to snap back to reality at the crucial moment.' He placed her scone plate on the bedside table and put her cup and saucer into her hands. 'Now, drink up, you deserve it. I'm going to have a shower. Much as I'd love to ravish you again, you're squeaky clean now and I'm still grunchy and grubby.'

'I don't mind.'

He shook his head and began to walk away. At the door, he turned and nodded towards his laptop, still set on the bed beside her. 'You can look me up while I'm in the shower . . . I know you want to.'

'How do you know I haven't already?'

He gave her a steady look. 'I just know . . . There are things you would probably have mentioned. I'm surprised, though. Most women in your line of work would probably have checked me out thoroughly before now.'

Most escorts probably would. If they were really escorts.

'Do you trust me so much that you'd let me fool about on a laptop full of your crucial data?'

His lips quirked a little. It wasn't quite a smile . . . or was it?

'Yes,' he said, then disappeared into the bathroom.

Now why the hell did I do that?

Why had he done it? Admittedly the most sensitive material on his laptop was encrypted and, clever as she was, he didn't think Bettie was a hacker as well as a naturally talented if inexperienced prostitute. But still, there were revealing enough documents she would easily be able to open.

And yet he trusted her. Without knowing why, he knew he'd be safe in her hands. Perhaps it was because she put her trust in him? She hadn't been in the life long, he was sure of it, and she had no one to protect her if he had happened to be a dangerous psycho. Yet she still came to him, and still allowed him to touch her and spank her.

Bettie wasn't a stupid woman, but she was almost sweetly naïve in some ways. And she made him feel that way too, as if all was new and fresh and untrammelled by the past, and its weight of associations . . . and regrets.

He smiled as he stepped into the shower, then laughed at himself as the water teemed down. Hell, he was just as wet behind the ears as she was. With a world of resources at his fingertips, he could have found out exactly who she was, where she lived, what kind of circumstances might have predicated her choices, everything about her, probably within half an hour. But he hadn't done it. He hadn't even looked to see if she had a website.

*I just want the here and now, and our game, Bettie. If that is
your real name? I don't want the past . . . or the future. Just a little
while, like this. That's all.*

So why, as he soaped his body, and wondered whether
to deal with the demands of his erection, or save it for the
woman just beyond the door, did his usual modus operandi
suddenly oppress him?

Why did he feel unsettled? Yearning? Wanting more?

Where did one start, looking up a man called *John Smith* on
the internet? Surely there must be thousands, hundreds of
thousands of them, and that horde not even including those
who used it as an alias.

She clicked the 'x' to close Chrome, even before she'd put
'John Smith' into Google. It was probably pointless trying
anyway.

The screen mocked her. There was no revealing screen-
saver, no wallpaper. Just plain blue, the screen matte
and unrevealing, in a businesslike and sombre high-end
machine. Eyeing the email program logo, she pursed her
lips. No, she couldn't go there. That was private. John had
trusted her.

Then, about to open Chrome again, she noticed an icon
in the upper left corner.

JS Intranet.

JS? His company or whatever? It was a bit understated.

She clicked open the browser and plugged 'John Smith
business' into it. She was just a very average Googler, not a
clever web sleuth, so she selected the Wikipedia link at the
top of the results list.

In the course of the next few minutes, as the shower ran
reassuringly in the next room, Lizzie gasped, aloud, several

times. His Wiki entry was frustratingly skimpy, but had enough to blow her mind anyway.

Good God Almighty, no wonder you think nothing of blowing a grand for an hour or so with an escort.

John Smith was a very rich man.

John Smith really was a 'John Smith', well, after a fashion. He had other names too. Not to mention a title he didn't use because of some hinted-at family estrangement.

John Smith had been married, but apparently wasn't any more.

Oh God, what if he'd still been married?

The fact that she hadn't even thought about it chilled her marrow. Obviously it wouldn't have mattered to a real escort. Married men sought out escorts all the time. But she wasn't one, and she didn't believe in doing over another woman by sleeping with her husband, no way. She remembered her own mother's anguish over her father's brief fling. They were reconciled now and, to the best of her knowledge, happier than before. But still, the sound of Ma's bitter tears still rang in her mind.

You've turned my head, John Smith. Made me forget stuff I've sworn never to forget, goddamn you.

Chastened, Lizzie frowned over other information, just as stark and jaw-dropping in its own way. More so . . . much more.

A conviction for dangerous driving? So serious that he'd served a stretch in prison? How bad must the offence have been to merit incarceration? Good grief, had he killed someone?

The details were brief and unrevealing, but did she even want to know more? How could she judge him? He didn't seem like the kind of callous brute who'd deliberately harm anyone – in fact, quite the reverse. He'd been exquisitely solicitous of her welfare. It was hard to believe any ill of him, but at some time during his youth, over twenty years ago, he'd driven so recklessly they'd put him in prison.

Suddenly, she decided she didn't want to know more. The John of today was a good man. She knew it in her heart and her gut. Whatever he'd done, he'd paid a price, and no doubt still felt remorse.

Frantic digital scrabbling around for celeb gossip and titbits about his love life seemed trivial and rather silly now, so she pushed the laptop away and reached for her tea. Surprisingly, it was still quite hot.

It had only taken a few moments to see her 'client' in a whole new light. Or lights.

The bathroom door swung open as she was nibbling her scone, and John ambled in, bath sheet around his hips, and rubbing his hair with a smaller towel. When he flung that away, his blond locks gleamed around his head, in angelic curls, making him look so much younger than his now confirmed forty-six years.

'Uh oh,' he said, seeing her face.

'I only did a search with Google. I didn't look at any of your stuff.'

'I never expected you to look at my stuff, but I can see your search proved fruitful.' He strolled to the side of the bed and retrieved his cup, and replenished it before turning back to her. Then he pulled up a chair to the side of the bed, and sat down, his face serious. 'So, let's have it, what do you want to know about first?'

'I really don't know where to begin. You're full of surprises.'

And of temptation too.

Faced with him, all damp and tousled in his freshly showered beauty, none of the revelations seemed to matter much as they *should* have done. Real as they were, they still seemed a million miles away, and about some other person. She hesitated to say *her* John, but what she'd discovered on the web was about a John, one who existed outside of their own magic bubble. Whatever he'd done and whatever and whoever he was, she just couldn't find it in her to think less of him. He was still the man who turned her head. Still the man she was infatuated with, in body and mind. A breathtaking fortune, a title, an ex-wife and, hell, even a prison record, none of it made her feel different. She still just wanted him.

He continued to stare at her, though, his eyes luminous yet full of shadows and a dark hint of apprehension, so she grabbed at something, the least problematical thing. 'Well, I thought you were loaded, but I didn't realise you had, like, a billion squillion pounds and owned about forty businesses . . . and what on earth are you doing at a place like the Waverley? I mean, it's lovely. I think it's the nicest hotel I've ever been in, but it's quite small, really, and apparently you own a much bigger hotel only ten miles away . . .' A thought occurred. 'You're not buying the Waverley too, are you?'

John regarded her steadily for what seemed like an eternity, and it seemed as if she were far more revealed to him by her omissions than he'd been by anything on the internet. Then he nodded his head, as if accepting her desire not to examine certain areas . . .

With a rueful shrug, he said, 'I'd love to buy the Waverley. I've made them an offer, but they won't sell. They want to keep it exclusive and family owned, and I can't really blame them.'

'I don't either. I'm glad they won't sell out. You plutocrats shouldn't have things all your own way.'

His guarded expression became a smile again, and it was as if he were thanking her, grateful for the return to a simple playfulness of mood. His head came up and he gave her a provocative look. 'You don't always say that. Sometimes you like me to have my way.' He paused and took a sip of tea. 'What's wrong, are you thinking now that you should have been charging me more?'

Oh, back to her own issues, her deception . . . If only she'd told him sooner. If only they could *both* be dealing openly. The truth hovered on her lips, but again, she stalled. This no-strings relationship was what he wanted, and to change things now would look as if she was some kind of gold-digger, and trying to trap him emotionally as well.

'No, like Sherlock Holmes, my fees are on a fixed rate. I think I'm a pretty good value mid-range prostitute but it'd be cheating to ask for more, just because you've *got* more.'

'Well, I must say, that's a very rational and non-acquisitive way of looking at things, Bettie, and I'm very impressed. I'm not sure others in the same position would be so forbearing.'

Ah, but nobody was in quite the same position.

'Well, I have to feel good about myself.'

'True.' He paused and eyed her, his expression assessing. It was like being subjected to a subtle, unspoken third degree. 'So, no more questions?'

Despite her resolution a moment ago, dozens of them surged, clamouring in her mind, almost deafening.

How serious had that accident been? Who else had been involved? Why had he divorced? Was there someone else in his life now? Why, when he'd grown up at a beautiful stately home like Montcalm, wasn't he staying *there*? It was only a twenty-minute drive from the Waverley . . . was he really so estranged from his family that he never visited them? She'd had her own problems on that score, disappointing her parents and not following their plan for her, but the love was still there, despite all.

Stop it, Lizzie, it's not your business. He's that cliché . . . the ship that's passing in the night.

She pursed her lips, actively suppressing any further enquiry. She was sure he didn't really want her to ask. He knew this was all transitory too, so why spoil it while they had it?

'Not right now. You are what you are, John, it makes no difference to me. You're a wonderful client. Nothing changes that.'

For a moment his eyes narrowed, and again, she teetered on the brink of spilling her own secret, but then he smiled his dazzling sunrise smile and all thoughts of the best way to tackle it dissolved like mist. She just wanted to touch him and to be with him. All the questions would be locked in a box for the moment. Perhaps for ever . . .

The line was drawn. Now they moved on. Their agreement silent, yet total.

'And you're a wonderful companion, Bettie. A wonderful lover,' John said, rising from his seat, setting aside his cup, and striding around to the other side of the bed. Closing the laptop and moving it aside, he flung himself down beside her, leaning on his elbow. 'I thought I was just about sated. That I'd doused my fires in the shower. But somehow, I find myself wanting you again.' Still staring into her eyes, he unfastened his robe and revealed the evidence, his cock, hard and high, gleaming and ready for action.

So beautiful. So familiar to her now, after just a couple

of days. Reaching out, she touched him, folding her fingers lightly around him and loving the heat and the silky texture of his skin there.

'Oh yeah . . .' His lashes fluttered and he drew in a deep breath, then smiled as she massaged him with her thumb.

'Did you deal with yourself in the shower?' If he had done, his powers of recuperation were truly phenomenal. Especially after his performance . . . his *performances* in the woods. As he nodded, she licked her lips, remembering the taste of him and how he'd not really allowed her to give him pleasure there, but had just taken it. Coming up on her knees, she tried to move into position to correct that situation, but he stopped her with a hand on her thigh.

'Uh oh . . . your turn, I think. Humour me.' He pushed her gently onto her back, and opened her robe now, baring her body to him. Reaching for a bottle of water that stood on the bedside table, he took a sip. 'Just clearing my palate,' he said, with a wink.

Lizzie shuddered, watching the stroke of his tongue across his lips and already feeling it between her legs. She wanted to move again, to writhe in anticipation, and to hell with any lingering soreness in her bottom. In fact the heat there only made her more excited and hungry to be feasted upon.

John came up on his knees and flung off his robe. His body was magnificent, smooth, beautifully formed; not a muscleman but toned in all the right places. His cock swung heavily as he moved.

'But what about that?' she asked, nodding at his erection.

'Don't fret. He'll get his turn. Now, open your legs wider. I want to see your gorgeous pussy.'

She obliged, pressing on the insides of her knees, stretching the tendons. The room was warm but the cooler

air on the moist surfaces of her sex made her shudder. John
shuffled into position and slid his hand beneath her buttocks,
his fingers finding her stripes. She shook a little and he
looked up into her eyes, his questioning. Was it too much for
her? The lingering ache?

In answer, she wriggled in his grip, pushing her crotch
forward, opening herself more, inviting and encouraging,
rubbing her bottom against his palm and fingers.

John plunged in. Parting her pubic hair with his free
hand, he pressed his face to her pussy, tongue darting out
and diving in between her labia, going straight for her clit.

'Oh . . . oh,' she moaned, astonished at how ready
she was. Talking with him, her desire had been diffuse, a
murmur in the background. But just one touch of the point
of his tongue, right at her heart, and it was screaming loud
again.

'Mm . . .' he purred against her, the vibration making her
toes curl up. Rising on her heels, she shoved herself at his face,
gasping with each lash of his tongue against her quivering
clitoris. She grabbed at his hair, burying her fingers in the
damp gold of his curls, fingers pressing against his scalp. The
way she clung on hard was probably more painful to him
than the pressure of his fingers against her bottom was to
her. But it was impossible not to clasp at him as he tasked her
with an over-welling of exquisite sensations.

He flicked and licked. He swivelled his tongue about,
circling her centre, lapping at the convoluted folds of her
sex, pausing to suck them between his lips. Playing around,
he nuzzled with his nose while thrusting his tongue deep into
her entrance.

Again and again, he went back to her clit, blowing on it,
dabbing at it with the furled point of his tongue, then finally

and, remorselessly, drawing it between his lips and sucking, sucking hard while lashing at it too.

'Jesus . . . God . . . Oh hell!' Lizzie shouted, coming so intensely that her head seemed to whirl while delicious pleasure pulsed beneath John's stroking tongue. He gasped into her pussy as she rocked and bucked, and mashed her sex against his face, and dimly she was aware that she was tugging hard on his beautiful hair, and catching his arms and shoulders with fearful kicks as she squirmed about.

But it was impossible not to hurt him as the waves of orgasm surged and crested like a white unstoppable sea.

'Oh . . . please . . . enough . . . I think,' she panted, her sex still fluttering as he began a new onslaught. 'Oh, John, John, John . . . I just need a minute. You're too bloody good . . . I think you're going to drive me insane!'

'Really?' he murmured, and his soft laugh was a caress in itself against her flesh. Cresting again, she collapsed back, overwrought by pleasure, no longer having the energy to hold on to him, but just floating, floating.

Eventually, though, she came down, settling lightly as if in slow motion. She smiled to herself as John kissed her chastely on her belly, and then the inside of each thigh, before finally sitting up.

'Still compos mentis?' Leaning forward, he whispered the words into her ear, filling her head with the scent of his cologne.

'Just about.' Her own voice sounded odd to her ears, as if it had no weight, no force of breath behind it. He'd knocked all that out of her with a sheer intensity of pleasure. Snapping open her eyes, she feasted on him all the same: his handsome, seasoned face, his drying hair, all mad curls, and his body, his superb naked body still rampant and ready.

'Think you could manage to spread your legs and let an old man have a quick fuck?' He twinkled, he literally twinkled at her. She couldn't have said whether it was his eyes, or his mouth, or his whole self, but the phenomenon was breathtaking.

'Well, *if* there were any old men lining up to shag me, perhaps I would. But seeing as there's only you, a magnificent stud-muffin in his prime, you'll have to do.' She shuffled into position, spreading her thighs. Her bottom twinged a little bit, but it was lessening in severity all the time. Soon it'd be barely noticeable, thanks to the ointment, and perhaps the healing power of orgasms. 'Just wake me up when you've finished, will you?'

'Cheeky cow.' He gave her breast a little squeeze, more companionable than anything, and reached beneath the pillows for the always handy condom. He seemed to make a habit of tucking a supply there; smart thinking.

Lounging like an odalisque, her arms stretched behind her on the pillows, she watched him roll on the contraceptive. He made even that necessary task into something elegant and precise, but there was almost a domestic quality about the moment. An accustomed lover, making a routine preparation, and doing it so naturally, so easily.

Dangerous thoughts gathered in Lizzie's mind. What would it be like if this was a domestic scene, an everyday occurrence in a shared life?

But that couldn't happen. John was an exalted man of business, a constant global traveller, always on the move. He had a home of sorts, because he was the scion of a great aristocratic house, but by the sound of it he wasn't welcome there, and neither did he want to be.

He was too complicated, too different, and had too much

history for her. He'd never be a regular, 'nine to five, uxorious sex with the little woman every night' kind of man. He couldn't be the sort of guy Lizzie had never even anticipated wanting, ever. The sort she wasn't even sure she wanted now; apart from the bit about seeing John every day, and being fucked and spanked by him on a regular basis.

Stop it!

She squashed her thoughts again rigorously, on seeing him frown at her, his enrobing complete. He was so sharp, so intuitive, and she blushed, convinced he'd detected her mad yearnings.

'What is it?' he asked, moving between her thighs, supporting himself on one arm while he touched her gently, parting her pubic floss. His fingertip glided over her still sensitive clit and she shuddered like a racehorse, then it dipped into her opening, paddling in her silky arousal.

'Nothing, just mad bits of thoughts, flitting in and out of my otherwise empty head. Nothing of consequence, and nothing you'd be interested in.'

For the most minute fraction of a second, he hesitated, but then he went on smoothly, 'Oh, thinking mad bits of thoughts, are we? While you're waiting to be fucked by me?' Fitting himself at her entrance, he slowly swung his hips, sliding himself into her. 'That's not very flattering, Bettie, is it?'

For a moment she was speechless, rapt in the familiar sensation of a man, this man, possessing her. The bigness. The heat. The closer than closeness. The living flesh of another, embraced by hers.

'Well, I did warn you I might take a nap.' She tilted her hips, parted her thighs wider, allowing him deeper.

'True.' He nestled in, taking advantage of her moves to

accommodate him. 'But I'll give you a bonus if you manage to stay awake. Double if I can coax another orgasm out of you.'

'Deal,' she said, closing her eyes, and folding her body up, locking her ankles at the small of his back.

To him it was perfectly natural to reference their business arrangement as he pushed his cock into her. To him, it was what it was. Whore and client, simple and easy and nothing wrong in that. It was only she who was harbouring stupid thoughts about it being more.

She kept her eyes tight shut to hide the threat of tears, and gave herself up to the delicious feeling of John sliding in, out, in, out, his rhythm and angle perfect for her. Each in-stroke knocked her tender clit, reawakening slumbering pleasure. As he fucked her, his weight on one arm, he stroked her face and her hair and peppered little kisses against her brow, her ear, her cheek. She grabbed at him, his back and his flank, loving the warmth of his skin and the flex of his muscles as he powered into her.

'You're so beautiful, Bettie,' he whispered, working her, 'You're a very special woman . . . a special lover. The best I've had . . .' He kissed her eyes, then the corner of her mouth, then her jaw.

It was arrant nonsense, of course, just the sex talking, but the fact that he said it, and so sweetly, touched her as profoundly as the stroke of his cock inside her. He was a devastatingly handsome, ludicrously rich, and sharp, intelligent, quite famous man. He could have any woman he wanted, and probably *had* had any woman he wanted. Great beauties, women of culture, the very finest of high-class courtesans who knew tricks she herself had no clue about . . . and yet he took a moment, in the midst of his own pleasure, to make her feel she was more special than any of these.

Her heart swelled with emotion, the most perilous one of all, and it was this, over and above the divine sensations of his lovemaking, that tipped her over the edge and made her come and come again.

11

An Invitation

'You mean you've already checked up on him and you didn't tell me?'

Home again, Lizzie confronted Brent. He looked even more white-faced than usual and, judging by his bleary manner and his red eyes, he'd been drinking as well as hitting Google on her behalf. Behind his back, Shelley shrugged, looking worried.

'Somebody had to,' snapped Brent. 'You seem to be sailing into all this without a care in the world. The first thing any escort, or any half-way sensible person, would do in this situation is check the guy out as much as they could. But you seem to be taking him completely on trust.'

But I do trust *him!*

Aware that after only three days of knowing John, that was a stupid and irrational statement, it was nevertheless what she felt, even after her own online discoveries. On the other hand, though, she could understand Brent's animosity, given his own traumatic history of guilt and self-blame over a road accident. He wasn't the one to cut John any slack on that score.

I need to make allowances. In a few days John will be gone, and I'll be little more than a fleeting memory to him. But I'll still be here with Brent and Shelley, who've always cared about me. They matter.

Both her friends had been there for her in tough times. And Brent especially, when she'd dropped out of uni, fallen out with her parents, and generally wondered what the hell she was doing with her life. So she owed him a bit of extra consideration now. She'd loved him once too, or thought she had. Maybe she still did, as the brother she never had who'd looked out for her when her own high-achieving sisters had been as confounded as her parents over her career choices . . . or lack of them.

'Yeah, it was a bit daft not to check him out, I fully admit that. But I thought it'd only be the one time . . . maybe two at the most. I didn't think it'd come to anything more than that, so I didn't bother.'

And it might not come to anything more than that either.

The thought made her despondent. Hell, much more than that. Her heart was on a plummeting elevator at the moment. She and John had parted slightly awkwardly when the hotel porter had delivered her dress and jacket, all dried and pressed from their valet service. She'd got the sense he'd wanted to say more, and she'd definitely wanted to say more, but somehow, their last fuck had been so intense . . . so . . . so intimate that it had almost been too much.

She wanted more. He didn't want more. Or, he didn't *want* to want more. It'd been as if a million confessions, protestations, pleas and admissions had been bubbling beneath the surface, and neither of them had been able to say anything.

John had kissed her in a vaguely melancholy way and then

bade her farewell. He'd made no new appointment, nor any mention of one. And she hadn't asked.

And now Brent was upset too.

It was the combination of John's history and bad timing. Tomorrow was the anniversary of Brent's own accident. The crash when Steve, his lover, had died, leaving Brent bereft and racked by a guilt that still endured. He blamed himself, although from what Lizzie and Shelley now knew, it had *not* been his fault.

Reaching out to touch her friend's arm, she ignored his flinch and said, 'I probably won't be seeing him any more, so all's well that ends well, and I'm not going to spend hours and hours poring over web pages about the one that got away . . .' She attempted a smile. 'It was fun while it lasted, though. Fancy . . . fucking a real-life billionaire and an aristo to boot. Definitely one for the scrapbook, to grin over in my old age.'

'We should all be so lucky, you jammy sod,' chimed in Shelley.

Lizzie glanced at her female friend, who was making tea for them. Had there been a wistful note in Shelley's voice? Quite probably. Lizzie knew that the other girl was dissatisfied with her own love life . . . or lack of it. What would have happened if Shelley had been the one to take refuge from the birthday party in the Lawns bar at the Waverley? She was delicately pretty with natural blonde hair and elfin features, a smart, sweet girl; she could easily have been the one John had taken a fancy to.

As Lizzie shuddered over the twists and turns of fate, she saw Brent brighten, and crack a grin. 'Yep, only you could manage that, Miss Bettie Page. Not even a real working girl and you manage to snag a punter any self-respecting whore would give every last square inch of her La Perla for a crack at.'

'And I say again . . . jammy sod,' concurred Shelley bringing the teapot to the table. She seemed in high good humour, and full of suppressed curiosity, but Lizzie still wondered . . .

'I know, I know . . . But I think I've probably had my run with him now, despite what he said about being around for a while. I've a feeling he could tell that I liked him too much, and he doesn't want that. A man with his gazillions must get a lot of unwanted female attention, I guess.'

Her heart sank a few more floors in the elevator. She *did* like him too much. But not for his money. A man like John Smith could be as poor as a church mouse, yet still be the most desirable male creature on two legs.

'And yet he was the one who encouraged you to Google him.' Brent gave her a shrewd look.

'Well, that's probably why. To let me know that I was just a passing fancy.'

'I'm not so sure,' opined Shelley, pouring tea. 'Perhaps he's fallen desperately in love with you, and wanted be sure you still fancied him, even if you know about his sinister past.'

'But if he is sinister, surely he'd want her *not* to know about it,' Brent pointed out.

'Well, whatever, I don't care . . . It was what it was. He was fun. The sex was amazing. And even if I send most of the money back, I'll keep a smidge for "expenses" and we can cover our rent and all our utility bills for a bit too.' Squaring her shoulders, she ignored the pangs, the yearnings for something more, nothing to do with money. 'And I'm sure he won't mind if I give a bit to Cats' Protection too.' She glanced at Mulder, who was currently curled up on the kitchen table, amongst the tea things, where she knew she wasn't supposed to be. 'Let's all get some fish and chips, shall we? Make pigs of ourselves. I had a fantastic lunch and a huge afternoon tea . . . but somehow I'm still starving. And I know she won't say no.' She scratched behind the small feline's ears, and got a whisker twitch in response.

Expecting a complaint about calories from Shelley and Brent saying he wasn't hungry, Lizzie was surprised when both her friends agreed to a fish supper. Her spirits lifted.

It'd be such a relief to do something completely normal, and enjoy a much loved and everyday treat after her strange days and nights in John Smith's company.

A few days passed. Lizzie paid some bills, and made some charity donations, but put the rest of her 'John' money in an envelope and stowed it away in the mini filing cabinet where they kept household papers. If she didn't hear from John, she'd try to get a forwarding address from the Waverley and send what was left on to him. Despite the fact that part of her insisted that she had in truth earned it, and provided exactly the same sexual services that a real escort would have done, it just didn't seem right to keep it all. That would really make her into a prostitute, even if it was just with this one man, and her feelings were a muddled turmoil about him already.

If she kept the cash to buy things for herself, she would always look at those things and know he'd paid for them, and for her. And if she didn't keep it, she could pretend it had been a very short love affair.

So, a clean break was better. No ties. Just a few memories, free and clear, to keep as treasures.

Life settled into a normal groove. Shelley took off to stay

with her beloved Auntie Mae for a week, because the older lady was a bit frail and always perked up after a visit from her niece. Brent seemed to cheer up, surprisingly, despite the anniversary of the accident. Or at least he appeared to. The garden centre seemed to be doing him the power of good.

Lizzie herself checked in with the temping agency, and looked for the hundredth time at brochures for various courses – design, fashion technology and the Open University. She'd have to do *something*, now more than ever. When the alternative was to brood about a certain beautiful, blond man who could spank her bottom and make her scream with pleasure with his hands, his mouth and his cock.

But it was difficult not to dwell on him. Difficult not to lie in her room, and find her fingers straying to her clit as she replayed the scenes she and John had shared, like frames from a sophisticated porn movie.

It was afternoon, and she was a hair away from an orgasm, with her hand in her knickers, when the phone rang.

'Fuck off,' she gasped, her head full of John, and the feel of him fucking her, pounding into her from behind, his fingers gouging at her well-spanked bottom as he held her steady.

Then suddenly she stopped. Pleasure not quite forgotten . . . but . . . interrupted.

It was her 'Bettie' phone that was ringing, not her normal one.

She sat up, grabbed a tissue and scrubbed her fingers. She straightened her clothes, and breathed deep. The phone chimed on.

Finally composed, she reached for it.

'Hello?'

'Hello, Bettie, how are you? Do you fancy a weekend away at the seaside? At your full per hour rate, of course.'

Well . . . just like that. Silence for days. Now an invitation. She opened her mouth to rebuke him, then checked. She had no cause to get cross. She was in a service industry, sort of, and the customer was always right. He owed her nothing, and he certainly wasn't obliged to dance delicately around her sensibilities.

And a seaside break did sound tempting. She hadn't had a holiday for ages, and with John she could expect five-star luxury all the way.

Not to mention five-star . . . no, six-star pleasure between the sheets.

The only thing, or person, that gave her cause to hesitate was Brent, with Shelley being away. But her friend actually seemed much calmer, and had even got out his bike and done a bit of road training. A very good sign. Healthy. If she and Shelley made sure to oh, so casually phone him every so often, he wouldn't feel too alone, surely? Especially as he had Mulder to keep him company. She made a note, too, to remind a couple of their other mates from the pub to call him for drink.

'Are you still there, Bettie? Are you all right?'

'I'm fine. Yes. And that sounds very reasonable.' The words were out before she could debate the issue of Brent with herself any further.

John laughed. 'Sorry, I was a bit abrupt, wasn't I? And sorry I've not been in touch. I've been in Scotland on an interminable round of stinking meetings. All I could think of was getting back here and then whisking you away for a nice trip. Will you come? Really?'

'Of course. I'd love to go to the seaside. How many days shall I pack for? How posh?'

He seemed to think for a moment. 'You always look

wonderful, Bettie. But, well, fairly posh. But bring jeans too. Hopefully we'll have time for some normal touristy things, ice-cream on the sea front or whatever.' He paused, and when his voice issued from the speaker again it was low and sultry. 'And bring some delicious lingerie. I'm looking forward to fucking you senseless, sweetheart. Not to mention spanking that glorious bottom of yours again. I've been thinking about that in the boardroom these last few days. It's the only thing that's got me through. I swear, without the image of your gorgeous body and the prospect of making your bottom red as a cherry again soon, I'd have lost it more than once and blown a very sweet deal.'

'So, I'm mental therapy now too, am I?'

'You're the best medicine, Bettie. I've missed you.'

It was spoken lightly, but she strained her ears to hear deeper meanings. Real emotion. Even after he'd rung off, leaving her with instructions to be ready good and early in the morning, so he could pick her up, she kept replaying the words in her head, trying to read more into them.

In the end, she decided they were what they were. A simple statement; not any kind of declaration.

He was taking an available, willing and fairly presentable woman with him on a trip, and paying her very splendidly for her services.

Nothing more.

'I'm Mr Smith's driver, ma'am,' said the handsome but brawny looking individual in the dark suit, standing on the doorstep, 'May I come in and collect your bags?'

Driver? John had a driver?

Of course he has a driver, you idiotic dolt! He's a sodding millionaire! Or billionaire . . . Whatever . . .

A man of John's wealth, racing between high-powered meetings, wouldn't descend to grappling with the traffic and swearing at other road users himself. He'd sit in cocooned comfort while somebody else dealt with the hassle. He probably had a plane, too, or a helicopter, or even both, awaiting his whim at the nearest airfield. He was a man of almost infinite means, after all.

'Yes, of course, please do.'

As she let the driver in, another thought occurred. With his history, maybe John didn't ever actually drive himself? Perhaps he'd been banned for life . . . or maybe he simply didn't feel right behind the wheel anymore, even after all these years?

A few minutes later, her sombre thoughts faded as she found herself standing before the open passenger door to what could only be described as a limousine. Pausing only to wave to Brent – who seemed almost as excited about her trip as she was, and who was hanging out of an upstairs window to observe this blatant example of obscene capitalism – Lizzie peered into the vast interior of the car, and met John's dazzling smile, and the gorgeous rest of him, awaiting her.

'Good morning, Bettie,' he said, leaning forward and putting out a hand to help her into the car. He'd obviously not been twiddling his thumbs waiting for her. The paraphernalia of business was all around him. Laptop on a small swing-out table, files, papers various, his briefcase. 'You look glorious, as usual. Looking forward to our trip?'

'Yes, very much.' She drank him in. He looked glorious too, and every inch the tycoon this morning. 'And you . . . well, you look like a boss, Mr Smith. Which I guess you are, to lots and lots of people.'

'Very true,' he said, shifting some of his documents aside

and reaching over to help her with her seatbelt. As the car door thudded shut, with the heavy note of quality, sealing them in a tinted glass capsule, his hand brushed her breast through her cotton top as he manipulated the belt.

When Lizzie gasped, his blue eyes flared and he smiled at her, subtle and tricky.

'It's like that, is it?' The hand that had brushed, cupped her now, thumb settling on her nipple and rocking.

The caress was light, almost inconsequential, yet it affected her. It was like that. Nine in the morning, she'd been with him all of thirty seconds, and she was alive with instant desire. Goodness alone knew what she'd be like after an hour or two, alone with him, in this secure and private space, his body so close.

Especially looking the way he did.

When she'd first set eyes on him he'd been wearing a fabulous three-piece suit, and this one, if anything, was even more sharp. He had a knack for picking the perfect colour to flatter him, and this was a grey that just might have been a kind of blue too, a subtle melt-down of the two shades. Whatever it was, it made his eyes look bluer than ever, and the pristine white of his shirt highlighted the very light tan of his complexion. His tie was a shade darker and a shade greyer than the suit, in a subtle pattern, and she smiled to herself, thinking of a book that she'd read not all that long ago.

'Yes, of course it's like that,' she said, steadying her voice, 'I'm on your time, John, the least I can do is be ready, willing and able on demand.'

Best to be up front about that. No use lapsing into loopy romantic reveries about this being anything other than a rich man buying a sex companion for a trip.

Strictly business, nothing more. Despite the fact her body

was singing from only the merest, lightest touch.

'That's very diligent of you, Bettie.' He squeezed her breast again, the contact still measured, but with more weight. She could see a darkness in his eyes, his desire as much a wildfire as hers. He leant forward, his fingers still curved around her flesh, and set his mouth on hers in a soft, tantalising kiss. His breath tasted of mint as if he'd not long cleaned his teeth, and his delicious cologne was an intoxicating vapour. Lizzie trembled, even though the kiss was brief.

His expression was radiant as he drew away, releasing his hold on her. 'I wonder if it was a mistake inviting you . . . I do have a little work to do, and you're such a temptation.'

Contrary swine!

'Well, I can get out then, in that case. Wouldn't want to interrupt you in the process of making even more money. It's not as if I haven't got other things . . . and people . . . I could be doing.'

He gave her a long look. 'I haven't got *that* much work to do. Indulge me a little while, Bettie, you know it'll be worth it.'

Oh, yes it would. Even just riding with him, sitting like a quiet mouse while he shuffled his papers and sent emails or did whatever he had to do, was a thrill. He only had to sit beside her, so lithe and dazzling and beautifully groomed, and it was almost like having sex without even touching. Her body was excited just by looking at him; her breast aching for more of his touch, her pussy heavy and yearning and sticky. She supposed she was his treat to himself, a rich man's temporary toy, but he was far more of a treat to her. A real escort would be thrilled to have captured the attention of a man so wealthy, and so generous with it, but for her the greatest asset on offer was the man himself.

'I'll hold you to that,' she said, offering him her most amenable smile.

John laughed, as if he'd seen right through her, but somehow she didn't seem to mind. She winked at him, and he shook his blond head. Did he know? And if he did know she wasn't a working girl, just exactly when was he going to tell her that he'd sussed her out? The uncertainty was another layer of excitement, another thrill that made her sex tingle and ache for him.

'So . . . I guess you've got questions for me,' he said, pulling his laptop close, and opening a file. 'You were surprisingly incurious the other day.'

Expecting questions herself, Lizzie was thrown for a moment. He really was the trickiest man.

'Well, you are what you are, John, and I am what I am. I thought we could just enjoy each other on that basis, sort of in a bubble, outside the real world.'

His fingers stilled on the keyboard, and he looked at her, visibly impressed. 'You're a very wise woman, Bettie. Another girl might have been pressing now, wanting more.'

Oh, I do want more! I want it all. But not the money.

The thought shocked her. The truth of it. The arrival of the knowledge, the recognition of 'the one', even after a few days and in the weirdest of circumstances. But she had to lighten up, steer away from the most dangerous of ground.

'No, I only want to play . . . nothing more . . . Perhaps we could role-play "ruthless sexy filthy rich tycoon and palpitating female victim"?'

John typed a few lines of something, apparently absorbed in it. 'We *could* play that, although I don't see you as a victim in any way, shape or form. You're the most powerful and well-sorted woman I've ever met.' He paused, typed a few more words. 'Except perhaps my ex-wife, and she's several decades your senior and enormously wealthy and cosmopolitan, so you'd expect her to be strong.'

He turned to her, and she could see him almost willing her to start quizzing him. She decided not to oblige, even though curiosity was killing her.

'Well, maybe I'm not a palpitating victim, but you *are* a filthy rich tycoon. Your role will be easy.'

'Exactly so.' He quirked his sandy eyebrows at her, suddenly very much the dastardly ladykiller, even though he'd barely moved a muscle. 'And in that case, little Miss Victim, I order you to take your panties off and give them to me. I want to imagine your cunt untrammelled and accessible, even if I haven't quite got the time to investigate it at the moment.'

Lizzie glanced at the tinted glass, dividing them from the chauffeur, and then at the scene gliding by outside. They'd come quite a long way, she realised. Even though they didn't seem to be speeding, the powerful limousine was like a magic chariot, that could shoulder aside lesser vehicles that hindered its progress.

'It's all right. The glass is one way. Nobody can see us, and nobody can hear us . . . unless we want them to. And it's probably not a good idea for Jeffrey to hear anything at all "heated". His concentration on the road is second to none, but you never know.'

Heated? Good God, she was heated already, just from John's words. And his presence beside her.

'So, are you going to get them off?' John said, rolling the words, salacious and fruity, 'or do I have to take them off for you?'

'All right, already.'

Fishing beneath her full skirts, she hooked her fingers in her waistband and, hitching herself up off the seat, she pulled down her beige lace knickers. She tried not to show her nervousness, her excitement, but she fumbled, tugging them off over her heels, and they got caught. Leaning over, laptop still on his knee, John untangled them and took them from her.

'Gorgeous . . .' He held them up, on the end of one finger, letting them swing. Lizzie blushed furiously when he inhaled, drawing in her aroused scent. 'Now, let's put these in a safe place, shall we?' Crumpling the underwear into a little bundle, he stuffed them into a pocket in his pigskin briefcase. 'There, that's better. Now lift your skirts from beneath you, and sit directly on the leather. They all do that, in the stories, don't they? *Story of O* and all that.' One-handed, he snapped shut the briefcase and pushed it away in the foot well. 'You have read *The Story of O*, I take it?'

Yes, she had. Once, a long time ago, reading it for a dare, at school, not really knowing what she was taking in. Parts had made her hot, in a confusing sort of way; other parts had been incomprehensible. What man, loving a woman, would casually give her away to someone else?

'Of course I have,' she replied, shuffling her skirt and petticoat from beneath her. He was being a bit contrary, so she wouldn't give him a flash, at least not yet. Tentatively, she settled down on the leather seat. The hide was fine and silky, and at first it felt cool to her skin, but as a natural substance it quickly warmed to match her heat.

What a relief the leather was dark, because she was so wet she would have made a mark on pale-coloured upholstery.

'How does that feel?'

'Very sexy. You should try it.'

For a second, his eyes flared, and she saw his fingers flex, as if about to stray to his belt. 'Maybe another time.' He returned his attention to his laptop.

Was that it? He'd primed her engine. Left her sitting her feeling aroused and exposed, yet not exposed, by the leather against her bum, and now he was back to work again. Men! She felt stirred up, yet defiant. She wanted to look out of the window, watch the passing scenery, and occupy herself with that, ignoring him. But she couldn't. The kiss of the leather was inescapable, and it was like his hand constantly caressing her. Her sex was heavy, agitated, more and more in need of his real caress, goddamn him.

'I would imagine that you'd rather like to masturbate right now.' The *ding* sound of an arriving email issued from the laptop, and John appeared to read it with close attention, as if he'd not said anything out of the ordinary. Perhaps he hadn't . . . for him.

'No, I'm fine. Just enjoying the ride.'

'Liar.' His voice was amiable, but he didn't even look at her. He appeared to be answering the email he'd just received.

Discreetly adjusting her position, Lizzie watched him. Anything to distract herself. He was actually working through emails, answering some, deleting others, writing new ones himself.

'Don't you have a P.A. to do all that? A man like you must have a thousand drones on call at the snap of his fingers. It seems a bit weird that you do all your own correspondence.'

Pausing, John turned to her. 'Yes, I do have drones, a whole army of them.' His mouth curved wickedly. 'And normally I travel with my P.A. and sometimes other staff. But I gave Willis some time off, to spend with his family, because

I rather fancied taking this trip on my own.' He looked her very levelly in the eye. 'In fact, I rather fancied having an adventure this time around . . . and here you are.'

Lizzie shivered inside. Being thought of as an adventure excited her. Of course, deep, deep down there was still that stupid part of her wanting to be more than that, but here in the semi-real world of what was actually possible, being his adventure worked for her.

Bearing down on the seat, she savoured the kiss of the leather, imagining it was John's hand . . . or even, oh yeah, his face. He wanted her as his submissive, but, she sensed, there might be a time when he'd be prepared to let the tables be turned.

But not now, though. His sharp, blue eyes narrowed. He'd seen what she was doing. She sensed he was about to reprimand her, so she asked the first mad question that came into her head. 'So you have a male P.A.? What's he like? Is he as good looking as his boss?'

John looked impressed, as he'd sussed her tactic, and applauded it. 'Willis? Yes, I would say he is rather a dish. His wife certainly thinks so.'

A dish?

Pressing her sex against the slinky, slithery leather, Lizzie was assailed by crazy visions. John had called the man a 'dish', almost as if he'd fancied him himself. She didn't think he did, but who knew? The dishy man beside her was a sexual experimenter, and she had a feeling he was probably game for anything and had tried most kinks in his time.

Could John be bisexual? The idea of him in a hot clinch with another gorgeous man made her tremble. Would he be dominant there too? Or perhaps . . . not so much.

Ooh, John, bent over a chair, being fucked, his beautiful

face contorted in pleasure-pain as some unknown stud pounded into him.

Suddenly, in the real world, John laughed and shook his head. His blond hair was immaculately groomed this morning, but the action made one curl dislodge and dangle over his forehead slightly. Lizzie longed to reach out and touch it.

'You're a woman of secrets and private thoughts, Bettie, but in this case I can read you like a book.' He smirked, then, for a second, snagged his lower lip between his teeth. 'You're wondering if Willis and I have ever fucked, aren't you?'

She grinned back at him. 'Well, you're gorgeous, and if he's "a dish" too . . . It's the sort of thing a lot of women think about. Two men together, twice as sexy, twice as much male pulchritude . . . twice as many cocks.'

'Is that a fact? Women like to fantasise about men shagging men?'

'Well, maybe not all women, but I do.'

True, one of her fantasies when she and Brent had briefly been lovers had been to see him with a male partner. It had never happened, but she'd still thought about it. And even now, very occasionally, the thought still drifted into her mind from time to time. It seemed a bit icky to imagine her born-again platonic friend *in flagrante* now. But there was nothing to stop her picturing her new friend, John Smith, with some blatantly handsome and willing P.A.

'I'm sorry to disappoint you, sweetheart, but Willis is very, very strictly heterosexual. He'd be horrified if I came on to him, and he'd leave. Which would be bad for him, because I pay him very well, and bad for me, because he's superlatively good at his job.'

'But if that wasn't the case, would you come on to him?'

Good grief, why was she pushing so?

Blue-star eyes narrowed. 'So, you're asking me if I'm bisexual?' There was an odd, very sharp note in his voice, and he paused, drawing in a deep breath, almost as if to keep her on tenterhooks. 'The answer will cost you, beautiful Bettie. Do you still want to know?'

She had to know. She'd probably expire from curiosity if he didn't tell her now.

She nodded, too excited to speak.

'Very well. I'm not currently bisexual and I've no plans to change that. But I can't say I've never experimented.' The laptop beeped softly, telling him more emails had arrived, but he closed the program. 'There were some caprices at public school . . . but who didn't have a fling there? There were crushes.' For a moment, he looked far away, the expression on his face stark. 'Mostly other boys with crushes on me, though. I was just as gorgeous then as I am now.' He seemed to be making light of it, yet his eyes were troubled and he frowned, as if confused for a moment.

It was Lizzie's turn to make light, to deflect dark. She sensed he needed it. 'And just as modest and self-deprecating too, I'll be bound.'

'Ah, but *I* was a dish then. Fresh and bonny, and my hair was much lighter. I was a golden-haired cherub and there were quite a lot of lads who wanted a piece of me.'

'You're a dish now.'

The smile he gave her was dazzling and strangely grateful. Logging off his computer, he closed the lid and put it aside, before retrieving the briefcase, and taking out a file of papers and a pen. Lizzie was surprised to see it was an ordinary bog-standard rollerball, such as she might have used herself, bought from a supermarket or paper shop.

Shouldn't a tycoon of his stature be using a solid gold Mont Blanc or something?

'Flatterer,' he said mildly, making a swift notation on the top sheet. 'Anybody would think you wanted me to tell you a lurid tale of my misspent youth. It'll cost you a damn sight more than just a few sugary words.'

'Name your price!' She gave him a bold look. The offer was irresistible, whatever the cost.

'Well, first I'd like you to masturbate to orgasm, here and now, while I tell you. Then, I'll want to spank you when we reach our destination. And, finally, I'll almost certainly want to have your arse at some time during this jaunt.' He stared at her, unblinking. 'That's my price.'

'You drive a hard bargain. You ought to be in my game. You'd make a fortune with your negotiating skills.'

Again came that not quite happy expression on his face; and Lizzie could have kicked herself. It could have been something to do with the work he was doing but she didn't think so.

'Well, you could say that I did once sell my body for money . . . but that's an entirely different story. For another time.' His pen stilled, hovering over the paper. 'What's your answer?'

What had he done? When? And who with? The questions jostled, but she knew it was counterproductive – and perhaps painful – to go off on that tangent now. And she was desperate to know what had happened, back at his public school.

'It's a deal. Let's have that story. Your sleazy exploits in the dorm or whatever.'

'Oh, it wasn't sleazy. I was infatuated, and so was he. For about three weeks we thought it was lurrrve.'

'Who was *he*?'

'Uh oh, this is a deal, remember?' He nodded in the general direction of her groin.

Fishing under her skirt and petticoat, Lizzie slipped a hand between her legs. She was hot and wet, and when she touched herself, she had to suppress a gasp. At this rate, the first portion of his price would be easily paid.

'I hope you're wet. I wouldn't like to think you're sitting there unmoved by all this.'

'Don't worry, I am . . . I'm saturated. Making quite a pool on your lovely upholstery.'

'Wonderful. And his name was Sherwood. Benjamin Sherwood. He was in my year. I even knew him socially. His family were part of our county set.' For a moment, John looked dreamy, as if the memories were very fresh. 'He was tall and rather skinny, but elegant with it. Hair black as ink, and curly. He wore it longer even than I wore mine, much to the consternation of our house master.'

'Were you just boys?' She felt a bit strange, thinking about teenage boys.

'Upper sixth, both eighteen . . . There was a hell of a lot going on between lads of all ages, but I didn't get into it until it was almost too late. Although perhaps it was better that way, less time to get found out, cause a scandal and enrage my father even more than I usually did.'

For a moment, she wanted to ask him more about his family, and what she suspected was a long-standing estrangement, but he went on, whisking the opportunity away.

'One afternoon we both had a free period. It was hot, oppressive, unbearable inside. I'd seen him heading off for a walk in the woods, and I followed him.'

'Ah, the woods . . . You seem to have a thing for shagging in the woods.'

John smiled, and shifted slightly in his seat. She couldn't see his groin for the folder of documents, but she would have bet her life on him already having a hard-on, stiff and massive.

'I do indeed. So did he. We'd sort of skirted the subject previously while out on a hike . . . but done nothing. Well, not much. Just a kiss or two and a bit of rubbing through clothes.' He gave her a sly, sideways look. 'But following him, I was ready, you know? I was as infatuated as he seemed to be . . . and I wanted the Full Monty. I was prepared.'

'In what way?'

John nodded at her. 'Let's see some action first.'

Slowly, she circled a fingertip around her clit, slithering and sliding in the well of moisture. She hardly dare press on, she was so near, imagining young John ready to go into action with his paramour. There was no way of knowing what this Benjamin really looked like, except in the broadest terms, so she pictured him as a tall, dark, curly-haired actor off the telly that she rather fancied.

'I'd got condoms. A tube of something. As I set out, I honestly didn't know exactly who'd be using what . . . but I didn't care. I just wanted to get off, with Benjamin. And to kiss him. He was a fabulous kisser. His tongue was almost as clever and tricky as yours.'

'So . . .?'

'You first. Make yourself come, right now, and I'll tell you all.'

She started to rub in earnest, but suddenly put on the spot, she tensed up, and the desired orgasm seemed to speed away from her like a receding light. Spreading her legs wider, she rocked a little, but she couldn't seem to get it.

'Sod it . . . I . . .'

'What's wrong?' His brow crumpled, and he seemed to be genuinely concerned.

'Sometimes I can't always do it to order . . . you know, come.'

A look of enormous wonder seemed to light John's face from within. He looked for an instant like that eighteen-year-old cherub, beautiful, almost untouched, but curious.

'You could have faked it. I would have thought that was standard operational procedure?'

Yes, for real escorts, she wanted to say, but didn't.

'Not for me. I like to give the client a bona fide experience. No sham or fakery.'

Putting aside his papers, he slid along the seat. 'Well, for that, I'll help you. You're a sweet, honest whore, and I like that.'

Well, I'm probably none of those three, but who cares?

Sliding his hand beneath her skirt, he gently nudged her fingers away, and replaced them with his own. They were bigger, but still deft, almost as intuitive as her own as he gently settled his middle finger right on her clit and slowly rocked it. The desire that had drifted away came flooding back. Relaxing, she let her own hands settle beside her on the seat, giving herself up to him.

'I found Benjamin waiting in our so-called trysting spot. A little hut in the woods, a sort of summer house, half tumbled down, but it was still reasonably private if someone should happen by.'

Sensation gathered beneath his clever finger and she bore down on it, already right on the brink. He flicked her and she fluttered, letting out a moan.

'He came to me immediately and started to kiss me and, while his tongue was in my mouth, he unzipped my trousers and took hold of my cock. He was a bit rough. He didn't quite know what he was doing any more than I did, but I didn't mind the discomfort. In fact, I liked it.' He leant against her, kissing the side of her face. 'See, I was already into kink at an early age.'

His finger circled, rocking trickily from side to side and, as John kissed her, his tongue in her mouth, just as Benjamin's had been in his all those years ago, she hit the tipping point. Uncouth sounds issued from her, grunts of pleasure stifled by his possession of his lips, controlling her.

Her vagina clenched hard, and she almost bit his tongue as her legs kicked out and her hips pumped. It was a rough, quick orgasm, almost too soon, but still heavenly. She clamped her hand over his, holding in the pleasure, and didn't release it until the spasms started to ebb.

12

Come into the Garden

'Do you want to hear the rest of the story?'

Lizzie blinked, dropping back into herself after the flight of orgasm. Somehow, she was in John's arms, her head cradled on his shoulder, but she wasn't quite sure how that had come about. Had the pleasure been so intense she'd passed out?

'Hell yes!' She straightened up, smoothed down her skirt, feeling suddenly energetic, as if she'd been recharged by the grace of John's hand.

'Good, I'll tell you it over coffee. We're just at a stopping place I know.' He gestured out of the window, just as the gliding car left the A-road they were travelling on, and pulled into the forecourt of what looked like an old-fashioned, ivy-clad roadhouse-come-café. Lizzie was astonished. She'd been so absorbed in herself, and John, and what he'd said and what they'd done, that she hadn't even realised they'd left the motorway.

'It looks nice. Much better than a services.'

'It is nice,' said John with a smile, smoothing his hair and plucking imaginary lint off his trousers. 'The coffee's second to none, and they do a lemon cake to die for, if you're hungry?'

Lizzie noticed he was still slightly erect, but it didn't seem to bother him. Maybe he liked to flaunt his junk in public? Who knew? He was a very strange man, as well as a very sexy one.

Walking through the garden of the Bluebell Café, to one of the outside tables, she had a feeling she was almost more aware of John's cock and its condition than he was. There were only a few other patrons there at this time of morning, but none of them seemed to notice anything untoward. A couple of elderly ladies fluttered and smiled when he wished them a 'Good morning' but she couldn't blame them. It was as if the god of the sun had passed by them, between the tables, bestowing his gracious light upon them. Lizzie grinned to herself, wondering what might happen if they happened to glance southwards, but they seemed mostly enchanted by his handsome face and his dazzling smile.

'So, your story,' she prompted, when they were seated at a table right in the corner of the garden, furthest from anybody and with a view of fields sloping down to a river. The coffee was just as sublime as he'd claimed, and the cake, mmm, heavenly.

John looked around. The nearest of the other patrons was yards away. 'So, yes . . .' He paused to eat a morsel of cake, licking the crumbs off the tips of his fingers. 'I believe we'd got to the part when Benjamin grabbed my cock, hadn't we?'

'Yeah, and you said he was rough and you liked it.'

'True. I was very keen on him, and keen on my dick being handled, although before that it'd been confined to my own efforts. Having another man's hand on me was as scary as it was fabulous. At the time . . .'

Some slight change in the timbre of his voice caught her attention, and she eyed him closely. Despite his previous avowals, she wanted to ask, *and now, would it still be fabulous*? He'd claimed not to be bisexual any more, but who knew? He could be spinning her lines just as much as she was spinning them to him.

'He rubbed me for a while, and I probably did a lot of moaning and groaning. It was a wonder I didn't come all over his fingers straight away, but, somehow, I managed to hang on. I grabbed his arse and he started humping against my leg. He was as hard as a stone inside his trousers.' He flashed her a grin. 'I'm surprised he didn't come straight away too, but clearly he had powers of endurance, just like I had.'

Lizzie took a sip of coffee, loving its aroma and the hard caffeine hit that sharpened her senses. She didn't want to miss a syllable of John's account.

'What happened next?'

'We kissed some more, and then he got his cock out, and we rubbed against each other. Lord, he was bloody enormous, thick as a club. And you wouldn't have thought it, because he was skinny and slight, even though he was quite tall.'

Lizzie tried to imagine this tall, dark and presumably handsome man caressing John. The golden angel and the saturnine devil, what a delicious contrast. She pictured herself in the woods with them – what was it about woods? – watching while they fondled each other. Touching herself while they touched one another. She shuffled on her seat, wanting to do that right now, and reached for her cake as a minor distraction from the ache between her legs.

'I don't think Benjamin had really thought through what we were going to do next . . . but I had. I'd seen him in the showers, and I knew what other guys were doing with each other. I'd decided I wanted him in me.'

'Oh!'

Pausing to sip his coffee, John eyed her. 'Why so surprised?'

Why indeed? Just because he was master of the universe with her, it didn't mean he wasn't sexually omnivorous, and prepared to play other roles.

'Do you think because I act the dom with you I can't understand and enjoy the flipside of the coin?' He toyed with his teaspoon, as if it were a proxy for toying with her or with long ago Benjamin.

Lizzie looked into his eyes. They were mild, yet somewhere, far back, there was a flare of darkness. What had happened to him? Something other than his dalliance with Benjamin . . . There was light and shade in his history, she could swear it. But she'd probably never know him long enough to learn his secrets.

'No, I'm not surprised. I think that's *why* you are so good a dominant, because you understand the submissive role too.' She gave him a steady look. Should she dare? 'I think that before you move on, Mr Smith, you should let me get the better of you. It might be quite diverting . . . and very sexy . . . to see you on your knees ready to take some of your own medicine.'

John nodded. She could tell he was impressed. 'I might take you up on that, beautiful Bettie. It wouldn't be a hardship to submit to you. Not in the slightest.'

'Good . . . very well . . . For the moment, I order you to go on with your story!'

'Your wish is my command, gorgeous,' he answered, rather more flippantly than was appropriate if he was supposed to be obeying her order, but she didn't care. She was dying to hear more of him, and of his long-lost paramour Benjamin.

John paused, sipped his coffee, then stared at her, his

eyes alight. 'I told him to take his clothes off. He seemed nervous about stripping, even with his dick on show, so I led by example. I thought he was going to come at just the idea of it, he was so excited, but he managed to get naked without losing it. He was gorgeous . . . as I'm sure he still is today . . . so tall and slender yet so massive where it matters.'

Again, Lizzie tried to imagine this paragon, but somehow, all she could see was John, and his beautiful body. 'What happened next?'

'I told him what I wanted him to do to me. I gave him instructions. I think he was surprised, and he was expecting to be the one who was fucked.' John's voice was low, like velvet, but still Lizzie glanced around. Nobody seemed to be in the slightest bit interested in them. Even the admiring old ladies had gone now. 'I told him to think of trigonometry while I put the condom on him, and then lubed him up. I always found that thinking of complex figures slowed me down a bit.'

'So, have you been counting your billions while you've been shagging me?'

He laughed. 'I'm a lot older now. I have much more control. And don't forget my fabulous biofeedback techniques . . . They've never helped much with my sleep issues but they've been brilliant for staying power in the sack.'

'Tell me about it . . .' Suddenly she wanted to ask about the sleep issues again, but now wasn't the moment. No way.

'Really. Anyway, we got down on the floor of the hut, and I was on my hands and knees, and I told him to lube me in return . . . but he was shaking too much. I had to manage it myself . . . The stuff went everywhere.'

Oh God. The temptation to reach beneath the tablecloth

and touch herself, as she'd done back at the Waverley, was almost unbearable. Wishing she knew biofeedback herself, she ate a bit more cake, barely tasting it.

'Eventually, we were sorted, and I told him to push into me. He hesitated. He said he wasn't sure he could do it. I had to get a bit sharp with him. Order him to do it.'

Why didn't that surprise her? John liked to be in charge, regardless of what he said, and even as such a young man, about to be buggered, he'd clearly still been calling the shots.

'So, basically, you were topping him from the bottom. Always like a boss, eh?'

He shrugged, still smiling at her. 'Yes, I suppose so, and it must have worked, because he seemed to get his act together and he . . . managed to get his cock into me, somehow.'

On the point of asking him what it felt like, Lizzie paused. As an experienced escort, she was supposed to know that. But, well, she wasn't experienced, not in that. And she supposed it was different for a man, with different anatomy.

She just said, 'Wow.'

'Wow, indeed. Fuck, it hurt. He wasn't very gentle. We were both pretty much virgin idiots. He didn't know how to push smoothly and, bossy as I was, I was excited as hell and didn't know how to relax properly. There was a lot of moaning and most of it wasn't in ecstasy, I can tell you.' He drew in a deep, sharp breath, as if back there, tense and tight, not knowing whether he was enjoying himself or hating every minute. 'But after a bit, we seemed to get a rhythm, and it started to be nice . . . very nice. I wanted it to last, to go on for ever, but that was never going to happen. He started to come, and come like a bloody jackhammer. We fell in a heap, and I was face down, chewing the floorboards, but in heaven. I thought he'd lost it completely and forgotten about me as anything more than a tight arsehole, but just as I was about to come, he scrabbled around beneath me and held my cock as I shot my load . . . I think that's when I really thought it was love . . . Because he thought of me, and tried to make it nicer when it mattered.'

Silence descended over them. A blanket of deep thought, of mild shock perhaps. John stared away across the garden, as if he was staring away across time, and Lizzie stared at him, as thunderstruck by the degree of intimacy he'd shared with her, as she was profoundly aroused by his description.

'Do you ever hear from him?' she asked, after a while. She felt hot and bothered, stirred and confused still, but it would be time to move on soon, and they needed to act normally, somehow.

John turned to her. He looked tranquil, as if unaffected by his trip down memory lane, but fondness crept into his blue eyes as he spoke. 'I get a Christmas card from him every year. Sometimes with a note. He lives in Scotland now. Married and as straight as straight can be, but blissfully happy by the sound of it. I'm glad for him. He's a good man, and he was good to me when I needed it.'

'So, you were just a youthful fling?'

'More or less. Like I said, we barely lasted a few weeks at school, but it was sweet at the time.'

Were all his relationships like that? Sweet at the time, but transitory? What about his mysterious marriage, that she knew from the internet had been to a much older woman? And other relationships, surely, surely, there must have been some? Many? Who knew? She wished she'd trawled the web more assiduously now, or taken more notice of Brent's Googlings.

His life is none of your business, Lizzie. He'll be gone in a week or so. You're just a fling yourself. Don't start obsessing and yearning for more.

John looked at his slim but probably ruinously expensive watch. 'I think we should be moving on now, sweetheart. Are you ready?'

'I'll call at the ladies' cloakroom, if you don't mind.'

Awash with wistful thoughts, her desire still hadn't waned in the slightest. She wanted to touch herself again, but to have the moment alone. In case tears came at the moment of truth, when she couldn't fool herself.

But in the pretty, immaculate, pink-painted cloakroom of the Bluebell Café, her body and her mind wouldn't work together. She was aroused, but her head whirled with thoughts, and she was left uncomfortable, unresolved and confused.

Her own fingers weren't what she wanted. She wanted John. His touch. His voice. Hurriedly she spent a penny, and washed her hands, then stared at her flurried face in the mirror. Her eyes were bright and a bit wild. She looked like an ingénue, not a supposedly confident woman of the world. She just wanted to get back to her man, even if he was only hers in the most temporary and superficial way. He'd gone to chat with the proprietors of the café, in the kitchens, where his driver Jeffrey, a friend of the family who owned the establishment, was enjoying his own coffee and presumably that delicious lemon cake.

While she was combing her hair, the cloakroom door swung open. It was a small room, and there was no way she couldn't immediately react to the presence of a newcomer . . . especially as it was John himself.

'What are you doing in here? This is the ladies' room . . . the *ladies'* room!'

'I know,' he said, reaching her in two long strides, then grabbing her, and her bag, and propelling her towards one of the toilet cubicles. 'But I'm not sure it's a lady I want right now.' He hustled her inside, and then bolted the door. The Bluebell was an old building and the cubicles were generous-sized, with enormous antique toilets like shining white porcelain thrones complete with sturdy wooden seat covers. 'I want a woman. I want you. A delicious, randy hussy who's always ready for my cock.'

Dropping her bag to the floor, he cupped her head in his hand and pushed her up against the side wall of the cubicle, kissing her fiercely and hauling up her skirts to slide his hands between her legs. Whatever had brought on this sudden surge of lust, so intense it compelled him to seek her out in the seclusion of an all-female enclave, she did not know. But it was as thrilling as it was fierce and unexpected.

She wanted him. She always wanted him. He grunted with approval, still kissing her as he found her wet and ready.

Marauding her mouth, he rubbed the edge of his hand against her clit, gripping her. The caress was rough and intense and she ground herself against it, gasping hard. He leant his other hand on the wall now, for purchase, inclining towards her and pressing with all of his body.

Every nerve on fire, Lizzie surged towards orgasm, but just as she was about to reach it, he snatched away his hand and stepped back, chest heaving. Glancing around the small space, he seemed to assess its possibilities. 'You'll have to ride me, gorgeous,' he said with a wicked wink, then flipped down the seat cover and settled down on it, unzipping his flies. His cock sprang out of his underwear as he pushed it out of the way, a thick, ruddy rod. He'd told her his youthful lover Benjamin was huge, but Lizzie couldn't imagine John's paramour being any bigger than he was himself. Her mouth watered and, unbidden, she dropped to her knees, reached for him and started licking his hot glans, lapping him with her tongue.

'You dirty, greedy girl.' He dug his hand into her hair, to control her. 'I was thinking about touching you all the time while we were out there. I was talking about Benjamin and him fucking me, but I was really thinking about fucking you. Especially when you were wriggling in your seat, hitching about with desire . . . so horny and ready.'

What was it about him? He'd looked so pensive, so wistful about his former lover, and yet, somehow it had been a mask, perhaps one of many he wore. But the slick head of his cock didn't lie. He was running with pre-come, as horny and ready as she was. She jabbed at him with her tongue, seeking a tender spot, and he gasped, then grabbed her hair. He didn't pull, he just held, delicately menacing.

'Oh no, you don't. I want to be in you. I'd like to be in your arse, but I'll settle for your cunt on this occasion.'

The raw language made her tremble, shake in her entire body, and ripple between her legs, longing for him.

'Here,' he said, fishing in his pocket for a condom and putting it into her hand, 'cover me. Hurry. Someone might come, and I don't want it to be me until I'm buried deep in your tight, delicious pussy.'

Fumbling a bit, she nevertheless managed to get the contraceptive on quickly, then, not sure how he wanted her, she got to her feet, looking into his blazing eyes for direction.

'Turn around and pull up your skirt. Show me that wonderful arse of yours.'

She complied, feeling somehow both shameful and glorious.

'Now wiggle a bit . . . part your legs . . . show me what you've got.'

Blushing, and feeling sweat pop out on her brow, and beneath her breasts, she obeyed him, rocking her hips and circling her bottom. She bent her legs, thrusting at him, the action lewd but infinitely exciting.

'God, you're fucking fabulous, you are, Bettie. There's no one like you. I've got to be in you. Now sit down on my cock.'

She started to turn. 'No . . . facing away. So I can play with you at the same time.'

Her skirt and petticoat in a bunch, she faced the door, holding the bundled cloth at her waist. As she positioned herself, she felt the touch of John's fingers on her sex, opening her, dividing her labia to give himself easy access.

'That's it. Sit on me, you dirty girl. Do it now.'

His glans butted her entrance. Huge. Hot through the latex. Demanding. Unstoppable. Once he'd pressed in a little way, he grabbed her by the waist and jammed her right down on him. Lizzie could have sworn her eyes crossed, and could almost imagine the top of her head flying off.

He filled her, filled her more than ever before and, as he adjusted her position, the movement tugged on her clit and made her whimper even before he'd touched her there. The bare skin of his belly, and the sensation of his pubic hair tickling her bottom, felt wickedly intimate and she rocked against him, drawing a sound from him too, more of a growl again, though, than a softer sound like hers.

'Yes, that's it. Sit right down. Take as much of me as you can.'

It didn't seem possible, but she tried, feeling the pushing pressure of his rigid length displacing her own inner structures in a way that made her want to take him even deeper. She braced her feet, ground down harder.

'Grip me. I know you can do it. Grip me and caress me from inside. Do it! You've got the cunt of a goddess!'

She clenched her inner muscles, grabbing him as hard as she could, embracing him fiercely. The effort set her on a hair trigger. Her thighs shook. Her clitoris trembled.

'Touch me, you bugger. You said you would!'

As he started to obey her, the outside door to the cloakroom swung open and someone came in.

Lizzie froze, suspended between pleasure and apprehension. It was as if she and John were a still life, a tableau, and yet at the same time her senses were sharpened. The smell of the pot-pourri in the bowl on the window sill was almost overwhelming, especially when combined with John's cologne and a faint hint of some pine-scented cleaning product. It was like a cocktail that made her even dizzier than she already was, and she swayed as she listened to the footsteps beyond the cubicle door. The newcomer seemed to pause by the mirror a moment, and their stillness only made the fear of discovery escalate.

Shaking, Lizzie was almost relieved when John's hand settled gently but firmly over her mouth, but that sense of relief shattered when he continued his efforts to fulfil her demand. She tried to struggle as silently as she could, even digging her nails into his trouser-clad thigh beneath her, but it was hopeless.

Like an evil magician, he found her clit with his fingertip and initiated a slow, circling caress.

His touch was divine, despite everything. Maybe even more divine because of it, because of the gathering dynamic tension, the pressure building, building, building as he touched her. Moans bubbled up inside her and, sensing them, his hand clamped harder across her face. When he bestowed a series of fast, remorseless flicks against her clit, she closed her teeth on the muscular pad at the base of his thumb.

John made not a sound, but inside her head, she heard his hiss of pain and his curse. Between her legs, he went at her with greater fervour, rubbing her hard and rough, deliciously fierce and unrelenting.

As the unknown someone knocked against their door, she came in a rush of silent white ecstasy. She was still riding the gorgeous waves, when John called out 'Occupied!' in a higher, assumed, but not entirely unconvincing voice.

Still immersed in the pleasure of climax, it was almost as difficult not to laugh out loud as it was not to whimper and cry in ecstasy.

'Sorry,' came the response, and a moment later, the sound of the other cubicle door being closed and locked. Fortunately, with the building being old, that meant proper walls between them . . . and a moment of respite.

Lizzie shook her head, dislodging John's hand, and twisted her body a bit on his lap, so she could see his face out of the corner of her eye. He was grinning his golden wicked grin, and his eyes were like black stars, pupils enormous with arousal. He flicked her clit again as she glared at him, but she clamped her lips together, keeping in her gasp.

Devil! Bastard!

Bracing herself, she sat down hard on him, as hard as she could, and at the same time clenched her inner muscles fiercely around his cock. Gripping him she rocked a little, as much as she could without making any noise, and her triumph was sweet as she strained to look back over her shoulder again.

This time it was John who was in trouble.

With his teeth gritted, and his face a mask of stress, he was somehow more beautiful than ever, and when she massaged him yet again, his eyes almost rolled up in their sockets as his long lashes fluttered down.

Touché!

With that thought, she too succumbed again, inevitably, to pleasure.

13

Uneasy Lies the Head

She was sleeping. Lulled by the smooth glide of the car, or rendered drowsy by a surfeit of pleasure, he knew not which. It could be neither. Might she simply be feigning sleep to get a break from him?

Whatever the cause, she looked adorable.

Talking of feigning, you finished your business correspondence ten minutes ago, so where's the difference?

Setting aside his laptop, John laced his fingers together and let his hands rest on his abdomen, and his gaze on Bettie. She was dozing in her seatbelt, her phone on the seat beside her. A few strands of normally immaculately styled black hair lay across her cheek, and though he wanted to brush them aside, he couldn't bring himself to disturb her.

What was it about this woman? This girl? She was only in her twenties, and he was a good twenty years older than her, but somehow she had a depth about her, a humour and a sweet sense of gravitas that made him feel almost as he had back with Benjamin, back when life was simpler . . . less marked by time.

He wanted more, but he knew there just wouldn't be

more. He was merely passing through, his business already almost all completed, and she lived where she lived, with a life of her own.

Don't be stupid, man. It's just a fling. A very nice interlude, with a woman who's somehow more special than most, but you are what you are. Not the settling down type now, and certainly not with a frisky, tricky young woman half your age, whom you're letting play a rather expensive game with you.

Bettie wasn't a prostitute. Well, certainly not a full-time one, he knew that now. Armed with her address, his investigative people had easily turned up her identity. She was Elizabeth Aitchison, aged twenty-four, and she worked as an office temp. She and Shelley Moore and Brent Westhead shared a rented house, and were apparently long-standing friends. There was much more in the dossier, but somehow he'd felt reluctant to delve deeper. Even though she'd taken his money, she was far less about selling her body, if truth be told, than he'd once been. But she seemed to be having fun *pretending* to be a working girl, and he was fine with that. It added even more of a delicious edge to their sex together.

She also seemed to lap up BDSM play like an experienced *connoisseuse*, even though he had a shrewd idea she was little more than an ingénue. It was rare that one so inexperienced understood the heart of the mystery, but Bettie seemed to.

Smiling, and feeling a stirring – again – in his cock, he let his mind roam back over the escapade in the ladies' cloakroom at the Bluebell. How was it that a hurried little shag in a toilet cubicle could be as stirring as a long, extended session on silk sheets in one of his high-end hotels? It'd been a thrill. He'd felt like a goat. But he still wondered why he'd initiated it in the first place.

Maybe it was because she'd got to him, too deeply, and

unawares. Somehow, she'd wiggled her way through his rigorously constructed defences, and triggered feelings he didn't quite understand, or want to accept. And hustling her into a rough, low-down, sleazy little fuck in a lavatory had been his subconscious way of getting everything back into his comfort zone.

Where everything, though pleasurable, was physical and temporary.

It's better that way. Much better . . .

She'd shown no sign of wanting to push for hearts and flowers or any big romantic gestures. Pragmatic and realistic despite her masquerade, he sensed, she seemed to be perfectly happy to be along for the ride, and the more rambunctious and kinky a ride, the better.

Hell, she thinks far more of that house-mate of hers than she does of you, you idiot.

He tried to ignore the absurd pangs of jealousy he'd experienced as she'd sat beside him, texting Brent, occasionally smiling. 'He seems in good spirits,' she'd said, on his enquiry about the other man. 'I was a bit worried about leaving, with Shelley being away too, but it sounds as if he's OK on his own, and he insists that he's eating. And look he's sent me a lolcat of Mulder lying in a daft position.' Not quite sure what the hell he was going to see, he'd found himself looking at a picture of a small, rotund black cat, stretched out on a rug with its legs stuck up in the air.

Yes, she had her life with her house-mates, and her cat, and she was devoted to them. Especially this Brent. The jealousy surged again and he squashed it. One of these days, the romantic relationship between Bettie and her Brent would rekindle, he suspected, despite what she'd said about her friend's supposed sexuality. They'd probably marry.

Maybe have kids who'd end up playing with that cute little cat?

A weight seemed to press on John's chest, and he dragged in a deep breath. Once, foolishly, he'd wanted that, the kids and the cat. Hell, he'd wanted it twice, with the same woman, and the second time he'd even *known* it was an illusion . . .

But now he knew better.

Looking out of the window at the gliding sight of trees in a vast plantation at the side of the road, the scene suddenly seemed grey and flat, despite the yellow sun overhead.

She'd been dreaming again. Fragments stayed with her as she woke.

In a white room, tied to a big white bed, and wearing a vast and fluffy white gown, she was being whipped by John. He was using a riding crop; she could see it as she looked over her shoulder at him, and yet she barely felt anything when it landed on her flesh. The sight of him filled her mind; his face, his shining hair, the vintage garb of a Victorian gentleman he was wearing. Smiling, he threw down the crop and launched himself upon her. In the dream, his trousers and underwear opened as if by magic and he thrust into her. She couldn't discern whether he'd entered her pussy or her arse, but it didn't seem to matter. He filled every part of her from the crown of her head to the tips of her toes, and she sobbed with relief and joy, completed.

Snapping awake, she wondered if she'd cried out. She felt dislocated from reality. Glancing to the side, she saw John staring at her. Weirdly, he looked shaken himself, blinking and a little bit out of it.

'Are you all right, Bettie?' His voice wasn't quite normal either. There was a trace of unsteadiness, and he rubbed his jaw with the flat of his hand as he spoke. 'You were making little noises. Were you dreaming?'

'Um . . . yes, I think so, but I can't remember what about,' she lied, unsettled because he seemed unsettled too. Turning, she glanced out of the window and saw they were driving over a bridge across a familiar deep valley towards the centre of a fine old town. It was their destination, a seaside resort she was fairly familiar with from holidays and day trips.

'We're here, by the looks of it.' She turned back to John, who was fussing with papers, shutting down his laptop, preparing for arrival. He was frowning. 'Are *you* all right?'

He gave her a sharp look, then his face relaxed, and he smiled. 'Why do you ask?'

'Just that you seemed a bit on edge, and you're not usually like that.'

'It's just business. Thinking about the deal ahead. I'm determined to get this hotel because I couldn't get the Waverley. Well, I want the chain, really, but I want it at my price.'

It seemed odd to be with John, the man of business, when up until now, he'd been John the sensualist, John the lover, John the effortlessly thrilling dominant. She'd no doubt he was as amazing in the boardroom as he was in the bedroom, though.

'Are you mega rich?' she asked, observing their progress through the finer, more exclusive area of the resort, the end of town she'd not much frequented on her previous visits. With Brent and Shelley, and sometimes a few of the pub chums, it had always been the touristy haunts they'd frequented. Fish and chips on the front; cheap shared flats; Kiss Me Quick hats, worn ironically. With her parents, it had been more traditional, very old-fashioned holidays, spent in genteel buttoned-up boarding houses, a bit stuffy but not entirely without their charm.

'Fairly,' replied John as the limousine pulled into the semi-circular driveway of one of the town's handful of five-star hotels. 'It's taken me some years to get quite to this level, but yes, I'm a very rich man.'

'A self-made billionaire?'

He laughed. 'They're very fashionable, aren't they?' He gave her a wink, as the car started to slow. 'Not sure if I'm actually a billionaire, though. I'm thereabouts. I have a very good few millions, and I'm sort of self-made.'

'What does that mean?' Still watching him obliquely, Lizzie cast about for her bag, and found it half-kicked beneath the seat. Had she been thrashing about in her weird white dream?

'It means that I generated the majority of my fortune myself, but that, originally, somebody else bankrolled me.' He gave her one of his tricky, edgy little smiles, full of irony, but she knew not about what. 'I earned that money too, but in a different way.'

'What way?' she demanded, snatching up her jacket and her bag as the passenger door clicked smoothly open, revealing Jeffrey ready to assist her from the car.

For a few moments they were caught up with porters and instructions about luggage. 'What way?' she repeated as they strode through the foyer together. It felt like the arrival of some visiting king or maharajah. She half expected low bows and the doffing of caps. It didn't quite get to that, but it must have looked like the arrival of some kind of royalty because other guests in the foyer glanced around, or looked up from what they were doing, as if drawn by some silent wave of glamour that emanated from John and washed over them.

His arm on her elbow, he leant close without breaking stride, and whispered in her ear. 'I'll tell you all about it later . . . but let's say that you're not exactly the only one here who's been handsomely paid as an escort.'

Without the warm touch of John's fingers sustaining her, Lizzie might have stumbled, but because he was there, and she didn't want to spoil the effect the pair of them were having, she kept it together, and maintained her poise throughout the effusive greetings, at the reception desk, from what seemed like all the hotel's senior management.

John was treated like a god, and that deference extended to her too. It was hard not to giggle though when he introduced her as his companion, 'Miss Page'. She realised that he'd never actually enquired after her second name, and she'd never given one, sticking to 'Bettie', so it tickled her that he smoothly extemporised with the surname of the more legendary 'Bettie'. The younger members of the greetings party didn't seem to think there was anything out of the ordinary, but one of the more senior looking fellows, a polished looking guy with twinkle in his eye, seemed to smile to himself, and take a closer look at her, clearly taking in the classic styling of her shoulder-length black hair, and the vintage dress and jacket she had on.

Their regal progress continued as the manager escorted them in the lift, to their suite. The pleasantries floated over Lizzie's head as she examined the import of John's 'escort' remark. Somewhere, somehow, he'd had sex for money too. But not as a working boy, surely?

He'd been married, though, hadn't he? Details on Wikipedia had been lean, and she reminded herself that she'd not followed links to find out more about his wife, for very feminine reasons. She hadn't wanted to think about that marriage, even though she'd only be in John's life for a few more days. It was just the way she always was with film stars she fancied, and her other crushes. If she didn't think about their romantic entanglements, they didn't exist. They could still be 'hers'.

But now, she knew she would have to get over that, and either ask him about his wife, or find out for herself. Even if it hurt.

Their suite was sumptuous, enormous, the best in the hotel, naturally, and a universe away from the comfortable, cosy kitsch of the Waverley. With spacious separate bedrooms, and en-suites for each of them, it was an ocean liner of cream and powder blue, and the shared sitting room had more floor-space than all the rooms in the house she lived in stitched together. But of the two hotels, she would choose the Waverley, for preference. She'd always choose it . . . It was the place where she'd first fucked the man she loved.

Oh hell!

Sharply, she glanced across the room. It was absurd. He couldn't read her mind, yet somehow, he was looking at her, a furrow on his brow as if he *could*.

'It's gorgeous. You should definitely buy it. I think I like the Waverley better, though,' she babbled, turning away.

'It is. I will. And I agree,' he said, crossing the room to her, and grasping her by the upper arms, so he could look down into her face. 'Are you all right?'

'I'm fine . . . just in a new place, that's all. That was . . . um . . . an interesting journey. Usually, when I come to the seaside, I'm all squished up on a train, and it's a bacon sandwich and a magazine to read. It's not quite as eventful.'

'Even with Brent?'

It was her turn to frown. What on earth did he mean by that?

'Of course. I explained to you. He and I are just friends. We have been for a long time. Long before we were a couple. And I hope we always will be.'

His blue eyes searched her face. His brow cleared. 'Yes, it's good to have friends.'

Do you have any?

Slowly, he kissed her, as if savouring her, trying to print the taste of her on his memory. Loving the touch of his lips, she tried to imagine his life. Travelling from one deal to another, in limousines or jets, confronting men like himself over polished tables covered in reports. Women in hotel rooms, for a few hours. Was he lonely?

'Do you remember what you promised, in return for that story?' he asked as he lifted his mouth from hers.

'Indeed I do . . . but have you time? They seem to be expecting you for a power lunch.' Despite her words, she moved against him, pressing herself against his crotch. He was erect, of course. A man of forty-six, he still had the wellspring response of a male half his age.

'There's always time.' Behind her back, he was at work, plucking at her skirt and petticoats, pulling them up. Holding the bunched fabric with one hand, he explored her naked buttocks with the other, fingertips palpating her flesh.

Lizzie squirmed. The contact was light, but incendiary. Everything John did to her moved her out of all proportion. His erection was like a fulcrum on which she turned, and she buried her face against his shoulder, to hide her face, afraid it would betray more than lust for him.

'I love your body. I love the way you move,' he murmured,

gripping her bottom cheek firmly, almost pinching. 'I love that you don't fake anything.'

'What if I'm just a very good actress?' she said, the words muffled against the fine cloth of his suit. Escorts *were* good actresses, wasn't that what the media said? Although it wasn't desire that she was falsifying, just the sudden, profound depth of her feelings that she was masking. Or trying to.

'Your pussy doesn't lie.' His fingers dipped into her cleft from behind. She was simmering wet, and they slid in the abundant moisture.

Unable to speak, she rocked against him, sometimes rubbing his cock with her belly, sometimes trying to ride his probing fingers. The angle was awkward, though. He couldn't exert the pressure she hungered for, on her clit. Her arm still around his waist, she used her other hand to drag at her clothing, this time pulling her skirt up at the front, so she could wriggle her own hand between their bodies and touch herself. Her fingertips knocked against John's in her cleft.

'Yes, that's it . . .' he breathed, 'touch yourself . . . bring yourself off while I slap your bottom. Do it, Bettie, do it!'

Gasping, she flicked her clit, anxious to centre on herself before the spanks began. He seemed to pause, as if waiting for her to find a rhythm, then withdrew his hand.

Touching herself, stroking herself with him so close felt like him doing it. His gorgeous spicy cologne filled her brain, his presence every part of her body. He was fine and strong against her as she started to rub herself.

His hand was hard and hot like a thunderclap of fire as he struck her bottom.

It wasn't actually a heavy blow. Holding her, he wasn't able to swing his arm. But it impacted more in her mind, and between her legs, than on her arse. Sensations spun around, winding about her clit and her fingers. She wasn't sure if it was pleasure, pain, yearning, exultation or desperation. She rocked against her own hand, pressing it and herself against him, still feeling him hard, against the back of her wrist now.

He slapped her again and again and again. The impact fused with her own ministrations. She was almost there, on the very brink but still awhirl, still confused. And he seemed to sense it.

'Come!' he commanded, his voice velvet fierce as his hand landed in another lazy slap, angled to jolt her finger and make it the agent of *his* caress. 'Come now, Bettie, now!'

It happened. Her vagina clenched hard, exquisite sensation bloomed, her knees went weak. John held her close, clasping her sizzling bottom cheek now, not spanking it. Keeping her tight against him as she rode the shattering wave.

Limp, she slumped, knowing she was safe and he would hold her up. He didn't even let her sway, but just supported her, his body sure against hers.

His cock was still hard.

Starting to surface, Bettie nuzzled him like a kitten. Her smacked bottom was hot, but as full perception returned to her, she knew it was just a mild sensation, and would be gone soon. The blows had been light, their impact falling more in the imagination than in reality.

But the erection against her belly certainly wasn't imaginary, and something would have to be done with it if he were to attend his meeting . . . and rule it.

She smiled, feeling excited and exhilarated. He'd wielded power over her, and he would in the boardroom, but it was as if he had so much that it had leeched into her too, by osmosis. She straightened in his hold, and pushed away, hands on his chest. There was surprise in his face, but he let her go.

'Bettie!'

There was a pure astonishment in his voice as she sank to her knees, reaching for his belt as she descended.

'Bettie, you don't have to do this. I don't expect anything.'

Smiling, she stared up at him, attempting to compel him with her eyes, the way he so easily did her. 'Shut up, John. I don't care what you expect. This is what you're going to have.' Still making him look at her, she unfastened his belt, then his trousers, and pushed down his shorts.

The desire to laugh welled up in her, but she contained it, even though she didn't know which was most amusing: the way his cock sprang up, hard and reddened in front of her face, or the expression of pure, flabbergasted astonishment on his face. He looked like a thunderstruck angel with a massive hard-on . . . adorable.

She plunged her mouth over his glans and began to suck like fury.

'Oh, Jesus God, Bettie, please.'

His hands were in her hair, and she could sense his ambivalence. At first, he still seemed to be trying to prise her off him, and yet somehow he was holding her there at the same time.

'Bettie . . . this isn't . . . oh!' His voice rose as she jabbed her tongue into the groove beneath the head of his cock, making his hips jolt.

For a moment, she released him and gave him a fierce look. 'Just shut up and enjoy yourself.' Before he had time to respond, she caught him again, and sucked even harder, flicking him with her tongue at the same time. Punishing him with her mouth, she pushed and scrabbled at his clothing so she could stroke his bottom at the same time, and tease his anus.

When she pushed her finger there, he cursed a blue stream, jerked his hips . . . and flooded her mouth with a jet of his come.

14

Reflections

'You could come to lunch with us, if you like? You're an honoured guest here, just as much as me.'

John straightened his tie, emerging from the bathroom. He'd taken a quick shower, and changed his suit. He was wearing a very dark blue one, navy almost, with a fine chalk stripe. He looked all business now, a prince of commerce. It was hard to imagine him shouting profanities as he filled her mouth with semen.

Well, maybe it wasn't too much of a stretch, but still.

'Thank you for the invitation and, much as I'd love to see you doing your tycoon thing, I wouldn't want to prove a distraction to you and bollocks up your deal.'

He smiled and strolled over to her. She was loafing on one of the huge, cream-coloured settees, in a bathrobe, and he leant down quickly to kiss her. 'I think you're more likely to bollocks up the deal for the opposition, especially if you came to lunch like that.' His hand drifted briefly between the panels of the robe, caressing her thigh.

'Is it likely to be boring?' She shuddered finely, amazed to find herself stirring again.

'It could be. A bit . . .' He shrugged. 'I'm afraid movies and television and books glamorise business too much. And most of the moguls involved are terrible old fogies. In fact I'm probably amongst the very few that are half-way presentable and generally unlikely to be kicked out of bed.'

'And so modest too.'

'What can I say?' He shrugged again, smirking as he straightened up.

'I think I'll pass on the business lunch, then. Perhaps I'll just loaf about here as your odalisque . . . or maybe I'll go for a roam about. I could get some cockles and candy floss on the seafront . . . or see if they still have donkey rides on the sands.'

For a moment, John's expression gentled and became quite wistful. 'That sounds cool. I'd rather do that than grapple this lot down a million on the deal.' He gestured vaguely around, to encompass management of this hotel, and perhaps . . . probably . . . the entire chain. 'Maybe tomorrow, eh? I'll have some free time then.'

'I'll look forward to that.' Her mind filled with a vision. John in jeans, strolling along the front with her, their hands entwined. Laughing . . . No cares, no business, no deceptions.

'And now, alas, gorgeous, I have to get down there. I'm keeping a bunch of anxious executives and two cadres of lawyers, theirs and mine, waiting.' He grinned, as if he was quite pleased about the latter, then slid his hand into his inner jacket pocket and brought out his wallet. 'If you feel like going shopping . . . perhaps a bit of lingerie or whatever . . . here's a card you can use. The PIN is four, seven, nine, three. And if there are any problems, ring this number.' He handed her the credit card, then one of his business cards, with a phone number hand written on the back, 'and one of my financial people will deal with it for you.'

Lizzie sprang up. The credit card was black. She'd never seen one of these, but she knew what it was, and it was too much. 'I can't take this! I mean . . . thanks and all that. It's very kind of you. Incredibly kind. But you've paid me well over the odds already. If I want to go shopping, I've got all the money you've already given me.'

John made a little sound of mock exasperation and rolled his eyes. 'You really are the strangest escort, Bettie.' He folded his hand around hers, around the cards, gently squeezing. 'Please take it. Just indulge me, eh? I don't like the idea of you carrying a lot of cash on the streets. I don't want you to be at risk from muggers.' He leant forward and kissed her cheek, a little frown appearing on his brow, then fading again. 'Maybe you could buy a really nice dress? Something a bit special. A cocktail dress . . . There's a party I thought we might go to this evening, if you fancy it. I can't tell you all about it now, but I will later when I've bought this bloody hotel.' With one last squeeze of her fingers, he let her go and gathered up his briefcase. Checking his watch, he strode to the door.

'I hope this doesn't take too long. I begrudge every moment spent away from you.' In the doorway, he paused, 'Ciao!'

'Knock 'em dead,' whispered Lizzie, but he was already gone.

Swanning through the hotel foyer with a clutch of big, shiny carrier bags, and other less glamorous plastic ones, Lizzie almost laughed at herself.

I really am living the Pretty Woman *experience here. Where's the once haughty but now kindly hotel manager to smile on me approvingly?*

But there was only a receptionist on duty to offer a smile and a cheery, 'Good afternoon.'

Back in the vast suite, Lizzie settled into a chair in the sitting room and put her feet up for a minute or two. She'd walked quite a bit on her shopping expedition.

Contrary to John's preferences, she'd mostly used cash he'd given her to make her purchases. A few nice items of lingerie, because that was what he'd wanted her to get. One or two little bits and bobs for herself, plus some books and magazines; several cute tops and a souvenir mug for Shelley; games and more books for Brent. She'd even purchased a few extravagant cat toys from the pet department of one of the stores for Mulder.

She hadn't been down to the sea front. Somehow, she wanted to save that experience to share with John. This trip wasn't a romantic idyll, just a bit of a sex jaunt, really. But a stroll by the seashore together might constitute a vague facsimile of romance, if only for half an hour or so.

She hadn't eaten either, but a glance at the room service menu earlier had looked reasonably enticing.

Closing her eyes, she tried to clear her head of everything but the simple pleasure of being away for a few days in a new town with a handsome, sexually ingenious man. That was easier said than done, though. The complications rushed on in.

After the shopping trip, she knew she had to tell John, the next time she saw him, that she wasn't an escort. It'd been a game at first, a dare to herself, a bit of a lark. But she'd never expected to be with him more than the once, or perhaps a couple of times. Now she was hooked. She'd fallen for him, and she wanted and needed to be honest, especially as she might never see him again after tomorrow, or the next day.

Which was why she'd spent only a modest amount of his money, and not touched the credit card . . . except for one item.

The special dress. She'd known the moment she'd seen it in the window of the sort of boutique of which she never usually even crossed the threshold.

It'd been another *Pretty Woman* moment. Although her look was far from Vivienne's street style, she'd felt like some kind of peasant as she'd walked into the shop. This was the sort of place John's real women might patronise – women of celebrity and possibly blue blood – not his temporary playmate. But she'd held her head high and assumed an aura.

She smiled again now. How wrong can a person be? The assistants had been lovely, super-friendly and helpful. It'd been all, 'Oh yes, it will look fabulous on you!' the instant she'd asked about the golden dress in the window.

It was what might once have been called a sheath dress, a beautifully crafted garment that skimmed the body without clinging, and somehow both tastefully and sensually suggested curves, without grabbing them. As if she was really living a movie, it fit her to perfection, a poem of creamy, buttery gold shantung, overlaid with fine cream lace, tailored immaculately. Lizzie imagined Audrey Hepburn wearing it rather than her beloved Bettie Page, and she'd slipped into a chemists and got the fixings for putting her hair up in a sophisticated chignon to create that sleeker, more soigné impression.

'You'll love it, John,' she said to herself as she unpacked the dress from its cocoon of tissue, in order to make sure any creases fell out, ready for his mysterious special party.

It glistened, almost shone at her. Never mind *Pretty Woman*, in this she would truly be Cinderella, the belle of whatever potentially outré ball John was planning to take her to. And like Cinders, this might be her last big night with him. As soon as she revealed how she'd deceived him, the fairy tale might well be over completely, kaput and for ever. So she had to make the most of every precious hour before the bell tolled.

I want it all, John. Everything you can do for my body, while you're prepared to do it. I might never be with a man again who knows quite as well what he's doing.

He'd made promises, and a mock bargain with her when he'd told her the story about his student amours with his male sweetheart Benjamin. The thought of it made her wriggle, imagining, wondering what it might feel like . . . anal sex . . . sodomy. She wanted to try it. She'd always been curious. But never before had she felt she could trust a man enough. Not even Brent, when they'd been lovers.

Yet with John, she knew she'd be safe.

The meeting had been tiresome. The deal, meant to be straightforward, had become a hideous tangle of absurd complications. Usually impassive in such circumstances, he'd wanted to jump up, swear and tell them to stop screwing around and wasting his time because he didn't want to be in the room with them, haggling over piddling sums of money, when he could have been upstairs, in his suite, with Bettie.

Her beautiful body, her sweet, bright, witty personality, they were like a delicious mirage to him, shining before him, in the aggravating desert of the negotiating environment.

When the deal was finally signed, he'd sighed out loud,

drawing inquisitive looks from the assembled lawyers, executives and other drones. He'd snatched up his laptop and briefcase and almost run out of the room, hearing the offers of celebratory drinks as merely meaningless words.

When he reached his room, he didn't storm in, though. She'd done nothing wrong. No need to take his frustration out on her. Seek solace in her arms, or in play with her, yes. But vent his irritation? No, never that.

He smiled, setting his case and laptop on a side table. Bless her, she was asleep again. He'd never before met a woman, or anyone, who had quite the easy facility for dozing off that Bettie had. He envied her, and yet, earlier, in the car, hadn't he half nodded off himself while she was asleep? That still astounded him to his very core, and he wondered if perhaps it had been just wishful thinking and he hadn't slept.

You did, man. You did. You fell asleep.

And that had never happened easily, spontaneously, or without apprehension, since prison. It'd been impossible.

His mind shied away from the memories. The fear. Pain. Bone-deep exhaustion. Hatred of himself. Knowing he deserved every horror. He didn't go to that place often, because he'd learnt to deal with it, and with himself, and be whole again. After a fashion. With help, and yes, with hindrance too. Clara's double betrayal . . . When twice he'd believed she cared for him; twice she'd assured him she loved him, but then walked away.

He'd got past it all, but the sleep issues had stubbornly persisted. Or at least they had until he'd found himself falling asleep beside Bettie in the back of the limousine. And slept on, if only for a few moments, in the presence of another human being, and without strong chemical aid, for the first time in over twenty years.

And Bettie, his call girl who *wasn't* a call girl, was asleep again herself now. She looked peaceful. Angelic. Her dark lashes were like fans across her high cheekbones; her mouth soft and tender, still deliciously pink without benefit of her tinted lip-stain. Her gorgeous body was bundled in one of the hotel's thick, fluffy robes. Her curves were hidden, but he knew them. The image of her luscious shape was in his mind, like an elixir to harden his cock. She had her legs tucked up beneath her, in the big chair, and he let his hand hover just millimetres over her terry-covered haunch, imagining the feel of the muscle there, the firmness, the resilience when he spanked her.

The succulent curve of her bottom reminded him of what he'd bargained with her for, in return for his story about Benjamin. A tale elaborated upon, but true in essence. Would she be willing to give him her arse? His fingers flexed, to caress it, but he held back, reluctant to disturb her, even though his cock had stiffened to a rigid aching bar, just at the thought of sodomising her slowly and luxuriantly.

Let her sleep, man. Don't be greedy. Wait a little while.

Stepping away, he tried to ignore his gouging erection. There were carrier bags spread in the other chairs, her shopping presumably. Curiosity piqued him, and he wondered if she'd overcome her reluctance to use the card he'd given her.

In the bags he found lingerie, a variety of small accessories – a couple of belts, a pretty purse with stitched leather kittens on it that made him smile – and several women's tops and teeshirts, a souvenir mug, other gift items. And cat toys? There were also quite a few books: thrillers, several romances and a couple of rather advanced looking primers on dressmaking. And quite a stack of games.

John frowned, intrigued by the selection of items. Presumably most of the things were for herself, but some were clearly for her house-mates, human and feline. He'd certainly not pegged her as a gamer.

As they were mostly combat and sport, he guessed the games were for Brent. The *real* man in her life. Again, John tried to squelch his sudden jealousy. Bettie was devoted to her friend, and John feared she probably loved the younger man far more than she herself realised. At the moment. But the time would come and, for her sake, he hoped soon. She, at least, deserved to get her emotional life settled . . .

Even if I can't.

John sighed again, more heavily than he'd done in the boardroom.

If I was a decent man, I'd send her home right now. Send her back to the man she cares for. But I'm not a decent man, and I want her. Want her badly.

His time with Bettie wouldn't be long. But he'd be selfish and grab what he could, while he could. Moments of happiness, to remember and to treasure.

Leaving his lover to her dreams, he strode to his room, yearning for another shower. To cleanse his soul, not his body. To sluice away both the past and the presentiment of future loss.

As Lizzie woke, she experienced a sense of unease. She felt as if someone had been watching her, and when she glanced around she expected to see John in one of the other chairs, studying her, perhaps sipping a glass of gin while he contemplated their next erotic encounter.

Bring it on.

She wanted the distraction. The uncomplicated escape of sex, despite the games they played. Delirious pleasure with John, whose need for her was straightforward, simple.

And it was a good job things were that way with somebody. She knew where she stood with him. Not so with Brent, who'd been snappish, distant, then argumentative when she'd phoned him again earlier to see how he was doing, a world away from the fairly cheerful friend who'd seen her off. What had happened?

'Don't fucking well fuss! I'm a grown-up, Lizzie. I can manage on my own, you know. You and Shelley treat me like a little kid sometimes . . . I'm not going to do something stupid.'

But for all his bravado, there was a bleakness in his voice, and that worried her. She'd wanted to suggest that she come home straight away, but even as she'd hinted it, he'd almost bitten her head off again.

'Look, leave it, will you. Enjoy your fuck-fest. And you take care . . . worry about yourself, not me. I'll bet you haven't told him yet, have you?'

The conversation had petered out, leaving her unsettled and still worried about him. Brent just wouldn't stop beating himself up, after all this time, for the accident he'd believed he'd caused, and the love he'd lost.

I will go back home tomorrow. I will tell John the truth, and return to real life.

But in the meantime, in the hours she had left with him, she'd dive into every possible pleasure she could share with him. She'd give. She'd take. She'd experience everything: the new and the strange, and the familiar, intense sensations she knew he could give her. The sweet succour of his lips, his hands and his marvellous body. The miraculous illusion that she was just as much 'the one' for him, as she suspected he'd become for her.

Springing to her feet, she stood listening and heard a shower running, the sound emanating from the open door to John's bedroom, and the bathroom beyond. He was back, it seemed, no doubt the possessor of this hotel now. Well, she would help him celebrate his success by giving him something else he wanted.

15

Revelations

The water teemed down. John tried to keep his mind blank, and to settle into his senses. The flow pattered against his skin in a micro massage, and the scent of the soap he'd cleansed himself with was fresh and heady.

His cock was hard, anticipating the hand, the lips or the cunt of Bettie . . . or perhaps the snug embrace of her arse.

Oh, my beautiful girl, I know you'll be heavenly.

He imagined her wriggling against him, her body a-tremble as she rode the disturbing sensations that had to be sailed through to reach the shores of delicious, dark pleasure, and forbidden intensity. There was always that frantic moment, no matter how familiar the act was.

Taking himself in hand, he shuddered, suddenly back with Benjamin, that last time, in the grip of that moment of dangerous, terrible thrill when the nerve-endings inside sent messages of panic zipping around the body. He'd been scared that time, unsure whether he could tolerate it after what had happened since they'd last been together, but his friend had made it beautiful for him . . . just as he was going to make it beautiful for the woman sharing his suite.

'Bettie,' he gasped, the rushing water of the shower trickling over his lips as his chest heaved. The urge to masturbate furiously almost overcame him, but he resisted it, wanting to save himself for her. 'Bettie . . .'

As if summoned, she appeared, her shapely form distinct through the frosted glass of the cubicle, skin creamy, curves delicate, dark hair fastened up in some kind of loose knot, the triangle of her pubic patch just as dark, a stark siren call to his aching penis.

Sliding back the shower door a little, she asked, 'Can I come in?'

He laughed in the pounding water. 'I'll think about it . . .' Reaching out, he opened the panel wider, to admit her, then drew her by the arm into the cocoon of steam and moisture. 'There . . . I've thought about it.' With an arm already around her waist, he slid the shower door closed to contain them.

As if they'd showered together a thousand times, their bodies came together, wet, naked skin pressing against wet, naked skin. The points of her nipples were as hard as his cock felt to him. Her mons pubis brushed against his aching flesh, a soft caress to his rigidity. He closed his hands around the smooth, resilient lobes of her buttocks, loving their firmness, irresistibly drawn to the warm groove between them, pressing in with his fingers to tickle her anus.

A little moan escaped her lips and she rocked herself against him, rubbing him and enticing him. Whether it was an automatic response or deliberate provocation, he really didn't care. It just felt sublime. He pressed harder, rubbing and probing at the little vent, smiling against her haphazardly contained hair when she worked herself harder against his length, panting and making eager little sounds.

'God, you feel lovely, Bettie.' He kissed her brow, her

cheek, then her throat. 'Are you going to give me what I want?' He poised his fingertip against her rear entrance, gently pressing.

'Hell yes,' she panted, 'I want it too. But there's stuff I need to tell you first, John. Important stuff.' She was shaking in his hold, and he wasn't sure how much of it was to do with the prospect of anal sex. He *knew* what it was that was making her tremble. It was the moment of truth, or one of them, and he wanted to tell her that none of it mattered to him, one way or the other. She was a jewel to him, escort or otherwise. He didn't care about the money. Just her.

'What is it, Bettie? You can tell me. You can tell me anything.' He stroked her, fondling her rudely. He knew that perhaps he should just draw her out of the shower, bundle her in a robe, and sit her down for a proper talk. But he simply couldn't stop touching her.

'You might not like it,' she said, her mouth against his neck now.

'Let me be the judge of that. I can't think of anything about you that I could possibly not like.' True. So true.

She looked up at him. Her eyes were huge and dark, alight with lust, but shadowed with apprehension too. He bent to kiss her quickly, to reassure her.

'OK, then,' she said, still looking him in the eye when he lifted his face from hers. Her bravery thrilled him just as much as the warm, wet skin of her body against his. 'But the first thing . . . really. My name isn't really "Bettie".'

It wasn't a surprise. The name went with the style. It stood to reason it was as manufactured as her homage to the famous 1950s glamour star.

'So, mystery woman, what *is* your name, then?' He kept on stroking her, and she drew a sharp little breath.

'Well, I am an "Elizabeth" . . . but people call me "Lizzie", not Bettie. The Bettie thing is just a joke, because I look a bit like her.'

Lizzie. He tried it in his mind before on his lips.

Lizzie. It was cute, spikey, pert; just like her. In the blink of an eye, he knew he liked it. He liked real Lizzie even more than he'd liked the performance that was Bettie.

'It suits you . . . Lizzie . . . I'm sure I'll soon get used to it.' Her hair was tumbling from its up-do and he smoothed the wayward black strands from her face. 'What else have you got to tell me? What other dramatic revelations are there?'

Now she did look away, but only for a moment. He felt her brace up in his arms, her spine straightening. She was ready to face the music.

'I'm . . . um . . . I'm not really a call girl, John. I'm not an escort. I never have been. I've never taken money. Well, at least not from anybody but you.' She pursed her lips, and he could see her mind working, whirling. 'And I'll give you back all you've given to me . . . well, most of it. I have spent a bit of it. But if you give me time, I'll pay that back too.'

Abandoning his teasing touch, he enfolded her in his arms, hugging her in the water. 'Bett . . . Sorry, Lizzie . . . I *know* you're not an escort. I've suspected you weren't a real pro for a while, but when you told me your address I had my people do some checking. I carried on with the game because *you* seemed to be enjoying it.'

She struggled wildly in his grasp, thumping him on the back, quite hard. 'You beast! You've been playing me for a fool!' Still beating at him, she shifted her weight, almost as if she were about to knee him in the groin.

'No, not a fool! A sharp, clever, daring woman, not afraid to do something crazy to get out of the daily routine.' He hugged her harder. 'A beautiful, sensual woman, with the guts to take on a kinky bastard like me in order to broaden her sexual horizons.'

He felt her stiffen, as if bracing herself for another onslaught, then she went soft in his arms, pliant against him, her belly pressed to his raging hard-on.

And she laughed, rocking against him now, shaking with mirth.

'You *are* a kinky bastard. And an insufferable arrogant git. I should walk out right now, *and* take all your horrible money with me, for stringing me along.' A pang of sudden unhappiness shot through him, fear that she meant it, but then she reached down and grasped his still rigid cock, cradling it in a way that was both delicious and vaguely menacing. 'But seeing as you're such a colossally amazing fuck, I might just let you off . . . and I'll stay a while.' She paused, her thumb stroking the groove beneath his glans, slowly, tantalisingly. 'I need to pay that money back, though . . . otherwise I *am* really a whore, aren't I?'

'Can we discuss the financial details later?' He slid his hands down to her bottom again. Two could play at the distraction game. He settled his fingertips once more against her anus. 'I don't think my negotiating skills will be at their sharpest right now. The blood that should be refreshing my brain cells seems to have settled elsewhere.' Stroking her as she stroked him, he rocked his hips, pushing his erection through her cradling fingers.

'All right. But I mean it, you know.' She shimmied against him, and he could feel the musculature of her arse flexing and tightening as if she were trying to entice his searching fingertips.

'I know you do. But for the moment, I'd rather focus on

one of our other bargains.' He pushed his finger hard against her rear vent, testing the muscle ring. 'You know which one.'

'I've never had anal sex before. That's why I needed to tell you. An accomplished call girl has probably done anal hundreds of times . . . but I haven't.' She was nervous, he could tell, but from the way she paused, and breathed deeply, he knew she was trying to relax herself and let his finger in. 'I'm a virgin back there.'

Something atavistic in him stirred. Something primal. He'd never have expected a woman her age to be a virgin, even if they'd met under the most normal of circumstances, but he experienced a strangely chest-beating, he-man thrill to know he'd be her first, in this one thing at least.

'Good.' He pushed a little harder, but she was tense. Standing here in the shower wasn't the way to do things. He needed to make it easy for her, as comfortable as possible.

And yet, as he pictured himself looming over her, about to push in, his imagination presented her bottom to him as rosy, freshly spanked, and his cock kicked hard in her fingers. Kinky bastard, indeed.

Biting his lip, he centred himself, breathing deeply. Did she sense his hair-trigger readiness? Her hold on him now was light as a feather, as if she did.

'Let's get out of this water, shall we?' he suggested, reaching to turn off the flow. 'Let's get comfy and then we can have some naughty, forbidden fun. You'll love it, I can promise you. Take it from someone who still remembers what it's like to have a cock in his arse.' With Benjamin, it *had* been good. It *had* been pleasure.

'You're a filthy devil, you are,' she growled at him, but she was smiling as they stepped out of the cubicle.

*

Lizzie smiled, but her heart was pounding and she felt as if she might fly apart at any moment. She'd told John, and he was OK with it. He still wanted her, at least for the moment.

Of course he fucking wants you, you nincompoop! You're about to let him put his dick in your arse. He's hardly likely to tell you not to darken his doorstep any more, when anal sex is on offer any minute, is he?

'What are you laughing at, Miss Lizzie?' he demanded, then pulled her close again for a deep hard kiss, body to body, his cock boring into her belly.

'Nothing,' she demurred when they broke apart again. 'I thought you might tell me to piss off when you found out I wasn't really an escort . . . but then I realised no man in his right mind would turn down anal sex first.'

He smiled down at her, water dripping from his curly hair where it dangled across his brow. 'Even if I weren't about to plunder your luscious bum I wouldn't tell you to go. We're having a good time, aren't we?' His eyes glittered. There was good humour there, but, was there something else? Perhaps not. 'We're two grown-ups who enjoy each other's bodies and both like a bit of kinky fun.' Reaching up, he swept the wet hair out of his eyes, then did the same for her, where strands were plastered to her face. 'And don't worry about money. I always give presents to people I like and I like you, Lizzie. So there's an end of it.'

She ran her hands down his body, savouring his hot, wet skin. 'So, we're like temporary sex friends now, instead of punter and escort?'

He paused for half a beat. 'Well, yes, I suppose that's a good way to put it . . . temporary sex friends. Yes, I like that . . . Do you?'

It sounded stupid, and she wished she'd never said it. But she could hardly tell him she might have fallen in love with him after just a few days of spanking and fucking, could she? That was infinitely more stupid. Even if it was the truth!

'Yes. Now shall we get on? Where . . . where do you want me?'

John glanced around the bathroom, his eyes lighting on the fluffy deep-piled bath rug and the heaped piles of fresh towels and bath sheets. 'There,' he said, pointing to the soft, thick rug, then flashing a wickedly saturnine grin at her. He looked like the very devil. 'I want you doggie style on that rug, with your beautiful bottom in the air all ready for me.' He gripped her buttocks hard, fingertips in the crease. 'And I'd like to spank you a little bit first. I want to see your bum cheeks pink as I push in.'

Lust surged in her belly. Lust and a delicious, roiling apprehension, imagining herself presented to him thus, rude and available, marked by his hand. She looked into his eyes, and the grin was gone now. Not the humour, that was still there, but his expression was more fiery now, resolute. Masterful.

She wanted him so much she almost floated to the ceiling, borne up on a wave of longing. It was the most natural thing in the world to lower her eyes, his submissive.

'Good,' he said again, and she knew he'd understood everything. Naked and dripping wet he was an assured and dominant god. 'Now, down you go.'

Trembling, Lizzie obeyed him. She felt klutzy and ungainly, but he made a low sound in his throat when she assumed the position he'd specified, obviously of approval.

'Oh, baby, you look so delicious like that. Your arse is perfect, you know that, don't you? A heavenly work of art.

And it'll be even more adorable when I've made it red. Hell, yes . . .'

Then he was on his knees beside her, touching her hair. Deftly he loosened the scrunchie that held it, and then smoothed it out, sweeping it to one side, over one shoulder. 'Be quite still,' he specified, then started touching her again, his fingertips gliding over her back and her flanks, then reaching under her to squeeze her breasts. He pinched her nipples, pincering them firmly between finger and thumb, one after the other, then, even as she began to squirm and shift her hips, he withdrew and leapt lightly to his feet again.

'Hold that position for me, beautiful. Just like that.' He walked around her, moving behind. 'Ah, that's lovely, but I'd like you to part your thighs a bit further. Show me more.' With his bare foot, he pushed against the inside of her knee, nudging her apart. 'Yes, better. Now stay exactly like that.'

She heard him padding softly away, barefoot, heading for his bedroom.

Moisture trickled down the inside of her thigh . . . but it had nothing to do with the shower.

16

Au Fond

Lizzie held the position perfectly, because he'd told her to, but it was difficult. Her pussy was puffed and aching for contact. His hand . . . hers . . . she didn't care. Arousal was welling and overflowing between her sex lips, more copious than ever before.

It was easy to obey him. Easy to do what he wanted. Anything was easier than thinking about complications. This, kneeling where he'd told her to, and simmering like a pressure cooker of desire, was the simplest thing in the world.

Tensing the muscles of her buttocks, she imagined his hand landing hard on first one, then the other, igniting the now familiar burn of pain. Pain that transmuted like alchemical gold into rich, dark pleasure. And how much richer and darker would it be to feel his cock pushing into her arse? She was ready for it, and prepared . . . but also *not* ready. She'd struggled when he'd just tried to insert his fingertip.

But he was John, and he'd never *truly* hurt her, so she trusted him more than anything to make it all feel good.

The door swung open again, and she heard the clink of

glass. A moment later he was on the rug beside her, setting down his haul. She saw a couple of tubes of lubricant – goodness, that much? – and a box of condoms. Not the type they'd used thus far; they were labelled as a thicker gauge. *Au Fond*, the brand name said, and if there'd been any doubt what they were designed for, the sleek line of a toned buttock on the box dispelled that, although it was hard to tell if the bum was male or female.

The clinking glass sound had come from two tumblers. Holding them together by the rim, John set them down on the rug at her side. The fluid was clear, and the balsamic, almost medicinal scent was unmistakeable.

Gin.

'A little drink will help relax you,' he said, picking one glass up again. 'It's not good to get legless in these situations, but a drop of gin might calm some of the nerves.'

Was he meaning to hold the glass to her lips while she knelt? Twisting to look at him, she sent him a questioning glance.

'Oh no . . . I wouldn't do that. That would be demeaning. Roll onto your side, love. Have a little sip.'

Lizzie slithered onto her side on the thick, fluffy rug, her knees tucked, and accepted the drink. She'd never really liked gin before she'd met John, but now, it hit the perfect spot with its silvery fire. It was a crystal elixir and it did exactly the job he'd described. A few mouthfuls of the neat alcohol sent a glow speeding through her veins that lightened her spirits and smoothed away anxiety.

Yet it did nothing to minimise her desire. Looking at John, who looked back at her over the rim of his own glass, she wanted him more and more. That unknown territory, her dark virginity, was his for the taking.

'Nice,' she said, taking a last sip, then handing the glass back to him. The intermission was over. He was her master again and, as gracefully as she could, she got back onto her knees, dishing her back to display her bottom to him.

'Nice,' he echoed, and the glasses clinked again as he put both aside.

Her head fell forward, and her hair swung around her face, as his hands settled upon her. He gripped her buttocks in a rude, firm grip, squeezing and pulling the flesh this way and that. It felt like the touch of an experienced stockman handling a prized animal. She knew it was meant to feel that way too, and the deep sense of submission made her ache and softly groan.

'Nice,' he whispered again, pulling apart the lobes of her bottom to expose her anus to him. The sensation of stretching made her want to weep with lust and plead with him to push into her right now, without preparation, without lubrication, without hesitation. Her own fluid welled again, and she knew it would be visible, shiny, on her thighs. Even as he manipulated her, she moved, swaying her hips invitingly, shifting herself around to open even more to him.

'Jesus, you're a horny little cat, Lizzie. You really want it, don't you?' He stretched her open, more, more. 'Tell me what you want. Tell me everything you want.'

Held wide open, she gasped. A gentle waft of air flowed over her vent. He was blowing against her in a whisper of a caress. Her face flamed, imagining how close his face must be to her bottom.

'I want you to fuck me. To fuck me hard. I want you in my arse. I don't care if it's uncomfortable. Or if it hurts. I just want you to have me there. Be the first . . .'

'And other things?' For just a moment, his lips settled on

the upper slope of her bottom, first one side, then the other, as if marking out the territory he wished her to refer to.

'Yes, I want you to spank me hard and make my bum hot and sore first. I want to be red for you when you bugger me.'

Where is all this mad stuff coming from? I only had a few sips of gin. I feel as if I've gone slightly off my head.

It was a thrilling feeling, though. A sense of total submission. Total surrender to this beautiful man who'd suddenly and accidentally arrived in her life and who would just as suddenly leave it again soon.

She must have him now. Have everything. Give everything.

'Oh please, John, do it. I can't bear waiting any longer. I'm aching.'

'I know, sweetheart. I know . . . I can see your delicious pussy dripping. It's divine.'

She let out a sharp, high cry when he swooped low and dipped his tongue into her cleft from behind, lapping at her silk. He shouldn't be doing that. He was the master. She should be the one abasing herself before him. And yet he was bowed down low, licking her sex, like a worshipper.

Pressing herself towards his questing tongue, she gasped. 'You . . . you shouldn't be doing that . . . should you?'

His answer was to grab her by the thighs, hold her, and thrust his tongue into her vagina, jabbing hard. He laughed when he pulled his face away, then kissed her on the crown of each buttock. 'I thought I was supposed to be in charge here? I'm the boss. I can do what I want.' He ran his hands over her thighs and flanks possessively. 'I've a good mind to carry you to that bed out there, tie you up, and lick you until you beg me for mercy because you can't come any more. How would you like that, you uppity minx?'

'You'd get cramp in your tongue.'

'Probably.' He leaned right over her, kissing the top of her spine. 'But I still might have tried it if I wasn't so desperate to fuck you in the arse.'

'Well, get on with it, then.' Arching her body, she pressed back against him, rubbing her thighs and her bottom against him, working her cleft against the hard prow of his cock.

'You're an outrageous sub, you know that, don't you? Don't think I haven't noticed you trying to top me from the bottom all the time. I should spank you hard for that.'

Twisting, she looked at him over her shoulder, using her eyes to tell him to get a move on now, instead of her voice. He shook his head, making his drying blond curls flutter like an angel's, and grinned back at her before kissing her hard on the spine at the base of her head, rubbing his face in her hair.

Then he straightened up, kneeling beside her with his cock pointing rudely. Without warning he landed a lazy, open-handed slap on her right buttock, then another on her left, making her yelp in surprise.

'You're a delicious, bad, beautiful woman, Lizzie . . . Lizzie whatever your name is.' He spanked her hard, another blow landing, then another, as if he could compel her surname out of her by main force.

'Aitchison. My name is Lizzie Aitchison . . .'

'Is . . . that . . . a . . . fact?' he pronounced, whaling the under-hang of her bottom with a slap for each word.

Sizzling heat roasted her buttocks, sinking into her crotch, almost making her come. She pitched forward, her elbows on the mat, forehead pressed against her arms, trying to compose herself. 'But if you've had your snoops checking up on me, you knew that already, didn't you?' she accused, the words muffled by her hair. 'And why won't you tell me *your* real name?' She knew it . . . just as well as he'd known hers . . . but it seemed important to ask the question.

'You know my name. It's John Smith.' His hand settled flat on her blazing flesh, as if she'd caught him by surprise.

'No, your *real* real name. The one you were born with.'

'You know that too, if you've looked me up.'

'I . . . I do . . .' A couple of particularly stinging slaps landed, angled cleverly, striking her right across the vent of her bottom and making her whine and churn her hips.

'Right, then . . . I'm Jonathan Llewellyn Wyngarde Smith, and I'm going to fuck that gorgeous, sumptuous, insolent red arse of yours, Miss Aitchison. I'm going to plough you until you come in a howling orgasm and turn cross-eyed. How does that sound?'

'It sounds fabulous, your lordship.' She gritted her teeth as he found that same uniquely tender spot again.

'Uh oh, I think you know that I don't use my title either. I haven't for twenty years. It's completely meaningless.'

Dishing her back, she thrust her bottom at him, inviting more, inviting everything. 'Well, that's a shame. I was hoping to be able to tell my grandchildren in my dotage that I'd once been buggered by a lord.'

'Well, for this one time only, consider me a lord, then.' He laughed and grabbed hold of her hot buttocks, squeezing them.

'Yes, your lordship. Thank you, your lordship.' Even though his fingers tightened, punishing her sore flesh and making her want to whimper, she still found herself giggling at the absurdity of it all.

'You won't be laughing soon, you cheeky mare,' he threatened, but she could hear the smile in his voice . . . the affection? Leaning over her again, he kissed her back and shoulders repeatedly, even while he handled her tingling buttocks. 'Dear God, I want to be inside you . . . right in you. I can't wait any longer.'

'Then don't wait,' she said, her body wracked by a long shudder. Was it fear, or was it longing? She couldn't tell.

Giving her one last squeeze, John pulled away. 'Would you like another sip of gin?' His voice was tight, as if he was having difficulty containing a great emotion, and was maybe as confused as she was. Her heart turned over, touched, even in the midst of sexual madness, that his thought was for her nervousness, her inexperience.

'Just a sip . . . yes . . . that would be good.' She rocked onto her side, hissing as her bottom pressed against the floor, and took the glass as he held it out to her. The bite of the spirit was fortifying, though; even one sip buoyed her up, and she put the glass aside and slid back onto her knees.

John was beside her, and she turned to look in his eyes. They were dazzling, almost navy blue, his face an illuminated icon of desire. An agreement passed between them. Her assent, and his acknowledgement of it. She let her head drop as she saw him reach for the tube of lubricant.

The stuff was cool when it touched her, and she imagined it as silvery as the gin as he slathered it into the hot crease of her buttocks. It was silky, but thick and unctuous, and it clung to her there, coating her anal vent and oozing down as he applied more and more.

And then it was more than application. He began pushing the stuff inside her, thick dollops of it. Odd sneaky feelings began to gather, and she shivered again.

'Relax . . . don't be scared . . . just relax.' His voice was low and hypnotic as he began to pack the sticky gel inside her. Panic surged, but he bent over her, kissing her back and breathing against her as he worked.

His words calmed her. His lips against her skin were far more potent than the gin. Her body yielded, accepting his ministrations and the sensations of heat and fullness. The fiery glow from her spanking seemed to spread through her entire sex and her pelvis, warming her and inciting her needs. She wondered idly if he'd used a whole tube of lubricant on her. It felt like that. As she shifted her thighs slightly, she imagined she heard the squelch of it.

'Stay still, my sweet,' he said against her back then straightened up. She imagined him looking down on her, pleased with his handiwork and with the sight of her submissive and presented before him, her thighs parted and her anal cleft glistening. There came the small tearing sound of him opening the contraceptive package, then dead quiet as he concentrated on sheathing himself. She didn't look round. To see him might overwhelm her. She was safe within the thick curtain of her black hair, dangling around her face.

Breathe . . . Breathe . . .

Apprehension welled again, but she compelled it to retreat, focusing on simply drawing air in and out, and not trying to anticipate or analyse. Better not to get ahead of herself, either in the moments that lay ahead, or the hours, days, weeks or years that lay beyond that.

She was just a body, ready to be possessed, ready for him.

'Hold yourself open for me.'

A moan tried to escape her, but she captured it, pursing her lips as she pressed her forehead against the piled-up towels, to support herself, then reached around. A heavy slicking sound told her he was slapping more lube on his condom-covered cock, and her heart pounded as hard as her body shook. Holding her bottom cheeks apart she barely registered the soreness of her spanking.

Again, she imagined herself, the rude, wanton sight of her own fingers on her flesh, facilitating his entrance. How lewd a snapshot of her now would be. The ultimate porno pic. And yet it didn't feel that way, not at all. It felt wonderful, and sacred . . . almost orgasmic. Her pussy fluttered, as if he were already possessing her.

'Jesus Christ, Lizzie . . . you're gorgeous . . . the hottest . . . the most wonderful . . .' His voice was ragged now. She knew he was exerting control, but there was a deep dark thrill at the thought he might lose it. Despite her inexperience, she wanted him to. Drawing apart her cheeks even further, she waggled her bottom to entice him, to stir him up.

'Lizzie,' he growled, pressing forward.

The slickened tip of his cock pushed against the forbidden entrance. It felt huge, and she gasped, but before she could falter, she pressed back against him, encouraging him. He was guiding himself with one hand, but with the other, he reached around and beneath her, seeking her sex.

'Oh . . . oh God,' she moaned as he found her clit.

'Relax, sweetheart,' he said again. He was pushing slowly, but she could feel him struggling with her tightness, the resistance she didn't feel in her mind and heart, but which her body still held on to. 'I know it feels . . . feels peculiar at first, love, but don't fight it. I won't hurt you. I'd never hurt you. Trust me.'

He pressed harder, the fat head of his cock stretching, stretching, stretching . . . It seemed impossible, and sweat broke out all over her body. Droplets pooled at her hairline, between her breast and in the creases of her groin. Another little push and his glans entered, and she couldn't help herself, a strange, high mewling sound did escape her lips this time. Dreadful yet wonderful sensations roiled in her vitals and she snatched her hands away from her buttocks, now he was in, and pitched forward onto thick-piled rug, folding an arm beneath her head and laying her face against it.

'That's it. That's it. Easy, my sweet girl . . .'

His voice, his wonderful, low, beloved voice was like a balm that soothed her fears, and flowed through her body, gentling its panicked reaction to the new sensation.

'My dear, sweet girl . . . that's wonderful . . . *you're* wonderful . . . that's it . . . stay relaxed. You're doing beautifully.'

All anxiety seemed to melt away like mist. The unpleasant fearful sensations dissolved with it, only to be replaced by an intense, all-consuming voluptuousness and sense of being possessed and cherished. John's hot cock slid into her easily now, her resistance was gone. He felt huge and potent, and the might of him found areas of sensitivity and susceptibility she'd never imagined could exist. He wasn't in her pussy, but it was as if he was there, and in her brain and heart too. His fingers strummed her clit and seemed to meet a pressure wave emanating deep inside, amplifying the divine stimulation of it. He was grasping her thigh now too, for purchase, and the way his thumb dug into the spanked flesh of her bottom cheek only added another note to the symphony of perception.

'Oh God . . . Oh God . . .' he groaned as her body rippled and gripped around him.

Lizzie was beyond words, but she crooned and moaned as hot pleasure bloomed in a great swelling wave that engulfed her loins. Her empty vagina clenched and grabbed, embracing the memory of the cock that now possessed her arse. Her clitoris fluttered and leapt beneath his gentle, puissant fingertips.

Tears trickled from her eyes, and flowed over her forearm, seeded by an emotion so great she could barely quantify it right at that moment. Joy. Ecstasy. Whatever the hell people called it when they were in a glorious evanescent place they might never reach again.

She only knew, as John shouted and came, his body shaking and slapping against hers, that she loved him completely and utterly . . . and always would.

Afterwards, John bundled her in a bath sheet and carried her in his arms to the bathroom adjoining her own room, answering her request for a little time to herself. It wasn't so much that she wanted privacy to cleanse herself, although she certainly did want that; it was more that she needed to be in her own space to gain emotional composure too.

If she stayed close, she was afraid that he'd be kind, and sensitive to her current state of fragility, and then she'd not be able to stop herself blurting out her silly feelings to him. Impossible, stupid feelings that could come to nothing. She was the one who'd posited the notion of 'temporary sex friends'. But John had embraced it without demur. It suited his needs. She was just a passing diversion for him, whether he paid her as a prostitute or not.

That didn't mean he wasn't a good man, though. He was just a good man who didn't want a relationship.

And the sooner she accepted that, the better it would be for both of them.

17

Eyes Wide Open

'So, tell me about what you really do for a living, Lizzie?'

They were eating late in the hotel's restaurant. Lizzie had jumped at the chance to dine out when John had suggested it. The atmosphere in their suite was too intense, too claustrophobic, even though the rooms were vast and spacious. There, she seemed to canon into her own ridiculous hopes and yearnings as if they were tangible objects, and John too seemed to be relieved at a chance to avoid them, even though neither of them had touched on anything more than the practical. As she'd expected, he'd been solicitous and thoughtful in every way.

It might have been much easier if he'd been a selfish alpha bastard.

'Well, as I'm sure you know, I mostly do secretarial temp work. It's a bit boring, but it pays quite well and I'm not tied down to one office and one boss that I might not like.' She gazed down at her plate. The simple chicken dish she'd chosen was exquisitely prepared, and one of the nicest she'd ever tasted, but her appetite kept flickering in and out of existence. 'But I also sew a bit. I love dressmaking . . . which is handy, because it's not easy to get "Bettie Page" outfits off the peg. I make clothes for my friends and friends of friends too. It's not really a business or anything. They always buy their own fabric, and pay me by buying a bit of fabric for me at the same time.' She put down her knife and fork, giving up on the chicken. 'I'm not sure how the taxman would view it, but what he doesn't know . . . well, it doesn't hurt. You won't tell on me, will you?'

John smiled. He looked almost fond for a moment, then seemed to sharpen up. 'Of course not, don't worry. But if you're ever looking for a bit of capital to start up your own design house, I'm your man. Don't hesitate to approach me.'

She could imagine it. Writing to him. Getting a formal reply from Willis, his treasure of a P.A. She'd no doubt he'd be a canny but generous benefactor. But there'd probably be no actual contact between them. Which would probably be worse than never ever having anything to do with him ever again.

'Well, that's an incredibly generous offer, but I'm not really a designer. I just use patterns and adapt them a bit.'

'It's a skill, nevertheless. And you'd be better off pursuing something creative like that, and using your gifts, than getting bored in an office.'

'True. And I'm not a very good temp anyway. I'm probably actually a far better call girl than I am a secretarial assistant or database clerk.'

John's expression lightened, and a familiar puckish twinkle appeared in his eyes. Lizzie felt lighter too and more relaxed all of a sudden. Sex and kink seemed far less perilous territory than talk of purpose in life, and emotions.

'Well, you've certainly got the gifts for that, too. If you really were to go down that path you could be the most sought after courtesan in the land!' He took a sip from his water glass, and waggled his eyebrows salaciously at her. 'I'd certainly give you a glowing reference.'

Yes, this was much safer ground. Erotic flirtation. She gave him a slow, sultry look in return.

'I'm pleased to hear it. I did try to give value for money.' Reaching out, she stroked the back of his hand where it rested on the tablecloth. His skin was warm, and the elegant shape of his fingers reminded her of how they felt, touching and exploring her. 'Although if the tables had been turned, I'd have valued *your* services at twice the fee you paid me.'

Her memory pinged as she said it. What had he told her? That he'd once sold his body too. John's blue eyes narrowed as if he'd read her thought.

'I've been paid a lot more than that for my body,' he said slowly.

They were straying back into dangerously iffy territory again, but curiosity gouged at her. 'What do you mean? Can you tell me? Don't worry if you can't . . . I'm just being a nosy cow.'

Twisting his hand beneath hers, he gave her fingers a squeeze then withdrew his hand to pour them some wine. They'd both been drinking mainly water, but now it seemed as if he needed a jolt of alcohol.

'I married for money, Lizzie. It's as simple and as complicated as that.' He took a sip from his glass. 'I don't know how much you've learnt about me from the internet, but I had a rocky time, to say the least, in my twenties . . . and became completely estranged from my father, and my family. I'd brought shame on them . . .' His face tightened, his mouth a thin line. She could almost see the younger John, angry, confused, ashamed of himself . . . totally alone. 'I was a mess. I knew I had a talent for business . . . but I had no capital. And then a friend came to me, someone I'd always liked, but . . . well . . . never seen as a woman before.'

He shrugged expressively. 'That probably sounds stupid, but it was . . . circumstances. Suddenly we found we could talk and talk, and because she was witty and kind and a lovely woman, I found I could tell her things.' He reached for his glass again, but seemed to have second thoughts, withdrawing his hand. 'I said I had plans to go into business and make a sodding great fortune, just to spite the old man. He thought commerce was beneath us, so much so that what money we did have was avalanching away, and we were in danger of losing Montcalm.'

'But I thought your family were loaded. Montcalm is one of the most fabulous stately homes in the country. Everybody knows how amazing it is.'

'It is *now*. Back then it was falling to bits.' He winked at her, his wry expression speaking silent volumes. She understood immediately who had shored up the family fortunes. In secret. There was so much she still didn't know about him, and probably never would.

'This woman . . . Caroline . . . offered me a bargain,' he went on, his voice low and level. 'After the death of her first husband, she'd been lonely. And more than that. She really missed sex. She said she thought I was the most beautiful man she'd ever seen . . . and that I'd been sorely wronged.' He paused, his lips twitching as if part of him wanted to laugh . . . and another part didn't at all, perhaps the reverse. 'She said if I'd marry her, and give her a taste of the good sex she was missing, she'd bankroll me to the tune of any sum I cared to name.'

'Crikey!'

'Crikey indeed. I was completely gobsmacked when she came out and suggested it, but . . . well . . . it seemed to make sense. We could both give each other something we needed. And I was a young man, in a bit of a mess . . . and hell, I was flattered too.' He shrugged.

But you're still beautiful, she wanted to say. *You're certainly the most beautiful man I've ever seen. Even now you're at least twenty years older . . .*

'And it wasn't as if I didn't like her. She was . . . she is . . . an incredibly attractive woman. Witty, sexy, very warm and wonderful company. The circumstances were weird, to say the least . . . more than you can imagine . . . But it was no hardship to fuck her,' he said in a very soft voice. 'We enjoyed ourselves in bed.' He did his sexy eyebrow thing. 'I tried to give the best value I could . . . the best bang for her bucks.'

Lizzie laughed out loud. 'God, you really are the living end. I thought I was being outrageous, pretending to be an escort . . . but you . . .' She shook her head. 'So, what happened? Obviously you're not together any more. Did she get tired of you?'

'Not exactly. But we did, gradually, become more and more just good friends than lovers. We could have rubbed along like that, but she met someone else.'

Lizzie knew her surprise must be patent on her face, because John smiled wryly. She still couldn't see how anyone could chuck him over for somebody else, though. Had she been mad? Had his older ex-wife gone gaga?

'I know . . . hard to believe. But this man was the childhood sweetheart she realised she still loved, two husbands notwithstanding. He was her true love, but he'd been living in the Far East two decades and now he'd come back, a widower.'

'So what happened . . . was it . . . was it ugly?'

John smiled, his expression far away, complex. 'No, exactly the opposite. We'd both known all along that it was only a temporary marriage. It was a gentle, amicable parting . . . and she was very generous. My "settlement", if you want to call it that, was all the seed capital I needed to consolidate the evil plutocratic business empire I control today.'

Lizzie gaped at him. No wonder he didn't have any qualms about paying for sex. No wonder he thought nothing of the pile of money he'd lavished on her.

'Wow,' was all she could manage.

'Yes . . . just described cold like that, it probably seems an obscene arrangement, but it wasn't like that at all. She picked me up when I was in a bit of a pit, and we were friends, we still are . . . and we were passionate lovers for a while. I still have dinner with her and her husband from time to time. And I paid her back every penny within three years.'

'Might take me a bit longer than that to pay *you* back.'

'There's no need. I *do* understand why you want to . . .' His expression was strangely earnest. 'But you don't need to, Lizzie. I'm a rich man. I enjoy giving gifts to friends. Just consider it as that. Donate the money to charity, if you must, but don't give it back to me. I don't need it and I don't want it.'

It still felt wrong.

'Look . . .' He seemed to sift through ideas, gauging the best way to make her keep his money. 'Why not take your house-mates away for a holiday somewhere fabulous? It sounds as if your pal Brent needs it, if he's been through the mill. Caroline took me to the Caribbean when we first got together . . . and the sun and the pampering did me a world of good.'

Lizzie narrowed her eyes. What was he up to? Why this fixation with Brent? Was he trying to set them up romantically again, so that he wouldn't have to worry about her himself when he was gone?

And yet . . .

'That's not a bad idea, actually.' Watching his face, she tried to determine his response, but he wasn't a master negotiator for nothing. He gave nothing away. His expression was mild. No apparent jealousy.

You dolt, you didn't really expect him to be bothered, did you?

'There. See. Problem solved,' John said briskly. 'Now . . . are we going to go to this party or not? It's entirely up to you, sweetheart. You look gorgeous in that dress, though.' He gave her a hot look, as if savouring what he could see, and what was currently hidden. 'You're just as sexy as Audrey Hepburn as you are when you are Bettie Page. I'd be the envy of every man there with you on my arm.'

Yes, a party would be fun. Away from the jittery intensity of being alone together. Away from the danger of revealing herself far more profoundly than by any kind of nakedness.

'Yes, I could fancy a party . . . What kind of a "do" is it? You were a bit mysterious.'

John didn't speak straight away. His eyes were bright and, for a moment, he pursed his lips.

'Well, it's a sex party, if you're up for that. Couples only. Single guests usually bring an escort along, but a "temporary sex friend" would fit the bill just as well.'

Good grief. Just like that. Well, that was one way to stop her getting nosy about his past and asking questions. A dozen images of writhing bodies flooded into her mind. Strangers fucking. Hot eyes, looking at her, wanting . . . expecting her to participate. Apprehension followed closely in the wake of the inner pictures. Was this really something she wanted to do? Even to please John?

'Um . . . I don't know . . . What's involved?'

John laughed softly, but his eyes scanned her face, recording her every response. 'Sex, of course, although all *you* have to do is watch, love. Nothing more than that. There'll be more than enough exhibitionists to go around. Have you seen the film *Eyes Wide Shut*?'

Yes, she had. She nodded, remembering the bizarre, unsettling orgy scene, set at an enormous, secluded mansion. It had been arousing, but in a detached sort of way. She'd always been aware it was a construct for the camera . . . not real.

'Well, it'll be a bit like that only with much less chanting, weird ritual stuff and murder.' He reached out and clasped her hand. 'In fact, absolutely no murder at all. And quite a bit more BDSM . . . so just up our street, really.'

Did she want to go? The idea befuddled her. Part of her had never imagined getting a chance to experience a private, luxurious, sex orgy, and natural curiosity cried out yes, yes, don't be a wimp. She'd plunged into the fantasy of being an accidental call girl and had the time of her life, so why not this, too?

And yet, another part of her was just Lizzie, completely normal, a woman of modest sexual experience who'd never really, truly had an adventure until she'd walked into a bar a few days ago and set eyes on the most gorgeous man she'd ever seen in her life.

She just wanted to return to their suite and have John all to herself for as much time as remained to her.

'You don't fancy it, do you?' he said, his voice gentle. 'That's OK. That's fine. We won't go. I don't want you to feel you have to do something you don't want to. I wouldn't enjoy it at all if I knew you were unhappy . . .'

He meant it, she could tell. His expression was understanding; he didn't seem in the slightest disappointed.

And it was that, the fact he put her first, over his own preference, wishes, whatever, that made her think again. Why be afraid? He'd said he'd never hurt her, and that meant whatever wild thing was going on at this sex shindig, John would be there to protect her, and guard her limits. How the hell could she doubt him?

He'd keep her safe and, oh lord, she'd have a story to tell afterwards!

'No! Actually . . . I think I do fancy it! How often does a girl get to try the *Eyes Wide Shut* experience? Especially when there's no murder involved . . . and none of that stupid chanting. As long as it's just watching . . . I'd love to go to the party.'

John beamed at her. She'd made the right choice. She was sure of that . . . wasn't she?

'Outstanding . . . you're a bold girl, Lizzie. And I promise . . . We're strictly there as spectators.' Decisive as ever, he crumpled his napkin and then dropped it on his side plate. 'Shall we go now? You don't seem to be making much headway with that.' He nodded to her barely touched chicken. 'And I'm not really hungry either. There's always a pretty lavish buffet at these affairs, anyway, if we get peckish later. Some people like to snack while they watch the "show", and those who participate always seem to work up quite an appetite.'

'Yes, let's go.'

Before I change my mind, she thought, rising from her seat.

The limousine wove down a long, dark country lane, sometimes barely squeezing through between high, straggling hedges. At other times, they broke out into more open country, cruising between fields bounded by walls and lower hedges, the pastoral view dusted with magic by a high, brilliant moon.

John seemed to be lost in thought, and didn't speak, though from time to time, he smiled at her in the hushed intimacy of the back of the car, and once or twice squeezed her hand, which he was holding.

After what must have been a little more than twenty minutes, a pair of imposing gates hove into view, and Jeffrey the chauffeur slowed the car to a halt, then jumped out and spoke into a small speakerphone set to one side, in a boundary wall. John's name alone was clearly a VIP pass, because almost immediately the gates swung smoothly open.

The car proceeded on its way, up a long and winding drive. 'Not quite as grand as Montcalm,' John remarked as they glided between lines of trees that Lizzie couldn't identify, 'but still a pretty impressive pile.'

'Do you ever go back to Montcalm?'

John's eyes glittered in the dark. His fingers tensed infinitesimally around hers. 'No, I haven't been back in years, and then only on the sly to see my mother. But that might have to change . . . My father isn't well. He'll never summon me, so it looks like I'm the one who's going to have to cave in, and visit him. If he'll see me. I'd never forgive myself if he died and we hadn't made peace.'

'Oh God, I'm so sorry.' She paused, sensing frustration and, yes, the ache of sorrow in him. 'I'm not exactly the apple of my parents' eyes, what with me dropping out and wasting the education my father cherished so much . . . But we've all come to understand each other a bit better nowadays, and I see them sometimes, and we manage to get on reasonably OK. Christmases and birthdays mostly.'

'That's good. I'm glad. You should never burn bridges. I wish I hadn't now.'

'Surely he cares for you deep down?' She twisted her wrist, to hold and squeeze his hand.

'I don't know. The things I did . . . have done . . . He's a proud man. Entrenched in old-school, aristocratic views. In his mind, I shamed him irreparably. And I suppose I did . . . And I let him down in other ways too. He was furious when I didn't want to live the life he had planned for me. Joining his regiment, being part of the county set, marrying the fertile young daughter of one of his old army friends . . . and then I topped it all off by marrying a woman old enough to be my mother, and destroying his hopes of passing the title down the line of one of his sons.'

Lizzie frowned. But John had brothers, didn't he?

He was watching her in the flickering light of torches that lined the drive, his face more troubled than she'd ever seen it. He answered the frown without her having to ask. 'My elder brother's wife couldn't have any more children after their daughter was born. My niece is a fabulous woman and very capable, but of course she can't inherit. And my younger brother is gay, something the old man refuses to accept consciously, although I think underneath he knows the score.'

'Oh dear . . . no wonder he's angry.' So many complications. So much baggage. It made the little ups and downs of her own life seem simple and easily negotiated by comparison.

A million questions surged to Lizzie's lips, and she would have had a hard time suppressing them, and minding her own business as she knew she must, but at that moment they broke through the trees and the drive widened and curved in a semi-circle before a house that was indeed a 'grand pile'.

Pale stone gleamed in floodlighting, the roof crenelated like a castle, great windows like rows of aristocratic disdainful eyes glaring out.

Now wasn't the time to quiz John about anything.

Least of all his future marriage plans.

The night was balmy and warm but John saw Lizzie shudder as she settled the delicate gold chain of her little evening bag on her shoulder.

Was she cold? Was she nervous? Worse, did she despise him? For his implied cruelty? In his father's eyes, he'd brought shame on the family, but John knew he could, should have healed the rift, tried harder. Been the bigger man. Been kinder and made allowances. And yet he'd hadn't and he'd been unyielding, and denied the old man even a chance to effect a rapprochement.

She probably thinks I'm a cruel bastard. Maybe I am? Why does she make me question myself after all this time?

He'd always tried to avoid this moral 'black spot' of his by running his business empire ethically, and being a silent yet extravagant philanthropist. But no amount of charitable donations, and secret funding of Montcalm, would ever make a stubborn old man happy . . . and maybe it was unforgivable to have left it so late?

'What is it?'

He jumped at the sound of her voice, and realised he'd been wool-gathering.

'Nothing . . . I was just wondering if I'd done the right thing, bringing you here?'

The simple answer, but not irrelevant. The final confirmation of his suspicions about her had rocked him. Even though it *was* exactly what he'd expected. He'd guessed that she wasn't the accomplished call girl who'd done every sexual thing under the sun, and who wouldn't turn a hair at a gathering like this.

More guilt swept through him, Lizzie-guilt. There was a big difference between suspecting something and having it confirmed. Far from being an escort, she was a fresh young woman who probably wasn't all that experienced, despite her intoxicating enthusiasm and a natural sensuality that rendered him awestruck and rigid with yearning for her.

But it was more than that.

His friends here were sophisticated, and good people, despite their recherché appetites. In a feast of BDSM, there wouldn't be anything here tonight to really hurt anybody, just intense, rarefied pleasure. But he was still swamped by an urge to protect Lizzie, to whisk her away to some safe stronghold and cherish her.

'Are you really sure about this?' He grabbed her hand, feeling idiotic, like a boy on his first date, scared that the most gorgeous girl in school would suddenly change her mind. 'You don't have to do this just to please me . . . I mean, I think you'll enjoy yourself, but if you have doubts, any doubts at all, we needn't bother. We can go back to the hotel.'

Shit, she thinks you're a complete idiot now!

'We're here . . . and you promised me a movie experience. Let's give it a whirl, shall we?' Imperious, she drew him forward, flashing him a smile, then turning that full-beam beauty on the security men standing at the door. 'I'll tell you if I don't like it, and we can skedaddle then, eh?'

John knew he was an articulate negotiator. He wouldn't have achieved what he had done without persuasive, silver-tongued skills. But he was lost for words. Awed by this beautiful young woman, years his junior, blown away by her poise. If she felt any apprehension, she didn't show it. Her façade of confidence was as spectacular as his own.

Huge pride filled him as they walked forward into the vestibule. The security men's eyes followed Lizzie, and even the imperturbable butler who greeted them, taking her pashmina, seemed impressed as he offered them their masks on a silver tray.

John felt as if he was ten feet tall. He'd escorted some exquisite women in his time, and sometimes to events like this, but never before had he experienced this primitive thrill. The knowledge that the most splendid woman of the evening had chosen him to squire her.

Oh dear God, what's happening to me?

But as she turned to him, a soft smile of pleasure on her face at the sight of the pretty carnival mask in her hand, John Smith was as confused as he was filled with wonder and lust.

18

Belle of the Ball

'It matches my dress. How on earth did you manage that?'

The eye mask was a gleaming, creamy gold, covered in damask silk with an edging of delicate lace. It wasn't an absolute exact match for her frock, but it was only a few shades off. How the hell had they known to have one ready to go with a dress she'd only bought that afternoon?

'I texted the hostess a picture of your dress while you were showering and asked her to pick out the best mask to go with it.' John reached for his own mask, which was plain black silk with no trim. It still looked stunning, though, as he fastened ties at the back of his head, dramatic and dangerous, and a stark foil for his golden angelic colouring. 'Here, let me help you,' he offered, taking the golden mask from her hand and moving around behind her.

Unsurprisingly, it fit perfectly too, and John's fingers were deft and gentle, fastening it in place without disturbing her carefully arranged hair. Satisfied with it, he drew her towards a long mirror that hung on one wall, presumably placed so guests could check their appearance before they joined the party.

Lizzie caught her breath, her lingering doubts evaporating. What a couple they made. John elegant and tall in his dark suit, snowy shirt and plain dark tie. He wasn't in evening dress, but he cut a perfect figure all the same. Beside him, she should have seemed an ordinary girl . . . but she didn't. She didn't even seem to be herself with this new look. A princess stood beside her prince, taller and straighter and more stylish than she'd ever looked before, even though her shoes weren't the most toweringly high.

It was difficult to see his expression behind the mask, but Lizzie could have sworn John was just as stunned as she was. He opened his mouth, as if to say something, then shut it again, just smiling.

Beside her, the security man said, 'Your phones, please, if you would. And, of course, any cameras.' He proffered the tray again.

Of course, they wouldn't want anyone sneaking risqué photographs at an event like this, even if people were masked. Lizzie took her phone out of her bag, but felt a pang. It was irrational, but what if something happened? What if Brent rang? Despite being drenched in John's presence, thoughts of her friend still surfaced in her mind. He'd told her to go, to enjoy herself . . . or he'd be cross with her. But still she couldn't help worrying about him, and how brittle he'd seemed lately.

She turned to John, watching her from behind his mask, mysterious and inscrutable. She could almost imagine he'd read her thoughts, the impression she so often seemed to get from him.

'Shall we?' He offered her his arm and she slid her hand under it, relishing its solidity. They were in a dream, but he was real beside her. The man who'd touched her and pleasured her and let her see new things. She'd never felt inferior to him – she didn't have that kind of complex – but she acknowledged that knowing him had changed and broadened her horizons.

Even when he was gone, she would never be the same.

They entered a vast, high-ceilinged hall, flanked by pillars that supported a balcony above. Soft classical music was playing in the background, but she couldn't have put a name to it, and there was a lively hum of voices as a counterpoint. Advancing into the room, they were greeted with discreet smiles, and the occasional 'Hello, nice to see you again,' aimed at John. The masks were obviously a formality. Everybody seemed to know everybody else, but John's hand over hers, where it clasped his arm, seemed to induce a protective field of safety and confidence around her. She didn't feel shy.

It was a diverse gathering. Many people were in formal evening dress, but just as many were in cocktail wear, most of the men in the sort of suits that had become a major turn-on for Lizzie since she'd met John. A waiter appeared beside them, offering a selection of drinks on a tray, Champagne, glasses of what looked like whisky and gin, and also softer stuff, fruit juice and water. Lizzie took a Champagne, resolving it would be just one, to take the edge off her nerves. She couldn't help grinning when she looked beyond the tray. The masked waiter was bare chested and wearing leather trousers. She would've thought him a stunning hunk if she hadn't already been with the most handsome man present.

Taking a sip of Champagne, she looked further into the room. 'OK?' said John beside her, running the backs of his fingers down her bare arm.

'Yes . . . fine . . . This is all very glamorous, isn't it?' Her gaze flitted hither and thither as she trembled at his touch.

'And . . . um . . . interesting too,' she added, eyes widening.

There was more than just posh evening wear on show. Observing the throng more closely, she saw fetish wear too. Men and women in leather and vinyl. Corsets. Cut-outs. Collars. Chains. Masks that were far more forbidding than their own party-wear versions. Gimps and executioners. Dominatrices and masters.

'Good to see you again, John,' said a low, husky voice from just behind them.

They turned to find a stunning blonde smiling at them. She was quite tall, and her hair was a beautiful cap of platinum curls. Her gown was strangely retro, power wear from the 1980s almost, with big, big shoulders and flounces. With it she wore long, tight black satin gloves that reached above the elbow, and her mask was glittering with precious stones.

'And to see you too, Joanna.' Lizzie watched John's face closely, looking for tell-tales. Was this a former lover of his? She was certainly beautiful enough, and her confident presence was breath-taking. 'I'd like you to meet Bettie, a close friend of mine.'

Smiling at his use of her *nom de voyage*, she felt the touch of his hand on her back as pure energy. Her confidence surged again. He was proud of her. His eyes told her he was getting a thrill, presenting her like this, as if she were some special goddess, just as exalted as the glamorous Joanna.

'Lovely to meet you, Bettie.' The blonde paragon caught her in a brief, but surprisingly warm hug. 'Are you a regular at dos like these? I'm sure we haven't met before.'

'No, this is my first time. John teased me with the prospect of an *Eyes Wide Shut* experience and it was just too tempting to pass up.'

Joanna grinned, suddenly looking much younger and far

less intimidating. 'Ah, I remember my first time . . . It was like being Alice in twisted Wonderland. But luckily I had a man just as wise and wonderful as your John to guide me through . . . and I've never looked back.' A fond look crept into the blonde woman's face. A look of love.

'Where is he, by the way?' said John, glancing around.

'Oh, he's paddling some slave or other in the cellar, I think . . . or fucking him, I don't know. I watched for a while then I fancied a wander around.'

Lizzie sipped her wine quickly, not really tasting it, even though it was luscious. Clearly, Joanna was far from the jealous type. The blonde gave her a searching look. Had her shock been so obvious? What a faux pas. This was supposed to be any anything goes sex party; it didn't do to react like an outraged virgin.

'I think I'd better go and check on him now, though,' Joanna said cheerfully. 'Kevin has a habit of getting swept away on a wave of his own bullshit sometimes. It's probably about time I brought him down to earth again.' She winked. 'Maybe give him a taste of the medicine he's dishing out.' She squeezed Lizzie's arm. 'Enjoy this gorgeous man, kiddo. Ciao!'

They watched Joanna glide away, elegant and confident, like a queen. 'Is she a dominatrix?' Lizzie asked, gathering her own confidence. The woman was a beauty, but wasn't she one too? Every now and again, she intercepted admiring glances her way.

John smiled, his hand flexing against her back as if he'd noticed her little moment, and wanted to reassure her. 'Sometimes . . . yes . . . but like a lot of people who enjoy pain and pleasure games, she's a switch. She makes a beautifully composed submissive on occasion.'

Lizzie could see that. Her own conclusions seemed to tally with those who really played. You could still be strong, even if you submitted to someone and let them spank you. And people didn't always want the same thing, all the time. She still had to ask the question, though.

'Have you punished her?'

'Yes, a couple of times, as part of impromptu scenarios.' His shrewd blue eyes narrowed, 'And no, in case you were going to ask, I've never fucked her. She and Kevin do have a fairly open marriage, though.'

Does he think I'm jealous? Why would he care if I am?

They wandered along through the party. It seemed convivial, and relaxed, but quite normal at first . . . until they passed through another, smaller reception room, and encountered a gathered group, who seemed to be all observing the same thing. The avid watchers seemed happy to open their circle and let in newcomers, however.

A woman in a gorgeous electric blue evening dress was bent face down over a table, with her frock pulled up and folded over her back. Her bare bottom was striped with crimson red, lurid against the paleness of her skin, and she was being rogered furiously by a completely naked man wearing only tight-fitting black hood. Somehow he was managing to perform with his hands bound behind his back and his vision obscured by the mask. His bottom was red too, and the chain attached to the collar round his neck was held by another woman sitting beside the couple, on the table.

Lizzie's heart pounded as she watched the moaning woman scrabble at the table as the hooded man laboured away inside her. Her feelings were as confused as her body was excited. Did she want to be the woman being fucked?

Or the woman in charge? The one in a short black dress, holding the chain? The dominant girl's eyes glittered behind her mask, and her face was flushed. It was easy to imagine her demanding service from any man that took her fancy any minute now.

Or any woman.

Lizzie wondered. In this world of fluid sexuality, anything would go. She didn't feel threatened, but somehow, she wasn't ready to plunge in. Turning her head, she caught John's eye and realised he was watching her, not the performance. Their gazes locked.

What do you want? Do you want to show me off that way?

He didn't answer, and his expression grew guarded for a moment, then he smiled and caught her arm. 'How about we find the buffet, eh? We didn't really do justice to our dinner, and suddenly I'm hungry.'

'Me too.' It was true, she realised. She was hungry. And she felt lighter, somehow, too. As if a pressure were released. John really did expect nothing of her here, save that she enjoy herself; and if that meant simply observing the various spectacles rather than becoming a part of them, well, that was fine.

They strolled through the next room, and the next. The house seemed to be an enormous labyrinth of luxurious furnishings and beautiful works of art, and everywhere they looked there were human tableaux too. Men spanking women. Men fucking women. Women sitting like queens in antique armchairs while men pleasured them with their mouths. Men on their knees. Everywhere. Lizzie noted that the percentage of dominant women tonight was higher than that of men, but she had no way of knowing if that was always the case.

She asked John when they were settled in the spacious salon where the buffet was set out, with plates of delicious hors d'oeuvres and other titbits, and glasses of iced water.

'It varies. Sometimes it's all female subs. Sometimes it's like tonight, with women mostly in charge.'

Caught in the act of popping another heavenly prawn confection into her mouth, Lizzie felt as if she'd been hit by a thunderbolt. Something in the way he'd said it seemed to suggest . . . invite . . . provoke.

'So which do you prefer?' she flung out, then concentrated on her food, waiting for his answer.

John took a sip from his glass, his beautiful throat undulating. He'd slipped off his tie and put it in his pocket a short while ago, and Lizzie loved this look of the rakish masked man with an open collar. He was powerful, yet the triangle of bare flesh offered a strange vulnerability too.

'You know my tastes . . . I like to play the dominant. I think it's my natural forte.' He paused, took another sip, then set the glass down on a side table. 'But I have been known to switch too . . . for the right woman.'

It couldn't have been a clearer clarion call to challenge if he'd pulled a white glove out of his pocket and flung it down.

In a room where people were talking, where music played, and there was even the occasional clatter of cutlery or glassware, a cone of silence seemed to descend around them. Lizzie wondered if her heart had stopped too.

John's eyes were clear, blue as the sky, full of his message. *Take it. Take the power. It's yours.*

'Is that a fact?' she said softly, gazing right into his eyes, not flinching, not blinking, not backing down.

'Yes.' He glanced downwards for a moment, barely for a

picosecond, but he might as well have fallen to his knees and kissed her shoe.

Lizzie nodded, acknowledging what had barely been visible. She put aside her plate. She no longer needed food. Or water or wine or anything. She was incandescent with energy. She could do anything.

'I've had enough of this. Let's walk.' She rose to her feet and began walking towards a door at the opposite end of the room. She hadn't a clue where it led to, but she was the Belle of the Ball, she was in charge, she would compel a space somewhere to be suitable for her needs.

Head high, she glided as Joanna before her had glided, but this time, she knew she had a man walking dutifully behind her, in her thrall.

They found themselves in a wide corridor, with a fine Persian carpet runner, and doors stood wide along the length of the space. As if she had willed it, a room presented itself, a smallish, intimate space, something like a private study, lined with bookshelves, a small fire burning, leather-upholstered armchairs before it. It was a man's sanctum, obviously, but she would rule it. She swept in, heading for the fireplace, aware of John behind her.

'Close the door,' she commanded softly.

Enclosed in the space, she felt her confidence falter momentarily, but glancing around and spying a leather-topped desk, she braced up, regaining her power.

Amongst newspapers, books, various desk paraphernalia, she spied a ruler. A simple wooden strip, not whippy like John's plastic one, but fit for purpose.

She hadn't even looked at him since he'd followed her in, but she knew he'd seen it too.

Turning, she regarded him, hoping her expression was

stern enough without her looking like an idiot. The mask helped, but she was on new ground here, in yet another new world. She had to trust her instincts.

John stood by the desk, his own expression inscrutable, impossible to decipher behind the plain black domino.

'And what are you looking at?' Lizzie said softly, the instincts she was relying on guiding her along the path John had always shown her. No shouting. No histrionic strutting. That approach seemed to be working quite nicely for some of the dominas out in the party, but she knew it wasn't her way.

John's eyes dropped immediately, and he shifted position, his hands clasped behind his back. She imagined him back in his public school days for a moment, up before the beak. How adorable he must have looked back then, a golden young Adonis.

'That's better.' She advanced upon him, but not too closely. Even in her heels, he was taller than her, and distance granted a better perspective. Breathing evenly, she cast around for a key, something to hang the scene on, and almost instantly it came to her.

'You were stringing me along, weren't you? You knew I wasn't an escort, but you still let me believe that you bought my story.'

He nodded in answer, and she realised he was waiting for permission to speak. It was amazing how completely he'd slipped into his role. She knew he was acting, and that it was all a façade, but wasn't that what their games were all about? She felt a momentary pang, wishing for something real amongst the theatrics, then stiffened her spine again.

'You may speak . . . but only when you're kneeling.'

His head shot up; there was shock in his eyes. She quelled

him with a small frown, and he sank onto his knees, all grace and beauty.

'Yes, mistress. I knew.'

A strange intoxication bubbled in her veins like the Champagne they'd drunk.

Mistress.

Suddenly she could be her, that dominant woman.

'For how long?'

'For quite a while, mistress. I suspected you were inexperienced. I sensed you were acting.'

There was no trace of humour in his voice; the words were quiet and neutral. Passive.

'Were you laughing at me, all the time?'

'No . . . no, not at all, mistress. I was in awe of you. Filled with wonder.'

He lifted his head a moment, and his eyes were bright. She believed him. And when he shuffled just a little on his knees, his jacket slid sideways a little and she saw his erection, enormous and rampant. She glared at that then, too, even though it made lust surge in her belly; and at the same time she wanted to laugh. Good God, he was an amazing actor too. Somehow he even managed to manufacture a blush, seeing her look at his cock.

'I didn't give you permission to admire me, or to get hard.' She moved in close now that he was kneeling, and stood right up against him. He barely had to sway to kiss her crotch.

'I'm sorry, mistress,' he whispered and, unable to resist, she let her fingers settle on his blond hair, loving its softness and silkiness. Sliding her hand down the side of his masked face, she cupped his jaw, and he turned in towards her touch, like a puppy, nuzzling for affection.

'I just don't know what I'm going to do with you.'

It was the literal truth, but she managed to inject a note of the weary schoolmistress into her voice. It seemed to work, because he bowed his head a little lower.

'Any suggestions?' She took a lock of his hair in her fingers, not pulling, but creating a bit of tension.

'You could beat me, mistress. I saw a suitable implement on the desk.'

'Do you want me to beat you?' She increased the tension, just a smidgen.

'I . . . I don't know. Only if it's your will, mistress.'

A sweet high thrill rushed through Lizzie's body, whirling through her sex, her heart and her brain. That hesitation, it was like a thousand words to her. She *had* actually rattled him, she was sure of it.

'Perhaps it is.' She swirled the lock of hair around her fingers, then released it. 'But first you must honour me.' Taking a step back, she plucked at the hem of her shimmering gilded dress and inched it up, sliding it over her thighs and her stocking tops, until the silky triangle of her coffee-coloured thong of lace and satin was revealed. 'Kiss it,' she commanded, 'but just a kiss. No funny stuff.'

Leaning forward, he pressed his lips to her pubis, his mouth against the delicate undergarment. She felt him breath in deeply, inhaling her fragrance, the scent of her perfume and the odour of her pussy.

'This slave begs to speak,' he whispered against her.

'You may, but it will cost you. And remember, my hand is not skilled with the implement. I could hurt you quite badly.' She wouldn't, of course, because she'd err on the side of safety, but the threat seemed effective because he gasped.

'This slave begs to pleasure his mistress with his lips and tongue.'

Lizzie almost faltered, her senses filled with the knowledge of what John Smith could do to her with his lips and tongue. He could make her into mindless, moaning putty in the space of moments. She'd have to be careful, but the temptation was just too great.

'Proceed.' She adjusted her stance a little, setting her thighs further apart.

Bowing his head first, as if he were a combatant in some obscure martial art, John set to his task, hooking his thumbs in the strips of lace-covered elastic that stretched around her hips. He peeled the flimsy garment down with slow reverence, working it over the tops of her hold-up stockings, then down to her knees. Looking up to her for permission to go on, his eyes were limpid pools of midnight blue, the pupils huge.

She nodded, and he skinned the thong right down to her ankles, then held still as she leaned her weight on him, grasping his shoulders as she stepped out of the garment, first one foot, then the other.

19

His Mistress's Will

The desk was just at her back, and Lizzie settled against it, making John shuffle forward on his knees. She parted her thighs a little, then buried her hands in his hair, urging him forward. In a weird, hysterical moment, she remembered being in a school play, years ago, and uttering the words, 'Attend me, slave', when she'd been cast as an exotic princess. It was a good job John was otherwise occupied, or her veneer of power would have been shattered by him seeing her fighting not to giggle.

All thoughts of past amateur dramatics fled away when he set himself to his task. His deft, gentle thumbs parted her sex lips and, his breath hot on her pussy, he began to lick her slowly and methodically. He gave the best head she'd ever had, she already knew that. But he seemed to be trying to outdo all previous performances.

He flicked, he teased, he fluttered his tongue, and he sucked. He panted against her sex, tantalising her with the flow of air, then returning to more assertive tactics. Pleasure gathered like a shimmering plasma in her loins, and without the desk against her buttocks and her grip on

John's hair, she might have tumbled to the carpet, felled by its intensity.

And yet, in the gathering euphoria, a still voice suddenly spoke.

You devil, you wicked devil . . . you're supposed to be the submissive here, and you're still trying to get the better of me!

She did laugh then and, despite the barrelling urge to orgasm, and orgasm hard, she gripped locks of his hair hard and tugged him off her. There was a delicious triumph in his yelp of pain and the blurred look in his eyes.

'Not yet, you sly devil,' she said, still holding his hair, her pussy only inches from his lips, so shiny with her moisture. 'I know what you were doing . . . trying to make me lose it. Do you think I'm so easy to get the better of?' He shook his head minutely, constrained by her hold on him. 'I'll come when I'm ready, Mr Smith, do you hear me? And not before. Now get up off your knees and stop grovelling around down there.' She released him and, as he sprang to obey, her dress slithered down around her thighs, denying him sight of her.

John stood a few feet away, head bowed. Lizzie had a feeling he was laughing inside, just as she still was, but his deportment as a submissive was perfect.

But what to do now? She had to hold her nerve. Casting around, she saw the ruler again. Well, now was as good a time as any to give it a try. She just hoped she didn't really, really hurt him because she didn't have much of a clue how to wield it with precision.

'Right. Across the desk,' she instructed him, snatching up the whippy strip of wood.

John glanced up, eyes wide behind his mask. She wondered if he'd sensed her doubts, in the way he was so prone to, reading her. Eyeing him steadily, she schooled her own expression as best she could, glad to be masked herself, so any lack of authority wouldn't be as apparent. John looked down again, moving to comply with her instructions.

'Wait. Take your jacket off first.'

He slipped off the fabulous item of tailoring, and set it aside. As was his preference, his suit was a three piece, and as he leant over the front of the leather-topped desk, the trim fit of his waistcoat only seemed to emphasise the firm, muscular rounds of his buttocks beneath his perfectly cut trousers.

Bare or clothed? What to do? Acknowledging her own inexperience, Lizzie decided it was probably better to let him keep the protection of a couple of layers of clothing. This was more a symbolic act than anything else. She didn't want to hurt him too much, or land more than a handful of blows. Her own desire was too ravenous for her to spend long on rituals. She wanted that huge erection of his inside her before too long.

John settled into his position, somehow managing to look graceful and strong even when at a disadvantage. He laid his bent arms forward out of the way, and rested his cheek against the surface of the desk, his face towards her. There was no apprehension in his expression. He was all calm. His eyes were closed, his long, thick eyelashes lying like shadows.

She didn't have to say anything, because mistresses didn't, but still she spoke. 'Are you ready?'

'Yes, mistress.' His voice was soft and though without inflection, it was just as thrilling as if he'd been lying in bed with her, about to possess her and fuck her.

I'm the one who's all nerves. I'm the one who's scared.

Lizzie smiled to herself at the irony, but just admitting it gave her confidence. She stepped forward, and laid the ruler flat against the crown of John's buttocks, letting it rest there a moment. With no idea quite how hard to hit, she landed a preliminary stroke, aiming for the point where the ruler had rested. He uttered not a sound, but she saw the muscles of his upper arms tense beneath the fine cotton of his shirt.

So far, so good.

It was surprisingly difficult *not* to hit hard. Lizzie let fly again, and again, with a little more force this time, focusing on the same location. It was safe. Prominent. Easier to concentrate on the centre of his gorgeous, tight bottom. She didn't want the ruler to wander about and land a cruel stroke on his most tender zone.

She'd meant to give him a few spanks, just four or five, but the process was strangely hypnotic. There was a dark thrill in watching his response. She saw him grit his teeth. Heard him gasp out loud. A wicked devil danced inside her, fed on power.

After the tenth blow, the power grew too much to contain. Its quality changed, transmuting and gathering in her sex, demanding service. She almost growled, imagining herself clutching the sore buttocks of her lover as he plunged into her, fulfilling his mistress's will.

'Oh fuck this! I want you! Move yourself,' she cried, tossing away the ruler and pushing at John's haunch and making him gasp again. As he stood up, pushing himself away from the desk, Lizzie launched herself forward, perched herself on its surface, shuffling into position and hauling up her skirt. 'Now make yourself useful, slave. Fuck me! Fuck me hard!'

She was laughing as she stretched her thighs open, inviting him.

'As you wish, mistress.' He was smiling, though. His eyes were bright and wild, and there was a dash of pink across his cheekbones. Were his other cheeks just as rosy? Lizzie sincerely hoped so.

'Oh, bollocks to that!' She pulled at his shirt sleeve. 'You know you've really been in charge all the time, you sneaky bastard.' She grinned at him, pleased to see him slip his hand into his waistcoat pocket and fish out a condom.

'Not completely,' said John, tossing the contraceptive on her bare belly as he worked on his belt and zip, and then his underwear. 'Does this look like I was in control . . .?' He turned away from her a moment, holding up his shirt-tails and pushing down his trousers and underwear to reveal the muscular rounds of his bottom, blotched with angry red.

'Oh, you public school boys, you know you love that sort of thing!' It was an impressive sight, though, bizarrely stirring her hunger for him.

'Apparently, I do.' He turned to face her, his hugely erect cock all the signal either of them needed. He pointed it right at her, jiggling it rudely before grabbing the condom and rolling it on in a hurry. 'At least he does.' He proffered his enrobed length to her, moving in close between her spread thighs.

'Who's in charge now?' gasped Lizzie, pulling him closer, wiggling so he could find her entrance. As he pushed in, she let out a low, happy cry, working against him, grabbing at his punished bottom to drag him in deep, loving his gasp at the pain revisited.

'Who the fuck cares?' he replied, a laugh in his voice as he shoved hard, plunging in deep. 'I think this one's a draw. We're both in charge. Everyone's a winner.'

As he reached between their bodies, to find her clit, Lizzie knew she was. It took but a couple of haphazard rubs and she was coming, shouting his name.

'Yes!' John shouted, as if it were his own pleasure, and half out of her head in the middle of an orgasm, Lizzie's ecstatic cries turned to laughter, just as ecstatic. The devil, the bastard, he'd got his way, exactly as he'd expected and just as she'd known he would.

Riding the delicious waves, she clutched him harder, her fingertips gouging the site of his punishment, her back arched as if compelling every inch of herself to every inch of him. She had no idea if it was the pain, or the intensity of their bodies slamming together, but as she soared again, he rewarded her with a harsh uncouth shout, and the so familiar hammer of his hips as he hit his climax inside her. The mighty old desk, solid oak or some such wood, rocked and slid slightly as they strained and bounced and pounded.

As it creaked in protest, they flew again, kissing and groaning mutual nonsense as they came.

'God, I could do with a drink. How about you?' said John cheerfully, straightening his clothing a little while later, and then dropping the used condom into the waste bin of whoever this great mansion belong to. Lizzie was on her hands and knees on the floor. She'd managed to retrieve her thong and wriggle into it, but she couldn't find the ruler. They must have kicked it out of reach when they were thrashing about in passion.

'Well, I don't know where it is.' She straightened up. 'Do you think they'll suspect anything?'

Tugging his waistcoat into place, John came across to her, and gave her a kiss on the cheek before brushing strands of hair away from her face. They'd both removed their masks, knocked half awry by kisses, and Lizzie touched the disaster zone of her lost hairstyle ruefully, then rummaged in her little evening bag – which she seemed to have dropped some time in the previous century – for her comb. She'd have to wear it loose for the rest of the night. Given what most of the rest of the guests were probably getting up to, a suddenly collapsed chignon wouldn't merit a second glance.

'I think our hosts would be astonished, and a bit disappointed, if they didn't find half of their rulers and other applicable instruments missing.' He reached out, took the comb from her and moved around behind her to run it deftly through her hair, teasing out tangles. 'It was probably left on the desk for the express purpose of prompting a scene like ours.'

Lizzie almost sighed with contentment. John's hands were gentle yet capable, combing her hair as if he'd been tending to it for years, then smoothing it with his hands. When he stepped away and handed the little comb to her, she checked her appearance with her compact mirror.

Her face was a bit flushed, and her lips were pink from kissing rather than from lip-stain now, but her hair looked spot-on, just as she would have arranged it herself.

'There's a career for you in hairdressing if the tycoon thing ever falls through.'

John beamed, running his hands through his own blond curls, and not doing too bad a job of tidying them either. 'Well, that's good to know. It's always handy to have skills to fall back on.' With a sudden, sultry look, he glanced towards the edge of the desk. 'And you'd make a superb dominatrix, if you ever decided to turn your hand to it.'

'I wasn't sure if I was doing it right . . . or whether you were enjoying it. Do you . . . um . . . do that often?' She stowed away the mirror, watching John shrug back into his jacket and smooth his lapels. The sleek man of the world was back, invulnerable in his armour of perfect tailoring.

'Not often.' He picked at an imaginary speck of lint. 'And I'm not sure I've ever really enjoyed it quite so much.' His eyes were intent beneath his sandy eyebrows. 'Like I said, you have a wonderful touch. Now, come on . . . let's find that drink.' He frowned a little, as if suddenly, some knotty problem had surfaced.

Lizzie's heart ached for the distance opening up between them. She knew the gulf would come, and sooner rather than later, but still it hurt. 'And the buffet too. I think I'm hungry again.' She did feel peckish. It seemed crazy. But food was always a sovereign comfort.

She almost laughed, but instead manufactured a smile for him.

'Are you all right, Lizzie?' he said, suddenly softer.

'Yes, fine . . . it's just all this stuff . . .' She gestured around. 'It's very intense . . . and I really am hungry.'

'Me too. Let's go. Masks on, sweetheart.' He closed the gap between them – the physical gap – and helped her with the golden mask. When his own was in place, he led her to the door.

In the corridor, he tucked her hand in his arm. Lizzie had no idea of the direction back to the buffet, the house was so vast, but John struck out along the broad corridor, flashing her a smile. They walked for a little way, and she began to recognise the pictures they'd seen before, and hear the sound of voices from the buffet room, but almost as they reached the door, the dignified butler approached them from a corridor running at right angles to the one they were heading along.

'Miss Page? I wonder if you could come quickly to the morning room. There's been a call on your phone . . . I think it's rather important.'

Lizzie's heart froze. Her step faltered, and John's strong arm slid around her, supporting her.

Brent.

It had to be Brent.

Oh, baby, what have you done?

Fearing the worst, she hurried after the butler, with John beside her.

20

The Real World

The vending machine coffee was horrible. It didn't taste of much, and was lukewarm, but Lizzie sipped it anyway, for something to do. Beside her, John had already thrown his plastic cup in the bin.

This is the real world.

The little waiting room off the men's medical ward at the local hospital was bleak. The old building was nothing like the equally venerable building she'd left, not an hour ago, that palace of luxury and perversion where rich and sophisticated people still went about their kinky pleasures.

A nurse hurried by the open door of waiting room, and Lizzie looked up anxiously. It wasn't news for her. They'd said she could see Brent when they'd settled him down, but it was taking a worrying while.

'Shall I make enquiries again?'

John reached for her free hand and held it tight. His beautiful face was grave, but it was difficult to know what he was thinking. He looked troubled, but as he didn't know Brent, it couldn't be her friend he was concerned for, could it? Perhaps he was worried about her? She had no illusions that he might harbour deep feelings for her, and she knew that she was just a passing fancy to him, but everything about him told her he was a compassionate man at heart, for all his business ruthlessness and sexual peccadillos, and he probably did feel a genuine, general sympathy for her and for Brent.

'Maybe in a minute?' she suggested. They hadn't really been waiting all that long. It just seemed like an eternity.

'Sure?'

She nodded, wishing she could make some kind of conversation with him. But she couldn't. This *was* the real world of unpleasant things happening and, to her, he was a creature of fantasy, a golden prince from her wildest dream.

He gave her hand a squeeze, and offered a small, strangely confused looking smile, then glanced away into the middle distance, leaving her to her troubled thoughts, and returning to his own. When she saw him frowning, she returned her attention to her unappetising plastic cup.

Back at the mansion, the call she'd been summoned to was one of many. Several had gone to voicemail, but her phone had kept ringing and the butler had finally answered in her stead. And then sped off to fetch her at the double.

Brent's voice had been slurred and indistinct in the messages. Sounding drunk, but somehow more. The words 'I just wanted to say goodbye' had chilled her to the marrow . . . but at the same time galvanised her to action. She'd called their landlady, who lived close by, and 999, in quick succession, all the time cursing herself for not being there. Then she called Shelley, and imparted the news as calmly as she could, so as not to upset the other girl. Shelley got upset anyway, and said she'd be on the next train home.

I should have seen it coming. I should never have left him.

And yet, hadn't Brent insisted she go? Oh God, maybe

this was why? He'd wanted them both out of the way to do this. She'd known his sorrow about his lost love was deep. Why hadn't she guessed he might seek the ultimate solace? The last comfort, beyond anything she could do to make him feel better.

All the while she'd been making calls, she'd been aware of John also in action. Summoning Jeffrey, making calls himself, frowning. It'd all seemed as if at a distance. When she'd finally leapt up, ready to leave, she'd swayed and he'd caught her and sat her down again. Then put a glass of brandy into her hand.

'Drink this. Sit a minute. Jeffrey is bringing the car round, but I'm just going to see if I can find someone. We might be able to get there much faster. Just hold on a moment.' He'd given her a hurried kiss on the forehead, then left the room, almost running.

Ten minutes later, they'd been in the back of a rather splendid helicopter.

'Is this yours?' she'd asked distractedly, as John had helped her buckle up, ready for take-off.

'No, alas . . . though I'd like one. It belongs to a friend who was also at the party. He's put it at our disposal for the time being. Here, you'll need these . . .' He'd passed her a headset.

Under other circumstances, it would have been a thrilling flight, her first ever, and she'd have been desperately curious about the 'friend'. But all she could do was offer thanks, and sit anxiously in her seat, willing the craft to whirl its way as fast as it could to their destination, not caring about the how and why of logistics. She hadn't a clue about such things and with Brent's slurred farewells in her head, she had no mind-space to care. Dimly, at one stage, she'd realised she was wearing John's jacket, with her pashmina round her neck and shoulders. She must have shivered on the way out to the helicopter and he'd bundled her up, but she simply couldn't remember it happening.

They'd landed in the park at the Waverley. It was the small hours of the morning, but many lights were lit in the bedrooms, as if people were peering out to see what the fuss was. John sped her towards a hired chauffeur-driven car that was waiting to bring them here, to the hospital.

It had all taken barely an hour, and they'd been sitting here twenty minutes.

Lizzie made to set her cup down on the floor beside her, but John took it from her and disposed of it. Returning, he took her hand again.

'Don't worry. They said they got to him in time, thanks to your quick action,' he said, rubbing her hand between his. Lizzie felt a hysterical urge to laugh; it was just what someone in a melodramatic film might do. 'He'll be fine.'

His voice was so quiet and composed, and his blue eyes were intent. For a moment she seemed to drown in them, even as her spirits lifted. Good grief, was he hypnotising her or something? It was ridiculous and impossible. How could Brent be OK, just because John *said* he would be? And yet, somehow, she felt more hope.

Swift, smart footsteps made her look around, breaking the spell that wasn't a spell.

'Miss Aitchison? Would you like to see Brent for few moments? He's very tired and naturally he's feeling a bit battered from having his stomach pumped, but I'm sure he'd like to see you for a minute.' The kind-faced nurse glanced from her to John. 'Just one of you, though. He's very sleepy and he needs to be quiet.'

'I'll wait here.' John's hand slid beneath Lizzie's elbow as she rose, as if anticipating the dizzy feeling that gripped her.

'Um . . . thanks . . . but you've no need to hang around, if you don't want to.'

What am I doing? Why am I sending him away?

'I'll wait here,' he repeated, giving her arm an encouraging squeeze. The look on his face was that of an old-fashioned, admonishing uncle. How bizarre that seemed, after all the passion they'd shared. It seemed like a million years since their last embrace.

'OK . . . Thanks.' In the grip of anxiety, she gave John something that looked more like a grimace than a smile and hurried after the nurse, heading for the small side ward where Brent was being treated.

Approaching the bed, she wished for John's strong arm again, but took a deep breath and braced up. Brent looked like a shattered doll lying there, hooked up to a drip and a monitor. His black hair was all awry, stuck up in curls and tufts, and his face was almost as white as the pillows and the sheet over him. Was he sleeping? She didn't know. He was very still.

When she reached the side of the bed, though, his eyes flicked open, looking weary and feverish.

'You look nice,' he said in a reedy voice. Lizzie felt a rush of relief when her friend gave her a weak attempt at a smile.

'You don't,' she blurted out, glancing quickly down at herself. She'd forgotten she was wearing her fabulous cocktail dress.

'Thanks for that.' It was clearly a struggle, but Brent maintained his feathery grin.

'You know what I mean . . . How are you feeling?' She wanted to be cross with him and demand of him what the hell he'd thought he was doing, but that seemed too cruel in his fragile state.

'Like shit . . . and don't worry, give me both barrels. I'm a fucking idiot, I know.'

Lizzie swayed, not sure what to say. How many hours had she been awake now?

'Jesus, Lizzie, get a chair. Sit down.' Brent struggled to sit up, then subsided back again.

Pulling up a hard chair, Lizzie said, 'You are an idiot, B, but I'm a poor friend. I shouldn't have dashed off like that on a sex jaunt when Shelley was away too. I should have noticed you were feeling so down. This is all my fault. I've been too obsessed with having a good time with John.'

'Don't be ridiculous.' From somewhere, Brent was finding a bit more energy. 'For one thing . . . this . . . well, it was sudden. Had some booze . . . and some . . . some other stuff. And I got a long, chatty email from some guy I know from way back. He had no idea about me and Steve and what happened and he was all "How's things with you?" and "Have you two tied the knot?" and everything just crashed down on me . . . and I lost my head.'

'Yes, but if I'd been at home . . . or Shelley . . .'

'Wouldn't have made any difference, believe me. And anyway, by accident or design, I didn't quite take enough stuff to do me in. So all it would have meant was that you'd have missed an exciting mercy dash from . . . from wherever you were.' He glanced at her dress again. 'My God, girl, that really is a posh frock. You look fucking stunning . . . what were you at, a fucking ball or something?'

'Something like that.'

Astonishingly, Brent's weary eyes sharpened. He could always sniff out wickedness and scandal, and clearly hadn't lost the facility in his current, enervated state. 'Spill it! I'm a sick man, remember. You've got to indulge me.'

Lizzie looked around. The door was still open. The other bed in the small side ward was empty, but a nurse could come in any minute.

'It was . . . it was a sort of orgy. A bit like *Eyes Wide Shut*, but much more friendly.'

Brent laughed. It was a thin one, but full of genuine surprise and amusement. Lizzie was glad and relieved to hear it.

'Right on, girl. Details! Details!' Brent glanced beyond her to the door. 'Incidentally, where is your billionaire pervert, by the way?'

'Waiting out there.'

A pang of longing gripped her. And one of guilt. Oh, for the warmth of John's arm around her, and his strong body against her for her to lean on. She was on such unsure ground here. She wasn't sure what she was doing, or how she should be. Brent had tried to kill himself, yet he was acting with a strange, forced brightness. She wanted to tell him to stop it, and to open his heart to her, so she could help him heal it. Yet she felt nervous and scared of going too deep. John would know how to act, and the best way to help Brent. He had years and far more life experience than she . . . he'd been through all sorts of mills himself. And yet, she *had* to deal with this on her own. God alone knew . . . Brent might be hiding a jealousy of the older man who'd swept her away. Not sexually, but emotionally; it was possible.

'Was he annoyed to be dragged away from his sex party?'

She looked sharply at Brent. Was she right? It was so hard to tell. He looked more exhausted than jealous, but even now, he might be pulling the wool over her eyes. He'd always been far better at performance than she was.

'No, not at all.' It was the truth. Preoccupied as she'd been, she'd still been aware of John's concern for her. It was as if he'd been able to compartmentalise the party, the pleasure they'd shared, the games, and put it all away so that he could focus solely on assisting her and helping her to get here. 'He's been great. Like an organised whirlwind. It's easy to see why he's so successful. He knows how to get things done as fast and as efficiently as possible.'

'A paragon.'

'Are you jealous?' There, the question was out.

Brent sighed, closing his eyes. Their few minutes must be up by now, and his energy level, such as it had been, was flagging.

'Maybe a little bit,' he said on a sigh, 'but I know I shouldn't be . . . I don't know . . .'

As if she'd sensed her patient under stress, the nurse bustled in. Checking Brent's vitals, she spoke to Lizzie over her shoulder. 'That's enough for now, Miss Aitchison. You can come back later today. You look as if you could do with some sleep yourself. Let your friend outside take you home. Brent will be fine with us. He needs his rest now too.'

'OK . . .' It was still hard to leave. She patted Brent's arm. 'Behave yourself. Don't be a pain and annoy the nurses.'

'Don't worry, I'll behave. See you tomorrow . . . or today . . . or whatever.'

His eyes were closed as she left the room, and there were tears in her own.

When the car reached her home, Lizzie turned to John. 'It's OK, you know. You don't have to come in. I'll be fine. I just need some sleep. I know you've got things to do . . . business or whatever.' She looked out of the window. It was morning.

She wasn't sure what time, but a watery sun was shining. 'I know you need to get back. And Shelley will be back soon too, so I won't be on my own.'

John gave her one of his steady looks. Mr Rational and Very Grown Up. 'You don't seriously think I'm just going to dump you here like a bundle of washing and go about my merry way, do you?' His arm was around her, but suddenly he squeezed her very tight. 'We either go back to the Waverley together, or I stay here with you. Which is it to be?'

'But . . .'

'No buts. Surprisingly for someone of my predilections, I don't actually like throwing my weight around all that much, but in this case, I won't accept any arguments. You can go back to being Ms Capable and Self-Sufficient tomorrow, when you've had some rest, but for the moment, I'm giving the orders. Which is it to be? Here . . . or the Waverley?'

21

Deliberations

She'd chosen here, and John was glad. She'd almost been dropping on her feet, and the nearest bed was the best bed.

And strangely, he was in it. With her. In this endearingly untidy room.

'But you don't sleep with other people,' she'd protested, eyelids drooping after he'd bundled her beneath the covers, and slid alongside her, stripped to his trunks.

'No, I don't. And I shan't this time. But I'll just lie here and think for a while. It's still rest.'

'Think about what?' He smiled. She was so stubborn and curious, even in this peculiar stressed-out situation, but before he'd even framed an answer, he'd realised she was asleep.

The bed was a queen-sized, narrow for two, but somehow, he managed to relax. Even Lizzie's luscious body, sweet and vulnerable in an oversized t-shirt, didn't disturb him for the moment. It wouldn't take much to get turned on over her; his need for her was like a constant simmer. But somehow it seemed more important, far more important, just to *be* with her for the time being, rather than to entertain thoughts of fucking her.

The curtains in her room were thick, but slices of light bisected the room, falling across the bed and also illuminating the clutter of her belongings; clothes, books, sewing paraphernalia. John had lost all sense of time. The party they'd left had begun after midnight, and they'd played. Then, there'd been their flight back across the county, time spent at the hospital. It was morning now, a new business day, and his schedule was full. But it was far more important to be here, watching over Lizzie as she slept, standing ready to be at her disposal if she needed to return to the hospital to visit her friend.

Her friend? Surely, it was more than that. John let his head fall back against the pillow as he stared at the ceiling. Why was he so jealous? Why? They both knew their relationship was fleeting, an interlude. She herself had coined the phrase 'temporary sex friends', and it was a good one.

So why the fuck are you wanting more from her, all of a sudden? You swore off all that after Clara. And it's worked . . . hasn't it? Why get these yearnings for a woman who has other commitments anyway, you blithering idiot?

Rubbing his hand through his hair, he turned carefully towards her, inching over so he wouldn't wake her up.

Without lip-tint and eyeliner, and with her black hair streaming loose across the pillow she was a far cry from Bettie Page or Audrey Hepburn, and yet, somehow, she still had a glamour for him. Her relaxed face was so young looking, reminding him that she *was* young, compared to him. Twenty-four to his forty-six. Not an insurmountable gap. Loving couples succeeded across much greater divides, but she might not want to negotiate it for the long term.

John sat up. 'What the hell . . .?'

Half-baked notions surged into his weary mind, but he fought not to go there. It was pointless and stupid. The only kind of relationship he could allow himself was one such as he'd had with Caroline, his wife; affection and expediency, nothing more. More . . . had only led to disaster, and pain.

'Fuck. Shit.'

You're an idiot man. You're an idiot. You just can't have it.

Shaken, he lay down again. He'd said he'd lie and think and that was what he'd do, turning on his side so he could see her face against the pillow, and her closed eyes, and her soft, sweet mouth. Behind those features lay a quick mind, a sense of fun, a spirit that was daring, yet honest and loyal to friends. Not without faults, but, paradoxically, all the more appealing because of them.

If he couldn't have her, he could still think about her, and secretly indulge in his fantasies. It'd be a torment, but he was powerless in the thrall of his imagination. Gingerly, he let his hand rest ever so lightly on her waist. He stopped breathing, waiting for her to stir, but she just let out a sigh, pressing her cheek against the pillow, and then settled again.

Her body was warm through the thin t-shirt, and inevitably it roused him. His cock stiffened. He couldn't turn off his desire, but it would be unthinkable to act on it.

Dreams were all he could allow himself right now, and they filled his mind, emptying it of negativity, stress, and the twists and turns of his life.

His eyelids drooped, heavy as lead, and he drifted into a dark, soft world, where paradoxically a brilliant light shined. A beautiful bright light whose name was . . . Lizzie.

There was light streaming in. What time was it?

John!

Lizzie blinked, disorientated, her mind fuzzy but for one thing . . . one person. Even before she was fully conscious, she sensed him next to her. Other stuff floated in her brain, but in her semi-dormant state, she frowned and pushed it away. Loving only the warm presence at her side, and his body touching hers.

John.

She could feel reality barrelling towards her, but she turned to him, her muzzy mind greedily snatching at wonder before fears and worries arrived. Light was flooding across them, through chinks in the curtains, illuminating a magical sight.

John, fast asleep, with the little cat Mulder curled up on his chest.

You're sleeping. How are you sleeping? I thought you said you didn't sleep with anyone else around. And you, you little furry monkey, I thought you didn't like strangers?

She didn't utter the words for fear of breaking the spell and waking the enchanted prince, and his companion, at her side. John's face was half turned away from her, cradled in his arm stretched back across the pillow, while his other hand rested on his chest, curved around Mulder's small body. A little smile played across his face and his strangely dark eyelashes lay thick against his cheekbones. Sleeping he looked a good ten years younger, if not more, and her thoughts flew back to her first reaction to him, back in the Lawns bar.

He was an angel. She breathed in, taking in the faint scent of his cologne and a hint of sweat. Their bodies were close and, even when not fucking, the proximity generated a lot of heat. She wrinkled her nose, knowing she wasn't as fresh as she might be herself.

Falling back into her body from her dream state, she cannoned into reality at last.

Brent . . . Oh, poor Brent. She'd left him on his own and he'd tried to kill himself.

Lizzie sat up, drew in a deep, quiet breath, and pulled her thoughts together. She needed to be logical and sensible. It was the only way to cope now. The only way she could stop herself screaming from the sensation of being torn in two, and shouting abuse at fate for giving something with one hand and then taking it away almost immediately. For tangling her life with that of two different men she cared deeply for, in entirely different ways.

Looking down at John, she longed to touch him and kiss him; and yet more than that. She wanted to know him, and understand him, and love him. Perhaps, with a little more time, there might have been some kind of chance with him, unlikely as it seemed. True-life fairy tales were rare, but they did happen. He seemed to care for her, and it was possible it might be more, but now she'd never know.

Brent needed her. Brent had been there for her when she'd lost her way and her confidence. He'd even made her feel better about herself sexually during their brief time as lovers. He deserved her loyalty, and her help and support. Shelley was a good friend to both of them, but didn't quite have the same bond with Brent that Lizzie did.

I have to give him all my support, with no reservations. No taint.

There would have to be no mooning about, nothing to give Brent the feeling that she was yearning to be somewhere else, with somebody else.

The man beside her stirred, frowning as if he'd sensed her decision, his slight movement disturbing Mulder. As the little cat unfurled herself and leapt lightly off the bed, a vice gripped Lizzie's heart.

But what if her decision would hurt John too?

Oh hell, life could be perverse. It could stab you with a spear of bitter irony sometimes. She ached to slide into John's arms now. Not for sex, divinely tempting as he was, but just for contact, for closeness. The chance to lie with him and talk, and begin the journey into knowing.

Come on, snap out of it, you fool. And grow up. Make the correct choice and live with it.

Silently admonishing herself, she lay down beside him, closing her eyes and keeping very still as she sensed John waking up. It would be far too complicated to let him know she'd seen him sleeping. That she'd stolen an intimacy from him he probably didn't want to give anybody, much less her.

She only hoped, as she felt him sit up beside her, in just the same cautious, edging way as she'd sat up only moment ago, that he wouldn't notice the single tear that slid across her cheek.

22

To Those Who Wait

'You don't mind if I do a bit of sewing, do you?'

Brent looked up from his laptop and smiled. 'No, hon, not at all. Go ahead. Although if you've a minute, I tore the pocket on my blue shirt and it could do with your magic touch to fix it again.'

'Rightie ho. Anything else while I'm at it?' She turned to Shelley who was watching the box, a rather ghoulish but fascinating documentary about plane crashes.

'Well, you could turn up my new jeans and there's a button missing off my black jacket,' the other woman said, gently tipping Mulder off her lap and getting up. 'I'll fetch them . . . if you don't mind, that is? I'll pay you, of course . . . and I think he should too!' She nodded at Brent.

Lizzie laughed wryly as she set up the sewing machine and took the first item from her basket. In the month since Brent vs. the sleeping tablets, and the departure of John, not long after, she'd packed in her temping job, and begun doing alterations and small sewing jobs for a high-end dress agency in town, as well as doing more dressmaking and general altering jobs for friends, and friends of friends too.

It was mostly routine work, and the income was modest, but it was much more satisfying to be working with fabric and her sewing machine than performing tedious office chores. It also meant she was around home more, and able to keep an eye on Brent.

The only downside of her new life as full-time seamstress was that she had more free time to think about John, and what might have been. Thus far, though, she was sure she was doing a pretty good job of hiding that from Brent and Shelley. Despite the fact that Brent in particular would keep on mentioning John at every available opportunity, and asking after him, almost as if he were as obsessed with the man as she was. Something that was weird, because Lizzie would have thought Shelley might have been the one most interested. Despite everything, Lizzie still smiled every time she remembered the other girl arriving home, and being introduced to John. Shelley's mouth had literally dropped open, and she'd seemed as dazzled as if she was meeting a real-life movie star.

I know, mate. That's the effect he always had on me . . .

I wasn't as if Lizzie had lost touch with her fabulous fling completely, even now. Far from it, although it might have been easier on the heart if she could have made a cleaner break.

'I'll stay around as long as you need me,' he'd said. 'If there's anything at all I can do, just say so. Anything.'

Oh, how tempting that had been. Almost irresistible. Mainly because his clear blue eyes had told her beyond a shadow of doubt that his offer was completely genuine, not just a polite man mouthing platitudes.

'It's OK . . . You've done so much already. We'll be fine now. You must have a ton of things to get back to . . . I mean, you've completed your business around here, haven't you?'

'Yes. I have. But I can stay if you want me to.'

Oh hell, I want you to!

She'd almost screamed the words, but, with difficulty, she'd restrained herself and politely declined. She hardly dared look at his face. She didn't want to see relief in his eyes. And yet, to her shock, she'd could have sworn she'd actually caught a hint of disappointment. Perhaps even pain.

But he'd complied. He'd left quietly and without fuss. Just one quick, very hard kiss, and a promise to stay in touch.

And then, to her astonishment, emails had begun to arrive. Not daily epistles swearing undying love, or anything like that, but a few times a week, easy, almost chatty communications arrived, jokes even. Contact from a friend, which was somehow far sweeter, and yet also more painful, than total silence would have been.

He offered thoughts about his business, and his travels, and once, revealingly, asked her opinion about his rift with his family. He was somewhat scant with the background, and as Lizzie had resolutely resisted morbid web searches about John, after the fact, she only knew the little she'd gleaned about him weeks ago. But still she gave her opinion; she'd nothing to lose now. She'd decided that, from now on, she'd keep in better contact with her own parents, and she urged him to do the same. In fact, everybody seemed to be doing it . . . Brent had reached out to his family as well, since his suicide attempt, and fences were being mended there too.

And John had sent gifts as well. In another life, she might have resisted them, told him not to, and sent them back. But he was crafty. He'd didn't lavish her with ostentatious billionaire consumer goods. He beguiled her with small, fun things. Books. DVDs. Tickets to a local costume exhibition, one that she'd never have expected him to even know about. Often the gifts were things she could share with Brent and Shelley. Computer games. Boxes of chocolates. Gourmet tea.

They were drinking some of that now. A lovely afternoon blend, made in a cute, kitsch teapot in the style of a country cottage. Another jokey gift from John. Lizzie finished the pocket on Brent's shirt, snipped off the thread, then took a sip of tea.

'What are you up to? You've been typing for fifteen minutes now. Proper typing, not just playing games or tweeting.'

Her friend abandoned his laptop, turning to her. He was looking so much better now, with more colour in his cheeks, and a bit more weight. His suicide attempt had been a catalyst for him, she sensed. Shown him what he had to live for. She'd never seen him so calm in all the time she'd known him. He wasn't even on any medication any more, and his sessions with his counsellor seemed to be doing him a power of good.

He sighed now, though. 'It's a letter to my mother.' He paused, drew in a breath. 'I'm going home to visit them for a bit. We might all end up arguing again, but I'm going to try to mend fences as best I can. And . . . well, I never really told them the full story of my . . . um . . . incident, so I thought it was kinder to do it face to face.' He paused, and gave her a cock-eyed grin, 'I feel guilty about sodding off, though . . . you've been so great. Both of you.' He smiled across at Shelley who'd returned with her jeans and jacket.

Lizzie crossed the room quickly and gave Brent a hug. Another brilliant sign. He was so much stronger now, and facing up to things. Just as she had to. John's emails would dry up eventually . . . He'd be reduced to a beautiful memory, a golden dream. But she'd cope.

'That's wonderful news! And it's right for you. Don't worry about us.' She nodded at Shelley, who was smiling encouragingly. 'Stay as long as you need to . . . and don't worry about the rent. I've . . . um . . . still got a bit of money in hand from you know what, so don't worry about the bills.' She gave him a quick kiss. 'In fact, I might nip to my folks for a weekend too, now we're better friends again.' Ruffling his hair, she went and resumed her seat. 'Looks like everybody is reconciling with their families. John's thinking about a rapprochement too.'

'I know,' said Brent.

She looked at her friend sharply. 'How? How do you know?' She swung her gaze to Shelley.

'Don't look at me . . . I don't know anything.' The other girl shrugged, visibly shuffling forward in her chair, curious.

'He left me his contact details. Just in case we needed anything . . . or anything happened to you.'

It was just a sign of friendship, she told her rampaging heart. He was just a benefactor now, someone who would always have her best interests at heart, even after the days of fine fabulous passion and kink they'd shared were long forgotten.

Three days later, Lizzie stood on the platform of the local railway station, waving to Brent as his train pulled away.

Shelley had said her goodbyes earlier, as she had a job that morning, and without her cheerful, settling influence the parting on the platform had been emotional. Brent had cried, and Lizzie had cried, even though he insisted his parental visit wouldn't last all *that* long. Lizzie had made a concerted effort to buck herself up and give him a grin, and a big bear hug . . . but it was difficult.

It reminded her so much of the last time she'd said goodbye to a man. And on that occasion it had been farewell for good.

There'd been no emails for several days either, and the weight of silence weighed on her, even though she'd begun bracing herself in readiness for it.

It's better this way. Dragging it out any longer would only make things harder. He knows that. He's actually being kind, ending it now.

With no particular commitments for the rest of the day, Lizzie felt gripped by lethargy. A sort of numbness. Staring across the tracks at a small municipal park on the other side, she decided to cross over the footbridge and go and sit there for a while. Then she'd go and buy a dozen cupcakes from her favourite shop in town, make her way home, and get on with her sewing whilst eating most of them.

Maybe she'd think a bit too, in the park, and later, while she waited for Shelley to get home. She had plans and decisions to make. John had casually assumed at one stage that she was a designer. Why not go for it, for real? Not big time, but there might be decent jobs she could get in the clothing business if she had some proper qualifications.

And at least it would be something challenging to do, a goal that would stretch her.

Her body seemed to weigh a ton as she wandered along the platform. At the end there was the footbridge to the park . . . or she just go home to the empty house? On the spur of the moment, she decided house, not park. She'd do some online research, get started, not shilly-shally about. And anyway, eating a dozen cupcakes would only make her feel sick.

As she left the concourse, she spotted a man, sitting on a bench at the other side of the car park. Sunlight glinted on his blond hair . . . and Lizzie's knees almost, but not quite, buckled beneath her.

Not John? Surely not John . . .

But as he strode towards her, pausing only to let a car speed by, she realised, to her shock and joy, that it *was* him. Her feet were frozen in place as he approached her, his legs long and lean in strategically faded denim. She noted the lovely soft blue of his V-neck sweater. The devil, she could swear he always chose those colours to highlight his eyes.

'I didn't know you were up here again. You never said,' she accused him. It was hard to think straight when faced with John in the flesh again. How was it possible that he seemed to be affecting her even more than ever before? She couldn't get enough of the sight of him. His blond curls, a bit longer and more tousled now, and his wicked, gleaming smile that made her melt and suddenly feel absurdly horny, despite the fact that she was cross as hell with him for springing himself on her.

'And it's lovely to see you too,' he observed with a teasing smirk. It seemed like yesterday since she'd watched him leave. An hour ago since she'd been in bed with him, or across his knee, being spanked.

'I'm sorry . . . it was just a bit of a shock. It *is* lovely to see you. Although I'm not sure quite why you're here.'

It's unfair, John. It's cruel. You can't just drop in now and again. It's not like I really am a call girl you can just pay and then forget, no harm done.

'Brent said I should come. In fact he insisted. He said that he and your friend Shelley were worried about you.'

Worried? Well, it was sweet . . . but she'd been so sure she'd hidden her sorrow from the pair of them.

'Well, I'm sure they mean well, but I haven't the faintest idea why they're worried about me. I'm fine. I'm better than fine. I'm doing great!' She narrowed her eyes at him, trying to look a bit fierce, so he wouldn't realise how she was nearly swooning at the sight of him, and struggling to keep from hurling herself bodily at him. 'And how come you're here right now? Did he tell you the time of his train or something?'

'Yes, that's pretty much it. He thought you might fancy a lunch, seeing as you're on your own today.' Without warning, John reached for her hand, grabbing it and squeezing it fiercely. It was an odd, uncoordinated, almost boyish gesture, and his handsome face was suddenly a mask of confusion, almost shyness. The change was so unexpected, so unlike the suave, confident man she'd been used to that she actually gasped.

'John, why are you here?' she repeated, befuddled by his eyes, and the strange fire in them, of yearning and hope and apprehension. His grip on her hand bordered on pain but she barely felt it. 'I mean . . . a man like you just doesn't pop up from wherever it is you . . . pop up from. Not just to take a casual acquaintance out for lunch because she's on her own for a day.'

'You're not a casual acquaintance. You never were . . . except perhaps that first evening.' He was so intent, his handsome face full of stress, but still a wonder to behold.

Lizzie tried to pull away her hand. She was the one confused now. Confused, and fighting a stupid, bubbling sensation. A feeling of hope and happiness and disbelief. 'But we were only "temporary sex friends" . . . nothing more than that. That was what you said you liked.'

He wouldn't release her hand, but the hold gentled somehow, became almost caressing, the sensation so sweet that Lizzie stopped fighting.

'I fancy myself as a clever guy, a sharp operator who always knows the score . . . but I'm a complete fucking idiot sometimes too.' He pulled her close to him, loosed the grip on her hand, and then flung his arms around her, hugging her against him. 'How could I ever think I could walk away from you? I must have been off my head. And a pathetic wimp too . . . Even if I thought you still cared for Brent that way, I should still have fought for you. The way I'm prepared to fight now . . .'

Oh, he felt so good. He smelt so good. It was as if something that had been wrong for a month was suddenly right. Mad, but right.

'What on earth are you talking about?' she said, her voice muffled against his shoulder. She suddenly had a mad urge to do what Mulder did, rub her face against him in ecstasy. Mark him . . . as her possession. 'I told you . . . several times . . . that Brent's just a friend. A very good friend, and I care for him, but nothing like the way I f—'

'Ah hah! You do care about me a bit, don't you?' A change seemed to surge through John's body. She could feel his confidence and his happiness rise. And not just that . . .

'Of course I care about you, you imbecile. And you're right. For a supposedly super astute businessman and a captain of industry, you *can* be a bit dense. I thought you'd figured out that I was totally dotty about you, and *that* was why you walked away! Because you weren't into relationships and whatnot.'

It was difficult not to just keep hugging and hugging him, to convince herself that he was real, he was here, and yes . . . that he did have a hard-on for her. Even in the middle of an emotional muddle, she loved that about him. It was simple and true and good.

But she pulled back a little and looked up into his blue remembered eyes. So full of heat. So full of joy. A joy she'd never dared hope for; the joy of seeing *her* again.

'I . . . I don't know what I'm into, Lizzie. I've screwed up relationships for so long, and let them screw me up . . . But now, I know one true thing, my darling, and that thing is that I have to be with you. I have to have you in my life somehow.' He inclined forward, and pressed his lips to hers in a soft, sweet breath of a kiss. It was tentative, but it hinted at burning depth beneath; a troubled depth too, not straightforward. 'God, I know you've got the guts to take me on, love, I knew that the moment I first set eyes on you. But I'm probably not being fair to you, you know that, don't you?'

She could feel turmoil in him, like an energy of conflict. She gripped his arm, trying to calm the furore with a touch.

'I can't do the full-on hearts and flowers thing, Lizzie, the way a special woman like you deserves. I'm . . . I'm not even fit for the "arrangement" kind of marriage I had before, and you're worth so much more than *that*.' He drew in a deep breath, the muscles of his arm tense beneath her fingertips. 'And there's stuff in my past too . . . shit that I want, and need, to draw a line under, and never revisit. And that means not telling you the whole of what I am.'

Lizzie opened her mouth to tell him it didn't matter, but then thought again. Did it matter? Perhaps she'd *need* to know those hidden things some day? But she sensed they were at delicate threshold now. He was trying to be as honest as he *could* be, and for the moment she just had to let him. She tightened her fingers on his arm, caressing, encouraging.

'Hell, that's what makes me feel so selfish.' He snagged his lower lip in his teeth for a moment, not playfully now, just perplexed. 'And yet I can't not want you, and not want to be with you. It's just impossible.'

He looked away from her for a moment, and when he met her gaze again there were shadows in his eyes. Anguish. The ghosts of those secrets it would be so painful to divulge . . .

Lizzie reached up and touched his lip, where he'd worried it, compelling him to relax, and to smile.

Could she take him on? It wouldn't be easy; their lives were so different, in so many ways, and he wasn't the straightforward man she'd always expected to end up with. But the more cowardly thing would be to walk away, and be a wimp, and she was done with backing down, giving up, living a half-life.

Besides all that, she loved him. She loved him with all her heart, regardless of his secrets. And regardless of whether he loved her, or was even capable of the kind of love she felt. He'd be a challenge, but nothing worthwhile in life was ever easy.

She smiled at him, and retrieved that slow, confident-looking, seductive smile she'd favoured him with in the Lawns bar.

'Look, Mr John Smith, I'm OK with all that. I'm not so needy I can't respect boundaries . . . but, by the same token, *you've* got to respect that I'm me, and sometimes I might knock up against those boundaries, and even bounce quite hard against them. You know what I mean?'

He nodded, and then drew her fingers to his lips again, shaping the mouth that she'd touched into a kiss, a pledge.

'Do we have a deal?' Lizzie fixed her eyes on his, compelling the words to confirm the action.

'We do. It's a deal.' The sunshine smile returned.

Before he could react further, Lizzie reached up, dug her fingers into his thick golden curls and drew him to her, assertively claiming his lips. She felt him still smiling against her mouth, but she subdued him, pressing with her tongue for entrance . . . and receiving it.

He hugged her hard, and she hugged him as they kissed like devils, devouring each other with all the hunger banked up in a month apart. Lizzie was vaguely aware that they were being watched, but she didn't care. It wasn't until they broke apart, both gasping that she caught sight of a woman who'd paused in the act of putting shopping into her car boot and was simply staring at them. Lizzie grinned at her, then tucked her hand beneath John's arm.

'Where to, boss?' she enquired. He was staring at her almost with almost as much astonishment as the shopping woman, but his fond smile was a wonder to behold.

'You're priceless, Lizzie. I haven't a clue what I've done to deserve you . . . but I'm glad you'll have me,' he said with a soft, husky laugh. 'I'm staying at the Waverley, and I need to get you back there as soon as possible. For lunch . . . or something.' He winked and, putting his hand over hers, he started walking, with Lizzie falling naturally into step beside him. 'And when we've eaten . . . and whatever . . . we can make some plans.'

Ah, the plans. The negotiations. Not as escort and client this time, but as whatever they were going to be from now on. Almost wanting to skip along at his side, she didn't fear the prospect.

Whatever their new journey was, it wouldn't be a simple path, and she had a shrewd idea that it would have more than its share of bumps. But whatever they were, and however big, she'd deal with them. *They'd* deal with them.

And all the time she'd be beside the man she loved.

Follow Lizzie and John's romantic journey in

THE ACCIDENTAL MISTRESS

coming soon from Black Lace

The Accidental Mistress

Having met under unusual circumstances when he first mistook her for a high price call-girl, Lizzie is now enjoying a passionate relationship with brooding millionaire, John Smith.

However, haunted by the demons of a past he won't talk about, John seems unable to offer her more than a no-strings-attached affair.

But will she ever be anything more than a rich man's mistress?

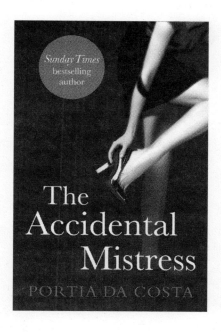